Wizard Omega

Book Four

Intergalactic Wizard Scout Chronicles

Rodney W. Hartman

ISBN-13: 978-0998216607 (R&K Publishing)

ISBN-10: 0998216607

Cover Design by Angie Abler

This is a work of fiction. Names, characters, places, and incidents are a product of the author's imagination. Any resemblance to actual persons, events, or locales is entirely coincidental.

DEDICATION

This book is dedicated to my daughter Emily. You are an inspiration to me. I am humbled by your willingness to go where you are needed without thinking of yourself. You are one of the bright lights in a sometimes dark world.

ACKNOWLEDGMENTS

My wife, Karen, has been and continues to be my biggest supporter. I can never thank her enough.

Books by Rodney Hartman

<u>Intergalactic Wizard Scout Chronicles</u>

Wizard Defiant   Book One
Wizard Cadet   Book Two
Wizard Scout   Book Three
Wizard Omega   Book Four
Wizard Rebellion   Book Five
Wizard Betrayed...Book Six

Website: www.rodneyhartman.com
Feel free to contact the author at: Rodney@RodneyHartman.com

CHAPTER 1

[Begin Transmission]

Intergalactic Time: Current Date minus 42 years

The battered escape pod floated in the emptiness of space. A dim light from one of the cockpit windows was the only evidence that the ship wasn't a derelict.

A starship drifted two kilometers off the escape pod's port side. The vessel appeared to be an Empire-class recon ship. The word 'Defiant' was painted in bold letters across the bow.

The airlock on the *Defiant* opened and a lone figure in a power-suit exited, then slowly jetted across the distance separating the two ships. Once the figure secured a safety line to the escape pod, the concentrated blue light of a plasma-cutting torch lit up the side of the pod. The illumination revealed the frame around the escape pod's hatchway was buckled. The figure slowly and methodically cut away strips of bent metal until the hatch began to wobble.

Just as the figure was about to pry the hatch open, a glint of light reflected off the pod's silvery surface. Whether it was due to the reflected light or a possible warning over the power-suit's com-link, the figure turned away from the pod to face the *Defiant*.

The recon ship was no longer alone. A black vessel of enormous size had appeared off the *Defiant's* stern. The dreadnaught's bow bore the outline of a black dragon with a red stripe down its side. A dozen beams of red, blue, and green leaped from the dreadnaught and exploded soundlessly against the *Defiant's* force fields.

Although outgunned, the smaller recon ship valiantly unleashed a flurry of missiles and plasma beams against the shields of the dreadnaught. Unlike the ancient Earth tale of David and Goliath, the giant didn't fall. Its defensive shields were too powerful for the *Defiant*.

Jets of flame from the lone figure's power-suit shot out in a desperate attempt to return to the recon ship. The figure must have known it was hopeless before starting. The distance was too great.

An orange tractor beam latched onto the escape pod and drew the pod toward a set of opening bay doors near the rear of the dreadnaught.

Despite the continued pummeling from the dreadnaught's weapons, the *Defiant's* shields continued to hold. The *Defiant* was obviously not a typical recon ship, and as if to prove that point, the *Defiant* interposed itself between the escape pod and the massive dreadnaught. A single missile shot out from the *Defiant* directly along the path of the dreadnaught's tractor beam. Captured by the orange beam, the missile sped straight through the small opening in the dreadnaught's force field and into the bay doors.

An intense white light that could only be the flash of a tactical nuke erupted. The dreadnaught shuddered but remained intact, giving evidence that its bay area was reinforced with an internal force field. Although the *Defiant* failed to destroy its giant opponent, the surprise nuclear attack succeeded in knocking out the tractor beam.

The escape pod once again floated free in space. But the little recon ship's success was not without cost.

The dreadnaught unleashed a flurry of energy beams and projectiles against the *Defiant*.

The recon ship's force fields began to weaken under the onslaught.

Apparently realizing their pending doom, the *Defiant* maneuvered to the far side of the dreadnaught while firing three missiles that struck the dreadnaught's force fields. Three explosions rivaling the light of small suns lit up all three ships as the tactical nukes exploded.

But the dreadnaught remained undamaged. Its shields were too strong for even tactical nukes.

Fortunately, through careful strategic planning of the *Defiant's* crew or blind luck, the dreadnaught's massive bulk and shields protected the escape pod and the figure from the radiation and shock waves of the nukes.

As the lone figure helplessly watched the battle, a stream of translucent light emanated from the stern of the recon ship. Its hyper-drive had been activated, and it was beginning to move away from the dreadnaught.

The black dreadnaught didn't seem inclined to follow until three more tactical nukes from the recon ship hit its shields. Apparently, the continuous affront of the recon ship's attacks was too much for the dreadnaught's commander to take. Streams of translucent light from the dreadnaught's stern moved its massive bulk in the direction of the *Defiant*.

As the lone figure watched, the two battling starships faded into the distance until they were indistinct pinpoints of light, then disappeared.

The lone figure drifted alone while staring at the spot where the starships had been. Undoubtedly the figure hoped for the return of the *Defiant*, which didn't occur.

After a full hour, the lone figure finally turned, jetted back to the escape pod, and finished prying open its hatch. For the next eight hours, random flashes of light appeared in the escape pod's cockpit windows.

When the flashes of light stopped, a translucent stream of light shot out from the rear of the escape pod as its hyper-drive activated. The little starship moved forward at an ever-increasing pace, then disappeared from sight. Only a few bits of stray metal floating in the emptiness of space gave evidence anyone had ever been there.

The brave *Defiant* was never seen again.

CHAPTER 2

Intergalactic Time: Current Date

Twelve massive Ultra Heavy Ambulatory Assault Vehicles made their way up the ridgeline in search of the lone Warcat scout. Their weapons' systems scanned left and right as if each of the mechanized behemoths were eager to be first to destroy the smaller scout vehicle.

UHAAVs were the main ground-assault armor for almost all advanced civilizations in the galaxy. The vehicles, or 'cats' as they were fondly called by their pilots, ranged in size from ten-meter high Leviathans to smaller Long Cats. Their intended victim was Wizard Scout Richard Shepard in a three-meter-tall Warcat scout.

Although his Warcat was an older model, its sensors were more than capable of picking up the sonic vibrations of the approaching enemy armor. As a wizard scout in the Intergalactic Empire, Richard was one of the best-trained scouts in the galaxy. But even wizard scouts were in trouble when they were outgunned and outnumbered twelve to one.

"Not exactly trying to hide, are they, Nick?" Richard thought in the space he shared in his mind with his battle computer.

"Why should they?" replied his battle computer. *"They've got three quads of cats against your lone Warcat. I calculate an eighty-seven percent probability that they think the outcome of any battle is a foregone conclusion. Personally, I think they're being optimistic. I only calculate a seventy-eight percent probability*

they'll kill you before you can get away."

All wizard scouts were assigned a battle computer, and Nickelo had been with Richard ever since his freshman year at the Intergalactic Wizard Scout Academy. As part of the process of becoming a wizard scout, a section of Richard's mind had been allocated as shared space with his battle computer. The rest of his mind was private, but inside the shared space, Richard and Nickelo could share information near instantaneously. Their 'speech' was more a series of feelings and images than words, which was fortunate, otherwise in combat conditions, he'd be dead before he could finish asking his battle computer for help.

Richard had ended his time at the Academy during his junior year when a surprise attack by a Crosioian task force destroyed most of the Academy's infrastructure a year ago. The loss of the only known DNA gas vent in the galaxy had been even more devastating than the loss of the Academy buildings. Without the DNA gas, no new wizard scouts could be trained. Richard's class would forever be the final class to graduate. He had been the last of his class to receive the coveted golden-dragon insignia of a wizard scout. Richard was the last of the wizard scouts. He was the wizard scout omega.

"Well," Richard thought back, *"I guess we'll just have to make sure we stay in the other twenty-two percent, won't we? Besides, we're only outnumbered twelve to one. We've had worse odds, haven't we? So what else is new?"*

"Oh, it's the same old, same old," said Nickelo with a laugh. *"I'll bet when you joined the Marines, your recruiter forgot to tell you they didn't give the milk-run missions to wizard scouts."*

Richard let his mind sift through the mass of information his battle computer was dumping into their shared space. *"It looks like we have two heavy cats and two medium cats working their way up the west side of the ridgeline. Those four cats should get here first."*

"Affirmative," said Nickelo. *"From the frequency of the sonic vibrations, I calculate you're up against two Leviathan heavy cats and two medium Long Cats."*

"Bummer," Richard said as he brought up the specs for a Leviathan UHAAV on his heads-up display.

The Leviathan cat was the largest of the armored vehicles.

Richard had fought them before. The ten-meter-high, six-legged Leviathan heavy cats were armed with a variety of anti-personnel and anti-armor weapons including missiles, plasma rifles, and a set of dual 240mm phase cannons.

"Don't forget about their armor," said Nickelo. *"They have half a meter of brerellium steel on their front and sides. Your Warcat's 40mm autocannon won't do more than scratch their paint. And you only have two anti-armor missiles. Two aren't enough to get past the Leviathan's force field."*

A normal Warcat was equipped with a small-caliber plasma rifle, but Richard's old maintenance chief, Sergeant Ron, had modified this particular Warcat with a higher-caliber 40mm autocannon. While deadly against light scout cats, even a 40mm armor-piercing round was ineffective against medium and heavy cats.

"Tell me something I don't know, old buddy," Richard said. *"Do you have any good news?"*

"Well, it looks like the second quad is setting up a blocking position a thousand meters to your rear. They'll have a clear field of fire if you try to leave these woods."

"Is that supposed to be the good news?" Richard said.

"Depends on how you look at it," said Nickelo with what sounded like another laugh. *"It means your death will be quick and relatively painless. I suppose you can think of that as good news if you'd like."*

"Ha, ha," Richard said. *"It's time to get serious, buddy. I could use a little help."*

After the demise of the Intergalactic Wizard Scout Academy the previous year, Richard had been on a variety of missions for the Empire as well as several unofficial missions for '*the One.*' For the last six months, he had been assigned to a mercenary outfit operating in District 2, near the Storis Nebula. After five years at the Academy, working with mercenaries had been different, to say the least, and he was still unsure of all the little nuances of his unit's command structure.

Richard thought back to his mission briefing, or lack thereof, the previous week. His commander had received encrypted, top-secret orders directly from the Empire's central computer. The orders had been marked with the seal of the Imperial High Council, the political arm of the Empire. The source of his orders had struck him as odd since they bypassed the normal military chain of command. However, they were legal, and orders were orders. He had been directed to proceed to a planet so nondescript it was known simply as Planet X3321. Once there, his orders were to infiltrate and retrieve data from a Trecorian research complex. According to his orders, the research complex's computer contained high-value information that might lead to the location of another DNA gas vent. Though suspecting he was being used in some type of political ploy, the possibility of finding a new vent was too important to pass up. If the Empire could find another source of DNA gas, then Richard was hopeful the Intergalactic Wizard Scout Academy could be reopened. Without additional wizard scouts, he doubted the Empire would survive its current war with the Crosioians intact.

According to his orders, the research complex was supposed to be lightly guarded. Military Intelligence (MI) believed the facility only had a few civilian guards. The only other troops on the planet were supposed to be a unit of preteens and teenage cadets apparently conducting some type of basic-training exercise. MI hadn't considered them a threat. Richard took MI's consideration with a grain of salt. He'd been burned by overly optimistic intel reports before.

Penetrating the security complex had been easy enough. Richard got to within four hundred meters of the complex in his Warcat. Once he'd exited his cat, he'd traversed the remaining distance on foot. Inside the research complex, he had quickly located the primary computer and begun to download the required data when everything went to hell in a handbasket.

The whole thing had been a trap. There hadn't been any data. The moment Richard plugged the retrieval device into one of the computer's access ports, alarms had gone off all over the compound. And the few civilian guards had somehow been supplemented by a squadron of hidden Trecorian cats.

If Richard had been a normal recon soldier, he would've been dead within seconds. But he wasn't a normal soldier. He was a wizard scout. He was sent on the most dangerous missions deep behind enemy lines and expected to survive. So far, he'd survived four hours since the alarms went off, but was unsure how many more hours he could evade his pursuers. He wasn't even sure if he could avoid a fight for the next ten minutes, much less hours.

Richard sensed a line of energy pass by him. The enemy cats were scanning in an attempt to pinpoint his position, but weren't having any luck in the heavily-forested area he had chosen as his current hiding position. A high concentration of magnetic ore in the rock below the forest floor was playing havoc with even the Warcat's advanced sensory equipment, so Richard figured the technicians in the Leviathans were having an even harder time of it.

"I'm glad I'm in a Warcat," Richard said. *"This model might be old, but Sergeant Ron's got it equipped with the best stealth equipment he could scrounge. I think they'll probably have to spot me visually before they can get their weapons targeted."*

Richard was lucky he had Sergeant Ron to maintain his equipment. For some unknown reason, Sergeant Ron had taken it upon himself to tag along with him after the demise of the Academy's wizard scout program. As a result, his Warcat was very well maintained.

"Well," said Nickelo, *"it's going to take more than stealth to get you out of this one. I calculate you have six minutes before the quad of cats coming up the west ridge spots you even if you remain stationary."* After a pause, Nickelo asked, *"What do you want to do, oh greatest of wizard scouts?"*

Richard thought he heard a muffled laugh from his battle computer. For some reason, Nickelo had a strange sense of humor during combat situations, which Richard usually chose to ignore. *"Plot me a route with the minimum chance of detection to one of the medium cats in that nearest quad,"* Richard said. *"I think we're going to have to narrow the odds before we can get away."*

"Plotted," said Nickelo as a green line appeared on the heads-up display of Richard's battle helmet. *"May I ask what you're going to do when you get there?"*

"I haven't quite figured that part out yet," Richard said. *"Don't rush me."*

Richard got the Warcat moving along the path Nickelo had plotted. Although the Warcat was three-meters tall and weighed a little over two thousand kilos, it moved relatively soundless through the undergrowth. Unlike its larger cousins, the Warcat had no control panel. Instead, the pilot was submerged in a thick gel that sensed its pilot's movements. The Warcat was more a large suit of armor than a vehicle. Inside the tight confines of the Warcat, Richard was dressed in his battle suit and battle helmet. They made for a self-sufficient environment that provided everything his body needed, including recycled oxygen and nutrients.

From the data in his shared space, Richard saw the four cats working their way along the west ridgeline. The closest cat was two hundred meters away. From the orange dot on his heads-up display, he knew it was a medium Long Cat. A red dot denoting a heavy Leviathan was following a hundred meters behind the Long Cat.

"I'd advise stopping by that set of trees to your right," said Nickelo. *"I calculate the Long Cat will pass ten meters to your front. I'm activating the Warcat's camo shield, with your permission, of course."*

"Of course," Richard said. *"Permission granted."*

A flow of energy enveloped the Warcat. While the camo shield didn't make it totally invisible, it did a decent job of blending the Warcat into the background.

Richard hoped the camo shield would buy him enough time to do what needed to be done.

The lead Long Cat moved into Richard's field of view. The Long Cat was seven meters high and walked on two massive legs. A 200mm phase cannon protruded from its chest. A circular pod with twenty-four anti-armor missiles sat on each shoulder. A set of four barrels protruded from the Long Cat's left appendage, which appeared to be 40-megawatt plasma rifles. Its right appendage held a 30mm chain gun.

Richard noticed the Long Cat approaching him was wider than normal and made out two pilots through the cockpit window.

"Wow," Richard said. *"They've got that bad boy loaded for bear."*

"A more accurate statement would be it's loaded for Warcat," said Nickelo making no attempt to hide his laughter this time. *"So what's your plan?"*

"Hmm," Richard said trying to think on the fly. *"If I got inside that thing, could you work the controls?"*

"If you gave me control of your battle suit I could," said Nickelo. *"But you've piloted a Long Cat before; you should be able to do it yourself."*

"Not well enough for what I need done," Richard said as he activated the battle suit's override. He had no problem admitting his shortcomings. At one time he might have, but no longer.

With the override on, his battle computer could do anything it wanted with the battle suit. Most wizard scouts refrained from activating their battle suit's override except in dire emergencies. Some wizard scouts refused even then. Richard was not one of those. He trusted his battle computer completely. Nickelo was not just his battle computer. Nickelo was his friend.

Just as the Long Cat drew even with him, Richard noticed the top of the Leviathan appear above the tree tops a hundred meters behind. The Leviathan was staying close enough to provide cover for the Long Cat while remaining far enough back to stay out of any possible ambush. As he watched, the top of the Leviathan disappeared from view as it stepped into a dip in the forest floor.

Taking advantage of the momentary window of opportunity, Richard dashed around the large tree he was using for cover. With two long strides, he was at the base of the nearest leg of the Long Cat. Jumping up, Richard got the Warcat onto the back of the Long Cat before its crew could react. After clamping the Warcat's claws onto the supports for the Long Cat's missile pods, Richard wrapped himself with Power.

All wizard scouts had a specialty. Some wizard scouts were healers while others were defenders, diviners, projectors, or shifters, to name a few. Testing during Richard's freshman year at the Academy had determined that he possessed all of the known abilities.

Richard used his shifter specialization to shift into the void between dimensions, then telekinesis to propel himself forward and through the metal skin of both his Warcat and the Trecorian's Long Cat. Once inside the cockpit of the enemy cat, he dropped his Power and shifted back into the physical dimension.

The Long Cat's cockpit was crowded. Two humans sat in cushioned seats in front of a control panel containing a complex array of computer readouts, buttons, and levers. One of the pilots turned in his seat and grabbed for a handgun in his shoulder holster.

Richard didn't give him time to finish the maneuver. At the thought of what he wanted to do, Richard felt his battle suit move as Nickelo took control. The battle suit reached out with both hands and clubbed each pilot on the side of the head.

The strength of the battle suit could easily have caved in the pilots' skulls, but Richard purposely weakened the blows to incapacitate instead of kill. His current mission was recon and data recovery. It wasn't to kill needlessly. While Richard wasn't averse to killing, he had no desire to take a life without cause. Besides, the Empire wasn't at war with the Trecorian Alliance. He preferred not to start one. The Trecorians were part of a loose alliance of star systems that had thus far remained neutral in the war between the Empire and the bat-like Crosioians. However, the Trecorians' home world of Trecor was located near an asteroid belt containing an abundant supply of brerellium as well as other valuable minerals. Both the Empire and the Crosioians needed the brerellium to feed their militaries' appetites for raw materials. The Crosioians had been successfully acquiring large shipments of brerellium by using Balorian pirates as their proxies to rob the Trecorians. The Empire also wanted a share of the Trecorians' brerellium but wanted to set up a trade system. So far, the Trecorians had refused the Empire's overtures.

Richard wrapped the pilots in Power and shifted them into the void. Using telekinesis, he lowered the pilots through the floor of the Long Cat. As soon as they were through the Long Cat's skin, Richard shifted the pilots out of the void and back into the physical dimension, then continued to use telekinesis to lower them safely to the forest floor.

"That was inefficient," said Nickelo. *"You know dimensional shifting is Power hungry. Your Power reserve is down to eighty-four percent now. You could have saved four percent Power by just dumping them out the hatch."*

Richard's Achilles' heel had always been the small size of his Power reserve. His main TAC officer at the Academy had often delighted in telling him and anyone around that Richard's Power reserve was the smallest of any wizard scout to ever attend the Academy. While well aware of his shortcoming, he wasn't heartless enough to kill someone just to save a little Power.

"It's over five meters to the ground," Richard said. *"The fall could've broken their necks. Besides, I didn't want to waste time fumbling with the hatch."*

Richard strapped himself into one of the pilot seats and stared at the complex set of controls. He had enough training in the larger cats to make them move and shoot but wasn't skilled enough to fight experienced opponents. Turning the Long Cat a hundred and eighty degrees, Richard spied the top of the nearest Leviathan just as it popped back out of the treetops.

"I could use some help, Nick," Richard said.

"That's what I'm here for," replied Nickelo. *"Just think what you want done, and I'll do my best to make it happen."*

Richard sent his plan into the shared space as a series of images. The arms of his battle suit began to move on their own volition. The battle suit's gloves became a blur as they moved across the Long Cat's control panel, touching buttons and moving levers. The Long Cat hunched down and began running at a forty-five-degree angle toward the side of the approaching Leviathan. A glance at his heads-up display confirmed the other two cats in the quad were a good four hundred meters away.

"Why hunch over?" said Nickelo. *"They know where you're at. By your actions, they're bound to assume this cat is no longer in friendly hands."*

As if confirming his battle computer's analysis, a feminine voice came over a speaker on the control panel. "Long Cat 26, stand down immediately or we'll open fire!" The voice sounded no nonsense.

Richard had no doubt the owner of the voice would do what she said. However, he kept running anyway. His only chance was to keep moving.

"They should have fired first without taking the time to give a warning," Richard thought. *"I would have."*

"I suspect they think their two friends are still onboard as prisoners," said Nickelo. *"They probably don't want to kill their own soldiers unless absolutely necessary."*

Richard was grateful the Leviathan pilot was concerned for her fellow soldiers. It was going to cost her. The precious seconds she'd lost giving her warning was all the time he needed to complete his plan.

Shifting directions, Richard rushed his Long Cat directly at the Leviathan. The tops of the trees hid the upper part of the heavy cat, but he wasn't interested in the upper levels anyway. Even the Long Cat's 200mm phase cannon would have trouble penetrating the thick armor around the Leviathan's upper areas. Not to mention the upper levels had the heavy cat's strongest force fields protecting its sensitive areas. The lower levels were a different matter.

Hunched over as he was in the Long Cat, Richard could just make out the front two legs of the Leviathan a hundred meters away. Richard almost thought the command to fire, but stopped.

"Wise decision, Rick," said Nickelo. *"You need to take out at least two side legs to do any good. The Leviathan could remain upright even with both front legs out of action."*

Richard sidestepped the Long Cat in an attempt to get a simultaneous shot at two of the Leviathan's side legs. He was pretty sure if he tried to take them out one at a time, the crew would avoid his second shot.

"Their weapons are charging," said Nickelo. *"They're going to fire."*

A second later, the tops of the trees exploded in a blaze of red as the Leviathan's plasma and phase weapons opened up on the Long Cat's position.

Fortunately, Richard's Long Cat was no longer there. He'd thought the command to activate countermeasures, and Nickelo had jumped the Long Cat to the side and switched on the electronic jammers.

Without being able to visually sight the Long Cat, the Leviathan's targeting systems were fooled long enough for Richard to evade most of the heavy cat's fire. Even so, a few rounds of phase energy found their mark. Thankfully, the Long Cat's force field held. The few phase and plasma rounds able to penetrate his shields glanced harmlessly off the sides.

The initial broadside from the Leviathan's energy weapons had cleared a path through the tops of the trees. Richard could now see the top of the Leviathan.

"Unfortunately," said Nickelo having intruded into Richard's thoughts, *"that means the Leviathan's gunners can now see you as well. They'll be firing everything they've got, including missiles, in another three seconds."*

Richard decided not to give the gunners another three seconds. All three of the Leviathan's left-side legs were visible, and the Leviathan's left-front leg was just being raised as the heavy cat started to take a step in his direction.

"Target the ground two meters to the side of the middle-left leg," Richard said. *"Fire everything the Long Cat has at that spot."*

"Are you sure?" came Nickelo's anxious thought. *"I calculate a forty-two percent probability at least a few of our Long Cat's weapons will penetrate the force field around the legs if you concentrate your fire on them instead."*

"Just do it!" Richard said.

Despite his battle computer's calculations, Richard had a hunch his Long Cat's weapons wouldn't be able to overcome the Leviathan's force field before the heavy cat's return fire took him out.

The Long Cat's weapons began firing almost at the same moment Richard thought his command. The ground around the base of the Leviathan's middle leg exploded in a blast of flying dirt, rock, and other debris. The force field prevented any damage to the Leviathan's leg. However, the ground under the middle leg's footpad disappeared causing the Leviathan to slip to the side. The slight shift in the Leviathan's stance threw off the aim of its gunners. Since Richard was still running for all he was worth in his confiscated Long Cat, most of the enemy's return fire hit the area behind him. The Long Cat's force field continued to hold against what little fire was on target.

"You need to take out more than one leg," said Nickelo. *"Should I shift fire to the rear leg?"*

"Negative," Richard said picturing an image of the bottom of the Leviathan's left-front footpad, now completely exposed mid-step.

"Understood," said Nickelo as he shifted fire to the front leg.

The bottom of the Leviathan's footpads were also protected by a force field in case of landmines, though weaker than around the rest of a cat to allow for gaining traction in slick terrain. By shifting fire to the underside of the exposed footpad, Richard hoped to take advantage of one of the heavy cat's few weak points.

Once again, every weapon on Richard's Long Cat concentrated

fire on a single spot. The force field around the bottom of the Leviathan's left-front foot held against the initial volley. Even the 200mm phase cannon round glanced off. A quick follow-up volley blew a hole in the force field large enough to allow two of the Long Cat's anti-armor missiles to pass through. Pieces of brerellium steel flew in all directions as the Leviathan's footpad was turned into a mangled mass of metal.

Once the Long Cat's phase cannon completed its half-second reload time, another 200mm phase round completed the footpad's destruction. The bottom third of the Leviathan's leg disappeared as the combination of plasma energy and solid creallium in the 200mm phase round did its job. Unlike a plasma round, which was composed entirely of energy, a phase round was a solid chunk of creallium surrounded by phase energy. Since creallium existed simultaneously in both the physical dimension and the void, even a fully-functional force field had a difficult time resisting the blast. The force field around the Leviathan's footpad was anything but fully functional by the time the second 200mm round hit.

As what little remained of the Leviathan's left-front leg continued downward, the heavy cat shifted left and forward. The other four legs on the cat scrambled for a hold as the pilots tried to compensate for the loss of their cat's two left legs. The pilots desperately tried to keep their cat upright, and the aim of the gunners was again thrown off. Streaks of phase and plasma energy passed all around Richard's Long Cat, but none struck home.

The pilots of the Leviathan were good. They almost saved their cat.

Richard suspected if the pilots had the full use of five legs, they could have prevented a fall. But the middle-left leg was still slipping into the hole Richard's initial blast had created. The Leviathan suddenly reached its point of no return and tipped left and downward. Richard decided to assist the planet's gravity by shifting his fire to the Leviathan's left-rear leg. His fire didn't penetrate the leg's force field, but the force of his plasma rounds was enough to hasten the fall.

Boom! The Leviathan slammed into the ground. Dirt and debris flew into the air in all directions.

Richard ran the remaining distance to the Leviathan and jumped onto the heavy cat's side, which was now its top. A few of the heavy cat's automated anti-personnel weapons began firing at him. None of the cat's heavy weapons were firing.

"I calculate the gunners might be a little shook up," said Nickelo. *"I recommend laying a few anti-armor mines to make sure they stay that way."*

"Agreed," Richard said.

The Leviathan was down, but it wasn't helpless. Richard was well aware he still had another two cats from the quad headed in his direction also. The last thing he wanted to do was leave a stationary pillbox in his rear.

Scanning the data Nickelo was feeding into their shared space, Richard confirmed his Long Cat had twelve ten-kilo anti-armor mines.

Richard took a look at the Leviathan lying on the ground. Even down, the heavy cat looked very large and the anti-armor mines looked very small.

"Set all twelve mines over the engine compartment," Richard said.

"Are you sure?" said Nickelo. *"I calculate a seventy-eight percent probability six mines will do the job."*

"I can't take the risk," Richard said. *"Those other two cats will be here in less than a minute. Use all the mines, Nick. I want this cat out of action."*

"Compliance," said Nickelo a little dubiously.

Richard's Long Cat immediately moved to the rear of the downed Leviathan and began dropping its entire load of anti-armor mines.

Boom!

Richard was jostled in his seat as the Long Cat was knocked off its feet.

"What was that?" Richard said. *"Are we damaged?"*

"One of the Leviathan's right-side 100mm plasma guns got a hit on you," said Nickelo. *"Its gunner must be back in action."*

"No kidding," Richard said as he stood the Long Cat back up and jumped off the side of the Leviathan. *"Tell me something I don't know."*

A quick glance at the Long Cat's computer readout showed Richard his force field was down to thirty-eight percent. The hit from the 100mm had taken a heavy toll, but fortunately, his cat was unharmed.

"Well, we're not going to let them get a second shot," Richard said. *"Take it out, Nick."*

"Compliance," said Nickelo.

The Long Cat squatted, then jumped high into the air. At the peak of its jump, the 200mm phase cannon fired. The creallium round hit the center of the pile of mines lying near the rear of the Leviathan.

Boom!

The explosion was so powerful the shockwave caught the Long Cat in mid-air and knocked it to the ground. The next thing Richard knew, he was staring at the sky through the Long Cat's windscreen.

"I tried to tell you six mines would be enough," said Nickelo. *"More is not always better. You should try listening to me more often."*

"Get me up, Nick," Richard said as he shook his head in an attempt to clear the after effects of the blast.

"Your wish is my command, oh greatest but most foolish of wizard scouts," said Nickelo.

The Long Cat rose to its feet, and Richard was once again able to see his surroundings. The Leviathan's 100mm plasma gun was no longer firing. In fact, none of the heavy cat's weapons were firing. Richard saw flames and smoke pouring out of a meter-wide hole near the rear of the Leviathan. As he watched, two crewmen exited an escape hatch near one of the right-side gun cupolas.

Richard heard a loud pop near the front of the burning cat. A meter-sized square piece of metal from the Leviathan's right shoulder went flying into the air. Two more crewmen scrambled out the hatch to escape their burning vehicle. One of the men had a limp, and the other appeared to have burns on part of his left leg. Since the men were moving post haste, Richard had a feeling their injuries weren't life threatening.

Richard pointed his Long Cat's 30mm chain gun at the fleeing crewmen. A wave of mixed emotions swept over him. The heavy cat's crew had been trying to kill him a few seconds ago. A part of him felt as if he should make them pay. At the same time, he hated the thought of being burned alive. Dying slowly in the merciless grip of fire was one of his fears. His nephew and niece had almost been burned alive a few years ago because of him. It wasn't a pleasant memory.

"No," Richard thought, *"being burned to death is no way for anyone to die. Besides, I'm the aggressor here. They're soldiers, just like me. They're only defending what is theirs. For all I know, they're good people with families and friends. I'll kill if necessary, but these guys are no threat to me now."*

"Time enough to get in touch with your feelings later," said Nickelo. *"Those other two cats are closing fast. The second Trecorian Long Cat is making a beeline straight for us."*

Richard kicked himself for letting his thoughts about being burned alive drift into his shared space. Thoughts like he'd been having were best kept private.

"Understood," Richard said. *"I've got the two incoming cats on my passive scan."*

Richard's passive scan easily picked up the Power from the approaching cats much like a person's ears heard sound. They were making no attempt to hide. Using a mixture of information from his battle helmet and his passive scan, Richard made a quick calculation of both cats' paths.

"I don't think the medium cat is heading for us, Nick," Richard said. *"It seems to be heading directly for the burning Leviathan."*

"Hmm," said Nickelo. *"I calculate you're correct. Unless it changes course, the Trecorian Long Cat is going to pass forty meters to your right."* After a short pause, Nickelo added, *"Strange, the pilot is leaving his flank exposed."*

Whether the advancing cat's pilot was aware of the danger or not, Richard didn't know or care as he acted instinctively to take advantage of the situation.

"Nick," Richard said. *"Target everything we've got on that Long Cat's right leg. We need to take it out before the second Leviathan gets here."*

"Compliance," said Nickelo. *"Target is acquired. I can fire whenever you're ready."*

"Fire!"

Every weapon on Richard's Long Cat opened up at the same time. The 200mm phase cannon, 40mm plasma rifles, 30mm chain-gun rounds, and a salvo of anti-armor missiles traced a path straight for the running Trecorian Long Cat.

Unfortunately for Richard, the pilot of the medium cat was no slouch and veered left to avoid Richard's fire. At the same time, the pilot jumped the cat into the air and twisted ninety degrees until the barrels of the medium cat's weapons were pointed directly at Richard's Warcat. A blaze of return fire shot toward Richard's location.

Thankfully, Richard was also no slouch when it came to piloting either. Or rather, Nickelo was no slouch. Consequently, Richard's Long Cat was no longer in the same spot when the Trecorian cat's rounds hit the ground. The battle computer had immediately put Richard's thoughts into action by shifting the cat to the side. A few rounds hit, jostling Richard around in his chair a little, but nothing of consequence was damaged.

"Shields are at seven percent," said Nickelo. *"Sorry. I tried to avoid the fire, but the pilot's good. Plus, I didn't compensate enough for that extra two thousand kilos hanging onto our Long Cat's back."*

Richard had forgotten his Warcat was still clinging to the back of his hijacked Long Cat. Red blinking-lights flashed on several parts of the control panel as a vivid reminder of why trying to fight a battle with a Warcat hanging onto your back was probably not the smartest thing to do. As it was, his Long Cat couldn't hope to match the maneuverability of his unencumbered opponent. The other pilot was in a position to gain the upper hand.

To Richard's amazement, the pilot didn't take advantage of his momentary vulnerability. Instead of taking the time to fire a second salvo, the pilot turned the Long Cat and once again ran toward the burning Leviathan. Richard noticed the flames had completely engulfed the back half of the downed cat and were spreading quickly toward the front.

"Target that Long Cat's right leg again and fire," Richard commanded.

Richard was knocked around in his seat as his Long Cat opened up with everything it had.

"Don't you want me to save some of the missiles for that second Leviathan?" asked Nickelo suggestively.

"Negative!" Richard mentally shouted. *"Fire it all. Give it everything we've got."*

Another salvo shot out from Richard's Long Cat and struck the backside of the right leg of his opponent.

The force field protecting the leg gave way. Pieces of brerellium steel exploded outward as the lower part of the cat's leg shattered. The Trecorian Long Cat fell to the ground, bounced once, and remained still. Lady luck was against Richard this time—the Long Cat fell in such a way that its 200mm phase cannon pointed directly at his cockpit window.

He wrapped himself in Power in preparation for shifting into the void.

Surprisingly, the Trecorian pilot didn't fire the cat's main gun. Instead, the escape hatch blew outward, and a single human dressed in an emerald-green jumpsuit crawled out of the cockpit and ran toward the burning Leviathan oblivious to the plasma and chain-gun rounds kicking up dirt around him.

"Cease fire, Nick," Richard commanded.

The Long Cat's weapons immediately stopped firing.

"Is there anyone else in the Long Cat?" Richard said.

Richard doubted there was since he didn't detect any life forms with his passive scan, but there was no use taking chances. There was always the possibility someone was inside with a stealth shield.

"Negative," said Nickelo. *"That's a single-pilot version of the Long Cat."*

In spite of the tenseness of the situation, Richard took a second to watch the fleeing pilot. From the cut of the pilot's jumpsuit, he was a male. And he wasn't trying to escape. The pilot was running toward the burning Leviathan with single-minded purpose and without making any attempt to seek cover.

Richard could easily have shot the pilot down with a burst from his 30mm chain gun but resisted the urge. The pilot's actions confused him. Through the smoky haze surrounding the burning Leviathan, Richard noticed movement inside the cockpit. The Leviathan's two pilots were beating against the inside of the cockpit's cracked but unbroken windscreen.

"The cockpit's escape hatch must be jammed or blocked," observed Nickelo. *"Too bad. You haven't had to kill anyone up until now. Oh well, I guess we should be grateful there haven't been more casualties."*

"Those pilots aren't dead yet," Richard said as he turned his

Long Cat in the direction of the burning Leviathan.

"*Rick, no!*" Nickelo shouted into their shared space. "*You don't have time. The other Leviathan's preparing to fire.*"

CHAPTER 3

Richard was thrown hard against the right side of his seat as something slammed into the side of his cat.

"Eject!" shouted Nickelo.

Richard still had his body surrounded by Power from his earlier preparation for shifting into the void and immediately used it to dimensional shift just as a jet of flame along with molten pieces of metal entered the inside of the Long Cat's cockpit. Richard pulled himself backward with telekinesis and into his Warcat, which was still hanging onto the back of the Long Cat. He released the grip on the Long Cat's missile pods and kicked backward with the Warcat's legs just as the Long Cat exploded. A blast of fire and plasma energy hit his Warcat, throwing it backward a good twenty meters.

This time luck was with Richard. The Warcat's force field held. As soon as the Warcat hit the ground, he tucked his cat's legs against its chest and rolled to reduce the shock of landing. After two rolls, he straightened the legs and ran toward the attacking Leviathan. He was no longer concerned with the fate of the crew in the burning Leviathan. Their fellow Trecorian would have to save them. He had worries of his own now.

The Leviathan lit up as all of its weapons began firing.

Richard didn't give the gunners on the Leviathan time to adjust their aim. He was a dodging blur in his Warcat. He freely admitted he was only a mediocre pilot when it came to larger cats, but all modesty aside, he knew he was one of the best Warcat pilots in the

Empire. It felt as if the Warcat was an extension of himself.

Richard jumped to the side as fast as his Warcat's assistors could move the two thousand kilos of metal and weapons. With only a little help from his battle computer, Richard zigzagged his way toward the attacking Leviathan while doing his best to avoid its fire.

"The Warcat's force field is down to twenty-two percent," said Nickelo. *"You can't take another hit from any of the Leviathan's larger guns or missiles. I calculate you'd have a sixty-four percent chance of getting away if you retreated to the south."*

"I'm a Marine," Richard said. *"Marines don't retreat."*

Richard continued running while attempting to make it as difficult as possible for the gunners to adjust their aim.

"Smart marines retreat when the situation dictates," said Nickelo. *"At least the ones who want to stay alive do. Besides, don't think of it as retreating. Think of it as attacking in the opposite direction."*

When Richard didn't reply, Nickelo said, *"Okay, I can see you're going to do what you're going to do regardless of what I say. So what's your plan, oh greatest but most stubborn of all wizard scouts?"*

"I haven't the faintest idea," Richard said as he twisted the Warcat to avoid a stream of plasma rounds. *"What's my Power level?"*

He was still fifty meters from the Leviathan and doubted he could close the distance before the gunners got him in their sights.

"Your Power reserve is at thirty-eight percent," said Nickelo. *"It's not nearly enough to form a defensive shield capable of stopping all that firepower."*

"That's not my plan," Richard said as he sent his idea.

"It might work," said Nickelo after analyzing Richard's plan. *"Two years ago, thirty-eight percent wouldn't be enough. But you've improved your efficiency significantly during the last two years. I calculate you'll have five percent Power remaining in your reserve if you don't dawdle."*

Richard didn't plan on dawdling.

Nickelo flashed the image of a dip in the ground to his left that was just large enough to hide the Warcat.

Richard dove for the depression, and as soon as the Warcat hit the ground, he wrapped himself in Power and shifted into the void. Using telekinesis, he moved below ground toward the Leviathan. Everything was black underground, but it was easy to keep track of the Leviathan with his passive scan.

"You need to pick up the pace," said Nickelo. *"You're down to eighteen percent Power."*

"I'm going as fast as I can," Richard said unable to think of any way to significantly speed up his progress. But he did change his destination from the back of the Leviathan to the front to save a few meters.

Five seconds later, Richard rose out of the ground and levitated upward until he passed through the Leviathan's outer skin and into its chest cavity, then dropped his Power and shifted back into the physical dimension.

"You've only got three percent Power left," said Nickelo. *"I've been telling you to practice your efficiency more. You're not that good yet at using telekinesis to move long distances while you're in the void."*

"Understood," Richard said. Moving while in the void continued to be one of Richard's weaknesses as far as efficiency was concerned. No one knew it better than him.

Reaching to the left side of his utility belt, Richard unhooked his phase rod and activated it in stun mode. A meter-long length of brerellium with a creallium core popped out of the handle of the phase rod. Phase energy resembling small bolts of red lightning ran up and down the length of the rod, which emanated a feeling of hunger as if it wanted to feed on the life force of the living creatures around it.

Wasting no time, Richard ran four steps along a metal catwalk and shoved his phase rod into an open hatch on his left. A female sitting behind a control panel for four gun ports was just starting to rise from her seat with a blaster in her right hand. Richard's phase rod caught her in the stomach. Her blaster clattered to the floor followed by her body as she rolled around struggling for breath.

Taking another step down the catwalk, Richard thrust his phase rod into a hatchway to his right. The gunner inside was faster than his companion. A burst of plasma rounds burnt holes in the thin-metal wall behind Richard's head. Ducking below the streaks of plasma energy, Richard brought his phase rod down on the man's knee. The man's scream was cut off when Richard brought the phase rod back up between the man's legs, to his groin.

Not waiting to see if the man fell, Richard jumped the three steps leading to the Leviathan's cockpit. The steel hatch to the cockpit was shut and battened down. Richard wrapped himself with Power and shifted into the void.

"You can't stay in the void long with only three percent Power," said Nickelo.

"I don't need to stay there long," Richard said. *"I only need to get through the door."*

Richard willed himself forward with telekinesis. As his shifted body got even with the hatch, he felt a sudden jar and bounced back.

"What the hell?"

"Drop your shift," said Nickelo. *"The cockpit's hatch and walls must be reinforced with creallium."*

Richard dropped his Power and shifted back into the physical dimension. Creallium existed in both the void and the physical dimension. He wasn't going to be able to pass through to the cockpit like he'd planned.

"Power, Nick?" Richard said.

"You've got a little less than one percent," said Nickelo.

"Good enough," Richard said trying to remain undeterred by his failure to gain easy access to the cockpit.

Pulling the pack off his back, Richard imagined a satchel full of quarter-pound blocks of J22 plastic explosives with electronic timers. He felt a small amount of Power leave his reserve.

The dimensional pack had been issued during his freshman year at the Academy, and as far as Richard knew, he was the only living wizard scout that had one. With it, he could summon just about any item he could imagine. The only problem was that the more technologically complex an item, the more Power it took to summon it. There were exceptions, but those were the general rules. Thankfully, J22s and timers were extremely low-tech.

Opening the flap of his dimensional pack, Richard pulled out the satchel full of J22 blocks. Removing a block and twisting the top off, he quickly squeezed the malleable plastic into the seam around the hatchway's upper hinge, then did the same to the lower hinge using a second block.

"Set two seconds on the timers," Richard said as he pushed an electronic timer into the plastic around each hinge.

"Compliance," said Nickelo.

"Activate," Richard said.

He jumped down the steps and into the hatch where he'd left the female disabled earlier. She was just rising to her knees when Richard entered. A quick slap to the side of the female's head with his phase rod knocked her back to the floor unconscious.

Boom!

Richard stepped back into the hallway. It was full of smoke, but the night vision filter of his battle helmet had no trouble seeing through the haze. He jumped up the steps to the hatchway and yanked the partially ajar door off what was left of its hinges. The steel hatch was heavy, but the battle suit's assistors were up to the task. The hatch clattered to the metal deck.

The cockpit was full of smoke as well. A male pilot was still in his seat holding both hands to his ears, blood running out of his nose. The female pilot was standing with a hand blaster pointed in the general direction of the cockpit's entrance. She got two rounds off before Richard's phase rod caught her on the side of the head. As she fell to the floor, he knocked the male pilot out with a backswing.

"You're taking too long," said Nickelo. *"There's another quad of cats coming in from the west. A third quad is already in a blocking position to your north. You're going to be caught between them if you don't hurry."*

"I'm doing the best I can." Richard jumped down the stairs from the cockpit and ran toward the back of the Leviathan. He had to disable the rear gunners before he could make his escape.

As Richard passed the hatch with the male gunner, he swung his phase rod downward. The man was still lying on the metal floor moaning and holding his groin with both hands. Richard's swing caught the gunner on top of his head. The groaning stopped.

"Is he dead?" Richard said as he continued running along the metal catwalk of the hallway. Richard had swung harder than he'd intended. But then, he was in a hurry, so he had a valid excuse.

"Negative," said Nickelo. *"I calculate he'll have a mild concussion when he wakes up, but he'll survive."*

Richard felt better. He had nothing personal against the crew of the Leviathan. Other than the fact that they'd been trying to kill him, of course. But they were soldiers, and they'd just been doing their job. He'd be doing the same in their boots.

As Richard ran, he slung his dimensional pack onto his back and the satchel of J22 over his shoulder to free both hands, then located the final two crewmen with a passive scan. They were both in a room at the rear of the Leviathan. The hatch to the rear room was open, and rounds of plasma energy burst forth as the crewmen opened fire.

The hallway at the back of the Leviathan was as full of smoke as the front, so the gunners' vision was obscured, but the hallway was narrow and lack of vision didn't inhibit their aim all that much. Richard had very little room to maneuver. He dodged several rounds, but two blasts of plasma energy glanced off the left arm of his battle suit. His battle suit's tough armor held. Even though the suit was the best the Empire's technicians could create, Richard knew it wouldn't hold up against multiple hits if they were straight on.

"Maybe you should start wearing a personal force field to supplement your armor," Nickelo suggested.

"I'll take that under consideration if I live through the next few minutes," Richard replied.

He hated it when his battle computer made suggestions too late for him to do anything about it. Besides, the equipment for a personal force field was bulky and would just get in his way.

Richard was tempted to throw the satchel with the remaining blocks of J22 at the rear gunners but didn't. Eighteen blocks of J22 were enough explosives to take out half the inside of the Leviathan. Only pieces of the gunners would remain.

"Yeah," agreed Nickelo. *"And maybe only pieces of you as well."*

Reaching down to the front of his utility belt, Richard felt for his two standard issue anti-personnel grenades and a starburst signaling grenade. Unhooking the starburst grenade, he pulled the pin and threw the grenade at the gunners as he simultaneously dropped to the metal deck of the catwalk in an attempt to avoid their fire.

"Switch to max filter, Nick," Richard ordered.

Everything went black as the battle suit's visor changed from its familiar red tint to a black-opaque color more suitable for looking directly at the sun than for normal vision. Richard could just make out several bright beams of plasma energy passing a meter over his head. Although the vision of the gunners was still obscured by smoke, Richard had no doubt they would soon think to fire at the floor as well as the center of the hallway. He needed to get them out of action before one of them got lucky.

Boom!

A flash of light lit up the hallway. Even with his visor at max filter, the light was bright enough to leave flashing red spots in front of Richard's eyes. Jumping to his feet, he thought the command to change the battle helmet's visor back to its normal night vision. The view of his surroundings took on its familiar red tint once more. Richard closed the distance to the two guards. Both females were holding their arms over their eyes and staggering around, bouncing off the walls. Richard knocked them both out with his phase rod.

"Time!" Richard said.

"I calculate you have a minute and forty-five seconds before the next quad of cats is in firing position," said Nickelo.

"It's going to be close," Richard said.

Grabbing an unconscious crewman with each hand, Richard started dragging them along the hallway toward the front of the Leviathan. Near the area by the front gunners, Richard stopped at an escape hatch he'd noticed earlier and pulled the emergency-release handle. The hatch blew outward, and an inflatable slide popped out of the doorway to the ground below. Richard threw the two rear gunners down the slide, then stepped into the hatches where the two forward gunners lay, pulled them back to the emergency hatch, and threw them down the slide as well.

"One minute and ten seconds," said Nickelo. *"Forget about the pilots. You don't have time for this."*

"I can't leave them inside," Richard said. *"I don't want to have to worry about them regaining consciousness. They might start taking potshots at my Warcat's back with 240mm phase rounds. That would tend to slow down my withdrawal a little, don't you think?"*

"Then throw the bag of J22 into the cockpit and be done with it," said Nickelo. *"Now's not the time to become a conscientious*

objector. I don't understand what's going on with you today. You've killed plenty of people before."

Richard didn't really understand why he was putting his life at risk for these soldiers either. But it didn't matter. Just because he'd killed before didn't mean he enjoyed killing. Regardless of his reason, Richard let his battle computer know what he thought of his suggestion by running back into the cockpit and dragging the two pilots to the escape slide. As soon as they were out the hatch, he threw his bag of J22 into the cockpit and jumped out the escape hatch, not bothering to use the slide. The six-meter drop to the ground was a short hop for his battle suit.

Richard grabbed two of the Leviathan's crew and dragged them a safe distance away, then did the same for the remaining four by taking them two at a time. Nickelo complained continuously that the quad of approaching cats was too close. Richard refused to leave the crew within range of the heavy cat in case it fell.

"Fine," said Nickelo. *"They're clear. You've only got twenty seconds before those other cats are within firing range. Now get back into your Warcat. It's time to get out of here."*

"Agreed," Richard said. *"Set the timers for twenty seconds and activate. And plot me a route out of here while you're at it."*

"Timers are set and activated," said Nickelo. *"I've marked the route on your heads-up display that has the highest probability of keeping us alive."*

Richard had just enough Power in his reserve to shift into the void and enter the Warcat. He raised the Warcat to its feet and shifted it into high gear. Bending low, Richard ran southward with all possible haste along the path his battle computer had marked. Just before he got to the crest of the ridge, Richard took a final look behind using the Warcat's rear visuals. The Leviathan he'd just left was still standing upright and unmoving on its six legs.

Glancing at the burning Leviathan he'd destroyed earlier, Richard noticed it was now engulfed almost totally in flames. Only the cockpit area remained free of fire. He figured even the cockpit would be completely enveloped within a matter of seconds. Heavy smoke was pouring out of its chest area, making it difficult to see the rest of the heavy cat. A gust of wind momentarily blew the smoke clear of the cockpit area.

What Richard saw caused him to bring the Warcat to a sudden

halt.

"Rick, no!" said Nickelo with a sense of urgency Richard seldom heard his battle computer use. *"There's no time. The other quad will be within firing range in twelve seconds. You're out of Power and you're out of options. Use your head, Rick. You've got to get out of here."*

Richard's head told him to leave, but the sight in the Warcat's rear visuals caused something to unexpectedly tug at his heart. He could just make out the form of a pilot beating furiously against the windscreen of the burning Leviathan's cockpit with a metal bar. Inside the cockpit, two pilots frantically beat against the windscreen with their bare hands from the other side.

"Why hasn't he gotten them out yet?" Richard said. *"All the larger cats have emergency overrides for their escape hatches on the outside."*

"Actually," said Nickelo, *"standard procedure on larger cats is to deactivate the outside overrides during combat engagements. If they weren't disabled, an enemy soldier could open an emergency hatch and toss in a grenade. You aren't in the large cats much, so maybe you forgot."*

Richard had forgotten. He preferred the smaller recon cats, which were too small to even have outside emergency overrides.

"Those pilots are going to be burned alive," Richard said. *"And that Long Cat pilot looks like he will as well. I don't think he has any intention of abandoning his friends."*

"Yes, very noble of him," said Nickelo without the slightest hint of compassion. *"So wish them well and let's be on our way. The other quad can help their companions when they get here."*

Logic told Richard to leave. But something he couldn't pinpoint continued to tug at his heart. He tried to force his head to take charge, but it was no use. The tug was too powerful.

"How long before the other quad will be in a position to assist the Leviathan's crew?" Richard said.

"Forty-two seconds if they don't waste too much time blowing holes in your Warcat," said Nickelo. *"Now stop stalling and get this cat hauling its metallic-butt south."*

Richard didn't move. *"How long before the flames reach the cockpit?"*

"I don't know exactly," hedged Nickelo. *"There are lots of*

variables."

"Guess," Richard commanded.

"Fine," said Nickelo. *"Those two crewmen will be dead in fifteen seconds. And that other pilot will probably be dead as well. And you'll be dead too if you don't hightail it out of here right now. The lead cat in the other quad will be within firing range in nine seconds."*

The strange tugging on Richard's heart continued. He wasn't used to this feeling. Deciding not to waste any more time trying to figure things out, he ran toward the burning Leviathan. Dense smoke once again obscured the cockpit area. Intense flames spouted from the Leviathan's main body, playing havoc with Richard's standard night-vision visor.

"Switch to radiation filter," Richard said as he ran into the smoke.

Everything turned to shades of white and gray as his battle helmet's visor flickered while it switched to radiation filter. The visor was more a force field than it was a physical object, so the switchover between filters was fast.

The radiation filter picked up the Long Cat's pilot. He was still beating against the Leviathan's windscreen with his metal bar. The man was in a normal-cloth jumpsuit and not a power-suit, but his blows were still powerful enough to bend his metal bar. In spite of his herculean efforts, the windscreen remained intact. The Long Cat's pilot was so intent on trying to break through the windscreen that he failed to notice Richard's presence.

"Move!" Richard shouted over the Warcat's external speakers. "Now!"

Startled, the pilot jumped, then froze mid-swing at Richard's yell. His eyes widened at the enemy Warcat racing toward him, then he threw his metal bar at the Warcat's windscreen, and quick as lightning drew a phase pistol from his belt and fired point-blank at Richard.

If the Warcat's armored windscreen hadn't been between them, the shots would have struck Richard dead-center between the eyes. As it was, both the metal bar and phase rounds bounced harmlessly off the Warcat's armor.

"Now that's gratitude for you," said Nickelo. *"I told you to leave them. You should know by now no good deed goes*

unpunished."

Richard ignored his battle computer and gave the Warcat's left arm a little flick. The end of the 40mm autocannon caught the man on the shoulder and shoved him none too gently out of the way.

The man continued to fire even as he was being thrown through the air.

"Eleven seconds until the flames enter the cockpit," said Nickelo finally resigned to the fact his wizard scout wasn't going to leave until the Leviathan's crew were freed. *"And you only have five seconds until the enemy quad is within firing range. I doubt they'll miss at this range."*

Richard didn't waste time answering. He saw the reason the Leviathan's pilots hadn't abandoned their cat on their own. The frame around the cockpit's emergency exit was buckled. Richard doubted even his Warcat had the strength to tear the hatch off the heavy cat.

"Target the weakest point on the Leviathan's windscreen with the 40mm," Richard said. *"Blast the windscreen open for the pilots."*

"Compliance," said Nickelo.

The Warcat's left arm moved to point the barrel of the 40mm auto-cannon at the lower right corner of the Leviathan.

"I calculate it will take four rounds to weaken the armored glass," said Nickelo. *"You'll have to finish breaking it out manually. If we fire a fifth round, the windscreen will shatter and the 40mm will explode inside. I calculate that would seriously defeat the purpose of this whole endeavor. You do remember those pilots were trying to kill you not five minutes ago, don't you? This is such a waste of precious time, in my opinion. You're going to get us both killed."*

"I don't care," Richard said as the 40mm fired its first round.

The half-second delay between reloads seemed an eternity. The first round did little more than bounce off the Leviathan's windscreen while only leaving a slight smear. Richard noticed the two pilots inside the cockpit diving for the far side of their tiny compartment. The Long Cat's pilot was back on his feet, firing phase rounds at the Warcat as fast as he could pull the trigger of his blaster. He might as well have been throwing water balloons for all the good it did him. The small-caliber rounds were no match for the Warcat's armor.

"I calculate he thinks you're trying to kill his friends," said Nickelo. *"That doesn't seem very logical to me. The fire is going to kill them in a few seconds anyway. Why would he think you'd bother trying to hasten their deaths?"*

The second 40mm round hit the Leviathan's windscreen. A small crack appeared in the corner of the armored glass. The third round caused the single crack to multiply into a spider web of cracks. At the fourth round, the cracks lengthened until they extended all the way to the far corner of the shattered windscreen.

Richard drew back the Warcat's left arm in preparation for ramming the autocannon's barrel through the windscreen.

"Incoming!" yelled Nickelo. *"Duck!"*

Richard's years of association with his battle computer caused him to instinctively obey without question. It had saved his life often enough in the past. He dropped the Warcat down to all fours. Half a dozen plasma beams along with a 240mm phase round passed through the area where the Warcat's head had been.

"Run, Rick! There's no time. The Leviathan's pilots are as good as dead. Save yourself."

Richard was tempted to run, and might have if it had been anything but fire. He hated fire. During a night of rioting when he'd been an orphaned teen living on the streets back on Earth, Richard had seen people being burned alive while trapped in buildings by rioting mobs and still had occasional nightmares of that horrible night. The screams of the victims were vivid in his memory. Fire frightened Richard. He wasn't afraid of dying, but being burned alive was one of his greatest fears. He didn't wish a fiery death on anyone, not even his enemies.

As Richard wrestled with his emotions, he noticed the first flickers of flames entering the cockpit from the door leading back to the Leviathan's main body. The sound of screams as the trapped pilots sensed their pending doom assaulted Richard's ears. They beat even harder on the cracked glass, their hands leaving streaks of blood.

The pilot outside the cat had finally abandoned shooting at Richard. He'd replaced his pistol with a head-sized rock and was furiously pounding away at the windscreen in a desperate attempt to save his fellow soldiers from a horrible death.

Both the pilots inside the cockpit and the one outside were wearing helmets with visors down, so Richard couldn't see their faces. But he didn't need to see them to understand their fear. He could feel their fear. He knew it was there as sure as if it had been something tangible he could see. The sensation of fear was as clear as if it was coming from within himself. Richard had never before experienced anything like the level of empathy he was feeling now. A part of his mind wondered if it was a side-effect of the DNA baseline he'd received the previous year. The other part of his mind didn't care. It just reacted.

In spite of the danger, Richard stood the Warcat upright and rammed the barrel of the autocannon into the center of the Leviathan's windscreen. The sound of breaking glass was followed by a small hole the size of a grapefruit appearing in the windscreen. Richard drew the Warcat's arm back for a second strike.

Before Richard could complete the blow, his Warcat was thrown forward by something slamming into its left shoulder. Even encased in his battle suit and the surrounding gel, Richard was bounced painfully around the inside of the cat. Red lights flashed all over the Warcat's instrument panel as systems overloaded and shut down.

"In case you're interested," said Nickelo, *"that was a 100mm phase round. It was a glancing blow, but it still penetrated part of your Warcat's armor. You're lucky it wasn't a 240mm round, or they'd be picking up your pieces off the ground in order to get enough to bury in a small can. By the way, the Warcat's hydraulics are offline. My recommendation is to get out now. But then, you haven't been taking my advice lately, so what do I know?"*

The Warcat fell to the ground. Richard tried to rise, but the cat refused to respond. Richard thought the command to eject. The emergency escape hatch blew outward, accompanied by Richard and a jet of thick gel. He rolled twice on the ground before coming to a stop.

"Up!" yelled Nickelo. *"Head south. The quad is closing the distance fast. I calculate a sixty-two percent probability they're going to try to take you prisoner. Believe me, you don't want that to happen."*

Richard leaped to his feet but didn't head south. Instead, he jumped back toward the burning Leviathan's cockpit.

The Long Cat's pilot had picked up another scrap piece of metal, jammed it into the hole in the Leviathan's windscreen, and was tugging on the end of the metal bar like it was a crowbar. Even with both of his legs braced against the glass, the windscreen didn't budge.

With zero time remaining, Richard grabbed the rod out of the man's hands and jerked back. The strength of his battle suit's assistors was strained to the limit, but a large section of the windscreen came out with the metal rod. The Long Cat's pilot was thrown to the ground along with the metal rod. Dense smoke from outside flowed into the new opening and large flames entered the cockpit from the main-cabin door as its seals were burned away.

Reaching into the opening, Richard grabbed both of the Leviathan's pilots and yanked them out. He was none too gentle, and the force of his throw sent the pilots rolling along the ground. He was barely able to step back from the cockpit before a blast of heat and fire erupted around him.

At the same time, a series of shocks hit Richard's back. Plasma beams ricocheted all around him. His battle suit reflected most of the enemy fire until a solid projectile wrapped in phase energy slammed him forward as it penetrated his battle suit's back armor. He was lucky the phase round had enough momentum to pass completely through his shoulder and out the front side of his battle suit as well. Otherwise, it would've bounced around inside the battle suit until its momentum was spent. A phase round could put a lot of holes in a human body before its energy was spent.

Falling to the ground, Richard screamed from the white-hot pain in his shoulder. With the loss of the battle suit's seal, the tubes in his mouth and nose retracted.

"Don't breathe, Rick," Nickelo warned.

Part of Richard's mind heard his battle computer and understood the reason for his warning. But his body didn't care. It reacted to the shock of the hit by drawing in a big gulp of air. Unfortunately, all he got was a lung full of dense smoke and immediately started coughing.

"Up! Up!" yelled Nickelo. *"Get on your feet and run, soldier. That's an order."*

Richard tried to stand but was too busy coughing and retching to obey. He could feel his body trying to self-heal. The pain in his shoulder subsided slightly as the Power in his healing reserve did its job. However, the dense smoke continued to damage his lungs as fast as his Power could heal it. The largest of his three reserves was only for healing any injuries his body acquired, and healing Power could heal ninety percent of an injury within a short period of time. The other ten percent might take several minutes or even hours. However, if the source of damage was continuous, the best the healing Power could do was keep the wizard scout alive. That is, it would keep the wizard scout alive until the Power in their reserve ran out.

If Richard had been by himself, he might have lain on the ground gagging from the poisonous fumes until he was captured or died from lack of Power. But he wasn't alone. He had his battle computer.

The legs and arms of the battle suit began moving, and the suit rose to a standing position as Nickelo took control. Richard felt himself begin to run left and right as his battle computer dodged both solid projectiles and phase beams. Within seconds, he was clear of the smoke and gratefully sucked clean air into his lungs. After a few quick breaths, Richard's self-heal removed most of the damage to his oxygen-starved body. While the wound to his shoulder still hurt, the pain was rapidly being reduced. Even so, he opted not to retake control of his battle suit. Phase beams were passing all around him, and a line of 20mm rounds from a chain gun tore up the ground to his right side. Richard was confident the incoming fire was too heavy and too fast for him to dodge for long on his own.

The battle suit jumped left just as an explosion erupted. Richard was thrown through the air and landed hard on his left side. He screamed in agony as the shock reopened his partially-healed shoulder.

Nickelo passed control of the battle suit back to him. Richard ignored his pain as best he could and rose to his feet on his own. He wasn't sure retaking control was the smartest thing to do at this point but trusted his battle computer.

"I calculate they're no longer attempting to take you prisoner," said Nickelo.

"You calculated that all on your own?" Richard said as he

sidestepped to the left to throw off the gunners, barely avoiding a stream of plasma rounds. *"Maybe you should keep control of the suit, Nick. My shoulder isn't fully healed yet."*

"Negative," said Nickelo. *"I'm too logical. The targeting computers on those cats are beginning to anticipate my moves. I almost got you killed with that last explosion. We need your randomness and free will to get us out of this. I've marked a new path on your heads-up display. If you can avoid dying for another thirty seconds, I calculate a sixty-four percent probability you can lose them in the boulder field to your east. You've got your best stealth shield up. Once those cats lose visual sight of you, they shouldn't be able to track you."*

Richard wasn't sure he could stay out of the line of fire for ten more seconds, much less thirty. His battle suit was fast, but it couldn't match the speed of ten-meter tall Leviathans. Fortunately, either due to the randomness of his moves or blind luck, Richard made it to the boulder field alive. Just as he entered the rocky area, two blue blips appeared on his heads-up display.

"What are those blue things?" Richard said.

"They're Trecorian transport shuttles," answered Nickelo. *"From their trajectories, I calculate a ninety-four percent probability they're going to drop a blocking force on the far edge of the boulder field to prevent your escape."*

Richard reached out with his passive scan and let the Power from the two transports flow into his mind. He didn't like what he sensed. He sent the results of the scan to his shared space.

"Hmm," said Nickelo. *"Either those transport shuttles are larger than I think, or they've jammed soldiers into them like sardines. I don't see how they can cram two hundred and twenty-five fully-grown soldiers into them. Plus, each transport has a quad of light cats onboard to boot."*

"Well, they've done it somehow," Richard said. *"Now what?"*

Nickelo paused for a nanosecond. *"Well, first off, I take back what I said about you having a sixty-four percent chance of escaping. I've decided to revise my calculations slightly."*

"I'm sure you have," Richard said. *"And what are my odds now?"*

"Oh, they're about the same as a snowball's chance of remaining solid in the middle of a supernova," said Nickelo.

"Maybe they're a little better, but not by much."

Richard heard the sound of crashing trees behind him as the first of the Leviathans on his tail came charging out of the woods. He had no doubt they would have him in visual sight soon enough. He had to do something quick.

"What's our distance to the rendezvous point?" Richard said.

"Twenty kilometers," said Nickelo. *"Sergeant Ron's already there with our recon ship."*

Richard's maintenance officer had dropped him off the previous day via high-altitude insertion from an advanced-tech recon ship named *Defiant II*. Unlike the recon shuttles Richard was used to, the *Defiant* was a fully-functional starship capable of making jumps between folds in the dimensional plane when required. And like frontline starships, the *Defiant* could travel at more sustainable speeds using its hyper-drive. The *Defiant* was not Empire issue. The Empire wasn't in the habit of issuing starships to wizard scouts who were assigned to nondescript mercenary outfits in District 2. The *Defiant II* was fully owned and operated by Sergeant Ron. Richard had known Sergeant Ron was an expert at maintaining cats, but not that he was also an expert at maintaining small recon ships. He also hadn't known Sergeant Ron had a long list of friends who happened to owe him favors he could call in whenever he encountered a maintenance situation he couldn't handle. The end result was the *Defiant* being incredibly fast and well maintained despite Sergeant Ron keeping it otherwise pieced together from equipment he occasionally found at salvage yards.

"Why is Sergeant Ron already at the rendezvous point?" Richard said. *"It's way too early if I'm still twenty kilometers out."*

"Why?" said Nickelo. *"Because you were supposed to be there four hours ago. I'm surprised the Trecorian's haven't discovered the presence of the* Defiant *already. You're lucky you summoned those parts Sergeant Ron needed for the ship's stealth shield before we left on this mission."*

Richard glanced at his heads-up display and merged it with the data from his shared space. The combined information confirmed what he'd already suspected. There was no way he could get to the rendezvous point before the Trecorians intercepted him. Even if he did make it to Sergeant Ron's location alive, he figured a well-aimed anti-aircraft missile would blow the *Defiant* out of the sky before it could clear the atmosphere.

Richard dodged around a large boulder just as a Trecorian Long Cat burst out of the forest to join the Leviathan.

"That was close," Richard said as he ran while trying to keep the boulder between the Long Cat and himself. *"Do you think they spotted us?"*

"Are they shooting at you?" said Nickelo. *"No, they aren't. I calculate a ninety-six percent probability that they haven't spotted you yet."*

Before Richard could reply, a series of plasma beams passed an arm's length over his left shoulder and a score of 20mm chain-gun rounds tore up the ground to his right.

"On second thought," said Nickelo. *"I've recalculated the probabilities. My recalculations indicate they've spotted you after all."*

"Thanks for the timely update," Richard said as he dove for a small ravine to his front. He hit the bottom on his left side, his shoulder still a little painful but almost back to normal. *"Send the abort signal to Sergeant Ron. Tell him I said to leave. Tell him we'll make contact via your security interface to the tele-network once we find a safe area."*

Richard said a silent curse at the Empire's central computer for denying his battle computer direct access to the tele-network. The central computer believed direct contact with Nickelo would emotionally corrupt other computers on the tele-network. Consequently, his battle computer was only allowed access through tightly-controlled security interfaces, which had greatly limited the battle computer's ability to function effectively on several occasions.

"You mean if we can find a safe area," corrected Nickelo. *"That's not a given. Message has been sent. Sergeant Ron has acknowledged and said for you to head toward the lake to our south. He said he'd meet us there."*

"Negative," Richard said. *"Tell Sergeant Ron I said he is to abort. Tell him I said that's an order."*

After a slight delay, Nickelo said, *"Sergeant Ron said screw your order and the horse it rode in on. He said he's been disobeying orders since before you were born and a wet-behind-the-ears wizard scout doesn't impress him much."* Nickelo chuckled. *"You know, Rick, you may as well accept the fact that he's not going to abort. My recommendation is to make tracks south and head for the lake."*

"Fine!" Richard said as he jumped to his feet and ran south again. As he ran, he imagined an M63 lightweight plasma assault rifle, reached over his shoulder, lifted the flap of his dimensional pack, and pulled out an M63.

"You might have been better off summoning an M12," said Nickelo. *"Those infantry troops are down now, and at least some of them are in armor. It'll take multiple rounds from your M63 to penetrate even low-grade armor."*

"I know," Richard said as he did a quick function-check on his M63. *"But I'm low on Power. I wanted the M63 because it's a freebie. Besides, I don't want to kill anyone unless I'm forced. Our mission was to find information on a possible DNA gas vent. It wasn't to create new enemies. The high-energy rounds from the M12 would have too great a chance of being lethal even against armor."*

"Have it your way, oh greatest of wizard scouts," said Nickelo. *"I'm only here to advise and serve."*

"Now's not the time for sarcasm," Richard said irritably. The stress of the situation was starting to take its toll on his nerves.

"Fine," said Nickelo. *"I'll try to be more serious. You do see the line of infantry to your front on your passive scan, don't you?"*

In point of fact, Richard did see them. And he was depending on those very soldiers to help him break out of the swiftly closing trap set by the medium and heavy cats behind him.

"The twelve soldiers at our eleven o'clock position are unorganized," Richard said. *"Their leader must be falling down on the job. I don't think they have a visual on me yet. They know I'm in the boulder field, but not where."*

"And your plan is?" said Nickelo with more than a hint of curiosity.

"I'm going to charge right into them," Richard said. *"I'm hoping the cats behind me won't fire for fear of hitting their own troops."*

"Well, I guess it's always nice to hope," said Nickelo.

"Whatever," Richard said. He was out of options, so it didn't matter what his battle computer thought. Richard noticed his battle

computer wasn't giving any alternate suggestions or probabilities, which normally meant Nickelo couldn't come up with a plan that had a better than five percent chance of success.

Fully committed, Richard changed direction to his eleven o'clock and ran full speed toward the spot where the group of soldiers seemed to be milling around. He had a momentary thought that they might be good soldiers for all he knew, but they definitely weren't marines. No marine sergeant he'd ever known would put up with their troops clumping together like that.

Richard was only three steps out of the ravine when a weapons-lock warning flashed red on his heads-up display.

"The Long Cat has a lock on you," came Nickelo's voice into Richard's mind. *"Dodge left."*

Richard dove left and hit the ground in a summersault.

A burst of plasma rounds hit where he'd been sending dirt and broken bits of stone flying into the air.

Rolling out of his summersault, Richard jumped to his feet and leaped to the top of a shuttle-sized boulder. With another leap, he was back on the ground and running straight for a dozen startled soldiers. Half of them were in armor and the other half in sand-colored, camouflage fatigues. They were all armed with plasma rifles.

For a split second, time froze and Richard made out every detail of the situation as Nickelo funneled all available data into their shared space. With a shock, Richard realized most of the dozen soldiers before him were not soldiers at all. They were too young to be soldiers. Two of the unarmored soldiers appeared to be preteens. Richard could only make out one adult in the group, and he appeared to be an old man in his late sixties.

The old man and two of the armored soldiers recovered faster than their companions. They overcame their initial surprise and started bringing their weapons to bear on Richard. The old man actually got a short burst from his plasma rifle off before Richard kicked him in the chest. The old man went flying one way and his plasma rifle went the other.

Richard did a spin in the air while at the same time switching his phase rod to full destructive mode. He chopped downward onto the arm of one of the armored soldiers. The armor was good, and Richard's phase rod glanced off. However, the rod's phase energy penetrated the soldier's armor and shattered the man's elbow. The man's plasma rifle fell to the ground.

No, not a man, Richard thought. Through the soldier's visor, Richard made out the face of a young girl with short-cut blonde hair and steel-blue eyes. She reminded him a little of his friend Liz from the Academy. The girl didn't look much older than his fourteen-year-old niece, Dren. But Richard didn't feel too sympathetic toward the girl. The weapon she'd been holding made her an adult as far as he was concerned.

"Actually, Dren is still thirteen," Nickelo said matter-of-factly.

Richard ignored his battle computer, instead thinking of his niece who had been sent a hundred and fifty-seven years in the past.

When the phase rod made contact with the girl's arm, Richard had noticed her eyes widen in fear, followed by an intense expression of pain. Not only had the energy from the phase rod basically disintegrated her elbow but the demon essence in the rod's creallium core had also sucked out some of her life force before ricocheting off.

The girl was still screaming in agony as Richard switched the direction of his swing toward the armored head of a second soldier trying to fire at him. At the last instant, he remembered his desire to avoid fatalities and angled the phase rod down onto the soldier's shoulder. Richard sensed muscle and bone give way before the rod's phase energy. The soldier screamed not only from the pain but from the loss of life force sucked out by the demon essence as well.

Richard felt a wave of emotions swirling around him. The feeling of hunger from the demon essence and its desire to consume the life force from every living thing within range permeated the area. Richard felt the fear of the young soldiers as they reacted to the demon essence. Some of the soldiers appeared to be so affected by it that they were momentarily paralyzed by their fear.

"Take advantage of it, Rick," said Nickelo. *"Put the rest of them out of action. You're running out of time. Those medium and heavy cats are closing fast."*

"Roger," Richard said as he kicked a plasma rifle out of the hands of another armored soldier. *"But I need help. Take out the*

unarmored ones." On a hunch, Richard added in command voice, *"Use non-lethal force."*

"Compliance," said Nickelo. *"And just so you know, there's a sixty-seven percent probability I might have used nonlethal force even if you hadn't ordered it."*

Richard felt the right arm of his battle suit swing from right to left. His M63 lightweight plasma assault rifle fired a long burst of plasma rounds at the legs of the unarmored soldiers still standing. All five of them fell to the ground. Another quick burst of rounds from the M63 caught two of the soldiers in their arms as they tried to bring their weapons to bear. Their rifles went flying as the plasma rounds shredded their unprotected arms.

"Keeping them alive is smart," said Nickelo. *"If you killed them all outright, those cats would be firing at you even now."*

Richard swung his phase rod horizontally at another armored soldier, a young boy. The phase rod shattered the boy's rifle and continued on to slam into the armor protecting the lad's side. The hit was straight on, and Richard felt the boy's armor crack as well as several of his ribs. He also sensed the rod's phase energy scrambling part of the boy's intestines. His scream of pain was abruptly cut off.

"Crap!" Richard said. *"I didn't mean to kill him."*

"He's not dead yet," said Nickelo. *"But you will be if you don't hurry. We need to get to the lake."*

"Then stop talking and help," Richard yelled into his shared space.

As Richard swung his phase rod at the knee of another armored soldier, he felt the right arm of his battle suit swinging toward a different armored soldier. When his M63 was aligned with the soldier's knee, he felt the finger of his battle suit's glove squeeze the trigger. The soldier's armor was good. Most of the light-plasma rounds were deflected off, but a couple of rounds penetrated a weak spot in the knee joint and found the flesh beneath. As the soldier screamed, Richard sensed the plasma rounds tearing the flesh and bone beneath his armor apart. One of the rounds failed to penetrate the other side of the armor. The plasma energy ricocheted inside the leg of the armor. The energy continued to ricochet until it dissipated. By then, there wasn't much left of the lower part of the soldier's leg.

While Nickelo continued to fire at his target, Richard took out another armored soldier by shattering the boy's kneecap with his phase rod. Once the boy was down, Richard turned to the armored soldier whose weapon he'd kicked out of his hands. The weaponless soldier was in the process of bending over to pick up a discarded plasma rifle. Richard brought his phase rod down on the small of the soldier's back. It was a weak spot in the armor. The phase energy easily penetrated the metal armor at the base of the spine. Particles of phase energy acted like miniature subatomic explosions as the soldier's spine turned into a glob of blood and powdered bone.

The soldier fell to the ground and no longer tried to grab his rifle.

Richard made the mistake of glancing at the soldier's visor. What he saw tore at his heart. The pain-filled face was that of a young boy probably no more than ten years old.

"What the hell is going on?" Richard said. *"What are they doing sending children against us?"*

"I don't know," said Nickelo. *"But this isn't the time to try and figure it out. Your path's clear now. Get moving. The nearest Long Cat will be here in twenty seconds."*

Richard's head told him to follow his battle computer's advice and get out while the getting was good. Unfortunately, the emotions of the wounded around him were overwhelming. He could sense the pain and fear of the children. He'd never before experienced this much emotional empathy. He didn't at all like it, but there it was.

Richard's passive scan told him what he needed to know. Two of the young soldiers were dying. He directed a quick active scan at each of them. The one he'd hit in the side had part of his intestines destroyed. Internal bleeding was already filling his body cavity. Richard had been around enough wounds to know that even if the boy lived long enough to get medical attention, there wasn't much a normal medic could do for him. And the other young boy wasn't any better off. The M63's plasma rounds had basically amputated the boy's left leg below the knee. The profuse bleeding Richard's scan picked up left him with little doubt that the boy would be dead before his companions could help him.

"What are you doing?" said Nickelo.

Richard imagined a half dozen tourniquet patches. A small amount of Power left his reserve. Reaching over his shoulder, he pulled the tourniquets out of his dimensional pack.

The old man Richard had first kicked was just scrambling to a sitting position while tugging at a hand blaster in a holster at his side. Richard jumped onto the old man and shoved him back to the ground. The weight of the battle suit combined with Richard's own body weight came to over two hundred kilos. Despite the old man's continued struggles to reach his weapon, he was helpless.

"No!" Richard yelled using his battle helmet's external speakers. He tore the hand blaster from the old man's waist, holster and all, then shoved one of the tourniquets into the old man's hands. "Get the boy out of his armor and put this on his leg. If you don't hurry, he's dead."

Without waiting to see if the old man complied, Richard threw the remaining bundle of tourniquets at the least wounded of the other soldiers. Hopefully, she knew enough first aid to minister to her companions. Richard figured he'd done about all he could do.

"Nick," Richard said. *"Take charge of the battle suit. Get us the hell out of here!"*

Richard reached out with his mind to the boy with the stomach wound and wrapped the boy's wound with Power. He imagined how the boy's intestines should be, then compared it with how the boy's intestines were now.

"Rick, no!" yelled Nickelo into their shared space. *"I forbid it!"*

It was too late. Richard was an emp-healer. Before he could heal someone, his own body had to take on their injuries. The right half of Richard's intestines scrambled into a pulp to replicate the boy's injuries. He heard the sound of a tortured animal screaming in the distance before blessed unconsciousness overtook him.

If it had been up to him, Richard would have fallen to the ground and been easy prey for the approaching cats. But he was part of a team, and Nickelo moved the battle suit at double-quick time.

Just before Richard passed completely out, he sensed the boy's extensive injuries being healed. It took almost a quarter of the Power in Richard's healing reserve to bring the boy's body back to normal. When his Power finally began working on the acquired injuries in his own body, he was immersed in the darkness of unconsciousness.

CHAPTER 4

Richard felt a mild vibration against the bare flesh of his back. The vibration was soothing, and he wanted to remain wherever his pain-free body now found itself. Unfortunately, a drop of liquid ran into his eye and demanded attention. Raising his hand to his head, he felt his hair. It was damp.

"Am I bleeding?" Richard opened his eyes to look at his hand. Although his fingers were indeed wet, the liquid was clear.

A nearby hissing sound accompanied by a mechanical voice drew Richard's attention.

"You wake. Good," said the mechanical voice. "I have work to do."

Looking in the direction of the voice, Richard saw a muscular humanoid with gray-scaled skin and four arms. A translator box attached to the humanoid's belt was the source of the voice.

"Charlie?" Richard said. "Where am I?"

Sergeant Ron's assistant mechanic was one of the Empire's reptilian races from the Sterilian system in sector one. Richard had first met Charlie while a cadet at the Academy, and liked the old lizard. What Charlie lacked in conversational ability, he more than made up for with honesty and hard work.

One amazing thing about Charlie was that he had a Power reserve large enough to qualify him for wizard scout training. But instead of going to the Academy, he had chosen to use his psionic abilities to maintain heavy equipment such as cats. Through some fluke of Charlie's Power that Richard didn't quite understand, the old lizard could seemingly communicate with equipment in a manner sufficient enough to diagnose pending malfunctions. During his time at the Academy, Richard had known Charlie was an excellent UHAAV mechanic. Since their time together in the mercs, he had also discovered Charlie's affinity for maintaining the various systems on small starships such as the *Defiant*.

"You on ship," said Charlie. "You jump in lake. We fetch."

Richard took note of his surroundings. He was lying on a table in the small room the *Defiant* used as its medical facility. He was naked. An antiseptically-white sheet was wrapped around his body tight enough to give him the feeling of claustrophobia. The sheet was very sheer, and he could feel the cold metal of the examining room's table underneath his back. Swinging his legs over the side of the table, Richard stood up while keeping the sheet wrapped around him, albeit a little looser than it had been.

"Where's my battle suit?" Richard asked.

"Your battle suit's in the cargo bay. Charlie was going to fix the holes in your armor, but I told him not to bother. I calculate it would be easier for you to send the damaged battle suit back to Storage for repair. You can just summon a new one for yourself in the meantime. After all, you've still got almost two hundred of them left."

"Nick!" Richard said. *"What happened?"*

His battle computer didn't answer with words. Instead, Richard's shared space was flooded with information. He saw his battle suit running while dodging fire from multiple pursuing cats. When the battle suit reached the lake, it jumped in and sank to the bottom. Although the information was just cold, hard data, Richard could almost feel the freezing-cold lake water pouring into the battle suit from the hole in its shoulder. Just before the battle suit touched bottom, a four-armed humanoid in underwater gear grabbed the battle suit and dragged it into the airlock of the *Defiant*.

The scene switched. Richard saw the *Defiant* exploding out of the water and reaching for the sky as dozens of cats along the shoreline opened up with plasma beams, phase weapons, and anti-aircraft missiles. The *Defiant* evaded most of the fire. What little fire found its target was kept at bay by the force field around the recon ship. The next image to flash through the shared space was the blurring of stars as the *Defiant* transitioned to hyperspace.

Richard had been told often enough that he got an 'I am not in this room anymore' look on his face whenever he was in deep conversation with Nickelo. Charlie must have figured he was talking to his battle computer, and gave Richard a nod of his head and turned to leave. The old lizard had more important things to do than babysitting an obviously well wizard scout.

After giving a nod at Charlie's retreating back, Richard said, *"How long have I been out, Nick?"*

"Not long," said Nickelo. *"You've been unconscious for just a little over fifteen minutes."*

"That seems longer than it should be," Richard said. *"I've healed worse wounds than that before without even passing out."*

"Well," replied Nickelo. *"Yes and no. You've healed worse physical wounds. But the boy's stomach wound was tainted by the demon essence in your phase rod. I think that made all the difference. You probably need to be more careful with demon enhanced wounds in the future."*

"It would be fine with me if I never have to deal with demons ever again," Richard said.

Richard doubted he'd be that lucky. During his freshman year at the Academy, he'd helped the elf Shandria steal a magical seed from the demon Efrestra. The demon had sworn to hunt him down and torture him for a thousand years. Richard hadn't had contact with Efrestra since but doubted the demon had stopped looking for him. He supposed his only saving grace was a master demon who'd forbidden Efrestra and his three brothers from hunting him in the physical dimension. Richard wasn't sure why.

"Oh, by the way," said Nickelo with a timely interruption to Richard's somber thoughts. *"Sergeant Ron wants to see you. I told him I'd give you the message as soon as you woke up."*

"Well, I'm awake." Richard walked out the open door of the medical facility, into the common room beyond.

The *Defiant* was a relatively small ship designed to comfortably hold no more than twenty-two occupants. At present, the crew consisted of only Sergeant Ron and Charlie. Richard didn't really count himself because everything he knew about operating a starship would fit into a thimble. He considered himself more a passenger than an actual crew member.

The *Defiant's* common room consisted of a couple of lounge chairs and a long table for eating. Five doorways on each side of the room led to various crew quarters, a kitchen, a supply room, the ship's armory, and a common latrine with four showers. A metal ladder at the back of the common room led down to the cargo hold and lower anti-ship weapon's array. The same ladder also led to the upper anti-ship's weapons. A double door near the ladder opened to a corridor leading back to the engine room.

Richard walked toward the front of the ship to his left and the metal, double-wide stairway leading up to the ship's control room.

"Uh, Rick," said Nickelo. *"This is just a suggestion, but maybe you should put some clothes on first. You look like you're getting ready to attend a toga party."*

"A what?"

"Never mind," said Nickelo. *"Just take my word for it. You should get dressed first."*

Richard glanced down at the thin sheet wrapped around his body, realizing he probably did look a little ridiculous. Turning away from the stairs, he headed for the center doorway across from the medical facility. A thick curtain served as a door for a cabin. Pulling back the curtain, Richard entered. The cabin was the crew-quarters assigned to him by Charlie.

His room was small. An upper and lower bunk was on one side of the cabin. Two metal half-lockers, one on top of the other, were attached to the bulkhead opposite the bunks. A small desk and chair completed the cabin's furnishings. As Sergeant Ron had often said, the *Defiant* was a recon ship, not a luxury liner. Richard didn't mind the lack of physical comforts. Growing up in an orphanage followed by three years living on the streets had taught him to do without.

Someone had laid his dimensional pack on the pillow of the lower bunk. Richard was tempted to summon a clean uniform from his pack but refrained. He had no idea how extensive the pack's supplies were and often worried about the day he would attempt to summon something unsuccessfully because he'd frittered it all away unnecessarily. Besides, he was extremely low on Power and couldn't afford to waste any.

Richard pulled out a black wizard scout jumpsuit that was crumpled on the floor of his locker. The only color besides black on the jumpsuit was the golden-dragon insignia pinned to the suit's collar. Richard took a quick sniff of the uniform. It wasn't exactly clean, but he thought it didn't seem too bad if he ignored the obvious wrinkles. He made a mental note to do his laundry before they got back to base. Reaching into the locker again, Richard grabbed his underwear, socks, hat, and boots.

After dressing quickly, he used his passive scan to locate his battle suit. He spotted it in the cargo bay along with the rest of his gear. That is, except for his battle helmet. He sensed it was located in the control room near a single life form. Richard recognized the frequency of the life form as Sergeant Ron. Not counting the rats that seemed to infest all starships, the only other sign of life onboard was Charlie, currently in the engine room.

Reaching out with his mind, Richard willed his utility belt and attachments to him. A black military-belt appeared in the air near Richard's hand. He grabbed it before it could fall to the deck. Attached to the utility belt were a holstered .44 caliber AutoMag with two clips of extra ammo, a canteen, an ammo pouch with two anti-personnel grenades, and his phase rod. Richard strapped the utility belt around his waist.

During his junior year at the Academy, the Commandant had shown Richard how to tag items with Power. Once an item was tagged, he could summon it to his location. It took a lot of Power to initially tag items. However, during his downtime since he'd left the Academy, he had made an effort to tag all of his standard equipment excluding ammo. Richard wasn't sure how far away he could actually summon his tagged items but suspected it was quite a distance. The advantage of tagging items was that after the initial outlay of Power, it took no Power to summon them. And the tagging effect was permanent. Of course, he did need to have at least a little Power in his reserve to make it work.

After making a final adjustment to his gear, Richard started to leave his quarters but stopped at the doorway. Turning back, he picked up his dimensional pack. After imagining a starburst grenade, Richard opened the flap and pulled the grenade out of his pack.

"Smart," came Nickelo's voice in Richard's head. *"It's part of your standard load, so it costs you nothing in Power to summon."*

"So you're admitting I can do some things right after all, eh,

Nick?"

"On occasions," said Nickelo. *"Rare though they may be."*

"Whatever," Richard said. He should have known his battle computer's praise would come with a disclaimer.

After throwing his dimensional pack back onto his bunk and attaching the starburst grenade to his belt, Richard left his quarters and headed toward the control room. He found Sergeant Ron leaned back in the pilot's chair with his feet propped up on the control panel, Richard's battle helmet hanging from the armrest of the copilot's seat.

"Sergeant Ron," Richard said. "The maid won't like it if she finds your feet on her nice, clean control panel."

Sergeant Ron's long, salt and pepper hair flew around as he twisted in his seat to look behind him. His skin was wrinkled and weather-beaten. But Sergeant Ron's eyes gave a glint more in line with a mischievous teenager than an adult. Richard had never asked how old his maintenance chief was, but the look in his eyes gave the impression of a man who'd never grown up.

"Well, well," said Sergeant Ron with a friendly grin. "Did you have a nice nap? You wizard scouts are too pampered. That's why you're always sleeping on the job while we hard-working sergeants have to take up the slack."

Richard smiled back. "Yeah, I know, Sergeant Ron. The military is run by its non-commissioned officers."

"Now you're learning," said Sergeant Ron still grinning. Then he lost his smile and said more seriously, "I thought we'd lost you there, old buddy. It looked like they had an entire armored battalion after you. They even had a bunch of ground pounders to boot. Not to mention a dozen or so attack shuttles circling around, waiting to get a piece of your rear end."

"So Nick told me," Richard said. "Thanks for getting me out. But I did order you to abort. You're supposed to be working for me, remember?"

"Ah, and what kind of sergeant would I be if I didn't take care of my leader," said Sergeant Ron with his grin back on his face. "My wife would never let me live it down if I let something happen to you. I think she's still waiting for me to bring her an autographed picture of the genuine hero she's heard so much about in the news."

Richard blushed. After the fiasco at the Academy the previous year, he had found been the center of attention on the Intergalactic Empire News. For a couple of months, it had been hard to watch a video broadcast without seeing his face splashed across the screen at some point. Richard had taken a lot of ribbing from his friends for his fifteen minutes of fame until the reporters found something more exciting to cover.

"Not funny, Sergeant Ron," Richard said. "So where do you have this bucket of bolts headed? Back to the asteroid belt?"

The mercenary outfit where Richard was assigned was based in an asteroid belt in the Storis system in District 2. It was only a single hyper-jump between Planet X3321 and Storis.

Starships had two types of propulsion. Using normal hyper-drive, a good starship could accelerate to about ten thousand times the speed of light. While seriously fast, a starship using its hyper-drive could still take weeks or even months to get to its destination. For longer distances or in emergency combat conditions, a starship could use its hyper-drive to jump between folds in the dimension.

Since his graduation from the Academy, Richard had taken up reading on a wide variety of topics during his free time. One area he'd found particularly interesting was dimensional theory. From what he'd read, dimensions were like pieces of paper someone had wadded into a tight ball. Under the right circumstances, a hyper-drive could jump a starship from one fold in a dimension to another fold in the same dimension. Consequently, a starship could travel from one side of the galaxy to the other very quickly by jumping across any intersecting folds. For shorter distances, a single jump might get the starship to its destination. For longer distances, the trip might take several jumps.

The problem with using a starship's hyper-drive to jump across folds was that it was very hard on the hyper-drive. For each jump, a hyper-drive's fuel cells deteriorated approximately ten percent. Since overhauling a hyper-drive was expensive and time-consuming, most starships refrained from making jumps except when absolutely necessary. Military ships were only allowed to make jumps with their hyper-drives when authorized by higher headquarters or circumstances met a complicated set of rules of engagement.

Fortunately, the *Defiant* was not a military ship. Sergeant Ron had full control over when and how often he wanted to use the hyper-drive for jumps. And unlike most starships, the hyper-drive on the *Defiant* only deteriorated five percent when making jumps. The increased efficiency was a direct testimony to the maintenance skills of Sergeant Ron and Charlie.

Of course, since the *Defiant* wasn't a military ship, the cost of any overhaul was fully upon Sergeant Ron and Richard. Since Richard tended to be broke much of the time, Sergeant Ron usually refrained from costly hyper-jumps when he could avoid them.

Taking his feet off the control panel, Sergeant Ron sat up in his seat and swiveled around to face Richard. He pointed at the copilot's chair. "Why don't you take a load off your feet, Rick, and I'll explain what's going on. A lot has been happening while you were out playing hide and seek with your Trecorian friends."

Before sitting down, Richard glanced around the control room.

"They're by the navigator's console," said Sergeant Ron without explanation.

Richard didn't need an explanation. The old sergeant had read his mind. Stepping over to the navigator's chair, he picked up a small sack from the console, opened it, and looked inside. Several protein bars and snack packs of crackers greeted Richard. There was even a cup-sized plastic container with an attached spoon containing a dark paste. Richard recognized the paste as a pudding of some type.

"Thanks, Sergeant Ron," Richard said. "I am a little hungry."

"Ha!" exclaimed Sergeant Ron. "When ain't you hungry?" Pointing at the copilot's seat again, he added with a grin, "Now take a seat and try to pay attention while you're stuffing your face."

Taking no offense at Sergeant Ron's comments, Richard took a seat and promptly opened a protein bar. He took a small bite and savored the taste in his mouth.

"So where are we headed?" Richard said as he nibbled on a cheese cracker.

"To?" answered Sergeant Ron. "You've been summoned by the Imperial High Council, my boy. Looks like you're going to be hobnobbing with the big boys."

Sergeant Ron's reply confused Richard. In the ten months since he'd left the Academy, neither the Imperial High Command nor the Imperial High Council had wanted much to do with him. He'd been assigned a couple of boring administrative assignments that could easily have been handled by normal soldiers. Assigning a valuable wizard scout to such mundane tasks was asinine as far as he was concerned. Six months ago, Richard had received additional orders attaching him to a mercenary outfit in District 2. The unit's mission was to protect convoys and mining settlements from raids by Balorian pirates. While more interesting than his first two administrative assignments, it was still a waste of a wizard scout's abilities.

"It's just as well," chimed in Nickelo. *"'The One' has been sending you on his non-Empire missions every two or three weeks. You've needed the downtime between missions to recover."*

Richard forced down a rising swell of anger at the mention of *'the One,'* the bane of his existence. Both Nickelo and he agreed *'the One'* was probably a network of computers using the tele-network to collaborate much of the galaxy's computer resources toward some unknown purpose. Ever since Richard's freshman year at the Academy, *'the One'* had been sending him on missions back in time to the magical dimension. Most of the missions were on a planet called Portalis, but some were on other planets. Some were even in places so distant and obscure, Nickelo couldn't figure out where they were.

During Richard's first mission for *'the One,'* he'd tried to rebel. Unauthorized authority figures irked him to no end. He had soon learned rebelling had a cost. *'The One'* just kept sticking him on more difficult missions until he finally acquiesced to do the mission correctly.

During the last ten months, Richard had tried to be unusually accommodating on his missions. He had to be. His nephew and niece, Brachia and Dren, had been teleported back in time 157 years to the planet Portalis. Neither Richard nor Nickelo knew how to travel through time. Nickelo had finally convinced Richard that his sole hope of rescuing his nephew and niece was to perform missions for *'the One'* to the best of his ability. Hopefully, *'the One'* would eventually send him to the time and place where his nephew and niece were located. After twenty missions in ten months, Richard was about ready to call his plan a failure.

Richard momentarily pushed aside thoughts of *'the One'* to

concentrate on the matters at hand. His recall to Risors by the Imperial High Council smacked of politics. Richard was a soldier. He hated politics. And was growing frustrated at being jerked around by both *the One* and the Imperial High Council.

"This makes no sense, Sergeant Ron," Richard said.

"I hear you," said Sergeant Ron. "But it is what it is."

As Richard was taking a swallow from his canteen, he noticed Sergeant Ron giving him a strange look.

"What?" Richard said a little defensively. He liked Sergeant Ron, but sometimes his chief mechanic made him uncomfortable.

"Well," drawled Sergeant Ron. "I was just thinking how you left on your mission in a Warcat—"

Wide-eyed, Richard coughed up some water that suddenly went down the wrong way.

Sergeant Ron reached over and gave him a slap on the back. "You may remember Charlie and I spent a lot of time getting that Warcat scout into topnotch condition. But when you came back, all you had was a battle suit with a hole in it."

"Look, I'm sorry," Richard replied after he'd caught his breath. He really was sorry. Both Sergeant Ron and Charlie had spent many a late night modifying his Warcat until it was probably the best in the fleet.

Sergeant Ron stared back.

"It was a trap," Richard said. "I don't think there was any information on a new DNA vent in the first place. The location was supposed to be lightly defended. Somebody must have gone to a lot of trouble to set up a stealth shield capable of concealing an armored battalion."

"Yeah," said Sergeant Ron as he drummed his fingers on the armrest of his chair. "I was able to see part of the battle through video from the tele-bots."

"You had access?" Richard was surprised. The microscopic robots were capable of sending audio and video data back to higher headquarters via the tele-network. That Sergeant Ron had apparently gotten access to the data was puzzling. Since Nickelo was cut off from the tele-network, even Richard couldn't get access.

"Yeah, I had access," admitted Sergeant Ron. "Although I have to admit it wasn't easy. I was able to sweet talk your friend Stella into having her battle computer relay the information to me."

"What?" said Nickelo over the battle helmet's external speakers. "You have a communication's link with Jonathan?"

"Had," corrected Sergeant Ron. "I had communications. I lost it when we made the jump with our hyper-drive."

"Oh," said Nickelo. "Can you re-establish communications?"

"Maybe," said Sergeant Ron. "But not right now. The point I wanted to make is that Charlie and I saw part of the battle, Rick. And you had more than one opportunity to get away unscathed. Why didn't you?"

Richard mulled the question over for a few seconds while nibbling on another cracker. His actions had been bothering him as well. "I'm not exactly sure," he hedged.

"Now, Rick," chimed in Nickelo. "Are you sure that's the truth? I calculate a sixty-seven percent probability you know the reason, but are afraid to admit it."

Richard thought it over a few more seconds. He did have a theory. During the attack on the Academy the previous year, he had been called upon to assist Nickelo and Jonathan in hacking their way into the Crosioians' master computer. The hack had required Richard and Nickelo to merge their minds to an even greater extent than normal. During the merging, Richard stumbled upon a ghost of a memory in Nickelo's databanks. The memory, or dream as Nickelo called it, revealed Richard's heritage. He'd been taken out of his mother's womb by *the One* as a fertilized egg. Parts of DNA from several magical races had been spliced with his. One of the parts had been DNA from a gnome. Since his graduation from the Academy, Richard had spent a lot of time researching magical races whenever he'd been sent on a mission for *the One.* The gnomes on Portalis were known for their tendency to make sacrifices for others, even if it meant endangering their own lives.

"You think that piece of gnome DNA is starting to affect my judgment," Richard said more as a statement than a question.

"Could be," replied Nickelo. "The little bit of orc DNA in you has certainly influenced your stubbornness over the years. It's about time some of your better qualities started bubbling to the surface."

"Well, regardless of whatever influence that DNA cocktail of yours had," said Sergeant Ron, "the end result is we're short one Warcat. General Stevens isn't going to appreciate you losing her cat."

Richard was still getting used to hearing the rank of General associated with the crafty-old special operations leader. He had served under her when she was just a commander. Now General Stevens was in charge of all special operations forces in Districts 2, 5, and 7. And Richard knew his battle computer was right. General Stevens would not appreciate him losing her Warcat. She'd gone out on a limb transferring her asset to a rundown mercenary outfit in District 2.

"Well, I'll have to make it up to her somehow," Richard said. "In the meantime, General Stevens will just have to order a replacement."

"Ha!" said Sergeant Ron. "You've obviously been out of the loop. Since the supply depot in District 11 got overrun last month by the Crosioians, spare parts are difficult to get. Even older models of cats are becoming scarce, much less a new replacement model."

"He's right, Rick," chimed in Nickelo. "The Empire's going broke. Without full tele-network access, I can't know for sure, but from the intermittent data I've been able to glean through my security interfaces, the Empire is on the ropes. They've started stripping equipment from planetary reserve units to equip their active-duty forces."

"Are you sure?" Richard said. "I saw a Deloris Conglomerate unit last week, and they had plenty of equipment. It looked nearly new as far as I could tell."

The Conglomerate was a loosely organized consortium of manufacturing companies led by the Deloris Armaments Corporation. The Conglomerate maintained a quasi-military force, which had slowly been replacing planetary self-defense forces to free up regular military units for duty on the front lines. Richard had fought with some Conglomerate units during the battle for the Academy's airfield the previous year. While their soldiers were brave enough, they were nowhere near as well trained as their active-duty counterparts like the Marine units Richard was accustomed to.

"Don't get me started on the Conglomerate," said Sergeant Ron.

"If you ask me, they're quickly becoming too involved with planetary defenses. I think they're more concerned about advancing the political ambitions of the Deloris Armaments Corporation than they are the defense of the planets where they're assigned."

Sergeant Ron got a disgusted look on his face. "If things keep going the way they are, half the Empire's going to be de facto planets belonging to the Conglomerate. The Conglomerate was a good idea when old Jacob Deloris first organized it eighty years ago, but it's changed over the last forty years. Jacob would roll over in his grave if he knew what his great-grandchildren were doing to his company."

"Uh, Sergeant Ron," Richard cautioned. "You should probably watch what you say. You know there's undoubtedly some tele-bots right here in the cockpit with us."

"So what?" Sergeant Ron was getting a little red-faced. "I wouldn't say anything behind the Conglomerate's lying back I wouldn't say to their face." Glancing around the cockpit, Sergeant Ron shouted, "Did you get all that, you bunch of political backstabbers? I'll repeat it if you need me too. I think you're trying to take over the Empire one little piece at a time before anyone knows you're up to no good."

"Sergeant Ron!" Richard was getting increasingly nervous by his maintenance chief's loose talk. He couldn't figure out why his friend was getting so worked up. He didn't like the Conglomerate all that much either, but it wasn't worth risking a court martial over. "This is no joke, Sergeant Ron. There are Conglomerate personnel on the Imperial High Council. They'll have access to any tele-bot data."

"Well, guess what, buddy," said Sergeant Ron gritting his teeth, "I don't care. And I've got news for you. Most of the tele-bots are manufactured by subsidiaries of the Conglomerate. I wouldn't put it past them to install unauthorized software to receive all the data even if they *didn't* have members on the council."

"Uh," Richard started. He'd worried about the same thing before but had always talked himself out of it as a silly idea. "I've always assumed all communications passing through the tele-network were secure unless they were being hacked by the Empire's enemies, of course."

"Well, you've assumed wrong," came Nickelo's voice in their shared space. *"I calculate Sergeant Ron's mostly correct. The Conglomerate probably does use the tele-bots to glean data they deem useful. The only exception would be information the central computer wanted to keep secret."*

"Like our missions?" Richard asked.

"Yes," replied Nickelo. *"Things like that."*

Richard made a mental note to encrypt even seemingly harmless messages from now on before he sent them over the tele-network.

"I don't think that would be wise," said Nickelo. *"Too many encrypted messages would just draw more attention to you. If I could make a suggestion, why don't you let me determine what should and shouldn't be encrypted?"*

Richard didn't have to think about his answer long. He had an above average intelligence but hated thinking about things that didn't interest him.

"Fine by me," Richard said. *"I'll set up an area in our shared space where you can use my Power to encrypt data packets when required."*

"Hey," interrupted Sergeant Ron. "Are you guys going to include me in the conversation? You've got that blank look on your face again."

"Sorry," Richard said. "Uh…we were just talking about how to go about repairing my battle suit."

"Sure you were," said Sergeant Ron. "And I've got some valuable swamp land back on Velos I'll sell you real cheap."

"Uh," Richard said. "I really don't need—"

"He was being sarcastic, Rick," said Nickelo through the helmet's speakers for Sergeant Ron's benefit. "He's just letting you know he doesn't believe you. Just so you know, I gave Sergeant Ron a copy of the book *Cute Sayings and Slang of 20th through 21st Century America* by Robert R. Fitzgerald."

"Oh, that's just great, Nick," Richard said hoping to sound sarcastic but not sure he was succeeding. "The last thing I need is another person speaking your little euphemisms. Thank you very much."

"You're welcome," said Nickelo and Sergeant Ron at the same time. They both started laughing.

After a few seconds, Richard laughed as well.

CHAPTER 5

After he'd slept for a couple of hours and cleaned up, Richard made his way to the *Defiant's* small kitchen looking for something to eat. He chose a packet of dehydrated stew from the pantry. Turning to the non-human side of the storeroom, Richard plucked a packet of dried Sterilian worms out of a cabinet. Returning to the kitchen, he dumped the contents of the packets into large bowls. After adding water to each bowl from the hydro-faucet, he placed covers over the contents and stuck them in separate heating units, then sat down to wait.

From months of watching Charlie prepare his meals, Richard knew Sterilian food had to be heated slowly. If he tried to cook the worms too fast, they wouldn't rehydrate properly and the worms would die. After making the mistake once, Richard had learned Sterilians hated eating food that wasn't squirming around on their plates. His ears still burned from the chewing out Charlie had given him for destroying perfectly good worms.

Richard set the re-hydrator for the stew at a higher temperature, but not too high. Surprisingly, he enjoyed cooking. It took his mind off more serious matters and helped him relax. Plus, he'd discovered he had a knack for it. He liked adding his own mixture of spices to items while they were cooking. He'd been forced to eat a lot of bland food over the years, especially when he'd been in the orphanage. A couple of years ago, he'd decided whenever he got a chance to make his food taste better, he was going to go for it. Like he'd told his battle computer, there was plenty of time to suffer when he had no other choice. Fortunately, he had a choice now.

In theory, fully-trained wizard scouts didn't need to eat or even sleep for that matter. But theory was a long way from reality. A wizard scout's healing Power considered lack of sleep or nutrition an injury. As such, it healed the wizard scout's body accordingly. However, it used Power from their reserve to do so. Consequently, most wizard scouts preferred to eat and sleep at least a little whenever possible to keep their Power reserve at maximum. Since normal wizard scouts only had a single Power reserve, any Power they used for healing themselves was not available for offense and defense, and vice versa.

Fortunately for Richard, he had three Power reserves. His smallest Power reserve could only be used for healing others. His normal Power reserve could be used for offense and defense. Richard's third Power reserve could only be used to heal his own body. His self-healing was hardwired in that it automatically healed injuries to bring his body back to baseline whether he wanted it to or not. Richard had been a little hungry and a little sleepy when he'd gotten his DNA baseline taken. Consequently, his self-heal ability considered it an injury if he overate, and it automatically healed him back to baseline. Unfortunately, that happened to be a little bit hungry and tired. Given the dilemma, Richard found grazing a little bit of food several times a day not only kept his hunger at bay but also kept his body from using too much Power from his self-healing reserve.

After the stew was ready, Richard ladled it into two bowls and took them to the cockpit. He gave Sergeant Ron the lion's share of the stew. Once they were done eating, Richard returned to the kitchen and stuck the bowls into the cleaning unit.

When he could put it off no longer, he opened the door of the re-hydrator where he'd placed the Sterilian worms. He wrinkled his nose in disgust. Apparently, he'd gotten the temperature right because the worms were lively. They had somehow raised the bowl's lid and crawled out onto the bottom of the re-hydrator. Scrapping the loose worms back into their bowl with a spoon, Richard replaced the lid and headed for the cargo bay.

Once Richard slid down the ladder, he spotted Charlie tinkering with a piece of equipment on one of the maintenance benches. "Come and get it," he said as he headed in the old Sterilian's direction.

Charlie put down his tools and sniffed the air. "Smells good. You learn well."

"I aim to please," Richard said laughing. "Besides, I've had a good teacher. The next time I link up with Stella, I'll be able to cook her a full-course meal of worms, bugs, and other squirming things I'd prefer not to think about."

Taking the bowl from Richard, Charlie placed it on the table. The old Sterilian didn't remove the lid right away. Richard was surprised. Charlie was normally one of those eaters who got down to business immediately.

Looking down at his bowl, Charlie said, "Yes. Wizard Scout Stella would be pleased. How is she?"

Richard noticed the skin on Charlie's chest darken to a deeper gray. He'd seen his friend Stella do the same thing whenever she was embarrassed.

"Uh," Richard said trying to find the right words. "I haven't spoken to her in a couple of months. The last I heard, she was on a mission in District 4."

"Oh," said Charlie.

Richard noticed the mechanic still hadn't opened the lid on his bowl.

"She good wizard scout," said Charlie. "She be okay."

"Well, of course she will," Richard said growing confused. "She's one of the best."

"Good," grunted Charlie.

With that, Charlie finally uncovered his bowl of worms, but he still didn't begin eating. Several of the worms took their momentary respite to escape across the table.

"I glad she be safe," said Charlie.

"Yeah, me too," Richard replied continuing to eye the old lizard.

Charlie began eating with gusto.

Richard turned away. While he'd eaten a lot of meals with other races over the years, he still didn't enjoy watching Charlie spoon squirming worms into his mouth. He took the opportunity to go over to the maintenance table where his battle suit was laid out. A fist-sized hole in its left shoulder drew his attention.

"That looks bad," Richard thought in his shared space. *"Do you*

think they can fix it?"

Richard had never been to the planet Storage where his equipment was kept. However, between information he'd gotten from Nickelo as well as his niece and nephew, he knew the population of the entire planet was dedicated to maintaining the items used by variables for '*the One*.'

"Oh, I suspect the technicians on Storage will enjoy the challenge," replied Nickelo. *"Just send it back. They'll send you one of your undamaged battle suits until they get this one fixed."*

Shrugging his shoulders, Richard willed his dimensional pack to him. Reaching out with his hand, he plucked the pack out of the air before it fell. Once he had the pack, he opened the flap and began stuffing the battle suit inside. Since the suit was un-energized at the moment, it was an easy feat to roll up and place in his pack.

Whenever his battle suit was un-energized, it had the consistency and appearance of soft leather. It was also similar in weight. However, when worn and energized with Power from its isotopic battery, the battle suit had the strength of brerellium steel. It also had the weight to match.

Once he finished sending his damaged battle suit back to Storage, Richard sat down in a convenient chair and turned around to face Charlie. Unfortunately, the old Sterilian was still eating. Richard stared at him for a moment, deciding to get his battle computer's take on his friend.

"What do you think the deal was with all that talk about Stella?" Richard said. *"Charlie sounded a little strange to me."*

"Rick, Rick," chided Nickelo. *"We've got to work on your emotional logic more. Charlie's a Sterilian. Your friend Stella is a Sterilian. One plus one equals ten. What do you think it means?"*

"Uh, one plus one equals two," Richard said. *"And I've never even seen Charlie and Stella speak to each other. So if you're trying to imply Charlie has a crush on Stella, I'll have to say you're crazy."*

"First off," said Nickelo. *"One plus one equals ten in base two. You made the assumption I was using base ten. And you know what they say about assumptions, don't you? In the same respect, you're making the assumption Sterilians' emotional responses work the same as yours. They don't. So call me crazy if you like, but I think*

Charlie's got the hots for your friend Stella."

"The hots?" Richard said as he tried to picture how anyone could think Stella was hot. Between her double row of serrated teeth and four muscular arms that could rip a man in half, the word hot was the last thing Richard would think to call her.

Shaking his head to clear the idea of 'a hot' Stella out of his mind, Richard said, *"Each to their own I guess. But Charlie's like seventy years old. I seriously doubt he's shopping for a girlfriend at this stage in his life."*

"Ha!" laughed Nickelo. *"You need to read more. Charlie is only seventy-two standard-years old. The average life expectancy for a Sterilian is a little over two hundred standard years. Charlie's still in his prime. And just how old do you think your friend Stella is?"*

"Uh, I don't know," Richard admitted. *"I assume she's about the same age as me."*

"Not hardly, grasshopper," Nickelo replied with a snicker. *"According to her battle computer, Stella was forty-three when the two of you graduated from the Academy. So there isn't really that much difference between Charlie and her ages when all things are considered."*

Richard took another look at Charlie just as the old lizard was scooping the last of the worms into his mouth.

"Nope," Richard told himself. *"Maybe he's not old, but it's going to be hard to think of him any other way."*

* * *

The next few hours found Richard helping Sergeant Ron and Charlie maintain the *Defiant*. As Sergeant Ron often put it, there wasn't any room for idle hands on a starship, even if one set of the hands belonged to a highly-trained wizard scout. While Richard knew very little about maintaining equipment on a starship, he'd always been good at sensing lines of energy. Plus, he had an affinity for detecting flaws in computer operating systems. While he couldn't program a single line of computer code, he could detect problem areas in their programming before they caused problems.

"And I'm telling you there's something wrong with the

starboard-side energy displacer," argued Sergeant Ron. "I can smell it."

Richard took a sniff of the air. He smelled nothing.

"It's just a saying, Rick," said Nickelo over the battle helmet's external speakers sounding a little smug. "Sergeant Ron didn't mean he could actually smell something."

Sergeant Ron gave Richard a wink. "Not to contradict you, Nick, but I really did mean something doesn't smell right. There's just the barest hint of Halocian hydraulic-fluid in the air. My guess is a line has a hairline crack in it somewhere."

"Hmm," conceded Nickelo. "I guess I'm in no position to argue with someone who has an actual nose. So I stand corrected."

"Regardless," Richard said. "I don't smell anything out of the ordinary."

"See, that's what's wrong with you young whippersnappers and your highfalutin wizard scout training," said Sergeant Ron. "You spent most of your time in the Academy studying how to fight when you should've been figuring out how to maintain your equipment."

Richard looked closer at Sergeant Ron to see if his old maintenance chief was joking. He didn't catch even a hint of a smile.

"They could've given me a full semester of training on maintaining equipment," Richard countered, "and I still wouldn't be able to smell problems."

"That's up for discussion," said Sergeant Ron, "but that's not what I meant. You're aware Charlie could've attended the Academy, aren't you?"

"Yeah," Richard admitted. "So?"

"So," replied Sergeant Ron, "Charlie chose to do something useful with his Power like learning how to use it to diagnose equipment. Didn't you, Charlie?"

Sergeant Ron's assistance mechanic was across the room taking sniffs with his nose around the starboard-side energy displacer. At Sergeant Ron's voice, Charlie looked up and nodded his head in an affirmative manner.

"Everything releases Power," said Charlie as he walked over to join Sergeant Ron and Richard. "Trick is to spot wrong Power."

Perplexed, Richard asked, "What do you mean by wrong

Power?"

"Come. I show," said Charlie as a line of Power snaked out of him in the direction of the starboard-side energy displacer.

Richard recognized the line of Power as the type of scan he'd seen Charlie use when maintaining the ship's equipment. Since Charlie was making no movement other than forming a line of Power, Richard took it as a sign the Sterilian meant for him to follow his scan. Forming an active scan of his own, Richard moved his line of Power until it was parallel with Charlie's.

"No," said Charlie through the translator on his belt. "Merge with mine."

"Nick?" Richard thought in his shared space. *"Do you know what Charlie's trying to have me do? Is it safe?"*

"He's obviously trying to teach you something," said Nickelo. *"I'd say pay close attention. From what I've observed, Charlie's not one of those instructors who's willing to say something twice. You better be paying attention the first time."*

"Fine," Richard thought back as he began merging his scan with the Sterilian's line of Power. *"Are you coming along with me on the scan?"*

"Not this time," replied Nickelo. *"It's all on you, brother. I calculate I'd just distract you."*

"Whatever," Richard said a little disappointed his battle computer wouldn't be with him to detect any nuances in Charlie's scan. *"Suit yourself."*

Once Richard merged his scan with Charlie's line of Power, he felt another presence on the outskirts of his mind. It wasn't as distinct as his battle computer's, although the effect was similar.

"Charlie?" Richard thought.

No words followed, but Richard felt a sensation of emotions and images that let him know without a doubt the other presence was Charlie.

A sensation from Charlie seemed to say '*come.*' It was just a sensation, but Richard understood it as clearly as if it had been a word.

Richard followed the mechanic's scan while matching movement for movement. Their scans entered into a wave of energy surrounding the starboard-side energy displacer. Richard followed along with Charlie's scan until they were deep inside the displacer.

"Feel the energy," said Charlie. *"Let mind become part of it."*

Odd as Charlie's command might have been to another, it made sense to Richard. While he'd been a young boy at the orphanage, Richard had discovered he had an affinity for manipulating lines of Power from all sorts of equipment. He'd eventually learned how to use his skill at tracing Power to circumvent security locks on the doors at the orphanage. The technique had come in handy when sneaking out at night to look for food. Richard's ability to bypass alarms was partially due to his ability to merge his Power with that of the alarm system and become a part of it.

Richard followed Charlie's instructions and merged his Power with the waves of energy from the starboard-side energy displacer. He began to feel the pulse of the equipment. He momentarily became a part of the displacer, although in a purely observational way.

"Feel strange?" asked Charlie.

Richard was pretty sure Charlie wasn't asking how he felt. Charlie was interested in the equipment.

"Uh, the energy feels okay, I guess," Richard said trying to remain noncommittal.

"Sure?" asked Charlie.

Concentrating harder on the energy around him, Richard felt himself drawn in a certain direction as if he'd been caught in a slight current. Without asking Charlie's permission, Richard allowed the energy to pull him along until he'd left the displacer. Richard's passive scan told him he was traveling down a tube of some type. He felt Charlie's mind moving along with him, but the old lizard was remaining quiet. Before long, they came to a point in the tube where a stream of energy was dissipating out of the tube in a small stream.

"You find leak," Charlie said. *"Now find where we are."*

Continuing to use his passive scan, Richard took note of their position. They were in the flooring halfway between the cargo deck and the engine room.

"Got us," Richard said. *"Do we go back now and tell Sergeant Ron?"*

"No," answered Charlie. *"Follow me. You learn."*

With those words, Charlie took Richard on a sort of behind-the-scenes tour of the *Defiant*. For the next hour, the old lizard took pains to point out problem areas in the starship that needed to be watched closely. He even took Richard deep inside the *Defiant's* hyper-drive.

Richard had always enjoyed watching Power in all its intricate designs. In Richard's mind, the waves and lines of Power in the *Defiant's* hyper-drive were a work of art. He could've watched it for hours without growing bored. However, Charlie had things to do, and eventually, the lizard succeeded in dragging Richard away from the hyper-drive and back to the auxiliary maintenance room where the starboard-side energy displacer was kept. Sergeant Ron was no longer there.

"Do you need help fixing the hydraulic line?" Richard asked.

"No. I fix," said Charlie. "You just get in way."

Taking his friend's words as a dismissal, Richard headed back to his quarters to take a short nap. He was a little tired.

"You're always a little tired," said Nickelo.

"Yeah," Richard yawned. *"Maybe so, but I'm more tired than usual right now. Charlie had me at that active scan for quite a while."*

With those words, Richard lay down on his bunk and went to sleep.

CHAPTER 6

The silver-haired elf crouched down hardly daring to breathe. Her delicately-pointed ears twitched slightly, stirring a few strands of her long, silver hair. The elf strained to hear any sound of her adversaries. Her molten-silver eyes darted back and forth as she tried to spot any sign of danger before it could take her by surprise. But no matter where she looked, the elf's eyes kept coming back to the pair of legs protruding from around the corner of the tunnel.

The legs lay sprawled out on the stone floor, motionless. The light-blue robe partially covering the legs as well as the fine-leather boots belonged to the elf's companion and fellow acolyte, Crystal. The elf took a few cautious steps forward until she could make out more of the prone body.

Jeehanathoraxen, better known as Jeena to her family and friends, and her companion, Crystal had been tasked with finding a silver-trimmed chest in the dank tunnel-system. Jeena knew at least two mages were trying to prevent her from achieving her goal.

Those two mages are good, Jeena thought. *They have to be. Crystal's one of the best acolytes in the priest guild.*

Mouthing a seeker spell, Jeena drew Power from her reserve and converted it to magic. She used the magic energy to form a translucent ball of energy in her hands. Jeena kept the energy as small as possible. Her stealth shield was not yet good enough to hide herself and her magic at the same time if her spell was too large.

With a puff of air, Jeena sent the seeker spell toward the corner.

As the spell moved down the tunnel, the ball of energy became ever more translucent until it disappeared completely.

Keeping part of her mind merged with the seeker spell, Jeena called a second seeker into being. A larger ball of energy formed in her hands. Jeena sent the second seeker down the tunnel in the opposite direction. She made no attempt to hide it. The second seeker was her decoy.

Jeena toyed with the idea of trying to follow both seekers with her mind, but she quickly abandoned the thought. She envisioned her mentor, Priestess Aldriss, chastising her for even considering such a foolish plan.

'You're not that good yet,' Jeena imagined the priestess saying. *'Simpler is often the better course of action.'*

Jeena let go of the second seeker and allowed it to go where it may. She focused on the first, smaller seeker. It had reached the corner of the tunnel. In her mind, Jeena saw what the seeker saw. Sure enough, the body crumpled on the tunnel floor was Crystal. Jeena noticed the fog of Crystal's breath in the cold air of the tunnel. Her friend was still alive, but that did little to help Jeena at the moment.

Jeena needed to find the chest first. Once that was done, she could return and help Crystal. Jeena forced herself to ignore her friend in order to complete her assigned task. As Priestess Aldriss would say, *'the mission comes first.'* Jeena didn't always agree with her mentor's philosophy, but in this case, it made sense. Finding the chest was too important to be waylaid by prematurely caring for a fallen comrade.

Sending the seeker farther down the tunnel, Jeena checked for any signs of her adversaries. She found none. Holding the wand in her right hand at the ready, she continued edging forward until she was at the turn in the tunnel. If she had wanted, Jeena could have prodded Crystal's boots with her own, but she did not. She needed to find her opponents first.

Jeena hoped her information was correct and that there were only two mages opposing her. She knew she'd already be hard pressed to handle two mages by herself. While it was possible Crystal had taken one of the mages out, Jeena had her doubts. The stun wands Crystal and she'd been issued were noisy, yet she'd heard nothing. And the few minor offensive spells they'd been taught were far from silent either.

No, Jeena thought. *The mages must have gotten the drop on Crystal. The mage guild tends to teach their apprentices offensive spells much sooner than the priest guild. I have to expect the unexpected.*

By this time, the first seeker was at the next bend in the tunnel about fifteen paces distance from where Jeena stood. She held the seeker there. Jeena decided to make sure the tunnel between the seeker and her current position was clear before proceeding. Drawing Power from her reserve again, Jeena transformed the Power into magic by whispering a detection spell. She released the spell into the tunnel ahead. The part of her mind connected to the detection spell blazed with energy as it picked up the Power signatures, or auras, of the unconscious Crystal and herself. Jeena filtered their auras out. Still, the detection spell blazed with energy.

Our wands, Jeena thought.

Following the procedure Priestess Aldriss had taught her, Jeena filtered out the auras of the wands as well. The detection spell cleared and showed no more signs of energy.

Strange, Jeena thought. *I would've thought at least some residual energy from the spell that downed Crystal would have remained near her body.* Jeena made a mental note to ask Priestess Aldriss about it later.

Writing off the absence of detectable magic as a lack of ability on her part, Jeena stepped into the tunnel and took two steps toward the next corner where the seeker spell was still holding its position.

Before ordering the seeker spell around the next corner, Jeena tightened her grip on her wand. She double checked the emblem engraved in the middle of the wand to make sure the wand contained only stun spells. Even in the dim light of the tunnel, Jeena's night vision easily picked out the small engraving of the Tree of Light indicating the wand contained priest spells. Jeena nodded her head. The wand would have been useless if she'd accidentally been given a mage's wand. But that was not the case. The engraving was the Tree of Light and not the All-Seeing Eye of the mage guild. The icon of a prone figure gave proof the spells in the wand were stun spells. Based upon the intensity of the icon, Jeena knew there were four spells remaining in her wand.

I've got to make them count, Jeena thought.

As a mere priest acolyte, Jeena had no doubt her own memorized offensive spells were too weak and unreliable to depend upon in a fight.

Drawing a deep breath, Jeena mentally prepared herself to send the seeker around the corner. If her opponents were there, the appearance of the seeker would undoubtedly trigger an immediate response from the mages. They would know their ambush had failed.

Jeena started to send the command to move the seeker forward, but she hesitated. The hairs on the back of her neck were standing on end as if she was forgetting something.

Is the Lady trying to warn me? Jeena thought.

While it was not normal for the Lady of the Tree to interact with acolytes, Jeena's silver hair and molten-silver eyes gave testimony to the fact she was anything but a normal acolyte. Still, the Lady had never communicated with her directly before.

Why would she do so now? Jeena wondered.

Shrugging her shoulders, Jeena once again started to give the command for the seeker to advance, but again she hesitated. The feeling something was wrong wouldn't go away. She wondered if Crystal had felt the same thing before she'd been attacked.

Looking down at her sister acolyte, Jeena had a feeling she might soon be lying on the floor alongside her friend. It was then Jeena noticed Crystal's wand. Something about the wand struck Jeena as out of place. Then she saw it. The wand didn't bear the engraving of the Tree of Light. It bore the symbol of the All-Seeing Eye.

Jeena drew in a sharp breath as she tried to bring her own wand to bear on the prone figure. At the same moment, the form of the unconscious Crystal wavered as the polymorph spell dropped to reveal a figure wearing the red robe of the mage guild.

The mage brought her wand up as Jeena brought hers down. The air was filled with shouted words of Power from two voices. A streak of light jumped out from Jeena's wand a split second before the mage completed her words of activation. The light from Jeena's wand struck the mage and knocked her into the wall.

A movement in the vision of the seeker gave warning of a second mage. Charging around the tunnel corner, the mage was raising his wand for an attack. Jeena dove for the floor. She put up a hasty defensive shield. A streak of red light hit her shield and glanced off into the dim light of the tunnel behind her.

Shouting a word of activation, Jeena fired a second stun spell from her wand. The beam of light hit an invisible barrier two steps in front of the mage. The running mage fired back at Jeena with his own wand. Again her shield deflected the spell, but she could feel her shield weakening.

That's no stun spell, Jeena thought as she crawled backward for the safety of the bend in the tunnel. *And that's no tenth-year mage apprentice either. What are they thinking?*

Jeena had no time to wonder why she was being pitted against a more senior mage apprentice. Her mage opponents were supposed to be evenly matched tenth-year students from the mage guild.

After a third spell from the mage's wand glanced off Jeena's shield, the mage decided to try a different approach. He stopped and stuck his wand in his belt as he began making intricate movements with his hands. He mouthed words Jeena heard but immediately forgot. A ball of magic began forming an arm's length to the mage's front as he called forth his spell.

Jeena fired a third shot from her wand in hopes of distracting the mage. All she succeeded in doing was lighting up the tunnel for a brief moment as the stun spell ricocheted off the mage's shield and continued down the tunnel.

With only one spell remaining in her wand, Jeena knew her options were disappearing rapidly. The mage's magic was growing in intensity. Jeena doubted her weak shield could resist the spell.

In the brief light remaining from her ricocheting spell, Jeena noticed a wand near her left hand. It was the wand dropped by the mage who'd been disguised as Crystal. Jeena grabbed the discarded wand and threw it at the male mage. The wand hit the mage's shield and bounced off. Jeena didn't care. She hadn't expected the wand to hit the mage. Jumping to her feet, Jeena shouted the activation word for her wand. The wand's final spell shot out and struck the rebounding mage's wand in midair.

The mage's wand exploded in a blinding flash of light.

Even at ten paces and partially protected by the bend in the tunnel, the blast of magical energy knocked Jeena into the opposite wall. When she regained her feet, Jeena shook her head in an attempt to clear the ringing in her ears. She stumbled into a wall and momentarily leaned against it for support. Fighting for control, Jeena pulled her dagger from her belt and half-ran, half-stumbled toward the fallen male mage.

Being closer to the blast, the mage was just starting to rise to all fours. Jeena ran to his side and shoved him face down to the tunnel floor. She pulled back on the mage's head and placed the blade of her dagger against his neck. Jeena always kept her dagger very sharp. She noticed a thin line of red where the sharp edge of the blade touched the mage's throat.

"Yield!" Jeena shouted into the mage's ear.

Before the mage could respond, an old, red-robed mage came running around the bend of the tunnel with wand raised. He said a word Jeena didn't recognize. A beam of green light left the end of the wand and struck her in the upper chest. Jeena was flung backward and hit the tunnel wall behind her. The dagger clattered out of her paralyzed hand and onto the stone floor.

Paralyzed but conscious, Jeena heard the sound of many feet. A slew of red, white, and light-blue robes passed across her vision.

"Is he hurt?" shouted the old mage who'd paralyzed her.

"Just a slight cut on the neck, Master Jathar," said a young, white-robed female bent over the fallen mage. "He'll be fine."

Master Jathar turned quickly to an old, white-haired, female-elf dressed in a light-blue robe. Pointing his finger accusingly at the old elf, Master Jathar said, "You assured me there'd be no danger. How could I have explained it to this student's family if he'd come to harm?"

"Calm, Master Jathar," said the old elf. "Our medic said he'd be fine. No harm has been done."

"No thanks to you, Priestess Aldriss," said Master Jathar.

Pointing down to the prone Jeena, he added, "Or to this young ruffian you claim as one of your acolytes. She has no business in the priesthood. I don't care whether she has the silver hair and eyes of her ancestors or not. Her actions are unsuitable for a priestess of the Lady of the Tree. Her actions and temperament have always been unsuitable. Sometimes I think she acts more like one of those human barbarians than a high elf."

Rather than giving an angry reply, Priestess Aldriss said in a calm voice, "Alas, you may be right, Master Jathar."

In spite of her paralysis, Jeena drew in a sharp breath. *Is Priestess Aldriss going to expel me from the priest guild?*

Jeena could well believe the old elf would. Priestess Aldriss had been a hard taskmaster these last ten years. While the old priestess had never been openly against Jeena, she certainly hadn't gone out of her way to make things easier either.

"But," said Priestess Aldriss, "it's not my decision to make. And my pardon, Master Jathar, but neither is it yours. Only the Lady may decide who will or will not be one of her future priests or priestesses."

When Master Jathar opened his mouth to protest, Priestess Aldriss said, "I wouldn't presume to advise you who should be in your mage guild, Master Jathar. I would appreciate the same courtesy from you."

Jeena could just make our Master Jathar's face. She saw his neck muscles tighten. A blood vessel under his chin expanded until Jeena thought it would burst.

Surprisingly, when Master Jathar spoke, it was in a reasonably calm voice. "I will be protesting directly to High Priest Questor."

Jeena saw the old priestess give a tight-lipped smile. "Please give my regards to the high priest when you see him. He's always interested in hearing about the progress of his acolytes."

"Humph!" was the only response from Master Jathar as he turned and stomped off.

By this time, a group of the white-robed medics and some of the red-robed mages had gotten both the male and female mage apprentices up and walking.

Priestess Aldriss said nothing until the medics and the mages were gone. Even then, the old elf remained silent until the last vestige of sound from the mage's footsteps had faded into nothing. Then and only then did Priestess Aldriss turn to look down at Jeena.

"Well, for once I get to speak without you interrupting me," said Priestess Aldriss.

Jeena noticed the priestess purse her lips as if trying to find the right words. Jeena braced herself for the tongue lashing she was sure was soon to come. Jeena knew she'd done wrong.

Why did I use my dagger? Jeena thought. *Stupid, stupid, stupid.*

Once again, she had acted without thinking. It had always been thus. While other elves acted with forethought and logic, Jeena knew her emotions often made her act irrationally.

"You were very lucky," said Priestess Aldriss. "You should have noticed the polymorph spell on the mage before you did. The only reason she didn't stun you first was because activation words for priest wands are faster than those for mage wands. Do you disagree?"

Still paralyzed, Jeena couldn't answer even if she had wanted. *She's right, and she knows it,* Jeena thought.

"Still," said Priestess Aldriss, "there aren't many tenth-year priest acolytes who could disable two twentieth-year mage apprentices on their own."

That shocked Jeena. *Is she giving me praise?*

"But don't let it go to your head," continued Priestess Aldriss. "You may soon face foes more dangerous than fellow students of the higher arts."

The old elf waved a hand and said a word Jeena didn't recognize. Magic flowed out from the priestess and enveloped Jeena. Warmth replaced the cold in her muscles. With the blessed relief, Jeena found she could move again.

"Your training is done for the day," said Priestess Aldriss. "Gather your things. High Priest Questor wants to see you tomorrow at mid-morning in his chamber. Don't be late."

"I will be there on time, priestess," Jeena said biting off several retorts straining to escape. She'd like to have told the priestess what she thought of being pitted against mage apprentices ten years her senior, but Jeena refrained. She knew it would do no good to whine. Priestess Aldriss was not one of those instructors who calmly listened to student's complaints. Besides, the old elf's comment about facing more dangerous foes intrigued her. Not to mention it was unusual for the high priest to meet alone with a tenth-year acolyte.

Well, Jeena thought as she stood up and began gathering her things. *I think tomorrow may turn out to be a very interesting day.*

CHAPTER 7

The next two days on the *Defiant* settled into a dull routine. Sergeant Ron assigned each of them to an eight-hour shift. Since the *Defiant* pretty much ran itself while in hyper-drive, the duties for the three of them consisted mostly of odds-and-ends maintenance on the starship. Richard tried arguing he could work longer than eight hours since he only needed occasional cat naps, but Sergeant Ron wouldn't hear of it. He was all about fairness. Still, Richard tended to use a lot of his off-time to help Charlie. The old, or depending on how you looked at it, not so old lizard was a wealth of information on how to use scans to monitor waves and lines of energy. Charlie even knew some tricks about interacting with computers that he willingly showed the *Defiant's* resident wizard scout. Richard learned a lot over the course of the two days.

On the rare occasions when he wasn't working, sleeping, or in the kitchen cooking, Richard was in the common room reading. During his youth, he hadn't gotten the opportunity to read much. Getting enough food to stave off starvation always seemed the higher priority. Even during his five years at the Academy when he'd had plenty to eat, any reading he'd done had consisted primarily of boring technical manuals.

After graduation, Richard's priorities changed. He had a lot more free time, especially on missions for '*the One.*' Thanks to his dimensional pack, Richard had an almost inexhaustible supply of books; real, honest-to-goodness, hardback books. Nickelo had created a list of 'ten thousand books you need to read before you die' and given it to Richard. Before long, Richard discovered he was a prolific reader at heart. Even so, he figured he was going to have to live a very long time if he wanted to make more than a dent in his battle computer's book list.

The afternoon of their third day in hyperspace found Richard sitting at the common-room table reading. He was dressed in a semi-clean, black jumpsuit with the top half unzipped and tied around his waist. Sergeant Ron liked to keep the inside of the *Defiant* cool, but it was not so cool Richard felt he needed more than his t-shirt to stay warm.

Richard was currently reading an ancient classic about a woman and a man who just couldn't seem to get together. Every time Richard thought the couple was going to work things out, one of them would let their pride or their prejudice get in the way.

Lowering the book, Richard thought about his own love life, or lack thereof. Since his breakup with Liz, he'd had a few dalliances, but nothing serious or long term. He was long past his infatuation with Liz. Richard had a feeling it might be hard for an outsider to understand his change in feelings. After all, he'd come close to telling her he loved her. But for Richard, the time was much longer than the year since he'd left the Academy. 'The One' had sent him on twenty-two missions over the past year. The unofficial missions spanned a total of eighteen years in the magical dimension. The additional missions made keeping track of time screwy for Richard. As far as the Empire was concerned, he was only twenty-seven years old with a physical age of twenty-six. Since wizard scouts didn't age, he'd always appear to be twenty-six physically.

"So," Richard said out loud. "Am I twenty-seven? Or am I forty-five? I don't feel forty-five."

"Are you asking me?" asked Nickelo over the external speakers of the battle helmet.

Richard had laid his battle computer and utility belt on the table when he'd sat down.

"Sure," Richard said out loud "That is if you have an answer."

"Oh, I always have an answer. It's just that sometimes my answer isn't what you want to hear."

"Is this one of those times?" Richard asked unsure whether he wanted to start one of those confusing conversations with his battle computer.

"I guess we'll see," replied Nickelo. "Logically, your age is forty-five standard years. However, the reason you don't feel forty-five is because part of your memory gets wiped whenever you return to the present after performing a mission for '*the One.*'"

"Yeah, I know," Richard said disgustedly. "Most of my missions for '*the One*' seem more like half-remembered dreams than they do real life. What I do remember doesn't even make any sense. You once told me '*the One*' is sending me on missions to prepare me for some big task in the future. Why bother if he wipes my memory whenever I return. I can't learn if I can't remember what I did."

"Ah, but that's where I see the beauty of his logic," said Nickelo with a hint of admiration. "The size of your human brain is limited. You're a stubborn man, Rick. '*The One*' may calculate it's going to take a lot of training to prepare you for your future task. '*The One*' may only be allowing you to retain memories that are in line with his eventual purpose for you."

"Well," Richard said beginning to grow a little heated. He didn't like being controlled, and he hated not being able to do anything about it.

"Well, what?" asked Nickelo sounding curious.

"Well," Richard said again trying to remember his past missions for '*the One.*' "There are at least two missions where I don't have any memory of what I did at all. By looking at my Power's timeline, I know I spent several months on those missions. But I've no recollection of them. Why does '*the One*' send me on missions if he's not going to let me remember them?"

"My guess would be that those were failed missions," answered Nickelo. "He didn't allow you to keep those memories because either you failed to do something important, or you did something contrary to what would help you in your overall goal."

"It's not my goal," Richard pointed out. "I haven't been told squat by '*the One.*' All I have to go on is what that master demon told me a couple of years ago. I'm supposed to make some kind of decision at some point that will affect the continued existence of three galaxies. I'm not sure I actually believe the demon. Even if I did, I'm not sure I want that kind of responsibility thrown on my shoulders."

"Whatever, Rick," said Nickelo apparently deciding to end the conversation. "You're the big, bad wizard scout. I'm just the subservient and humble battle computer."

"Well, say what you—," Richard started to say.

Richard didn't get a chance to finish. An all too familiar tingle ran through his body. His surroundings began blurring in and out of focus.

"Put up your best stealth shield, Rick," ordered Nickelo. "You're teleporting."

Richard did as he was told. He threw up his best stealth shield and made a grab for his utility belt where it lay on the table.

Just as his hands wrapped around the belt, a voice in Richard's head said, *"Heal them. Heal them all."*

Then the room disappeared and everything went black.

* * *

Nickelo turned the battle helmet's visuals onto the spot where his wizard scout had been sitting. The spot was empty. His wizard scout was gone. The helmet's visuals picked up Richard's utility belt still lying on the table. The black jumpsuit his wizard scout had been wearing was crumpled up on the floor along with his undergarments and boots. The battle helmet's sensors picked up Richard's dimensional pack. It was still lying on his wizard scout's bunk.

That sucks, Nickelo thought. *'The One' has sent him on another mission without any equipment and without me to advise him. I was afraid of that. I told him he should've been more cooperative on our last mission. But no, Rick wanted to be stubborn again. Will he never learn?*

Nickelo wished he had someone to talk the situation over with. Existence without his wizard scout was boring beyond belief.

There's Sergeant Ron and Charlie, of course, but they aren't as interesting as my wizard scout. Besides, I can pull my wizard scout's chain without even trying. Other people aren't nearly as much fun.

Five minutes passed, then another five. The seat where his wizard scout had sat remained empty. The nanoseconds passed interminably. Nickelo checked various calculations to pass the time. Without unfettered access to the tele-network, his ability to perform useful tasks was limited. He had no purpose.

"Nick," came Sergeant Ron's voice over the common-room's intercom. "Where's Rick? I'm not picking him up on the ship's sensors."

"My wizard scout is currently on a mission for *'the One,'*" Nickelo answered. "May I be of assistance?"

"Great. That's just great," said Sergeant Ron sounding like he was more worried than frustrated. "How long before he returns? I need to make a jump. I want to talk to him before I do."

"Hmm," Nickelo said using the time to make calculations. Their plan had been to make the run to Risors using standard hyper-drive. Their flight time was scheduled for a full two weeks. Making hyper-jumps was too expensive to do without a good reason. Routine meetings between a wizard scout and the Imperial High Council were not important enough to warrant the expense of a hyper-jump.

"I can only guess when my wizard scout will return," Nickelo said. "Normally, the elapsed time in the physical dimension is less than five minutes. The previous longest time has been thirty minutes."

"Well," said Sergeant Ron sounding none too happy. "As soon as he returns, have him report to the control room. Apparently, our mission's priority has been significantly increased."

"Wilco, Sergeant Ron," Nickelo answered. "Assuming Rick returns, I'll do as you request."

According to his calculations, the odds his wizard scout wouldn't return were extremely low. Of course, nothing was ever guaranteed. In any regard, Nickelo prepared for his friend's return by loading the memory backup for his wizard scout. Depending on the length of his wizard scout's mission, Nickelo calculated he might have to load parts of Richard's memory backup into his shared space to bring him up to speed on current events.

Thirty minutes passed, then another thirty. Sergeant Ron kept calling for status reports. Nickelo could only tell him his wizard scout was still missing. After a full two hours had elapsed, the battle helmet's sensors picked up a disturbance in the air around the table.

A moment later, Richard was sitting in the chair. He was naked, and he had a wild look in his eyes. Nickelo's wizard scout jumped to his feet.

"No! Not yet, damn you!" shouted Richard.

"Rick! You're back," Nickelo said out loud with a great sense of relief. "Where were you? What was your mission?"

Nickelo watched as his wizard scout took a quick look around the common room before collapsing in his chair and slumping forward with his hands over his face.

"Not yet, Nick," whispered Richard aloud. "Give me a minute to adjust."

Nickelo remained silent, although the wait was interminable. His friend didn't say anything for several seconds.

"I don't remember what we were doing when I left," Richard said finally. "It's been too long."

Nickelo gathered the information from his wizard scout's most recent memory backup and fed it into their shared space. He sensed electrical discharges in Richard's neurons as the memories were refreshed in the faded areas of his wizard scout's brain. The knowledge transfer took longer than normal. Nickelo calculated his wizard scout must have been gone a very long time.

"Better?" Nickelo asked trying to adjust his wizard scout back to the here-and-now as gently as possible.

"A little," responded Richard. "So we're on our way to see the Imperial High Council? How long was I away this time?"

"You left a little over two hours ago," Nickelo answered. "Uh, where were you, and how long were you there? That is if you don't mind my asking."

Nickelo's wizard scout didn't answer with words. Instead, Richard sent a stream of images into their shared space. Nickelo saw Richard's arrival on Portalis in a snow-covered land. His wizard scout was naked. A short sword was stuck in the snow at his feet. The sound of wolves could be heard in the distance. From the changes in the howls, Nickelo calculated the wolves were drawing closer.

The scene shifted. A fur-covered Richard was on a battlefield healing combatants. The battlefield changed to a city. Nickelo saw a long line of people waiting in front of a small table to let a robe-clad Richard heal their injuries. The scene was repeated a thousand times as his wizard scout wandered the land healing the injured and the sick of the various races. Dwarves, gnomes, humans, and even some races Nickelo didn't recognize lined up to see the Great Healer of the North.

A final scene showed Richard in a dimly-lit cavern. The cavern was filled with thousands of ebony-skinned elves with white hair lying on blankets or stretchers. Nickelo recognized them as dark elves. Other dark elves were hurriedly walking between their brethren wiping the brows of the sick and trying to ease their suffering. Nickelo saw Richard in a brown robe walking beside a group of dark elves carrying staffs. The group walked to the center of the cavern where they formed a circle around Richard.

His wizard scout's thoughts let Nickelo know the dark elves with the staffs were priests and priestesses. The circle of dark elves fed their Power to their high priest. He, in turn, directed the combined Power to Richard. Nickelo watched as his wizard scout used the Power of the priests and priestesses to draw the illnesses of the thousands of dark elves into himself. Nickelo watched as those around his wizard scout began to heal. Richard, on the other hand, fell to the ground. At the same time, thousands of the dark elves who'd been sick moments before rose from their blankets and stretchers. They cheered the fallen human. The cheers of thousands of more dark elves echoed throughout the cavern as they watched the healing of their brethren. After a time, Richard staggered to his feet.

Nickelo saw the image of his wizard scout begin to shimmer. He was being teleported out. The elapsed time from his first appearance in the snow-covered field to the healing in the cavern of the dark elves was just shy of twenty-five years. The flow of images in their shared space ceased.

"Oh," Nickelo said genuinely concerned for his friend. "I'm sorry I wasn't there to help you."

"So am I," said Richard. "Thankfully, most of the memories are starting to fade now. I know there was a lot of pain, but I'm starting to forget that as well."

"You were a healer?" Nickelo said just to keep the conversation moving. He didn't need Richard to confirm the question. The images had given mute testimony to his wizard scout's assumed profession.

"Not by choice," answered Richard. "But that's how it worked out." With a sigh, Richard added, "I really hate emp-healing."

Nickelo remained quiet. His calculations indicated it was best to let his wizard scout proceed at his own pace. After a few seconds, Richard spoke again.

"I did get more efficient at healing," said Richard. "And I didn't have to kill anyone this time. That was a pleasant change." Richard rubbed his temples with his fingers before continuing. "I'll admit I did like helping people. I just hated I was put in a position where I had to do some of it by emp-healing. However, I did spend a lot of time with healers of various races learning how to heal minor wounds and injuries without having to use my Power."

"And the healing of the dark elves?" Nickelo asked. "What was that all about? Was it your primary mission?"

With a shrug of his shoulders, Richard said, "I've no earthly idea what healing those dark elves was about. I guess I must've known at the time, but the memory's gone now. Since I was teleported out right after I did the mass healing, I assume it was my primary mission. I do know I couldn't have done the mass healing if I hadn't learned how to heal more efficiently first."

Nickelo waited a few seconds before saying, "I hate to push you, Rick, but Sergeant Ron needs to talk to you. I get the impression there's a change in mission. I'm sorry."

His wizard scout didn't answer. He just nodded his head and rose to his feet. Nickelo watched as Richard put on his clothes and boots. Once dressed, his wizard scout headed toward the cockpit of the *Defiant*.

As a computer, Nickelo knew he didn't have a heart. But even so, he felt as if his heart was being torn apart at the sight of his friend. It had obviously been a rough mission, and he hadn't been there to help. While Nickelo knew he had no control over his wizard scout's missions, he still had a nagging feeling he was somehow responsible. It was not an enjoyable feeling.

CHAPTER 8

Richard climbed the steps to the control room. By the time he entered, the memories from his last mission had faded to an indistinct blur with just a few snatches of clarity. He only vaguely remembered the mass healing. Richard felt as if he'd just awakened from a vivid dream, only to have the dream fade away under the harsh light of reality.

The events of the battle on Planet X3321 and their mission to return to Risors seemed to override the happenings of the last twenty-five years in the magical dimension. As far as he could remember, it was always thus upon his return. The physical dimension was his reality. Any time he spent in the magical or spiritual dimensions was just a dream as far as he was concerned. His missions could be very realistic and painful at times, but they still seemed like dreams. Richard had a feeling thinking of his missions for *the One* in this manner was the only way he could ever hold onto his sanity.

"Well, glad to see you're back," said Sergeant Ron from his seat at the pilot's station. "I was beginning to think you'd done gone AWOL on me. Now, that would've been a shame. I'd hate to have to do all that paperwork."

Although he was in no mood for jokes, Richard did his best to play along. "Nope, you're still stuck with me. Uh, Nick said you wanted to talk to me. He said it was something about a change of mission."

Richard suddenly realized he'd left his battle helmet and utility belt back on the common room's table.

"Yeah, shows how much you missed me," chided Nickelo. *"Don't worry. I can pick up everything through our shared space as long as you don't block me out."*

"Sorry," Richard apologized. *"I guess it's force of habit. I've been kind of sparse on equipment the last few years."*

"You going to be okay?" said Sergeant Ron sounding concerned. "You look worse than an ore shuttle working the outer rings on Paltos Minor."

"That bad, huh?" Richard said giving a hesitant grin.

As the memories of his last mission for *'the One'* continued to fade, Richard felt his mind returning to normal. He wasn't quite there yet, but he hoped he would be given enough time.

"Maybe a little worse," grinned Sergeant Ron. "Any hoot, that's not the reason I wanted to see you. While you were off to wherever you go, I got a change in orders from the Imperial High Command. They want us to expedite our trip to Risors. They've ordered you to report to Councilwoman Deloris at the planetary administration building on Risors by 0800 hours tomorrow standard time."

The request struck Richard as more than a little strange. It would take multiple jumps in hyperspace to make the meeting in time.

"To be precise," said Nickelo in their shared space, *"the* Defiant *will need to make four hyper-jumps to get there by 0800 hours."*

"Hmm," Richard said trying to stall for time to think. "What'd you tell them, Sergeant Ron?"

"What do you think I told them?" said Sergeant Ron grinning from ear to ear. "I told them to pound sand. I told them the *Defiant* was a privately-owned vessel, and we weren't going to pay for the wear and tear on our hyper-drive just for some politician's convenience. I also told them we'd be there in ten more days running on standard hyper-drive and the honored councilwoman would just have to wait. And if they didn't like it, they could just pay for a complete overhaul of the *Defiant's* hyper-drive along with some long-overdue upgrades; because that's the only way I'd consider making even a single jump without a military emergency."

Richard gave a little laugh. He was definitely getting back to normal.

"I'm betting they didn't take your response too cordially," Richard said.

"Well, actually, they surprised me," said Sergeant Ron as he scratched his beard thoughtfully. "The fools came back and told me the Deloris Armaments Corporation was going to pay for a full overhaul of the *Defiant* if'n we got back in time. They're even going to throw in two Zip fighters for our wing pods if we hustle."

"Hmm," Nickelo said. *"A full overhaul is over two million credits. Even small fighters like those zippers are over a half a million apiece. I calculate whatever's up doesn't bode well for you, old buddy."*

Ignoring his battle computer, Richard flipped the switch on the navigation console. A three-dimensional hologram of the star systems between the *Defiant* and Risors appeared. A purple line zigzagged between the white point denoting the *Defiant's* current position and the yellow point denoting Risors. Richard noticed four red dots along the route marking jump points between dimensional folds in the galaxy.

"Did you tell them you were going to do it?" Richard said. He wasn't sure whether he approved or not.

"No," said Sergeant Ron. "I wanted to talk to you first. Something must've changed that we don't know about. And I don't like the fact the money's coming from Deloris Armaments instead of being funded by the Empire."

"But the meeting's with the council," Richard said.

Sergeant Ron pointed his finger at Richard. "That's where you're wrong, Rick. Your meeting was originally with the council. Now it's with Councilwoman Deloris. I would highly advise you not to trust her. She's more ambitious than is good for her or the Empire."

"Well, I'll admit it does seem strange," Richard said. "But if my memory serves me correctly, the *Defiant* is down to forty percent service life left on her hyper-drive. An overhaul could come in handy."

Sergeant Ron rubbed his jaw thoughtfully. "Yeah, a free overhaul could be useful. And if Deloris Armaments is paying for it anyway, the overhaul might be modified to entail a few special upgrades as well. I know some people on Risors who owe me a few favors."

"I'll just bet you do," Richard said with a laugh. "By the way, what was all that about two fighters for our wing pods? What good will they do us? I don't know anything about flying fighters. Does Charlie or you?"

"No," admitted Sergeant Ron. "They fly different than the bigger ships. But I don't pass up free gear when it's offered."

"So we're going to make the jumps?" Richard asked.

"That's up to you, Rick," said Sergeant Ron.

"Me?" Richard said surprised.

"Yeah," said Sergeant Ron. "I told you when we left Velos I'd take care of flying the *Defiant*, but you'd be the leader of this little outfit. You do remember, don't you?"

"I told you then I wasn't a leader," Richard said. "You're the *Defiant's* captain. I don't even understand why you insisted on coming with me. What about your wife and family? How do they feel about it?"

"Oh no, you're not changing the subject," said Sergeant Ron. "I'm a sergeant, and that's all I ever want to be. I ain't no captain. I run this ship, but the why and wherefores are all yours." With a grin, Sergeant Ron asked, "So, boss, are we jumping or ain't we?"

Richard mulled the situation over in his mind.

"Nick?" Richard thought. *"What do you—"*

"Oh no, Rick," interrupted Nickelo. *"This decision is all yours. Make a decision and go with it."*

"Fine, Sergeant Ron," Richard said out loud. "Update the calculations and make the jump."

"They're already made," said Sergeant Ron as he slammed his fist on a large button near the center of the control console.

The *Defiant's* hyper-drive sounded its roar. Richard's cells were torn apart as the *Defiant* jumped the fold between dimensions. The *Defiant* was on its way.

* * *

The *Defiant* landed at berth 103 on the east side of the Aloran spaceport on Risors. The spaceport was crowded. It teamed with life. Starships of every kind were taking off and landing several times a minute from the spaceport's two hundred and twenty-three berths. From large cargo ships to giant luxury liners to small recon ships like the *Defiant*, the spaceport was alive with activity.

While Richard knew berth 103 wasn't the best docking station at the spaceport, he could tell it certainly wasn't the worst either. He was once again amazed at the number of contacts Sergeant Ron had up his sleeve. With just a couple of calls, the *Defiant's* captain had acquired a berth and a maintenance crew to begin the *Defiant's* overhaul. By the time Richard left for his meeting, a dozen technicians were furiously working on removing the hyper-drive's core out of the *Defiant*.

As Richard walked toward the spaceport's east transportation building, a half-empty hover-bus pulled alongside and offered him a ride. After some helpful directions from the bus driver, Richard soon found himself on a second bus headed for the planetary administration building twenty kilometers away.

The bus ride was peaceful, and Richard took advantage of the calm to take a short nap. He awoke a half hour later when the bus pulled to a stop in front of the doors of the planetary administration building. It was the home of the Imperial High Council as well as a slew of other government offices.

Once inside, Richard found the reception desk. A male android sat in a seat behind the desk.

"I'm looking for the office of Councilwoman Deloris," Richard said.

"Yes, Wizard Scout Shepard," replied the android in the emotionless voice Richard associated with sims. "We've been monitoring your progress from the airfield. Councilwoman Deloris is expecting you."

The android handed Richard a small rod and pointed to a line of clamshell-like chairs on the far wall. "Since this is your first visit to our building, I've taken the liberty of programming the route into this destination rod. Just insert the rod in the receptacle on the side of the chair."

Richard took the rod and looked at it closer. It was about the size of a pen, and it appeared to be a solid hunk of metal. His friend Telsa had told him about conveyances like the transportation chair when they were at the Academy, but this was his first encounter with one.

Since the android hadn't assigned a specific chair, Richard

chose the closest one. He sat down in the thick padding of the chair. It was very comfortable.

"I guess they don't want some high-level politician getting a blister on their bum," Richard said.

"Now, Rick," replied Nickelo. *"Don't start getting an attitude already. To the best of our knowledge, you don't have any enemies here yet. Wouldn't it be nice to keep it that way?"*

Richard was dressed in the black and silver-trimmed jumpsuit of a wizard scout. Although he wasn't wearing his battle suit, he did have his utility belt with his phase rod attached. As was typical for a wizard scout, his battle helmet was hooked to the left rear of the utility belt. He didn't have any other weapons. Building security officers tended to frown on visitors bringing weapons and live ammo into their buildings this far behind friendly lines. Most security officers made exceptions for a wizard scout's phase rod.

Inserting the direction rod into the obvious receptacle on the side of the transportation chair, Richard was surprised when the chair remained stationary. Instead of moving, a light-red glow surrounded the chair and began flashing. Richard noticed a team of three security guards headed his way. All three wore sidearms, but none of them had their weapon drawn.

"What now?" Richard thought.

"Excuse me, wizard scout," said the lead guard as he glanced at the computer readout on his forearm. The guard sounded like a person doing their best to be polite but expecting an argument. "I see your destination rod is programmed for the council chambers. That's a level five restricted area. No weapons of any kind are allowed there. We can hold onto your phase rod if you'd like, sir."

Richard noticed the trailing guards move their hands just above the butts of their sidearms. Richard's temper started to rise, but he pushed it back in its cage where it belonged. Richard's temper had always been one of his weaknesses. Thankfully, he was getting much better at controlling it.

Without a word, Richard unhooked his phase rod and handed it to the lead security guard.

"Thank you, wizard scout," said the guard sounding relieved. Gesturing toward a desk in the center of the reception area, the guard added, "You can pick this back up over there when you leave the building, sir."

"I'm proud of you," said Nickelo. *"They're just doing their jobs after all."*

"I know," Richard thought back, *"but senseless things get my goat sometimes. I can just summon my phase rod if I need it. They've gained nothing."*

"Well, they don't know you can summon items," said Nickelo. *"It's a time-commando ability, not a wizard scout one. Oh, and I like your 'get my goat' comment. I think you've been reading my* Quaint Sayings *book. Good for you."*

"Whatever," Richard said dismissively.

Richard had actually been reading a copy of the book. To be honest, he found it to be interesting reading, although he'd never admit it to his battle computer.

The guard passed his palm over the readout on the transportation chair. Richard heard a hum. Then the chair moved toward a chamber in the wall. The chamber was the same size as the transportation chair.

The chair entered the chamber. It was actually a tube more than a chamber. Magnetic fields running through thin-metal strips along the sides of the tube lifted the chair at a high rate of speed. Richard was pushed down into the thick padding of the chair. A moment later, he was shoved to the right side of the chair as it shot down a side tunnel to the left.

The planetary administration building was massive. Just the wing devoted to the Imperial High Council was over two kilometers in length. But the transportation chair made quick work of delivering its passenger. Within twenty seconds, the chair abruptly slowed and exited out an opening in the tube. The chair came to a halt in an ornate room filled with several dozen beings of various Empire races.

A tall, blue-skinned male approached Richard. At least, Richard thought he was a male. It was always hard to tell with Eorians.

"You mean it's hard for you to tell," quipped Nickelo. *"I calculate a ninety-nine point nine percent probability the Eorians have no trouble distinguishing the difference."*

"Wizard scout," said the Eorian as he or she gave a bow. "I am Councilwoman Deloris's chief of staff. Please follow me."

The Eorian didn't wait for Richard to answer. He or she just turned and walked toward a wide hallway across the room. Richard followed.

Halfway down the hall, two burly guards dressed in light-blue Conglomerate uniforms stood in front of a double door. They were armed with M63 lightweight plasma assault rifles. Both guards turned and glowered at Richard.

"This is Wizard Scout Shepard," said the Eorian. "Councilwoman Deloris is expecting him."

Without waiting for a reply, the Eorian gave Richard a bow, turned, and walked back the way they'd come.

"Friendly chap, isn't he?" Richard thought.

"Yes, he is, assuming he's a he," answered Nickelo. *"He reminds me of you a few years ago. You were ever the social butterfly."*

One of the guards held up a small scanner. A yellow light ran up and down Richard's length.

"He's clean," said the guard.

The second guard opened the door and ushered Richard inside. As he passed, the guard whispered, "You'd best not give the councilwoman any trouble. We'll be right outside."

"Ah," said Nickelo into Richard's shared space. *"Another devoted fan of the wizard scout corps."*

"Can it, Nick," Richard said. *"I'm going to need some help. I'm not very good at dealing with politicians and their conniving ways."*

"So I've noticed," Nickelo laughed. Then he added a little more seriously, *"Never fear. I've got your back, buddy."*

Once inside, Richard was referred by the receptionist to a second receptionist who referred him to the undersecretary for the councilwoman. After a fifteen-minute wait in a semi-crowded antechamber, Richard was led to another set of doors flanked by four guards in the light-blue jumpsuits of the Conglomerate. Like their earlier companions, all four were heavily armed. The scowls the four guards gave Richard as he passed by made the first two guards look like his best buddies.

"Friendly cusses, aren't they?" said Nickelo. *"They're loaded for wild pactar I might add. I calculate the councilwoman is concerned about her security."*

Richard didn't reply. The door shut behind him. The only other occupant in the room was a slim woman dressed in a light-blue pantsuit. She had the physical appearance of a woman in her late twenties, but Richard wasn't fooled. From her aura, he guessed her age was in the mid-forties. He'd seen her before. She was Councilwoman Deloris.

The councilwoman looked up from her desk and gave Richard a smile. "Ah. Wizard Scout Shepard, we meet again. How long has it been?"

"Ten months," Richard said keeping his answer terse.

The last time he'd seen the councilwoman had been when he'd graduated from the Academy. He'd never had any direct dealings with her, but he knew she was no friend of the wizard scout corp. From what his battle computer had told him, the councilwoman had been leading a charge to close the Academy when the Crosioians did the job for her by attacking. Richard trusted her about as much as he trusted a coiled rattlesnake from his home world of Earth.

"Oh, come now, wizard scout," said Councilwoman Deloris with a friendly smile. "I'm not your enemy. Surely we can be friends."

"Oh, she's good," said Nickelo. *"Her smile almost looks genuine. Watch what you say, Rick. Words are her weapons. You're outgunned big time."*

"Don't I know it, buddy?" Richard said.

Richard had always hated subterfuge and political niceties. He was still a Marine at heart, so he decided to take the direct approach.

"I'm just a soldier, councilwoman," Richard said. "I obey legal orders from my chain of command. But if I may be frank, I doubt we can be friends. My understanding is you were responsible for a lot of the Commandant's grief his last few weeks. You made it obvious you're no friend of wizard scouts. I'm not apt to forget."

"Ah. I suspected you might think unkindly of me, Rick," said Councilwoman Deloris. "You don't mind if I call you Rick, do you? Titles seem so formal. One gets tired of them after a while."

Richard shrugged his shoulders.

The councilwoman must have taken that as his approval because she continued, "And, Rick, you must call me Diane." She gazed into his eyes for several seconds. "You know, I owe you a debt of gratitude. How could I want to be anything other than your friend?"

Her words took Richard by surprise. "I don't understand. Gratitude for what?"

"Oh, Rick. You're too modest for your own good," said the councilwoman with a chuckle. "For starters, everyone on the council owes the Hero of Velos a debt. From all the reports I've read, you pretty much singlehandedly fought off the Crosioian invasion force."

Richard said nothing. Flowery words didn't inflate his ego anymore. Years ago they might have, but he was no longer the naive teenager he'd once been. He was an experienced wizard scout now.

The councilwoman waited a few seconds as if expecting Richard to reply. When he didn't, she said, "All right, maybe that's overstating it a bit. But I'm a politician. Exaggeration comes by force of habit. Please forgive me if I occasionally inflate the facts a little. However, I do owe you a debt, Rick. After all, you saved my son's life during the battle at the Academy's airfield last year. If you hadn't convinced him to trade his Warcat for your rifle, he would've marched off to his death."

She turned around to look at the wall behind her, raising a hand to her eyes. After a moment, she turned back around and said, "I don't think I could have recovered from that."

For the barest moment, Richard thought he saw the councilwoman drop the façade she used to shield herself from the world around her. For that brief moment, he saw the fear of a mother who'd almost lost the most precious thing in her universe; her child. Then the façade was back in place, and the moment was gone.

"Well, anyway," said the councilwoman. "I just wanted to thank you."

Richard wasn't sure how to respond, so he just remained silent for what he hoped was an appropriate amount of time. Finally, he spoke. "Councilwoman, why—"

"Diane, please," interrupted Councilwoman Deloris.

"Uh...okay, err...Diane," Richard muttered. "Really. Why am I here? You've had almost a year to thank me for the situation with your son. The council authorized hyper-jumps for the *Defiant* with a fully-funded overhaul to get me here by today. Why?"

The councilwoman started to frown, but she hurriedly changed the expression into a smile. "I've been told you were blunt and to the point. I fear your ship's captain is rubbing his bad habits off on you, but no matter. Please sit, Rick. You're making me feel uncomfortable standing at parade rest like that."

The councilwoman pointed to a thickly-padded chair to the left side of her desk. After pulling the chair to the front to keep the desk between them, Richard sat down.

"I've been meaning to thank you," said Councilwoman Deloris, "but I've been so busy with the war and all. Not to mention the destruction of the Academy has put a strain on the military. But you're right. Thanking you is not the primary reason your trip to Risors was expedited. It seems we've had a request from a very important interstellar government for you to be temporarily reassigned to them."

That got Richard's attention.

"Who and why?" Richard asked. He'd been denied wizard scout type missions for so long he was leery of any additional out of the ordinary requests. Being assigned to a mercenary outfit was bad enough. He was a regular military soldier. The fact he wasn't assigned to a standard military outfit left a bad taste in his mouth. His friends were off defending the Empire from the Crosioians while he played tag with Balorian pirates or got sent on wild-goose chases.

"Who?" said the councilwoman. "The Trecorians have made the request. Why? They say it's because they want you to help train their soldiers."

"What?" Richard said incredulously. "And the council believes them? The Trecorians were trying to blow holes in me not three days ago. They missed, and I don't plan on giving them a second chance."

"Hmm," said the councilwoman as she pursed her lips and touched the tips of her fingers together. "I'll let your chain of command discuss that with you. But just so you know, your reassignment has already been approved by the Imperial High Command."

Councilwoman Deloris gave Richard a sympathetic look. "Rick, I understand your feelings. Truly I do. But the Empire has been courting the Trecorians for the last three years; all to no avail. The

Empire needs their raw materials for our war effort. This is the first conciliatory overture we've gotten from the Trecorians."

She leaned forward before saying in a softer tone, "May I be honest with you, Rick?"

"Watch it, Rick," warned Nickelo. *"You can bet anytime a politician asks if they can be honest with you, that's the time they're probably going to be the most dishonest."*

Richard just nodded his head yes. The councilwoman took his nod as an affirmative reply to her question.

"I've read the report of your action with the Trecorians," she said. "Very impressive. Outnumbered twelve to one, you destroyed four of their cats and lived to tell about it. On top of that, you did it without killing any of their soldiers. The Trecorians were impressed as well. They've offered to begin limited sales of brerellium to the Empire if we reassign you to them for a few months."

Richard snorted disgustedly.

"Does the Empire get a bonus if I accidentally get a burst of plasma rounds to the back of my head," Richard asked in as sarcastic a tone as he could muster.

Councilwoman Deloris took Richard's comment as a joke. She gave a little laugh. "You military types and your coarse sense of humor continually amaze me. The Trecorians' ambassador gave the council Duke Bistoria's assurance you would only be involved in training well behind friendly lines. The Imperial High Council believes him."

From previous briefings, Richard knew Duke Bistoria was the pseudo leader of the Trecorians. "Do you believe him, Diane?" Richard said emphasizing the councilwoman's name. "Would you trust the life of your son on the duke's promise?"

Councilwoman Deloris looked long and hard at Richard. He didn't flinch. Richard figured he'd called her bluff. He assumed she was even now trying to think of a way to take her words back.

"As it so happens," said Councilwoman Deloris in a deathly-serious tone, "I am trusting my son's life on the duke's promise. My son, Matthew, will be accompanying you on your ship. If there's any treachery on the part of the Trecorians, my son will pay the price along with you."

Shocked beyond words, Richard just stared open-mouthed at the councilwoman. The list of additional arguments he'd been formulating in his mind disappeared into a puff of smoke. He could think of no arguments suitable against a mother willing to risk the life of her son.

"Maybe the honored councilwoman doesn't like her son very much," suggested Nickelo. *"Have you thought of that?"*

Richard brushed his battle computer's comment aside. He'd heard her son defend his mother the previous years. Richard seriously doubted the boy would be so loyal to his mother if there were any dislike in the relationship.

"You look shocked," said Councilwoman Deloris. "You needn't be. I've met the duke on several occasions. He's an honorable man, as are most of the Trecorians; male or female. You'll probably like them."

The councilwoman smiled. "The Trecorians have always reminded me a little of the old Spartans back on your home world of Earth. They're very militaristic. You'll probably fit right in."

Richard had read quite a bit on the Trecorians before he'd gone on his mission to Planet X3321. He nodded his head in agreement with the councilwoman. Like her, the Trecorians reminded him of the ancient Spartans. However, they weren't nearly as brutal. Still, they were similar in many ways. For instance, every Trecorian child began military training at an early age.

"It could still be dangerous," Richard said stalling for time to think. The councilwoman's declaration was definitely unexpected. He needed time to sort out all the information.

"And, I don't run the *Defiant*," Richard said. "Sergeant Ron's her captain. He has the final say on who can and can't be on his ship. He can be a little hardheaded at times."

A strange look came over Councilwoman Deloris before she got her emotions under control. The look was gone as quickly as it came. Richard couldn't quite figure it out, but something had definitely been there. His words had hit a sore point in the councilwoman for some reason.

"I'll handle the *Defiant's* captain," said Councilwoman Deloris. "I have an offer he can't refuse. Besides, we're upgrading your *Defiant* from top to bottom; new avionics, weapons, the latest hyper-drive, and two Zip fighters for those empty wing pods of yours. If my son's going to be on the *Defiant*, I want it to have the best protection credits can buy."

"Well, I didn't see that one coming," Nickelo admitted in their shared space. *"I wonder what her game is? I calculate a ninety-two percent probability there's more to this than meets the eye."*

"No, kidding," Richard shot back. *"Figured that all out by your lonesome, did you?"*

His battle computer didn't dignify Richard's comment with a reply.

"You're staying quiet, wizard scout," said Councilwoman Deloris. "From the look on your face, I gather you're conferring with your battle computer."

Richard mentally kicked himself. He was going to have to do something about controlling his features when he talked to Nickelo.

"We're just trying to figure out why you're doing this," Richard confessed. "From what I understand, the Conglomerate owns plenty of top-of-the-line starships. Why force your son to go on ours?"

"Ha!" said the councilwoman with what sounded like a genuine laugh. "I'm not forcing my son to do anything. It was his idea. And he can be as stubborn as me at times. As soon as Matthew found out you were coming here, he was adamant he was going to go with you. I'm afraid you've been somewhat of a hero to him since the battle at the Academy's airfield last year."

"Why don't you just tell him no," Richard asked. "The *Defiant* is a combat ship. There's a war on. Trouble has a way of finding us regardless of what your Trecorian duke might promise."

Councilwoman Deloris gave a knowing smile. "It's obvious you don't have teenagers of your own. The more you tell them no, the more they're going to try to do that very thing."

Richard gave a slight nod of agreement. She'd pretty much summed up his teenage years.

"Besides," said the councilwoman, "Matthew has too much of his grandfather in him for his own good. My father's parents tried to control him and force him to run the family business. They succeeded for a few years, but then he rebelled and joined the military when he was forty years old to follow some decrepit wizard scout. I'm not going to make the same mistake with Matthew. If he has to sow some wild oats, I'm going to let him get them out of his system now. Then he can come back in a couple of years and take his proper place in the business."

"Two years?" Richard exclaimed. "He can't be with me for two years. I'm a wizard scout. You know that. We're only sent on the most dangerous missions. It's no place for a boy."

Without speaking, Councilwoman Deloris stood up and walked around the table until she stood in front of Richard. She was a tall woman, and she hovered over Richard. He suspected she used her size to intimidate people. But he was a wizard scout, so it didn't work as well on him. Still, it was disconcerting having her hovering over him. Richard stood up as well. He was tall himself. He looked the councilwoman directly in her eyes.

"Are you happy with what you're doing, Rick?" Councilwoman Deloris asked in a quiet voice.

Her question took Richard by surprise. "I don't understand what you mean," he finally admitted.

"Oh, come now. It's a simple question. The Empire's at war. You're a wizard scout. Yet for the past year, you've only been assigned to second-rate missions."

She looked deeper into Richard's eyes as if trying to gauge his reaction. "Doesn't it bother you to know your friends—your fellow wizard scouts—are risking their lives every day while you're coasting along on missions better suited to reserve recon units than a highly-trained wizard scout?"

Richard opened his mouth to protest, but the councilwoman held up a hand to keep him silent. "Yes, yes, I know. The Trecorians almost killed you during your last mission. But that was a fluke, wasn't it? The mission was supposed to be a milk run, from my understanding. I suppose we should be grateful the mission didn't go as planned since it's opened up trade talks with the Trecorians. However, that wasn't the original intent of your mission. So I ask you again. Are you happy with what you're doing?"

The councilwoman's questions had Richard off balance. He didn't think fast, so was having trouble seeing where she was headed.

Hell, no, I'm not happy, Richard thought, *but I'm not going to admit that to you.*

In reality, it did bother Richard that his assignments during the past year had been low-grade missions. And it did bother him that his friends and the others in the dwindling ranks of the wizard scout corps were being pressed into ever more dangerous situations.

"Don't think of it that way, Rick," came Nickelo's thought. *"You've been on a score of missions for* 'the One' *that have been infinitely more dangerous than anything the others have done. You've been doing your share."*

"Those don't count," Richard said heatedly. *"Those missions seem more like dreams than reality. Sometimes I wonder if they really happened. Besides, I'm an Empire soldier. Nothing I do for* 'the One' *is helping our war effort. Last I heard, a third of my class was dead or disabled."*

"You don't answer," said Councilwoman Deloris. "But you don't need to answer. I can see it in your eyes. Of course you're not happy, so I'd like to make you a proposal."

She paused as if giving Richard's curiosity time to draw him in. After a couple of seconds, she said, "Why don't you leave the wizard scouts and come to work for the Conglomerate? I have a lot of pull on the Imperial High Council. Getting you out of your commitment as a wizard scout would be no problem. With the Conglomerate, you'd have missions more suited to your abilities. And the pay would be much better, I can assure you of that."

"My, she's full of surprises," said Nickelo.

"I'm a soldier," Richard said as if trying to convince himself as much as the councilwoman. "I have no desire to be some bozo security guard for an overpaid vice president in charge of making widgets people don't need or want."

"Oh, Rick," said Councilwoman Deloris with a tolerant smile. "You underestimate us. The Conglomerate wouldn't waste your talents, I promise you that. And you'd still be a soldier. We have every branch of the military in our forces as I'm sure you've noticed. We could use a man like you."

Richard noticed the councilwoman glance back at the clock display inset in the top of her desk. She looked back at him and said, "I have a meeting in twenty minutes with the other council members. Would you mind walking with me part way? We still have a few items I'd like to discuss, but my time is short."

"Of course, councilwoman," Richard said, "I—"

"Please, Rick" admonished Councilwoman Deloris. "Call me Diane."

"All right, Diane," Richard said. "I was just going to say the whole purpose of my trip was to meet with you. So I guess I'm at your disposal."

The councilwoman gave a halfhearted smile. "Ah, you overestimate my importance. There are others who wish to see you as well. I was just first in line." The councilwoman gestured to the door, saying, "Shall we? The time is short and our needs are great."

CHAPTER 9

Councilwoman Deloris led the way out of her office. Richard moved over to her left side. Just outside the door were four guards in the light blue of Conglomerate security personnel. Richard noticed the four guards fall in behind the councilwoman and him. When they did, Councilwoman Deloris stopped and held up her hand at the shortest of the four guards. He was an older man, probably in his sixties.

"Not this time, Carlos," said Councilwoman Deloris. "I'm heading for the council chambers. You know they don't allow private security personnel there."

"That's a dangerous rule," said Carlos with obvious distaste for the rule in his eyes and voice. "The council's guards aren't concerned enough about your safety. As many times as your life has been threatened, they should allow an exception in your case."

Smiling, Councilwoman Deloris turned to Richard. "Carlos has been watching over me ever since I was a child. Sometimes he's worse than a mother hen."

"Your security's no joke, councilwoman," said Carlos. "At least let us escort you to the hallway outside the Imperial High Council's chambers."

Richard thought he saw concern in the old man's eyes. Richard had a feeling the old man would lay down his life for the councilwoman if necessary.

"Nonsense," said Councilwoman Deloris. "All the council members get death threats from time to time. We can't please everyone. There will always be a few disgruntled souls out there."

"These latest threats haven't been the normal ones from some nut job, councilwoman," said Carlos. "They hinted you wouldn't live the week. I must insist we accompany you."

The councilwoman's smile disappeared, and her voice took on an edge. "And I must insist your guards and you stay here." After a second, the councilwoman said in a much gentler voice, "Besides, I will have the best wizard scout in the Empire at my side. Won't I, Rick?"

"Err," Richard stammered trying to figure out how he'd gotten involved in the exchange of words. "Actually, I don't even have a weapon."

"Ha!" said the councilwoman with what sounded like a genuine laugh. "You're far too modest, Rick. You're the Hero of Velos, remember? You are a weapon."

"Err," Richard said again trying to stall for time. He didn't like being called a hero. In point of fact, he tried to go out of his way not to be heroic most of the time.

Carlos eyed Richard as if sizing him up. Richard had a feeling the old man found him lacking. Carlos's words confirmed Richard's suspicion.

"If he's such a hero," said Carlos, "what's he doing here? He should be on the frontlines, not back in the rear taking R&R."

The animal which was Richard's temper rattled its cage a little. Richard forced his anger to stay in check. He consoled himself with the fact the acidity of the security guard's comment was due to his concern for the councilwoman.

"That's enough, Carlos," said Councilwoman Deloris. "You'll stay here. I'll call you after the meeting, and you can escort me back."

Richard noticed Carlos press his lips together as if trying to hold back a retort. The old guard apparently succeeded in his efforts because he just nodded his head.

After motioning the other three guards to return to their stations, Carlos looked at Richard. "You'd best keep her safe, wizard scout, or you'll have to deal with me."

Richard chose not to reply.

"That's smart, Rick," came Nickelo's thought. *"No use escalating the situation."*

When Richard didn't answer the old man's challenge, the security guard snorted and headed back to join his fellow guards.

Councilwoman Deloris began walking again. As she walked, she talked. "I must apologize, Rick. Carlos has always been very devoted to the Deloris family. He's been with us so long you'd think he was an adopted member of the family."

"Understood," Richard said although he really didn't. "Err...what was that about death threats?"

"Ah, that's one of the things I wanted to discuss with you, Rick. And it's one of the reasons I'm allowing my son to go with you."

"How so?" Richard asked.

"How much do you keep up with politics, Rick?" asked the councilwoman.

"As little as possible," Richard admitted. Politics had never interested him. And it didn't help that every two or three weeks *'the One'* sent him on missions back in time that could last for months or years.

"That's probably wise," Councilwoman Deloris laughed politely. "Politics aren't for the faint of heart, so I'll spare you the details. Suffice it to say the Empire has several camps, each of which strives for the political soul of the Empire."

"And the Conglomerate is one of those camps?" Richard said knowing full well it was.

"Ah, I sense a hint of bitterness in your voice," said Councilwoman Deloris. "Yes, the Conglomerate is one of those camps. There are always opposing views in government. That's just the nature of politics. But in the end, we're still on the same side, are we not? Take the Commandant for instance. He and I had different views on the fate of the Academy, but neither of us doubted the other's commitment to the success and well-being of the Empire."

Easy for you to say, Richard thought. *The Commandant's not around to naysay you.*

As they talked, the councilwoman led them deeper into the planetary administration building. As they walked, the crowds thinned until the corridors were nearly empty. They took a high-speed elevator down. When it stopped, Richard guessed they were at least five hundred meters below ground level.

The door of the elevator opened to reveal a large, stonewalled chamber over a hundred meters across and two hundred in length. Richard figured the ceiling was at least fifty meters high.

"Actually, it is fifty-two meters high," said Nickelo, *"but who's counting?"*

The councilwoman stopped a few paces past the elevator door. Richard joined her. The door shut as the elevator rose to attend to someone else's needs. The large chamber was devoid of life. He and the councilwoman were alone. She turned and faced him.

Councilwoman Deloris must have seen a questioning look on his face, because she said, "This is an emergency shelter in case of attack."

She pointed at an enormous stack of metal cases located about twenty meters away. It was one of dozens scattered throughout the chamber.

"These cases contain emergency supplies," she explained. "We can shelter five thousand people here for a week if necessary. A corridor on the other side of this chamber leads directly to the hallway outside the council chambers. I like to use this place as a shortcut when I go there. It avoids the crowds."

"So I see," Richard said in a voice loud enough to echo in the vast space. "I'm surprised there aren't guards."

The councilwoman looked around. "Hmm, so am I. There are usually two outside this elevator. It's just another reason I've been trying to convince the Imperial High Council our Conglomerate forces should be providing security for the more important Empire facilities. This war has created a shortage in the active military forces. They aren't even able to provide adequate security. The absence of guards only reinforces my point."

Richard was unsure of his position. The councilwoman was a high-level politician, and a very powerful one at that. Despite her insistence on calling him by his first name, he had no illusions he was treading in safe waters. Still, he refused to let her comment go unchallenged.

"Are you saying you want your Conglomerate forces to replace the active-duty security personnel like they did on Velos?" Richard said. "That didn't work out too well."

Just before the Crosioians had attacked the Academy the previous year, Conglomerate forces had completely taken over responsibility for security on Velos. All active security personnel had been shipped off planet to supplement the military on the front lines.

"Ah, Rick," said Councilwoman Deloris in what Richard assumed was supposed to sound like a hurt voice. However, he had a feeling it would take a lot more than a few words to hurt her. She gave him the impression she was a very tough woman.

"Let's be frank," said the councilwoman while she continued to stand facing Richard. "First off, they're not my Conglomerate forces. I'm the head of Deloris Armaments Corporation. I don't run the Conglomerate. I know people call it the Deloris Conglomerate on occasion, but that's far from the truth. It's a completely separate entity. And secondly, the attack happened the day after the Conglomerate had taken over planetary security. They didn't even have a chance to get settled before the attack occurred."

The councilwoman looked Richard in the eyes. "You fought alongside some of the Conglomerate units. Are you saying they didn't fight bravely?"

Richard thought back to the battle at the Academy's airfield. He actually owed his life to some Conglomerate fighter pilots who'd knocked out some Crosioian heavy cats at the cost of their own lives. He couldn't fault their courage.

"No," Richard admitted. "They fought bravely enough. They lacked experience though."

"Exactly," said Councilwoman Deloris. "And that's why I…err…I mean *we*…need you. I could pretty much guarantee your assignment as a general in our organization. We could use you."

Richard said nothing. He wasn't foolish enough to think he was qualified to be a general in anybody's military. If the councilwoman was dangling such an assignment in front of his eyes, he had no doubt she had ulterior motives.

"Now you're thinking, Rick," said Nickelo. *"I knew if you listened to me long enough you'd learn a thing or two."*

When Richard didn't answer, Councilwoman Deloris placed a hand on his chest just over his heart. She drew closer. He felt her warmth through the thin cloth of his jumpsuit. Although Richard knew the councilwoman's age was in her forties, the best cosmetic surgery the Empire could offer had kept her face youthful. She still maintained the looks of a beautiful woman in her late twenties. But

Richard wasn't impressed. He stepped back.

"I work for the Empire," Richard said.

"And what is the Empire, Rick?" said Councilwoman Deloris in a sharper tone. "This war has stretched the Empire to its limits. We're near financial ruin. Some new blood needs to take charge. I…err…the Conglomerate has many ideas that could end this war and bring back the glory the Empire deserves."

She took a step forward and placed her hand on Richard's chest again. "And just think, Rick. You could be there to help. I could reward you in many ways. Won't you at least consider it?"

Before Richard could answer, he heard the clang of a bell behind him. When he turned, the elevator door was just opening. A blonde-headed, young man in his late teens stepped out. Richard thought he looked vaguely familiar.

"Matthew!" said Councilwoman Deloris as she quickly drew her hand back. "What are you doing here? And where's your guards?"

Although he wasn't sure, Richard thought he heard fear in the councilwoman's voice.

"Hmm, she sounds concerned," said Nickelo. *"Councilwoman Deloris must think there's more to those death threats than she was letting on."*

"Mother," said the young man, "I thought you'd be here. Everyone knows you love to take this shortcut."

"I told you never to go anywhere without your guards," said Councilwoman Deloris. "You can't be here."

The young man was unperturbed by his mother's outburst. "Nonsense, Mother. You're just going to the council chamber. I left my guards with Carlos. If you can roam around without guards, then I can as well. Besides, I wanted to meet Wizard Scout Shepard again."

"How's your arm?" Richard said, remembering the young man had been wounded during the battle at the airfield the previous year.

Matthew raised his arm high above his head. "Good as new. One of the wizard scouts healed it after the battle."

Walking forward, the young man smiled and held out his hand. "Since my mother has forgotten her manners, I'll introduce myself. I'm Matthew Deloris. But please call me Matt."

Taking the young man's hand, Richard shook it. "I'm Richard Shepard. My friends call me Rick."

"All right, Rick," said Matthew apparently assuming Richard considered him a friend. "I understand we'll be trav—"

"You can't be here, Matthew," interrupted Councilwoman Deloris. "Err...I've important things to discuss with Wizard Scout Shepard."

Turning back to the elevator, Matthew pushed the button to send the elevator back to the top floor. "Fine," said Matthew as he turned back around. "Discuss away. You're always telling me I need to learn more about the family business."

The councilwoman looked at her son for a good eight seconds.

The young man didn't flinch.

To Richard, the two seemed to be having a battle of wills. He got the feeling they were evenly matched.

Finally, Councilwoman Deloris turned away and glanced nervously around the chamber. "Fine," she said as she looked back at her son. "But stay close. I don't like you being away from your guards. Some of the death threats I've received included you. That's the only reason I'm agreeing to you going on the *Defiant*. I want to get you out of the Empire's territory for a while."

Rolling his eyes so only Richard could see, the young man said, "Sometimes Mother thinks I'm helpless. I keep telling her she can't keep me locked up behind brerellium-steel doors all the time. I'm seventeen now. I'm not a boy. Tell her, Rick."

Richard didn't want to be drawn into a family squabble. Growing up in the orphanage as he had, he wasn't used to it.

"Why does he think I'll stick up for him anyway?" Richard wondered. *"I just met him."*

"Maybe he took a look at you and just assumed you're as hard-headed as he apparently is," said Nickelo. *"Or maybe he's just grasping at straws. Or maybe—"*

"Enough, Nick," Richard said. *"Just forget it."*

"Consider it forgotten, oh greatest of wizard scouts," said Nickelo accompanying his reply with a series of not so subtle laughs.

Councilwoman Deloris inserted herself between Matthew and Richard. She wrapped an arm in each of theirs. Her son tried to pull away, but the councilwoman held on tight.

"I mean it, Matthew," said Councilwoman Deloris. "If you're going to be here, you're staying close. You have no idea how dangerous the Empire is right now."

"You worry too much, Mother," said Matthew. "We've got a wizard scout with us. What could go wrong?"

CHAPTER 10

The assassin rose slightly from his hiding spot behind the set of storage boxes. He sighted down the scope of his Deloris sniper rifle. The rifle was top-of-the-line, as was the silencer at the end of the barrel. The version of sniper rifle he'd chosen for his task fired solid, stealth-slugs designed to be undetectable by electronics or wizard scout scans. His target was nearly two hundred meters away and partially hidden by boxes. But he was confident in his ability to make the shot. He wouldn't miss. Still, the presence of the boy was unexpected. The assassin had planned too well, and he didn't like the introduction of unknowns into his calculations.

The assassin checked his stealth shield. It was his best. The wizard scout at the other end of the chamber seemed oblivious to his presence. The assassin checked the control device for the explosives that were hidden in one of the storage cases near his target. The explosives were ready. He'd measured them out exactly to the required specifications. With a click of a button, the timer would activate. Four seconds later, the far end of the chamber would become an inferno. No normal human would be able to survive his ambush without help.

The assassin knew the wizard scout accompanying his target could do dimensional shifts. The assassin had no doubt the wizard scout could also shift his target into the void as well if he was quick. The question was would the wizard scout be able to react fast enough to escape the inferno. The assassin did a rough calculation in his head. He weighed the probability of his target being killed by either his bullet or the explosives against the reaction time of the wizard scout.

Finally, the assassin made his decision. It was a risk, but his mission needed to succeed, and it needed to succeed now. They wouldn't get an opportunity like this again. The assassin sighted his scope just above his target's heart. As soon as he fired, he would activate the timer for the explosives.

The assassin drew in a deep breath and let part of it out, then slowly increased the pressure on his rifle's trigger.

CHAPTER 11

Richard felt strange walking while locked arm-in-arm with the councilwoman and her son. He was reminded of a video the sisters at the orphanage had once shown of three people locked arm-in-arm walking down a yellow-brick road as they made their way to see some kind of wizard. They'd been opposed by an evil witch. Richard was glad there was no evil witch around to bar their way now. He checked his passive scan. He detected no other life forms nearby other than the two by his side.

Suddenly, Councilwoman Deloris was jerked out of his arm and flung backward. Her unexpected movement was accompanied by a spray of blood out of her back. Richard caught a glimpse of a red stain on the front side of her chest as well. At almost the same time, Richard sensed a buildup of energy from one of the cases buried in the stack of supplies ahead of them.

"Bomb!" Nickelo yelled into their shared space. *"And it's big."*

One thing Richard was very good at was reacting without thinking. He turned and grabbed Matthew as he dove for the councilwoman's body where it lay twitching on the floor. A pool of blood was already gathering underneath and around her body.

As he dragged the boy through the air, Richard wrapped both of them with Power. He reached out and wrapped the councilwoman with Power as well. When he landed on the councilwoman, Richard shifted the three of them into the void. Using his telekinesis, he moved them down through the chamber floor and into the solid rock below.

A blast of energy erupted above. Richard sensed parts of the ceiling falling down into a massive fireball swirling above the surface. Everything was dark below ground in the void. Richard sent out active scans to pinpoint his location as well as the boundary of the explosion.

"The elevator shaft's clear," said Nickelo. *"It's taking a lot of Power to keep the three of you shifted. Recommend you expedite moving to the elevator."*

It was several hundred meters to the floors above. Richard doubted he'd make it trying to drag two other people along with him. The elevator shaft was their only hope. He moved toward the shaft pulling the councilwoman and her son with him.

"Is she dead?" Richard asked.

"Negative," answered Nickelo, *"but she soon will be. The bullet hit just above her heart. I calculate she'll be dead in fifteen seconds."*

Richard took Power from his healing reserve and wrapped it around the councilwoman in preparation for healing her wound.

"No!" Nickelo mentally screamed into their shared space. *"You'll black out. When you do, you'll shift out of the void, and we'll all be dead. You have to wait until you're in the elevator shaft."*

Richard obediently withheld the healing, but he did as much of the preparation as he could while he was levitating them toward the elevator shaft. He imagined how the councilwoman's body should be and compared that with how it was now.

Although he was going as fast as he could, the time to travel the short distance to the elevator shaft seemed interminable. Eventually, he popped into the opening of the elevator shaft and pulled the councilwoman's blood-soaked body and her son up out of the ground. As soon as they were clear, Richard dropped their dimensional shift. As they solidified back into the physical dimension, Richard took note of the greasy metal walls around them. They were in the shaft itself, not the elevator. He remembered Matthew had sent the elevator car back to the surface.

Without waiting to analyze the situation further, Richard pulled the councilwoman's injuries into himself. He heard himself scream as a fist-sized chunk of flesh was blown out his back to emulate the councilwoman's wounds. As Richard blacked out, his last conscious thought was, *I hate emp-healing.*

* * *

The sound of pounding slowly brought Richard out of the darkness into which he'd descended. He smelled smoke. He also heard shouts in the distance, but couldn't make out the words. As his brain cleared, Richard realized the shouts were very close.

Opening his eyes, Richard saw Councilwoman Deloris and her son beating and clawing at the inside of the elevator shaft's door.

"They won't budge," yelled Matthew in a voice bordering on panic. "We'll be crushed."

"I'm sorry, Matthew," said the councilwoman as she continued clawing desperately at the elevator's door. "I'm sorry I got you involved in this."

"Nick," Richard said. *"Give me an analysis."*

His battle computer didn't waste time on words.

Richard received a vision of a blazing inferno outside the elevator shaft's door. Another part of his brain simultaneously saw a vision of the elevator coming down the shaft at a high rate of speed. He didn't need his battle computer to tell him all three of them would be crushed when it arrived at the bottom of the shaft.

With a series of images, Richard let his battle computer know his plan to shift the three of them into the void just before the descending elevator arrived.

"No!" Nickelo said nixing the plan. *"The door will open when the elevator gets here. You only have enough Power to keep the three of you shifted for twenty-two seconds. That's not enough time to reach safety."*

Before Richard could think of an alternate plan, he sensed a vision of him using telekinesis to lift the three of them up to meet the plunging elevator. He saw himself stopping and changing directions to match the downward speed of the elevator. Then he saw himself shifting his group into the void and allowing the elevator to catch up with them. The vision showed him shifting out of the void and hitting the elevator's emergency stop.

"It'll take perfect timing," Richard said. He had a momentary regret that he wasn't wearing his battle suit. Nickelo wouldn't be able to do the work for him. He'd have to do it himself.

"Yes you will," agreed Nickelo. *"You won't get a second chance, but it's the best plan I can come up with. The elevator will be here in twelve seconds, wizard scout. You better start hustling."*

Without another word, Richard jumped to his feet and grabbed the councilwoman and her son with his hands. With no time to explain, he wrapped the three of them in Power and began levitating up the shaft as fast as he could go.

The councilwoman screamed. Her son looked like he wanted to scream as well, but when he turned and saw Richard, he kept his mouth closed.

He's got guts, Richard thought.

Up the three of them went. Richard saw the bottom of the elevator rushing down to meet them.

"You should thank the Creator the emergency lights are still working," said Nickelo. *"Otherwise, I calculate a ninety-three percent probability your timing would be off, and you'd all be squashed flat."*

When Richard thought the distance was right, he stopped and reversed direction.

"You're too fast," said Nickelo. *"You've got to slow down enough to let it catch you, but not so slow it passes you by."*

"I'm trying," Richard said. *"My depth perception's off."*

"You should've put your battle helmet on," said Nickelo. *"I was hoping you'd think of it on your own, but I guess not."*

"Sure you were," Richard said.

"You've got four seconds of Power remaining," said Nickelo. *"It's now or never."*

Richard slowed his pace. As soon as he sensed the bottom of the elevator was about to slam into his head, he shifted into the void taking Councilwoman Deloris and her son with him.

"Two seconds," said Nickelo.

Richard's feet cleared the inside of the elevator's floor. However, the lower parts of Councilwoman Deloris's legs were still below the bottom of the elevator.

"Damn, she's tall," Richard exclaimed as he jerked on the councilwoman's arms.

Richard had worried he wouldn't be able to drop his Power at the exact moment necessary to clear the bottom of the elevator without part of their bodies going into the roof. As it turned out, he'd lost control of the situation anyway. His Power ran out on its own. Both his levitation and dimensional shift stopped at the same time. Richard materialized back into the physical dimension with his feet a half meter inside the elevator. He fell to the floor.

"You've got to hit the emergency switch," said Nickelo.

"I know," Richard said as he jumped toward the elevator's control panel.

He slapped the bright-red emergency switch. The elevator came to an abrupt stop. Richard was thrown to his knees.

Looking around, Richard spotted the prone figures of Councilwoman Deloris and her son, Matthew.

"Are you okay?" Richard asked. As far as he knew, the shift back to the physical dimension had partially embedded one or both of them in the floor of the elevator.

"They're fine," Nickelo assured him.

"I'm fine," said Matthew. "Mom! Are you okay?"

"I'm all right," said Councilwoman Deloris. "I just need to catch my breath."

"Nick," Richard said. *"I'm out of Power. Give me an analysis and possible courses of action."*

"Based upon my electronic scan," said Nickelo, *"the elevator stopped twenty meters above the bottom of the shaft. The shaft's door is currently holding against the fire, but some smoke is entering. You'll probably need breathing masks in a few minutes. I sense alarms going off, but you'll still need to use the emergency-communications console to let someone know you're here. I'm not connected to the tele-network, so I can't do it for you."*

As it turned out, Matthew was way ahead of him on making contact. By the time Richard turned to look for the communication console, the boy was already informing emergency personnel of their predicament. Richard heard him making liberal use of the words 'a member of the Imperial High Council trapped in here.' Richard wasn't sure the words would speed up the response, but figured it couldn't hurt.

After about five minutes, smoke began entering the elevator. By then, Richard's natural recharging had replaced a whopping one-third of one percent of his Power. It wasn't much, but it was enough. Richard summoned his dimensional pack from where it was located on the *Defiant*.

Using his pack, Richard acquired three low-tech oxygen masks. While not top-of-the-line, they were good enough to keep them alive.

Richard also summoned his phase rod from the security desk where it had been stored. Nickelo argued against it, saying it would reveal their secret, but Richard didn't care. As far as he was concerned, someone had tried to kill the councilwoman, and they might try again. The presence of his phase rod made him feel better.

It took another two hours for rescue crews to completely put out the fire and extract the three of them from the elevator. Once their rescue was completed, the councilwoman ordered her son back home. The young man argued he wanted to stay, but Councilwoman Deloris would hear none of it.

When Matthew continued to argue, the councilwoman brought out her big guns by saying, "I'm your mother, and I said go home. Now!"

Matthew went. Councilwoman Deloris sent an extra security team with him.

Once Matthew was gone, Councilwoman Deloris thanked Richard profusely for saving her son's life. She told him if he ever needed anything, all he had to do was ask. She also told him she was going to make sure the *Defiant* was upgraded with the very best equipment the Deloris Armaments Corporation could afford. When she said this, Richard mentally whistled. He figured the Deloris Armaments Corporation could afford a lot. He had a feeling Sergeant Ron was going to be a mighty happy starship captain.

Once the councilwoman departed, Richard was hijacked by security personnel for questioning. He spent the next six hours in a secured room being grilled by a never-ending array of interrogators. A couple of security personnel had initially tried to confiscate his phase rod and dimensional pack. Richard had informed them in no uncertain terms the only way they'd get them was over his dead body. A higher-ranking Conglomerate security officer made the wise decision to leave the equipment with Richard.

CHAPTER 12

Later that afternoon, Richard found himself outside the planetary administration building trying to decide what to do next. He was contemplating hailing a hover-taxi to return to the spaceport when a large, hover-car pulled up.

Since the hover-car was a type Richard associated with high-ranking government officials, Richard stepped away from the curb to make room. A well-dressed chauffeur got out and ran around the hover-car to open the rear-side door. The chauffeur looked directly at Richard.

"I am at your disposal, sir," said the chauffeur. "Councilwoman Deluth is waiting at her residence for you."

The chauffeur's comment caught Richard by surprise. Councilwoman Janice Deluth was the widow of Wizard Scout Thomas R. Jacobs, Richard's old commandant at the Academy. She was also Richard's mother, although she was unaware of the fact. He'd found out just as the battle for the Academy had begun. With the resulting death of her husband during the battle, Richard had deemed the time inappropriate to inform Councilwoman Deluth she had a long-lost son.

During the past year, Richard had not attempted to make contact with either Councilwoman Deluth, his mother, or ex-TAC Officer Gaston Myers, his brother. He'd figured too much time had passed. Since Richard had been secretly removed from his mother's womb as an embryo, she was unaware he'd ever existed. Because Richard saw no advantage in opening old wounds or creating new ones, he'd decided to let the matter lie. He had made his peace with the knowledge. Unfortunately, his peace was being shattered by the chauffeur's comment.

Now what do I do? Richard thought. He had an inclination to start running.

"Don't be a chicken," said Nickelo. *"Remember, as far as you know, Councilwoman Deluth is the only remaining time-commando. I'd recommend you see what she wants."*

The chauffeur waited patiently as Richard stood there staring at him. Richard figured the chauffeur was either well-practiced at keeping emotions off his face, or he was just used to dealing with temperamental politicians.

"Probably both," observed Nickelo. After a slight pause, Richard's battle computer said, *"Based upon all available data, I calculate getting in the hover-car is your best course of action."*

Richard didn't like being rushed, but he couldn't think of anything better. Steeling himself for what he thought might turn out to be an awkward situation, Richard nodded his head at the chauffeur and entered the car.

The vehicle was no ordinary hover-car. It was a government-issued limo designed for high-level dignitaries. Richard had been in a similar vehicle once before at the Academy. However, he hadn't been able to appreciate its luxuries then. TAC Officer Myers, the bane of Richard's existence during his Academy years, had been with him at the time. As Richard remembered it, he'd spent most of the ride sitting stiff-backed while saying as little as possible in order not to draw attention to himself.

Since he was alone, Richard took the opportunity to explore his surroundings. As the hover-limo took to the air, Richard opened a small cabinet to his front. The inside was lined with small bottles of various colored liquids along with several drinking glasses. Richard recognized a few of the bottles as expensive liquors, but most of the brands he'd never seen before. Drinking alcohol had been frowned upon at the Academy, so his experience with Empire liquors was limited, to say the least.

Shutting the doors to the liquor cabinet, Richard opened another set of doors to his left. He was met by an assortment of snack packages.

"Now that's more like it," Richard thought. *"I was getting*

hungry."

"You're always hungry," said Nickelo. *"What else is new?"*

Ignoring his battle computer, Richard grabbed a handful of snacks. He nibbled away as he taste-tested several of the items. He bit into one whitish-looking cookie and immediately regretted his actions. Richard spit out the obnoxious substance into a convenient napkin.

"That sucked," Richard said.

"Ah," replied Nickelo. *"From information in my databanks, that cookie is a delicacy from the Killorian system. It's very expensive."*

"Well, they can keep it on Killoria, as far as I'm concerned," Richard thought back.

Fortunately, Richard found several snacks that were quite delicious. He amused himself for the next fifteen minutes by tasting various treats and laying the empty packages on the seat next to him in descending order of taste.

"I don't know why you're bothering with eating," said Nickelo. *"You're healing reserve will keep your body adequately nourished."*

"First off, I'm a little hungry," Richard said. *"Snacking keeps the edge off. And secondly, I thought you told me eating keeps my body from having to use Power to keep it at baseline."*

"Yes, I did." Nickelo sounded a little reluctant to admit his wizard scout was correct. *"However, if you remember, I also specified eating in moderation."*

"Whatever," Richard grumbled. *"I can't win, can I?"*

"I'd say the fate of three galaxies is hoping you can," said Nickelo.

Richard didn't answer. He'd suddenly lost his interest in eating. Sometimes he hated his life.

A dark window near the front of the hover-limo reduced the image of the chauffeur to a barely-visible dark shadow. With nothing better to do, Richard resigned himself to looking out the passenger window. He guessed they were flying about five hundred meters above the ground at a rapid pace. The hover-limo had long since left the city center. They were now in a much less populated area.

"Actually, we're at five hundred and twenty-two meters AGL,

and our speed is four hundred KPH," said Nickelo. *"We're a hundred and twenty kilometers south of the city. According to my databanks, this area is reserved for the estates of various high-level politicians."*

The time was approaching early evening, but even so, Richard could make out the shapes of several large estate houses below him. As the sky turned to dusk, lights began popping on in many of the mansions and outbuildings all along the horizon. Richard toyed with the idea of putting on his battle helmet to see better but nixed the idea. He doubted it was considered good manners to show up at someone's door wearing a battle helmet and carrying weapons.

"No doubt," agreed Nickelo. *"I calculate it would probably be good manners to change your uniform. The olfactory sensors your nephew, Brachia, installed in the battle helmet indicates you reek of smoke."*

Richard was embarrassed he hadn't thought of the shape of his uniform before now. *"I should've changed before I left the planetary administration building."*

"Shoulda, woulda, coulda," said Nickelo, *"but you didn't. However, you still have time to rectify your error in judgment. The chauffeur hasn't begun his descent yet."*

Removing his dimensional pack from his back, Richard pulled out a black wizard scout uniform. It looked new, and it was neatly pressed. The silver thread sparkled in the hover-limo's cabin light. A shiny golden-dragon insignia was pinned to the left collar. Richard used the distance from the tip of his index finger to his first knuckle joint to measure the spacing of the insignia. It was centered perfectly on the collar. Satisfied, Richard stripped his dirty uniform off and replaced it with the new one.

"Somebody knows what they're doing," Richard commented. *"Everything's measured to Academy standards. Who maintains this stuff?"*

"A variety of races," said Nickelo. *"I doubt you'll ever get a chance to meet them. Just be thankful they take pride in their work. Some of the gear you're forced to use on your missions for 'the One' is hundreds of years old."*

"Yeah, tell me about it," Richard said as he strapped on his utility belt and attached his phase rod to the belt's left side. He was just thankful his phase rod and M63 were modern weapons. For

some reason, *'the One'* tended to force him to use older, antique equipment.

Before Richard could start complaining about the unfairness of *'the One,'* the dark window behind the chauffeur rolled down.

"We are three minutes out, sir," said the chauffeur. "My instructions are to wait for you as long as necessary. When you're ready, just inform one of the servants, and I'll come back to the front door to pick you up."

"Thanks," Richard said.

Looking out the forward window, Richard saw the lights of several small bungalows ahead. He saw nothing that looked like it might belong to a respected member of the Imperial High Council.

"Where's Councilwoman Deluth's house?" Richard asked as he began to get suspicious. He wondered if he'd meekly walked into a trap of some kind.

"The councilwoman's home is the one on the left," said the chauffeur.

"That little thing?" Richard exclaimed.

The chauffeur started to laugh before he caught himself.

"Forgive me, sir. You caught me by surprise. Councilwoman Deluth is not what you'd call pretentious. I was just imagining how she'd react if someone tried to force her to live in one of those monstrous estates we passed along the way here."

Richard gave his mother kudos for living a simple life.

"What'd you expect?" said Nickelo. *"She's a wizard scout and a time-commando to boot."*

"Yeah, well, Richard said, *"I guess I figured as a council member, she'd be wealthy. I thought all politicians were rich."*

"Well, you thought wrong," said Nickelo. *"However, you're right in the case of Councilwoman Deluth. She's wealthy beyond anything you can imagine; as are you."*

"Me?" Richard said. *"Have you looked at my bank account lately? That overhaul we did on the* Defiant *four months ago pretty much wiped my account clean."*

"Ha!" laughed Nickelo. *"You continually surprise me with your naivety. You've got the wealth of an entire planet at your disposal. All you have to do is summon it through your dimensional pack. You want a handful of Ackmar diamonds? Just summon them out of your pack. You want a metric ton of gold*

bullion? Just pull it out of your pack. But I'd recommend making sure you have somewhere to put it first."

Richard hadn't ever thought of doing anything like that before. He wasn't sure he could. And he wasn't sure he wanted to. Sure, he'd summoned a few local coins or small gems while on missions for *'the One'* when in the magical dimension to pay the bills, but he always tried not to go overboard.

"Well, what are you waiting for?" asked Nickelo with a strange tone to his voice. *"Summon some diamonds. Make them a gift to the councilwoman if you want."*

"No," Richard said. *"I didn't earn that stuff. There's a difference between summoning something on a mission and just summoning it because I'm greedy."*

"Yes, there is," said Nickelo. The strange tone was gone from his voice. *"I just wanted to make sure you knew it. I've no doubt the councilwoman does."*

"By the councilwoman, you mean my mother," Richard said as a statement and not a question.

"Yes," said Nickelo, *"your mother."*

At that moment, the hover-limo touched down so lightly Richard barely noticed they were on the ground.

"Once you get out, sir," said the chauffeur, "I'll be moving to another location in case someone else arrives. But I'll be nearby when you need me."

"Thanks for the ride," Richard said as he got out and stood in front of the bungalow.

The councilwoman's home was a tidy-looking place. Night was full on now, but small lights lit up the flower gardens lining both sides of the walkway leading up to the house. Richard strolled up to the door. He didn't see a bell. Instead, an old brass knocker was attached to the wooden door. Richard pulled the knocker back three times and let it fall. The sound echoed from inside the house.

Before long, the door opened. Richard assumed he'd be greeted by either a servant or Councilwoman Deluth. Richard assumed wrong. As the door opened, he saw a short, toad-faced man. The man was all too familiar. It was TAC Officer Gaston Myers.

CHAPTER 13

Jeena snuggled deep into her soft, down-filled covers against the morning chill. In spite of her desire to sleep just a little bit longer, she forced herself to open her eyes, albeit slowly.

That's what you get for staying up so late reading when you have an important meeting first thing in the morning, she thought.

In spite of her self-chastisement, Jeena pulled the thick covers closer around her neck. It felt good to relax even if it was just a temporary relief from the grueling day Priestess Aldriss had scheduled for her.

The morning was early enough to be still dark. But even so, Jeena saw everything clearly with her night vision. She surveyed her surroundings. While her night vision didn't see colors, the various shades of gray allowed her to detect even small details. Jeena took a moment to admire the intricate carvings in the wooden posters of her bed. The High Lord Carndador, her great grandfather fifty times over, had hand carved the bed himself. The bed had been in the family ever since. Over the generations, the bed had been carefully preserved by magic against rot and decay.

The furnishings of her bedroom were sparse. But they were all beautifully designed and ancient beyond belief. Much of the furniture in her home had been in the Thoraxen clan since the time of her ancestors, High Priestess Shandristiathoraxen and her bondmate High Lord Carndador.

A flash of pride in her family's heritage passed over Jeena before she pushed it away and buried it deep inside her where such silly things belonged. Pride was too easy a trap to fall into. She'd been blessed by the Creator to be born into the Thoraxen clan. Jeena knew she'd done nothing to deserve the privilege herself. Her mother had often reminded her of the fact during her youth.

"My name may be Jeehanathoraxen," Jeena whispered into the night air, "but I've done nothing yet to add honor to the Thoraxen name. So get out of bed, you lazy elf, and get the day started or half the population of Silverton will be up before you. Oversleeping won't impress the high priest."

Thus self-chided, Jeena eased the covers off her warm body and sat on the edge of the bed. She was careful not to knock over the scrolls and books piled all over her bed. She'd been so engrossed in the history of the elves last night she'd once again fallen asleep reading.

Jeena had enjoyed reading ever since she could remember. Even for an elf still in her adolescence, that was a long time. Jeena's thoughts drifted back to all the pleasant hours she'd spent in the library over the years. The library and its books had been her refuge during the dark times.

"Best get moving, Acolyte Jeehanathoraxen," Jeena said in a louder voice.

The air was cold enough a puff of fog came out as she spoke.

Jeena had always had a habit of talking to herself when no one else was around. Her adoptive mother, Lord Reale, said it was one of her quirks. Reale said everybody had quirks. According to her, some elves just kept them hidden better than others.

Jeena found her slippers with her feet and put them on. The luxamar fur of the slippers quickly warmed her feet.

They should, Jeena thought. *I spent enough hours combing luxamars to get enough fur for the slippers.*

Jeena liked luxamars. They were small rodents about the size of a rabbit. When they shed, the luxamars used their soft fur to make dens for their young. Humans were known to kill luxamars for their hides. Elves, on the other hand, tended to wild luxamars who were not yet expecting by combing their fur during the summer months to help them stay cool. Jeena thought it was a win/win situation. The elves helped the luxamars stay cool in the summer, and the luxamars helped the elves stay warm in the winter by providing the fur to line the elves' clothing. It was a natural balance.

Jeena smiled. She liked balance. The relationship between the elves and the luxamars seemed balanced to her. The elves had many such relationships with the animals and plants of the forest.

Before rising, Jeena glanced at the last scroll she'd been reading when she'd fallen asleep. It had disturbed her enough to cause nightmares. The story was a diary excerpt written by High Priestess Remozorz before she'd retired from her post with the elves. Even though she'd been a gnome, the High Priestess Remozorz had been one of the most devoted servants of the Lady of the Tree. Jeena didn't mind telling people Remozorz was her heroine. When she was a child, Jeena had often imagined she'd been with High Priestess Remozorz on the Highlamar Plains fighting the necromancer and his Northern Mages. Jeena normally enjoyed reading the writings of Remozorz. However, the diary entries she'd been reading last night were much darker and foreboding than normal for the usually cheerful gnome.

* * *

High Priestess Log - The Year of the Tree 11115, the 23rd day of Spring.

I am growing increasingly worried about Commander Kreathin. He has not been the same since the loss of his bondmate, Lillia. He is a good elf, and no one, least of all I, can find fault with the way he conducts his duties. Still, I sense a growing darkness within him. He blames the humans for the death of his bondmate. His hatred for them continues to grow and fester. He even blames my friend Rick for her death. I'm glad for Rick's sake they will never meet again. I have discussed Kreathin with the Lady. She says for good or ill, it's something he must work through on his own. I will continue to pray for him.

High Priestess Log - The Year of the Tree 11116, the 4th day of Summer.

Another elf has been killed in the forest. We found the bloodspot this time, but no trace of her body could be discovered. This is the third elf lost in the forest this year. Neither the Council of Light nor I believe it is an animal attack, although that is our official story. I fear it is something much darker. The trace of evil at the bloodspot was too powerful to ignore. I dread to say it, but it had the same evil taint I sensed when I fought the necromancer on the Highlamar Plains. Is there another necromancer within our midst? I do not know. I pray not. But I recognized the same foul demon-stench that corrupted the aura of the necromancer. I will pray to the Lady for guidance. What else can I do?

High Priestess Log - The Year of the Tree 11117, the 39th day of Fall.

I continue to worry about my friend, Commander Kreathin. I have not written of him in a while, but he has not improved. If anything, he grows more distant with each passing day. I begged him last week to let me help. He just laughed and said he needed no help. I think differently. Others are beginning to talk as well. If he does not speak to me of his problem soon, I will take the matter to the Council of Light. Only they have the authority to force Kreathin to accept help. I do not wish to embarrass him, but I cannot continue to ignore the evidence. I fear it will come to no good if I do not intervene.

High Priestess Log - The Year of the Tree 11117, the first day of Winter.

I have only myself to blame. I waited too long. I should have forced Kreathin to accept my help, but I did not. Now he is gone, and it is too late. We followed Kreathin's trail to a hidden chamber in the forest. What we found was too despicable to even think upon, much less write. I would never have believed the horrible evil of the place could have been instigated by an elf. How could an elf have been converted to a necromancer? Other elves have lost their bondmates and not fallen into such depths of depravity. Kreathin is gone now, vanished into thin air. I have lost my friend. Even if he is found, I have still lost him. It is more than I can bear. I will resign my position as high priestess. Would that I had died in battle on the Highlamar Plains rather than live with the memory of what my friend has become. This is my last entry in the log. I only hope the Lady chooses someone better qualified than I to be my replacement. I will spend the remainder of my days praying Kreathin does no more harm. He has done so many foul things already.

* * *

Jeena rolled the scroll shut. It was a sad tale. She lived in the Year of the Tree 99844. The events of the diary had happened over eighty-eight thousand years ago. Still, the thought an elf could be turned to such evil did not sit well with her. Jeena shoved her thoughts aside. She didn't wish to dwell on such dark matters today. She resolutely stood up to find what the morning would hold. Jeena made her way to her home's water room. She carefully weaved between the stacks of books and scrolls that seemed to cover every flat surface in her snug bungalow.

Once inside the water room, Jeena said a word of magic and released a small amount of Power from her reserve. A piece of quartz in the ceiling flashed with a momentary brightness before settling down to a pleasant glow. Jeena touched the reflecting stone above the washbasin and said another word of magic. The dark stone shimmered and changed color until it formed an image of the room and her.

Jeena allowed herself a moment to look at her own reflection. As always, her eyes intrigued her. They went well with her long silver hair. Only a few of the Thoraxen clan over the years had inherited the eyes of their forebear, the High Priestess Shandristiathoraxen. Jeena and her brother, Ceril, bore their great grandmother's features. As a child, Jeena had always enjoyed looking in the reflecting stone at her eyes. Their eternally-churning, molten silver seemed to hold all the answers if she could only find the right questions.

Looking away from the reflecting stone, Jeena splashed warm water from the basin onto her face. She scrubbed hard to wash the night from her eyes. When she was satisfied, Jeena began combing her long, silver hair. She was careful to comb her hair in such a way to highlight the points of her ears. She was proud of her elven heritage. Jeena was sure her mother wouldn't begrudge her this little flaw in character. She smiled at the thought of her mother. She missed her.

Once satisfied with her combing, Jeena pinned her hair in place with two broaches; one of gold and one of silver. The broaches clipped together to form two dragons intertwined in such a way it was near impossible to tell where one started and the other ended. The gold and silver dragons meshed so perfectly they seemed to form a single creature.

Glancing at the reflecting stone only long enough to survey the results, Jeena forced her eyes away. As a child, her mother had caught her looking into a reflecting stone admiring her own beauty. Her mother had drilled into her long ago that doing so was being vain. Her mother had said, "What the Creator has given as a blessing, he can easily take away."

Jeena had taken her mother's words to heart. She'd been told so often by so many elves she was beautiful that she had come to accept it as fact. But Jeena always reminded herself that her beauty was none of her own doing. It was a blessing from the Creator, and she'd done nothing to deserve the blessing.

Taking a quick look in the reflecting stone once again, Jeena smiled. "I'm not being vain, Mother. I have to see what I look like in order to get ready for my meeting with the high priest, don't I?"

Jeena hesitated a moment as if expecting a reply but, of course, none came. A pang of loneliness swept over her. She missed both her parents, but she missed her mother the most. Lord Reale did her best, and Jeena loved her adoptive mother dearly, but even the kind Reale couldn't take the place of her real mother. The deaths of her parents had been long ago, but the pain was still deep. Jeena supposed it was even harder on her older brother, Ceril. His memory of their parents was clearer than hers, and he kept his grief locked deep inside. Jeena didn't think her brother's method of dealing with his grief was wise, but there was nothing she could do about it.

She and Ceril were the first two elves to be born with the silver eyes and silver hair of their ancestors in over ten thousand years. Jeena had often wondered if that had something to do with her parents' death. Both Ceril and she were supposed to be with their parents when they had been attacked and murdered. That they weren't there was only by chance. Jeena wasn't sure whether their salvation was a blessing or a curse. Even with the tender attentions of Reale and her bondmate, High Lord Trenadine, those first few decades without her parents had been rough. Discovering the wonders of the library had been her salvation.

Jeena didn't bother putting on makeup. She seldom used it. Returning to her bedroom, she pulled a light-blue robe out of the closet and put it on. She tied a silver belt around her waist in such a way as to ensure the silver thread sewn in the design of the Tree of

Light was visible over her left breast. The emblem was the crest of the Thoraxen clan.

Satisfied with the effect, Jeena went into the kitchen and made a quick breakfast of grapes and cheese. She washed it down with a cup of spring wine. As she ate, Jeena reflected on what the morning might hold.

"I'm only an acolyte," she said out loud. "Why has High Priestess Questor singled me out among all the acolytes for a private meeting? Even Priestess Aldriss doesn't know the reason for the audience."

While Jeena didn't know the reason either, she did know it was an honor she didn't deserve. From years of association, she knew the other acolytes worked just as hard or harder in caring for the Tree of Light.

Once she finished breakfast, Jeena washed out the dishes and put them back in their proper place on the shelves. She did a hurried survey of the kitchen. Books and scrolls were stacked everywhere, but at least nothing was dirty. Jeena had often been told by Reale that her house cleaning skills were less than desirable.

"My home's not dirty, Reale," Jeena said with a fond smile. "It's just...cluttered."

Satisfied she was ready to face the day, Jeena opened the door and stepped out into the early-morning twilight.

* * *

The sun was just appearing over the mountains to the east when Jeena left her house. She took a moment to turn back and survey her home. The white marble of the small, single-storied bungalow was dulled by the years, but Jeena loved her home anyway. It held many pleasant memories, albeit a few bitter ones as well.

Jeena turned and resumed her path to the main thoroughfare of Silverton. The elven capital was normally a bustling city, but at this early hour, Jeena passed only a few elves on the street. For the most part, the city still slept. In another hour, things would be different. The streets would be full of elves and noisy with conversation and laughter. But for now, Jeena had the city mostly to herself. For a few minutes, Silverton would be quiet. The near silence gave Jeena a sense of peace.

Two guards in elven chain mail nodded their heads at Jeena as they passed on the last leg of their night patrol. She was unsure if their deference was in acknowledgment of the light-blue robes of the priest class or the emblem of the Thoraxen clan emblazoned above her breast. Jeena gave the guards a friendly smile and a nod of her head in return. The guards' night of toil was almost over. Her day was just beginning.

When Jeena reached the rotunda at the city center, she took a white-graveled path to the right that led to the city park. While taking the park trail was farther to the palace, Jeena didn't hesitate to take the longer route. She still had time before her meeting. Besides, she always enjoyed the beauty of the longer, less-traveled way. The park trail passed between ancient silver elms thousands of years in the making. Their branches interlaced overhead to form a silver-colored roof with their leaves.

As her friend, Elisinsar, the chief librarian had often told her, the silver elms used to glow at night, but they had stopped doing so a century before her birth. Elisinsar said it was because the Tree of Light was running low on Power, and the Lady needed to conserve energy. Jeena didn't know the reason. She just knew the trees no longer glowed. She felt a twinge of regret she would never experience what the older elves had seen. However, the silver elms were beautiful even without their glow. She could only imagine what they would look like lit up in all their glory.

The silver elms thinned until they disappeared altogether. Jeena found herself at the edge of the park center. The Tree of Light stood before her. No matter how often she viewed the tree, Jeena revered its beauty. The tree was the height of a hundred tall elves standing one upon the other. The tree's gigantic branches stretched out the width of a bow shot from its main trunk. The Tree of Light was awe inspiring.

The tree was ancient. From her earliest memories, Jeena remembered being told how High Priestess Shandristiathoraxen had planted the first silver elm seed nearly a hundred thousand years in the past. From that seed had sprung the Tree of Light. Jeena opened her senses to feel the immense strength of the Tree of Light. Legend said in ancient times, the Tree of Light had been even more powerful. If true, Jeena thought it must have been powerful indeed. The Tree of Light was the most powerful thing she'd ever encountered during her short 322 years of life.

"Hail, Acolyte Jeehanathoraxen," said a deep but friendly voice.

The voice came from Jeena's left. She didn't need to look to know it was her friend, Chief Forester Mistros.

"Good day to you, Mistros," Jeena said as she gave him a friendly wave. "The Tree of Light looks healthy and well on this glorious morning. May its seeds once again fall."

"Ah," said the old elf. "Perhaps the tree will seed once again. I for one have my doubts."

"Now, Mistros," Jeena said laughing merrily. "You're too gloomy sometimes. Look at the sky and the morning sun. It promises to be a beautiful day. Isn't that a blessing in itself?"

The chief forester smiled. "Ah, the optimism of youth. I too was young once, Jeehana, though you may not believe it."

"You should smile more often, Mistros," Jeena said. "It takes centuries off your face."

"Only centuries?" laughed Mistros. "Then I'll have to smile much more often in order to make me young again."

While Jeena would like to have talked to her friend longer, her time was getting short. Reluctantly, she took her leave from the old forester.

"I shall return this afternoon, Chief Forester Mistros," Jeena said formally. "I don't want you thinking I'm shirking my part in caring for the Tree of Light. I'm off to see High Priest Questor."

"I wondered at your choice of dress," said Mistros with a mischievous grin. "It seemed unsuitable for picking up broken branches and raking leaves."

"Ha," Jeena said smiling. "It's been years since you had me hauling leaves and limbs. I'm a full acolyte now. I tend to the flows of Power. You know that."

"Ah," said Mistros with a smile of his own. "I must've forgotten. Until this afternoon then, Jeehana."

"Farewell, Mistros," Jeena said as she quickly headed for a trail leading in the direction of the palace. She was eager to see what the day would hold.

CHAPTER 14

The entire universe was silent for an eternity, or was it just for a blink of an eye? However long it was, it mattered little to Richard. He just stood there looking at his nemesis dressed in a business suit. Richard had never before seen ex-TAC Officer Myers in civilian clothes, much less a business suit. The suit didn't look natural on him.

In Empire time, it had only been a year since Richard had last seen Myers. But in time-commando years, it had been over two decades. Even so, Richard found himself slightly intimidated by his brother. The word 'brother' was hard for him to even think, much less say, but the truth stood right there before him. Richard wasn't sure how he felt about the situation.

"Shepard," said Myers.

"Myers," Richard answered back.

With a nod of his head, Myers indicated a hallway behind him. "Councilwoman Deluth is waiting for you."

Myers turned around and began walking down the hallway. As far as Richard could tell, the man didn't bother checking to make sure he was following.

"He doesn't need to check," said Nickelo. *"He's a wizard scout like you. He knows you're following by his passive scan."*

The house was bigger than it looked from the outside. They walked down a long hallway. An open archway to the left revealed a sitting room of some type with a lit fireplace on the opposite side from the archway. Over the mantle was a large holograph of a man and woman smiling. The woman was dressed in a wedding gown, and the man was wearing the dress uniform of a wizard scout. Richard recognized the couple. They were the Commandant and Councilwoman Deluth. They looked happy.

A woman sat in a comfortable chair near the fireplace. When Myers and Richard entered, the woman rose. She was Councilwoman Janice Deluth; his mother.

"Ah, you're finally here," said Councilwoman Deluth. She smiled. "I think I must have dozed off for a bit."

Richard was shocked. The councilwoman appeared much older than when he'd seen her last. Physically she appeared to still be in her late twenties. But Richard's senses were attuned to more than what he could see with his eyes. As a diviner, he could sense and manipulate Power links. He could tell the line of Power connecting his mother to her Power reserve was thin and frayed. From earlier research, Richard knew the Empire had her official age at eighty-two. But he also knew she was a time-commando. Richard had a feeling she was much older than the Empire's official age.

The councilwoman started to sit back down, but her hand missed the arm of the chair. She started to fall. Myers was there in a flash to catch his mother and ease her back into the safety of her chair.

"I told you not to overdo it, Mother," said Myers. "You know what the medics said."

"Oh, pooh on those medics," said Councilwoman Deluth as she gave Richard a wink. "I was fighting battles that would make those medics' hair stand on end before they were even born."

"My point exactly," said Myers. "You promised me you'd take it easy if I brought him here."

"So I will," said Councilwoman Deluth with a mischievous grin. Her smile seemed to take years off of her. "That is, I will as soon as you get out of that ridiculous suit you're wearing, Gaston. You should be in your wizard scout uniform."

Myers didn't give even a flicker of a smile. "I'm not a wizard scout anymore, Mother. I'm chief of security for the Deloris Armaments Corporation. You know that."

The news shocked Richard. *"Not a wizard scout? At a time when the Empire needs every wizard scout it has? And he's working for Diane Deloris? How'd he get out of his active-duty commitment?"*

"Well, actually," said Nickelo. *"Wizard Scout Myers had over thirty years of active service when you were at the Academy. The average life expectancy of a wizard scout is five years. I'd say he's had more than his share of active-duty time."*

"Whatever," Richard said.

Richard wasn't all that impressed. Counting the years during his time-commando missions, he had a feeling he would soon surpass his old TAC officer in years of military service.

Ignoring her son's reply, Councilwoman Deluth motioned to a padded chair across from her. "Please sit, Rick."

Richard sat. He didn't know what to expect from the meeting. He supposed he did expect a little more formality. However, the councilwoman seemed bent on keeping things informal. She was even calling him by his nickname.

"Why does everybody seem to want to call me by my nickname?" Richard thought.

"Are you asking me?" said Nickelo. *"I calculate it's because you're such a friendly and outgoing person."* Nickelo laughed. *"Of course, I only calculate a negative two percent probability that's the reason."*

"My son," explained Councilwoman Deluth, "saw fit to resign from the wizard scout corps and accept employment with the Conglomerate. Thomas would roll over in his grave if he knew."

"Perhaps this isn't something we should discuss with outsiders, Mother," said Myers.

"Nonsense," said Councilwoman Deluth. "Rick's not an outsider. I told you. He's your brother."

Richard was floored.

"You know?" Richard asked the councilwoman. "How? When?"

"When?" said Councilwoman Deluth. "I found out shortly after your graduation from the Academy. How? I had Gaston sneak into the Empire's archives and snatch a sample of your DNA baseline. Your DNA is odd, to say the least, but the human part is a perfect match with Thomas and me."

Richard didn't know what to say. He'd been living with the secret of his family heritage for the past year. He hadn't wanted to upset the councilwoman further after the death of her husband.

"Did the Commandant…" Richard started to ask, but he couldn't quite get the words out.

"Did Thomas know you were his son?" said Councilwoman Deluth. "No. He did not. But he was quite fond of you nevertheless for reasons that will one day become apparent."

"Err, why?" Richard asked.

"I said one day, Rick," said the councilwoman with a smile to soften the blow. "I have my reasons for not telling you. You'll just have to trust me."

Richard nodded his head affirmatively.

"I didn't ask you here for a family reunion," said the councilwoman with her voice suddenly taking on a businesslike tone. "I wanted to know more about the assassination attempt this morning. I viewed the investigation videos, but I want to hear it firsthand."

"I'm not sure I can add anything else, councilwoman," Richard said. "I—"

"Janice," said Councilwoman Deloris. "Call me Janice. I think Mother might be pushing it a little at this point."

Richard nodded his head gratefully. Calling her Mother would be awkward. Biologically, she was his mother, but he'd been raised in an orphanage by the sisters. He and the councilwoman had no shared experiences to form any kind of deep-family bond.

"Very well, err…Janice," Richard said. "I pretty much told the security personnel everything. Naturally, I left out anything about 'the One' or about the workings of my dimensional pack."

"Gaston," said Councilwoman Deluth turning in her seat to face her son who had taken a chair next to hers. "You were there. Did you notice anything unusual?"

"I told you I was waiting in your office when the explosion occurred," said Myers. "Your office is hermetically sealed and lined with creallium to prevent eavesdropping or teleportation. I was unable to see or sense anyone. Once I heard the explosion, I immediately rushed outside and used my passive scan. I assume you're trying to find out if I sensed the presence of a Crosioian scout or one of those magic users we encountered at the Academy last year. I didn't."

"What I'm trying to find out is if there was anyone who could've slipped a weapon past security," said the councilwoman.

"What about you, Rick?"

"No, ma'am," Richard said. "I never sensed anyone, and I didn't see where the shot came from. Whoever it was must have had a very good stealth shield."

"My thoughts exactly," said the councilwoman. "And, my understanding is the assassin used a solid slug instead of a plasma round. I wonder why?"

Richard shrugged his shoulders. He hadn't thought about it.

"What are you trying to say, Mother?" asked Myers.

"I'm not trying to say anything," said Councilwoman Deluth. "I'm just pointing out a non-exploding, solid round was used. That's all."

"Well, it would've killed her for sure if I hadn't been there to heal her," Richard said. "The follow-up explosion almost got us all as it was. If I hadn't sensed the energy building up and shifted us into the void, we'd have all been goners."

"So the explosion wasn't instantaneous?" said the councilwoman touching the tips of her fingers together and putting them under her chin. "That's interesting."

"It almost was," Richard said remembering how he'd gotten the three of them shifted just in time. "A little less delay and I couldn't have done it. We were very lucky."

"Yes you were," said Councilwoman Deluth. "And thanks to you, Diane was saved."

"Well, err, uh," Richard stammered.

His mother abruptly changed the subject. "Did you know Councilwoman Deloris has been trying to convince the council for the past six months to allow Conglomerate troops to provide rear-area security in lieu of active troops?"

"I think she mentioned something about that," Richard said trying to remember exactly what he'd heard and where.

"Well, thanks to her near assassination this morning, she's going to get her wish," said his mother. "The assassination attempt scared several council members. They took a vote in my absence. Conglomerate security troops are going to take over most of the key, rear-area security duties within the next few months."

Without warning, Councilwoman Deluth pounded the arm of her chair with enough force to make dust fly out of the cushion. "I should have been there to knock some sense into their heads."

"You were too ill," said Myers. "You still are. And if you insist on getting worked up like this, I'm going to have to call this impromptu meeting to a close."

"I'll be fine," said Councilwoman Deluth in a much-subdued voice. "It just riles me when a manipulative woman like Diane always seems to get her way."

Councilwoman Deluth seemed to take a few seconds to compose her thoughts.

"Rick," she said. "I understand you're being reassigned to the Trecorians for a few months. You must've made quite an impression on them."

"Well, uh," Richard stammered trying to select his words as carefully as possible. "I'm not sure what's going on. They were trying their best to kill me the last I saw of them. I'm thinking they might take up where they left off if I go there."

"Oh, I don't think you need to worry," said Councilwoman Deluth in an assuring voice. "Although the Trecorians have remained neutral in our war with the Crosioians, they've been our allies on occasion in the past. I suspect they will be again at some point in the future."

"Maybe so," Richard said unconvinced. "But they even had their children out trying to kill me."

"Yes," said Councilwoman Deluth. "I watched your video report."

She turned her head to look at her son. "Gaston, would you care to explain to your brother."

The muscles in Myers's jaw tightened.

Richard got the impression his ex-TAC officer wanted to object to the use of the word "brother."

Looking at Richard, Myers said, "The Trecorians are a militaristic race. When their children are six standard-years old, they begin their military training. Based upon Councilwoman Deloris's discussion with Duke Bistoria, you got tangled up with a group of cadets on maneuvers. We think the fact you refrained from killing their children was a major factor in their request for your reassignment."

Richard wanted to question Myers why Councilwoman Deloris, who was his mother's political enemy, would be sharing information with him. But since his mother didn't say anything about it, Richard kept silent on the subject.

"I was almost forced to kill a couple of those kids," Richard said. "I'm glad I didn't have to. But even so, I don't understand why we should trust this duke."

"His name is Duke Bistoria," said Councilwoman Deluth. "I've met him several times. He's a man of his word. You can trust him."

When Richard still looked unconvinced, she added, "Did you know a significant number of Trecorians over the years have volunteered for military duty with the Empire?"

"No, I didn't," Richard said. "Are you sure we can trust them?"

The memory of a Trecorian round blasting its way through his left shoulder was still fresh in his mind.

Both Councilwoman Deluth and Myers laughed.

"Did I say something funny?" Richard asked.

He didn't mind getting laughed at by his friends occasionally, but he didn't like it coming from Myers. Besides, he at least wanted to know the reason why.

Richard's ex-TAC officer took it upon himself to explain. "Cadet 215 was, or rather is, a Trecorian. You may remember her."

"You mean Liz?" Richard was shocked. She'd never mentioned it to him. When Richard thought about it, he realized she'd been pretty tight-lipped about her family history. He'd convinced himself she was an orphan like himself.

"I mean Captain Elizabeth Bistos," said Myers as if enjoying Richard's confusion. "She's an up-and-coming-star in the fleet. The Trecorians have a habit of changing their names slightly when they volunteer for military service with the Empire. It has something to do with keeping their family's lineage straight. Captain Bistos real name is Bistoria."

Richard didn't think fast, but even he could put one plus one together.

"Are you telling me Liz is related to that duke you guys keep talking about?"

"None other," said Councilwoman Deluth with a knowing smile. "Your Liz is one of Duke Bistoria's daughters. My sources tell me you two were pretty friendly for a while."

Richard felt himself turning red. He and Liz had been more than a little friendly.

"Regardless," said Myers, "the circumstances have turned out well for the Empire. You'll be teleporting to Trecor tomorrow evening."

"Teleporting?" Richard said. "What about my ship?"

"The *Defiant*," explained Councilwoman Deluth, "is in the middle of a major overhaul. My sources tell me the Deloris Armaments Corporation is showering the *Defiant* with every piece of advanced equipment they can make fit. Your Sergeant Ron said it would be another month before the *Defiant* is flight ready."

"A month?" Richard said.

"Yes, a month, Shepard," said Myers. "And the Trecorians have requested your reassignment be given the highest priority. For some reason, the Creator knows why, they want you there ASAP."

Mulling the information over in his mind, Richard decided his best course of action was to remain silent. He'd never liked talking to Myers when he was a cadet. Richard found he liked talking to him even less now.

"Keep your temper, Rick," said Nickelo. *"He's not your enemy."*

"Well," Richard shot back, *"he sure as hell isn't my friend."*

"No, but he is your brother," said Nickelo. *"So deal with it."*

"I'm afraid I grow tired, Rick," said Councilwoman Deluth. "You're welcome to spend the night here if you'd like. Or...Gaston can have our hover-limo take you back to the spaceport."

Richard took a look at Myers. His ex-TAC officer didn't seem pleased with the prospect of a guest.

Well, join the club, Richard thought. *Sleeping in the same house as you would be no great thrill for me either.*

"Uh, thanks, uh...Janice," Richard said. "But I think I'll return to the *Defiant*. If I'm going to be teleporting out tomorrow evening, I've got some things to take care of."

"As you wish," said Councilwoman Deluth. "I doubt we'll get a chance to talk again before you leave. However, perhaps you wouldn't mind if we chat occasionally via the tele-network. I could have my battle computer, Danny, set something up."

"I'd like that," Richard said honestly.

"Good, so would I," said Councilwoman Deluth. Turning to Myers, she said, "Gaston, would you see your brother to the door and notify our chauffeur?"

"Of course, Mother," said Myers as he rose and walked out into the hallway without waiting for Richard.

Once Myers was gone, Richard's mother turned to him.

"My apologies, Rick," said Councilwoman Deluth. "The death of his father was a terrible blow to Gaston. They'd been at odds for so long they had trouble showing their affection for each other. But I know Gaston loved his father immensely. He just never got a chance to tell Thomas. I think Gaston resents the fact that you and Thomas spent so much time together at the end. Plus, you were there when Thomas was…" The councilwoman stopped talking for a moment and turned her head away from Richard. After a few seconds, she turned back around and continued with a steady voice. "You were there when Thomas was killed. I believe Gaston thinks it was his place to fight by his father's side. He never got the chance."

Richard had a feeling he should say something to the effect that he understood. But he didn't understand, so he decided to remain quiet.

"It's time for us to say goodbye, Rick," said Councilwoman Deluth. "And, I wish you the best of luck."

Richard rose from his seat. He took a long look at the councilwoman; his mother. She looked tired.

Will I ever see her again? he wondered.

Richard wasn't sure what to do. He was pretty sure a hug would be inappropriate, so he snapped to attention and gave a salute. "Sir!"

Councilwoman Deluth smiled.

"You remind me of Thomas," she said in a weak voice. "You did the very first time I saw you. That was so very long ago."

Then the councilwoman closed her eyes and went to sleep.

Richard stood there watching his mother for a few seconds. It was strange. Physically, she looked no older than he. But his senses told him otherwise. She was old; frail. Richard took a lap blanket off the back of the chair where he'd been sitting and gently laid it across his mother's legs and chest. He hesitantly bent over to kiss the top of her head, but he stopped himself before completing the act. Richard straightened and walked to the archway. He turned back around and took one last look at his sleeping mother. Then he turned the corner into the hallway.

Myers was not in the hall or by the door. Richard walked outside the house and found Myers standing on the path through the garden. The hover-limo was back in the same spot where it had been when the driver had dropped Richard off.

Heading for the limo, Richard brushed past Myers. His ex-TAC officer reached out and grabbed his arm stopping him from passing.

"Let's get one thing straight," Myers said through gritted teeth. "I don't care if we share a few bits of DNA or not. You're not my brother, and you never will be."

"That's fine by me," Richard said. His temper rattled the doors of its cage. "I didn't like you at the Academy, and I'm not too fond of you now."

Myers glared at Richard for a couple of seconds. "Just so we understand each other."

"I think we do," Richard said.

Richard started to move on, but he stopped himself. He hated talking to Myers, but he had a final nagging question he needed answered. Things just didn't make sense. He'd found they rarely did in his life, but in this case, things made even less sense. Richard forced himself to swallow his pride and ask Myers for the information he required.

"If it's so important for me to get to Trecor quickly, why the hell was I brought back to Risors? I haven't been told anything that couldn't have been said over a secured tele-network link. The *Defiant* could've been on Trecor by now if we hadn't come all the way here first."

Richard noticed Myers start to say something and then stop. The toad-faced man seemed to contemplate his words before answering.

"You'd have to take that up with Councilwoman Deloris. She's the one who requested to meet you in person. Mother didn't even know you were here until after the assassination attempt."

Although he couldn't put his finger on it, Richard had a feeling Myers knew more than he was saying. He noticed Myers had said their mother hadn't known, but he hadn't included himself in the statement. However, Richard saw no point in pressing the issue. He turned back toward the hover-limo and the waiting chauffeur.

He only made it a couple of steps.

"Shepard," said Myers.

Richard turned back around. Myers had a strange look on his face.

"I'd recommend taking Councilwoman Deloris's offer," said Myers. "You're wasting your talents with the Empire. You could go a long way in the Conglomerate. You know *'the One'* is just using you. Wouldn't you like to fight back?"

"I find it a little strange you think I have talents," Richard said heatedly. "I remember you saying the opposite when I was at the Academy."

Myers didn't answer for a few seconds.

"I was just doing my job," said Myers. "I'll admit I've never liked you, but my point is still valid. Do you enjoy being a puppet for *'the One?'* Diane, err…Councilwoman Deloris has made you a generous offer. Use your head for once and take her up on it. Once you get back from this Trecor mission, we could work together to find a way to stop *'the One.'* You know as well as I *'the One'* doesn't care one iota what damage he does to his tools. *'The One'* will chew you up and spit you out just like he did the Commandant. Don't be a fool. You know I'm right."

Anger burned deep inside Richard. He didn't like the tone of Myers's voice when he mentioned the Commandant's name. Richard didn't care if Myers was the Commandant's son or not. The Commandant deserved respect. Richard didn't like Myers's attitude. However, he forced himself to get control of his anger before answering.

"What I know is that I find it strange you're working for your mother's political enemy," Richard said barely keeping the resentment and suspicion out of his voice. "You should be helping our mother, not Councilwoman Deloris."

Anger burned in Myers's eyes. "You've no idea what you're talking about, Shepard. The Empire is on the ropes. It has been for years. Councilwoman Deloris and the Conglomerate are the Empire's only hope. You'd do well to hitch your future with them."

Myers seemed to try to give Richard a semi-friendly smile, but the hint of anger still in his ex-TAC officer's eyes ruined the effect.

"We aren't enemies, you and I," said Myers. "If we worked together, I know we could find a way to remove the control *'the One'* has over people. It's too late to save the Commandant, but we could save others from the same fate. You could save yourself, Shepard."

"Don't listen to him, Rick," cautioned Nickelo. *"He's angry at* 'the One' *for a perceived past grievance."*

Richard ignored his battle computer. He didn't like Myers. He doubted he ever would. But then again, he didn't like *'the One'* either. Seeing no point in making another enemy, Richard decided to take the middle ground.

"I told Councilwoman Deloris I'd think about it," Richard said. He couldn't remember if he had or hadn't, but it seemed like a safe answer.

As far as I know, it's the truth, Richard thought. *I am going to think about it. I owe nothing to* 'the One.' *I didn't ask for any of this. I'm loyal to the Empire. But isn't the Conglomerate part of the Empire?*

"You do that," said Myers as if giving a warning. "You think about it real hard."

Richard bit his tongue on an angry retort before it escaped his lips. Arguing with his brother would accomplish nothing. With an abrupt turn, Richard walked to the hover-limo. The chauffeur held the door open for him.

"Where to, sir?" asked the chauffeur.

"To the spaceport," Richard said. "I need to get back to the *Defiant.*"

CHAPTER 15

It was nearly midnight before Richard made it back to the hangar where the *Defiant* had been towed. Although it was late, nearly two hundred mechanics, armament personnel, and technicians of every imaginable type were busy hauling equipment in and out of the hangar. Even before Richard stepped inside, he heard the unmistakable pounding of plasma welding. The arcs of plasma energy gave an eerie strobe-light effect to the hangar's interior.

Capable of comfortably holding a crew of twenty-two, the *Defiant* was large for an Empire recon ship. However, the size of the *Defiant* was dwarfed by the size of the hangar. Once he was inside, Richard stopped and gazed in awe at the building's immenseness and the bustling activity going on around the *Defiant*.

Richard was on the verge of using his passive scan to find his crewmates when he heard a familiar voice.

"I don't care what standard procedure is," yelled Sergeant Ron over the noise in the hangar. "You ain't puttin' no Type III cable in my ship. It'll fail when I need it the most."

"But—," said a middle-aged man in an orange jumpsuit who was standing near a hover-cart loaded down with plasma cables.

"There ain't no buts," said Sergeant Ron cutting off the other man's protests. "You haul that stuff out of here and don't come back until you've got some Type V cable."

The middle-aged man's expression would have been comical except for the fact Richard had a feeling this wasn't the first time Sergeant Ron and the technician had butted heads. The technician said something to three other men dressed in identical orange jumpsuits standing near the hover-cart. Richard saw them nod their heads and begin dragging the cart away.

"And I don't want none of that cheap import stuff either," yelled Sergeant Ron after them. "I want the same quality cable your Deloris good-for-nothing executives use in their space yachts."

As the technicians walked past, Richard noticed they all had large Deloris Armaments patches on their backs. A smaller Conglomerate insignia was sewn on the left chests of their uniforms.

"I don't care how much overtime they're paying us for this job," muttered one of the technicians as they walked past. "That guy is a pain in the ass. He expects everything to be perfect."

Richard ignored the technicians and looked back at Sergeant Ron. The *Defiant's* captain was just starting to speak to a woman in a black jumpsuit wearing a set of welder's goggles. Sergeant Ron happened to look up. His eyes latched onto Richard.

"Rick!" said Sergeant Ron with a tired grin. "I was wondering when you'd drag your tired carcass back here."

"Here I am," Richard said smiling in return. Sergeant Ron was a crazy old coot, but it was hard not to like him.

"Yeah," said Sergeant Ron strolling over. "I hear tell you had a little ruckus this morning." With a laugh he added, "Just can't stay out of the news, can you?"

Richard shrugged his shoulders. "One does what one does best."

With another smile, Sergeant Ron waved a hand around the hangar. "Like what I've done with the place?" Giving Richard a wink, Sergeant Ron laughed, "I sweet talked a few friends into giving us a hand."

"So I see," Richard said. "I guess you heard we're going to have a passenger?"

"That's still up for debate," said Sergeant Ron. "I'm the captain of the *Defiant*, not Diane Deloris."

"But you're letting them install all this equipment," Richard said. "I assumed you agreed to the terms of the deal."

"Hmm," said Sergeant Ron. "I'm betting the good councilwoman probably assumes the same thing. I'm also betting she might be in for a surprise."

Richard sensed possible legal trouble coming their way. He wasn't sure of the cost of all the equipment and manpower, but he had a feeling it was double or triple the original cost of the *Defiant*.

"Deloris Armaments is going to be pissed if we don't take Councilwoman Deloris's son," Richard pointed out.

"Let her be pissed," said Sergeant Ron with a crazy laugh. "I've dealt with her before. What's she going to do? Take it all back? Ha! Let her try."

"It's not your ship, Rick," said Nickelo. *"Let Sergeant Ron handle it. You've got your own worries. You'll be teleporting out in eighteen hours."*

"I know," Richard thought back.

"All right, Sergeant Ron," Richard said conceding defeat. "It's your ship."

"Correction, Rick, old buddy," said Sergeant Ron with a slap on Richard's back. "It's *our* ship. I had the title to the *Defiant* changed this afternoon. You're now half-owner. From now on, we're partners; fifty-fifty."

Richard was confused. *"What the hell am I supposed to do with a starship?"*

"Don't worry about it," replied Nickelo. *"I've a feeling Sergeant Ron is going to be the brains of the outfit anyway."*

"Ha, ha," Richard thought back. *"Not funny."*

"Look, Sergeant Ron," Richard said as he yelled to be heard over the sound of all the plasma welding. "It's not that I don't appreciate it, but it's your ship. I haven't earned it. Besides, wouldn't I have needed to sign something or other to make it official?"

"Not when you know people," said Sergeant Ron with a smile. "And I know people. It's all done good and proper with all the correct legalese." With a wink, Sergeant Ron said, "Just don't go looking too closely at your palm print on the title. I took for granted you wouldn't sue me."

Richard looked at the smug smile on Sergeant Ron. It was hard to be mad at the old man. "No, I won't sue. But please ask me the next time."

"No problem, partner," said Sergeant Ron holding out his hand.

"All right, partner," Richard said as he shook Sergeant Ron's hand. "But if we're going to be partners, we can't be having any secrets between us. Agreed?"

"Agreed," replied Sergeant Ron. "My life's an open book. I wouldn't think of keeping secrets."

Richard would probably have taken Sergeant Ron more seriously if he hadn't winked and laughed when he'd said it.

For the next hour, Sergeant Ron gave Richard a tour of all the work being done. Afterward, he spent another half hour explaining the additional planned upgrades to be installed in the upcoming days. Most of the details went over Richard's head.

From Richard's understanding, the main changes were going to be an upgrade of their hyper-drive to a new prototype model developed by a Deloris Armaments' subsidiary. Supposedly, it would give them an extra twenty percent speed during normal hyper-drive, and they'd be able to make thirty hyper-jumps instead of their current twenty before requiring an overhaul. In addition to their engine, the *Defiant's* force fields were being beefed up along with their ship's weapons. Sergeant Ron assured him once the overhaul was completed, the *Defiant* would be the toughest recon ship in the Empire. The Deloris Armaments Corporation was even installing 200-gigawatt plasma cannons on the upper and lower decks. In addition, the *Defiant* would still have its normal battery of four one-hundred-megawatt anti-fighter plasma autocannons.

"That's a lot of firepower for a recon ship," Richard pointed out to Sergeant Ron. "Some destroyers only have 100-gigawatt cannons."

"Yep," replied Sergeant Ron. "I guess our dear councilwoman wants to make sure her son is protected. I'm betting some Balorian pirates will be in for a big surprise if they try jumping us."

"Our mission is to train Trecorians," Richard said. "We're not supposed to be doing any fighting."

"Yeah, right," Sergeant Ron said with a loud snort. "And if you believe that one, I think you should get your head examined."

Richard didn't say anything else on the matter. He didn't believe it either. Peaceful days weren't how things seemed to work out in his life.

At that moment, they happened to be passing a group of welders working on the right-side wing pod.

"What are they doing?" Richard asked.

"Oh, them?" said Sergeant Ron. "That bunch of yahoos wanted

to mount a Zip fighter directly on our wing pods. I told them hell no."

Although he wasn't a starship pilot, Richard knew Zip fighters, or zippers as they were called by their pilots, were single-seat fighters. While they couldn't make hyper-jumps, they were very fast under normal hyper-drive. Due to their small size, they only carried a double set of forty-kilowatt plasma guns and four 20mm chain guns. As a result, their usefulness was limited to recon and anti-personnel missions. A good pilot might be able to take on a shuttle fighter, but they were pretty much useless against larger ships.

"I'm making them reinforce our wing pods first," continued Sergeant Ron. "Also, I'm having them put in an enclosed tunnel system and air locks in each wing so our pilots can man the zippers while we're in flight."

"Our pilots?" Richard said. "What pilots are those? I don't know how to fly one of those things. You told me Charlie and you don't either, remember?"

"Yeah, that's true," admitted Sergeant Ron.

Giving a big grin, Sergeant Ron said, "But by golly, they'll make the *Defiant* look cool as hell when we land at spaceports from here on out."

Richard just shook his head.

"You look tired, Sergeant Ron," Richard said. "Why don't you go get a few hours of sleep? It's going to be a long day tomorrow. Charlie and I can watch things until you get back."

"Yeah, I think I will go lie down for a few minutes," said Sergeant Ron. "But I want to show you something else first."

Without further explanation, Sergeant Ron led Richard into the *Defiant's* cargo bay. The inside of the ship was as bustling with workers as the outside.

"What do you think?" said Sergeant Ron as he pointed to two black Warcats mounted to the sides of the cargo bay.

"Wow!" Richard said duly impressed. "They look new."

"They are," Sergeant Ron said with a nod. "They put the model you borrowed during the fight at the airfield to shame. These Warcats are the best Deloris Armaments have to offer."

Richard noticed the Warcats were missing weapon pods. He said as much.

"Yeah," said Sergeant Ron. "But we'll have plenty to choose from. These Warcats have quick-releases on each arm. We'll be able to pick and choose weapon pods depending on the mission. Our armory is being enlarged and upgraded. Our new weapons will be delivered in a couple of days. We're even getting some anti-ship missiles for the zippers."

Richard saw several workers cutting a hole in the metal plating at the front end of the cargo bay. The *Defiant's* armory was located on the other side. The current armory was more a vault than an armory. The *Defiant* had only been designed to be a reconnaissance ship, after all.

"I'm confused, Sergeant Ron," Richard said shaking his head. "What weapons? We've got a crew of three; or four if you decide to take on Matthew Deloris. We have no need for a lot of weapons." A thought hit Richard. "And how are we going to maintain them? We don't even have an armorer. You and Charlie already have your hands full."

"Well," said Sergeant Ron. "I always say take things when you can get them. You never know when they'll come in handy. As for an armorer, that's what I wanted to talk to you about. We need one."

"I'll go with whoever you say, Sergeant Ron. You know that. It's your ship."

"It's our ship," corrected Sergeant Ron.

"Okay, our ship," Richard said. "But you're the captain. If you say we need an armorer, then we need one. Do you have someone in mind?"

Sergeant Ron gave Richard a look he usually gave when he was going to ask something that tended to get Richard in trouble. Richard braced himself.

"Actually, I do have someone in mind," Sergeant Ron admitted. "However, he's a little indisposed at the moment."

"Who?" Richard asked suspiciously.

"Sergeant Hendricks," replied Sergeant Ron.

Richard relaxed. Sergeant Hendricks had been the Academy armorer before it was shut down by the council. He liked the good-natured sergeant. The armorer had even made Richard's one-of-a-kind boot knife. The knife had saved his life several times over the years.

"Sounds good to me," Richard said. "Do you know where he's stationed? Maybe between Councilwoman Deloris and my mother, err...I mean Councilwoman Deluth, we can expedite his transfer to the *Defiant*. Assuming he's interested in the position, that is. He may be happy where he's at."

"Oh, I'm betting he's not all that happy," said Sergeant Ron with a strange smirk. "And I'm pretty sure he'll jump at the chance to work on the *Defiant*."

"Then where is he?" Richard asked growing suspicious again.

"On Diajor," said Sergeant Ron.

Diajor was the military's prison planet. From what Richard had heard over the years, it was a miserable place. Only prisoners with very long sentences were sent there. Most of them never left alive.

"Uh, as a guard?" Richard asked hoping for the best.

"Nope," said Sergeant Ron. "He's there serving a thirty-five-year sentence. Seems when the Conglomerate took over duties at the Academy, Sergeant Hendricks took affront to the fact that they wanted to confiscate all the weapons from his armory. He put five of them in the hospital. One of them was the son of a Conglomerate admiral. Politics being what they are, Sergeant Hendricks got sentenced to Diajor as an example to anyone else who might want to try obstructing the Conglomerate."

Richard was shocked.

"You know," said Sergeant Ron growing very serious, "he'll never last thirty-five years on Diajor. And even if he does survive that long, he'll be a shell of the man he was when he finally gets released."

Richard knew Sergeant Ron was right. He hated to see the friendly Sergeant Hendricks destroyed like that. All Sergeant Hendricks ever wanted to do was work in his armory. When Richard was at the Academy, he'd heard rumors that whenever someone had tried to promote Sergeant Hendricks out of the armory, he'd done something crazy to get busted in rank so he could stay. Richard had a feeling the sergeant had gambled with the system one time too many.

"I'll talk to Councilwoman Deloris about it tomorrow when she brings her son," Richard said. "Maybe she can do something."

"You can certainly ask," said Sergeant Ron knowingly, "but it won't do any good. You're going to have to get him yourself."

"What?" Richard said. "That's crazy. Even if I could, the military police would just haul him off the *Defiant* and take him back to Diajor. Heck, they'd probably take us with him."

"Doubtful," said Sergeant Ron. "As of yesterday, and for the next six months, the *Defiant* is sovereign territory of the Trecorian Planetary Alliance. If we can get Sergeant Hendricks onboard, the Empire won't dare touch him."

"What can I do?" Richard protested. "I'm getting teleported out tomorrow evening, and the *Defiant* is out of action for the next few weeks."

"Then I guess you better figure something out quick," said Sergeant Ron with a conspiratorial wink. "I fly the ship. You're the wizard scout. These kinds of problems are all yours, partner."

Richard stared at Sergeant Ron. "You're asking the impossible."

"I know," agreed Sergeant Ron with an easy laugh. "That's why I'm giving you until tomorrow evening to get it done."

Sergeant Ron yawned. "As for me, I'm going to find me a semi-quiet place and get some much-needed sleep."

With that, Sergeant Ron turned and weaved his way through the workers in the cargo bay until he exited the ship. Richard watched him go.

"And I thought 'the One' was a conniving SOB," Richard thought. *"I've been set up."*

"So you have, Rick," agreed Nickelo with a not so sympathetic laugh. *"So you have."*

CHAPTER 16

It was early morning when Gaston Myers walked into the outer office of Councilwoman Deloris. The reception area was already full of staff and petitioners alike. The councilwoman was an early riser, and Myers knew she expected her staff to be there just as early as her. Prior association with the councilwoman had taught Myers the councilwoman's habits well. He was used to her schedule.

"The councilwoman will see you now, wizard scout," said the receptionist.

Myers nodded his head and went to the door. It opened just before he got to it as two petitioners in frilly suits exited. Myers did his best to keep the sneer off his face. He didn't like the over-dressed popinjays, but they were a necessary evil in the world of Empire politics.

Once the two had passed, Myers entered the councilwoman's office and stood in front of her desk. He heard the door slide shut behind him. Councilwoman Deloris said nothing at first. She just stood on her side of the desk and gave Myers a steely-eyed gaze. Her eyes were hard for Myers to read. He got the impression the councilwoman was trying to choose the right words before speaking.

A full thirty seconds of silence passed. Finally, Councilwoman Deloris walked around the side of her desk and approached Myers. When she was close, she reared her hand back and slapped him hard across the mouth. Myers could have dodged easy enough, but he didn't try. He'd expected some form of physical reaction. He just hadn't known what form it would take.

From past experience, Myers knew the woman had a temper. He'd weathered more than a few storms in the past, so he just stood still and allowed the councilwoman to vent her anger. He knew she would eventually tire. After a dozen slaps, she stopped.

"How dare you? What right did you have to endanger my son?" she said.

Although the councilwoman's temper had cooled slightly, Myers could see its remains smoldering in her eyes.

"I did what I thought was necessary," he told her. "You made it very clear we'd only have a single chance at success. Matthew was in no more danger than you; less in fact. I shot you, not him."

"That was different," said Councilwoman Deloris. "I was prepared to risk my own life. I wasn't prepared to risk our son's."

"Next to me, Shepard is the best the Empire has," said Myers. "I weighed the risk. Shepard had a full four seconds to shift into the void before the explosion. It was more than enough time. I knew he'd succeed. He could have made it in less time."

"It was not your risk to take," said Councilwoman Deloris.

"He's my son too," Myers said. "He may not know it, but that doesn't make it any less true."

That stopped whatever words were about to come out of Councilwoman Deloris's mouth. Her eyes softened a little.

"Shooting you was the hardest thing I've ever done, Diane," Myers said softly. "What if I'd missed?"

"I had faith you wouldn't," said Councilwoman Deloris. "I trust you."

Myers shook his head slowly. "Please don't ask me to do anything like that again. I felt your pain when the round hit."

Myers turned his head and looked at the wall for a couple of seconds. When he once again looked at the councilwoman, he said, "It was torture for me. I was prepared to wrap both of you in Power and shift you into the void myself if Shepard was too slow."

Myers glanced at the floor before looking back up. In a voice barely above a whisper, he said, "I couldn't stand to lose you, Diane."

Councilwoman Deloris's eyes glistened in the room's light. She touched Myers's lips with the fingers of her right hand.

"You're bleeding," she said as she removed a kerchief from her pocket and dabbed at the corner of his lips.

"It has already healed itself, my love," Myers said. "And our son was in no danger. I could have saved him from the explosion. But I couldn't have healed your wound. We needed Shepard to do that. You risked much, my love."

The councilwoman looked into Myers's eyes. "You do love me, don't you, Gaston?"

"You know I do," Myers said. "It nearly tore my heart out to hurt you."

She smiled. "You won't have to do it again. Yes, the risk was great, but the reward was even greater. The council is now in the palm of my hand. Conglomerate security forces will take over responsibility for the council's security by the end of the week. Within a year, we shall have our security teams in virtually all of the important areas in the Empire. Then we'll be ready."

Councilwoman Deloris cupped Myers's hands with hers. "I'll need you by my side when the time comes, Gaston."

"I shall be there," said Myers. "Fear not."

Councilwoman Deloris gave Myers a knowing smile.

An awkward silence ensued before Myers spoke. "It's all going as you predicted. With the modifications to the *Defiant*, its crew should be able to discover if what we seek is there."

With a final dab of her handkerchief, Councilwoman Deloris wiped the last specks of blood from Myers's lips. Once she was done, she asked, "Do you have the new control system with you?"

"No, not with me," Myers said. "But I'll have it before we go to the spaceport."

"Good," said Councilwoman Deloris. "And what if the Trecorians' anomaly is not what we seek?"

"Then we still have our backup plan," said Myers.

"So your contacts have found the missing bottles of DNA gas?" said Councilwoman Deloris. The excitement was evident in her eyes.

"Yes," Myers said. "But they're well-guarded. I can't recover them on my own."

"I, ah...I mean *we* must have the gas," said Councilwoman Deloris. "Then we can be together."

Myers looked at the councilwoman. "You know I would marry

you without it. You're a beautiful woman, Diane. You'll always be beautiful to me."

"No," said Councilwoman Deloris. "We can't be together when one ages and the other doesn't." She waved one hand at her face. "This is as far as the surgeons can go. They can do no more for me. What would you have me do? Would you push me around in a hover-chair when I'm too decrepit to walk?"

"You know I would," Myers said.

"I will not rehash the same arguments again," said Councilwoman Deloris. "We must either recover the lost bottles of DNA gas or find another DNA gas vent between dimensions. It's the only way we can ever truly be together."

"Then we will find one or the other, Diane," Myers said. "I give you my word of honor."

Without waiting for a reply, Myers took Councilwoman Deloris in his arms and kissed her. She didn't resist.

CHAPTER 17

By 0730 hours the next morning, a new shift of workers had rotated inside the hangar. A group of them were busy unpacking and preparing a large, octagonal metal-container that virtually glowed with energy. Large letters stenciled on the side of the metal object read XHD821. An equally large Deloris Armaments Corporation insignia was painted onto the container as well.

"I've never seen a hyper-drive outside its protective shield before," Richard said into his shared space. *"It looks simplistic."*

Richard yawned. He'd gotten a couple of hours sleep during the wee hours of the morning, but apparently not enough. In theory, he didn't need to sleep due to his DNA baseline. However, his mind occasionally demanded the rest provided only by sleep to continue functioning properly. Richard had a feeling he could have used another hour's rest as he yawned again.

"Don't let your enthusiasm run away with you, Rick," said Nickelo. *"Bystanders will think you're bored with all that yawning."*

"Whatever," Richard said. *"So what makes this hyper-drive so special?"*

"It's a prototype," said Nickelo. *"You heard Sergeant Ron explain the advantages, but I see you've shoved the conversation off to the side as usual."*

"Science doesn't interest me all that much," Richard admitted. *"As long as I know how to make something move and go boom, I'm satisfied."*

"You know, sometimes you infuriate me," said Nickelo, *"which is hard to do since I'm supposed to be an emotionless computer."*

"Which we know you're not," Richard said as he tried to keep his laugh internal so as to avoid drawing stares from the technicians around him.

"Well, that's your fault," said Nickelo. *"You're the one who's emotionally corrupting me."*

"Then we're even," Richard laughed enjoying the fact that he actually seemed to be getting the upper hand on his battle computer for once. *"You've gotten me to actually plan things out on occasion. I was quite happy jumping into battle half-cocked until you came along."*

"It's a good thing I did," Nickelo said in a chastising voice. *"If you'd been left to your own devices, I calculate a fifty-five percent probability you'd be dead by now."*

"Probably," Richard agreed. Changing the conversation back to his original question, Richard said, *"So what makes this hyper-drive so special?"*

"I'm not presently connected to the tele-network," said Nickelo. *"However, from what I can ascertain from my electronic probe and your active scan, the energy flow is significantly different from normal hyper-drives. I calculate Sergeant Ron is going to have a difficult time keeping the reactor from having a meltdown."*

"That would be bad, I'm guessing?" Richard said.

"Yes, that would be very bad," said Nickelo. *"Imagine fifty of the largest nuclear warheads on the dreadnaught Destiny all exploding at the same time. That will give you a little idea of what having a meltdown with this hyper-drive would be like."*

Richard tried to wrap his mind around the problem before answering. He didn't have to be a scientist to understand the dangers. *"Then why the hell are we letting them install this ticking time-bomb on the* Defiant? *I respect Sergeant Ron and Charlie's mechanical abilities, but I doubt they're experts at maintaining experimental hyper-drives."*

"No, they aren't," said Nickelo, *"and Councilwoman Deloris knows it. I'm withholding judgment until I see what kind of control system they install. It will need to be a very advanced computer system. I could do it, but my job's taking care of you. Plus, I'm not connected to the tele-network."*

"Yeah, life's a bummer, ain't it?" Richard said. *"By the way, you do remember we're teleporting to Trecor tonight?"*

"Uh, I forgot to tell you, Rick," said Nickelo sounding almost embarrassed. *"You'll be going alone. The central computer contacted me earlier and said I'd need to stay on the* Defiant *and help indoctrinate the new control unit. The central computer said the* Defiant *is part of some algorithm or other. The central computer's giving me a special security interface to work with the* Defiant's *new computer system."*

Richard was shocked and a little irritated. He was shocked the central computer, at the apparent direction of *'the One'* no doubt, had the audacity to think it controlled the availability of his battle computer. Sure, *'the One'* sent him on missions in the magical dimension occasionally without his battle computer, but this was different. Also, he was a little pissed at Nickelo for not mentioning it earlier.

"It's not my fault," protested Nickelo who'd apparently heard Richard's thoughts. *"I'm acquiring more of your personality the longer we're together. I calculate I'm getting a little forgetful, just like you."*

"Hmm," Richard said. *"Are you telling the truth, or are you stretching it a little?"*

"Well," confessed Nickelo, *"maybe there's a little stretching, but the end result is you'll be on your own on Trecor for the next month. Sorry."*

"I have a sneaky suspicion I'm the one who's going to be sorry," Richard thought.

* * *

At 1000 hours on the dot that morning, a fancy hover-limo slid to a halt twenty meters from the ramp to the *Defiant's* loading dock. After the chauffeur rushed around and opened the passenger door, Councilwoman Deloris and her son, Matthew, got out. They were followed by the figure of the short, toad-faced man Richard had come to dislike over the years. The man was Gaston Myers.

"What's he doing here?" Richard asked his battle computer. *"I didn't enjoy seeing him all that much last night. I'd hoped I wouldn't have to see him again for a long time."*

"Just deal with it, Rick," said Nickelo. *"Besides, look at the box he's carrying. Do you notice anything suspicious?"*

Richard did a quick check with his passive scan. He sensed nothing out of the ordinary. He told his battle computer his findings.

"Exactly," said Nickelo. *"In fact, I'll bet you don't sense anything at all. The box is made out of titanium, and it's got a charge running through it. Whatever's inside is completely isolated from the rest of the world. The box is like a miniature version of the armory I was locked in back at the Academy's airfield."*

Richard took a closer look at the box. It was about the size of a shoe box. Rechecking his passive scan, Richard confirmed his battle computer was correct. No Power readings of any kind were escaping the box. Even if the box was empty, the space inside should still have been giving off a slight amount of Power.

Taking a risk, Richard sent out an active scan and tentatively probed the box. Sure enough, the box was being charged with energy, which was temporarily turning the titanium into creallium.

As Richard's niece and nephew had explained it to him the previous year, when a certain energy frequency was passed through titanium, it temporarily turned into creallium. Brachia had even installed particles of titanium dust in Richard's battle suits. When charged, the particles turned into creallium that existed in both the physical dimension and the void. The setup provided Richard protection from creatures that could do dimensional shifts into the void.

Richard withdrew his active scan. Myers gave him a knowing smirk.

"The jerk knows I was scanning," Richard thought. *"He must know I didn't find out anything."*

"What'd you expect?" said Nickelo. *"In my opinion, next to you he's probably the best wizard scout in the galaxy. Heck, you didn't even wrap a stealth shield around your active scan. Even the worst wizard scout in the galaxy could have sensed your scan."*

Richard was saved from further conversation by the approach of Councilwoman Deloris and her son. Myers followed a few steps behind clutching his box. Using his passive scan, Richard sensed Sergeant Ron beating a hasty path from the *Defiant's* control room to the cargo bay. The *Defiant's* captain would be joining them shortly. Richard internally cringed at what he thought would be an explosive confrontation between the crusty-old Sergeant Ron and the strong-willed councilwoman.

"Wizard Scout Shepard," said Councilwoman Deloris with a well-rehearsed smile. "It's good to see you again. Our technicians aren't giving you any trouble, are they?"

Richard noticed the councilwoman had dropped the use of his first name in public in favor of his official title. He sighed with relief. He didn't like the false-friendliness politicians seemed to throw around with practiced ease. It made him feel like the councilwoman was just waiting for the opportunity to stab him in the back.

"Now, Rick, you promised me you'd watch your manners today," reminded Nickelo. *"After all, you're going to ask her for a favor. Don't forget about Sergeant Hendricks."*

"Yes, mommy," Richard thought back.

Getting back to the councilwoman's question, Richard said, "Not at all, councilwoman. They're all very hard workers. I have to admit, I'm overwhelmed at the…uh…investment Deloris Armaments is making in the Defiant. Sergeant Ron says we're going to need to take on an armorer to keep all our weapons maintained."

"Of course you will," said Councilwoman Deloris. "That's why the Conglomerate has graciously agreed to reassign several of their more experienced personnel to the Defiant. You'll require the best. Not only is your mission important but you'll have my son onboard as well. He's the future of Deloris Armaments, you know."

Matthew's face turned a little pink. "Mom, please. I told you I'd just be a normal crew member. You promised you'd stay out of it."

Turning to her son, Councilwoman Deloris said, "And I will, Matthew, as soon as I make sure you have the protection you need. That's why I'm personally selecting the members of the *Defiant's* crew."

"The hell you are," said an irate voice behind Richard.

"Ah," said Councilwoman Deloris with more than a little hint of disdain in her voice. "It's always a pleasure, Ronald."

Richard noticed Sergeant Ron cringe at the councilwoman's use of his first name.

"Hmm," said Nickelo in their shared space. *"Remind me never to call Sergeant Ron by his given name."*

"I'll second that," Richard said.

"The *Defiant II* is my ship," said Sergeant Ron. "That was the deal. I'm the captain. Deloris Armaments no longer has any ownership interest or say in the *Defiant*."

"Oh, really?" said Councilwoman Deloris with a sweep of her hand at all the activity around the *Defiant*. "We're investing a lot of credits and equipment in the *Defiant*. I believe we have a lot of say in the matter."

"You can believe what you want," said Sergeant Ron growing a little red-faced. "Take this crap back if you've a mind to, but the *Defiant II* is mine. You got control of the company and I got the *Defiant II*. That was the deal."

Richard glanced back and forth between Sergeant Ron and the councilwoman. *"What are they talking about, Nick?"*

"I'm not sure," said Nickelo. *"For some reason, my databanks have very little information about the Deloris family or their company. I've a feeling part of my databanks was wiped for some reason."*

"Now watch your blood pressure, Father," said Councilwoman Deloris with acid dripping from her words. "You'd hate to have a heart attack in front of your grandson."

Richard's jaw dropped.

"What?" he managed to stammer.

Councilwoman Deloris turned to Richard with an innocent-looking smile on her face. "Oh, didn't he tell you? No? Then let me be the first to introduce you to your ship's captain. This is Ronald Matthew Deloris, ex-CEO of Deloris Armaments Corporation and current hard-headed bastard who deserted his family in order to follow some broken-down wizard scout instead."

The sudden massive amount of information threatened to overload Richard's brain. But even so, he was pretty sure the councilwoman wasn't referring to him as the wizard scout in question.

"You mean the Commandant?" Richard said.

"He wasn't the Commandant then, was he, Gaston?" said Councilwoman Deloris without looking away from Richard.

Myers said nothing.

Richard looked at Sergeant Ron for explanation.

"I was going to tell you eventually, Rick," said Sergeant Ron. "I figured I'd wait until we were off planet."

"Grandfather," said Matthew. "I didn't mean to cause any trouble. I just—"

"I know what you were trying to do, Matt," said Sergeant Ron. "And I don't blame you, boy. If'n you don't make a break for it now, they'll pigeonhole you into a blue suit for the rest of your life. All you'll ever do from then on will be attend meetings with other blue-suits all in the name of scraping together a few more credits."

"Those credits are paying for the equipment on the *Defiant*," said Councilwoman Deloris with her voice increasingly rising in volume. "I don't remember you hesitating to use the company's credits to buy the original *Defiant*."

"That's not the point," said Sergeant Ron in a near shout. "The *Defiant II* was my severance package. I left ownership of the company to your brother and you. What more do you want?"

"How about a father and mother?" Councilwoman Deloris shouted.

"I didn't kill your mother, Diane," yelled Sergeant Ron in return. "And, I signed everything over to you kids. I left you with plenty."

"The keyword is left!" said Councilwoman Deloris her eyes blazing.

The hangar that had been full of pounding, welding, noisy motors, and every other kind of sound for the last twenty-four hours was abnormally quiet. Richard felt more than saw the stares of the workers around them. Richard caught the eye of Matthew Deloris. The young man turned away embarrassed by the outbursts of his mother and grandfather.

"Grandfather?" Richard thought into his shared space. *"Are you sure you didn't know, Nick? I find that hard to believe."*

"Honest," said Nickelo. *"It's not in my databanks. I'm not hooked up to the tele-network. If I ever knew, it's been wiped from my memory."*

Councilwoman Deloris and Sergeant Ron continued to stare at each other for several seconds. Sergeant Ron broke the silence first.

"Say what you want, Diane," said Sergeant Ron. "But the end result is as of yesterday, Rick and I are sole owners of the *Defiant II*. We pick our crew. And I say no to your handpicked lackeys."

Turning to Matthew, Sergeant Ron said, "Sorry, Matt, but that includes you. I sympathize with your situation, but I want a crew on my ship that's loyal to me, not your mother."

"Grandfather, please," said Matthew. "I need this chance. And...I'd hoped we could get to know one another. I haven't seen you a dozen times in my life. I.... Please."

Sergeant Ron looked from Matthew to Councilwoman Deloris to Richard.

"What do you say, Rick?" said Sergeant Ron. "You're half owner in the *Defiant* now."

Richard looked at the young man. Matthew had a pleading look in his eyes. However, the boy remained silent. Richard gave him kudos for not begging. While he couldn't empathize with a rich boy wanting to get away on own, he could appreciate someone wanting a different life than the one they'd been handed. During Richard's three years on the streets, he'd never had anyone try to help him change his lot in life. He wondered if things might have turned out different if someone had given him an opportunity to change.

"I like the kid," Richard finally said. "He's got guts enough for a battalion of Marines. I say let's sign him on." Richard shrugged his shoulders and smiled. "Heck, if he doesn't work out, we can always jettison him out the escape hatch."

Richard winked at Matthew. The young man nodded and returned a half-smile.

Rubbing his chin with one hand, Sergeant Ron said, "I don't know. Let me think about it."

"Before you decide," said Councilwoman Deloris, "I want you to sit in the car with me for a minute. There are too many prying eyes out here."

Sergeant Ron didn't say anything. He just followed the councilwoman to the hover-limo and got in. The chauffeur remained outside. They were in the hover-limo a long time.

"Thanks for sticking up for me," said Matthew.

"No problem," Richard said. "Heck, we fought together,

remember?"

"I'm not likely to forget," Matthew said as he continued to stare at the hover-limo. "I wonder what they're saying."

"I've no desire to know," Richard said. He meant it.

Looking at Matthew, Richard said, "I had no idea Sergeant Ron was a part of the Deloris family. What's the story, if you don't mind my asking?"

"I thought it was common knowledge," said Matthew continuing to stare at the hover-limo. "It's a deep, dark, family secret that isn't very secret. It pops up in the news videos every so often. However, I learned early on not to mention my grandfather's name around my mother. They say most families have a black sheep in their lineage. I guess my grandfather is ours."

Richard said nothing. He waited for the boy to continue on his own. After a few seconds, he did.

"When I was very young, I assumed both my grandparents were dead," said Matthew as if he were talking to himself more than Richard. "Their starship was attacked by some unknown pirates when my mother was just a child. As I said, I thought both of my grandparents had died in the attack. Then one day, my grandfather shows up at our door and demands to speak with my mother. I remember a lot of shouting coming from the library after they went in. I found out years later Grandfather signed over all rights and interests in Deloris Armaments Corporation in exchange for the *Defiant II*. Apparently, he'd been off chasing pirates in the *Defiant II* for years before that. Mother and the other board members were trying to get the *Defiant II* back. I guess they worked out a deal that day at the house."

Matthew sighed. "I don't think Grandfather ever found what he was looking for with the *Defiant*. He'd been working off and on at the Academy for decades as I understand it. A few years ago he ended his quest and began working full-time for Commandant Jacobs. I've only seen Grandfather a few times since he came to the house that day. Mother forbade him from ever returning."

"Wow," said Nickelo. *"The kid's an open book once you get him started. I'm glad you only asked him one question."*

"Hush, Nick," Richard said unamused. He could tell Matthew was hurting. Richard had once heard an unlimited supply of credits didn't buy happiness. He guessed whoever told him that was right.

Myers continued to stand off to the side, out of earshot, while clutching his box to his side.

Richard made no attempt to start up a conversation with his brother. They had nothing really in common.

After fifteen minutes, Sergeant Ron and Councilwoman Deloris got out of the hover-limo and joined Matthew and Richard. Myers wandered over as well.

"Let's see it," said Sergeant Ron.

Councilwoman Deloris nodded to Myers. He opened his box and removed a piece of dull brerellium no bigger than a fingernail. Richard sensed a blaze of Power coming from the chip. He recognized the Power's frequency. It was Margery, the Commandant's battle computer.

"What the—" Richard started to say before he caught himself.

"Are you sure she'll work?" said Sergeant Ron.

"Her databanks have been partially wiped," said Councilwoman Deloris. "Our computer psychs tell me giving her something meaningful to do is the best therapy she can receive. She was with the Commandant over seven decades. That's too long to expect her to bond with a new wizard scout, even if we had new ones available."

"Wizard Scout Myers," said Sergeant Ron. "The Commandant was your father. Do you agree with this? Seems to me you and your mother have a lot of say in the matter."

"Battle computers belong to the Empire, not individuals," said Councilwoman Deloris. "The Imperial High Council can reassign them anytime they want."

"Yeah, right," said Sergeant Ron in a tone making it obvious he didn't agree. "Well, Gaston?"

Myers looked at the processing unit in his hand for several seconds. Finally, he looked at Sergeant Ron. "Yes, I think it would be the best thing for her. The *Defiant* is familiar to her. So are you. You and the Commandant spent several years together hunting those pirates of yours. I think Margery will feel at home on the ship. Besides…"

"Besides, what?" prodded Sergeant Ron after several seconds passed.

Richard saw Myers look at him before turning his attention to Sergeant Ron.

"Besides," said Myers, "the Commandant connected a one-way link to Shepard during the battle at the spaceport. Margery will sense it. Mother thinks having the link nearby will help Margery cope with the loss of her wizard scout."

"Will someone please tell me what I'm missing here?" Richard said.

Councilwoman Deloris spoke first. "The new control systems on the *Defiant* have been designed to work directly with a battle computer. Margery will be installed inside the *Defiant*. She'll help control the new hyper-drive. I guess it'll probably be easier to think of the *Defiant* as a large battle helmet from now on."

Great, Richard thought. *That's all I need, another computer trying to control my life.*

CHAPTER 18

While Sergeant Ron and Councilwoman Deloris verbally clawed and scratched at each other a few more times over the next hour, in the end, they came to an agreement. The *Defiant II's* overhaul would continue as planned with no stipulations other than Matthew would be assigned as part of the *Defiant's* crew.

As predicted by Sergeant Ron, acquiring Sergeant Hendricks, who was apparently now Private Hendricks, as the ship's armorer was out of the question. Councilwoman Deloris made it plain the delicacy of the current political situation made such a request impossible. Barring some miracle, Private Hendricks would serve his full sentence on Diajor.

Even without a deal to release Hendricks, Richard thought Sergeant Ron had come out with the better part of the deal. After all, the *Defiant II* was getting a lot of advanced equipment for the measly cost of taking on one extra crewman.

An hour later, during a private meeting in the captain's cabin between Sergeant Ron, Councilwoman Deloris, Myers, and himself, Richard found out how wrong he was.

"We are not, and we will never be, a spy ship for the Conglomerate," said Sergeant Ron working himself into another frenzy. "You can forget it!"

"For once in your life will you listen to reason," said Councilwoman Deloris. "You act like the Conglomerate is the Empire's enemy. Nothing could be further from the truth."

"Wow," said Nickelo in Richard's shared space. *"She's good. I*

think she almost believes what she's saying."

"Well, guess what?" said Sergeant Ron. "The *Defiant's* not going to be a spy ship for the Empire, the Conglomerate, or anyone else."

"Will you be reasonable?" said Councilwoman Deloris. "It's not spying. All you have to do is try and locate an anomaly in the Trecorian's' sector of space and report its location back to us."

"You mean to the council, don't you?" said Sergeant Ron knowing full well it wasn't what his daughter meant.

Richard could tell the councilwoman was losing control of her temper, but once again she bit her tongue at the last second.

Myers looked at Councilwoman Deloris and said, "May I?"

Still biting her tongue, she nodded her head.

"They should know all of it, councilwoman," said Myers.

Councilwoman Deloris gave Myers a dirty look but then nodded her head in acquiescence. "If you think we must."

"All of what?" Richard thought.

"Are you asking me*?"* said Nickelo. *"How would I know? But if you pay attention, maybe we'll both find out."*

Myers opened the box he'd placed on the table earlier and pulled out the processor chip it held. "Once Margery is installed in the ship's control network, she'll be able to correlate the ship's equipment to pinpoint any anomalies in the Trecorians' sector of the galaxy."

"So?" said Sergeant Ron. "The galaxy's full of anomalies."

"You're correct, Sergeant Ron," agreed Myers, "but this anomaly is special. During my parents' last mission for *'the One'*—"

Richard drew in a deep breath and glanced at Councilwoman Deloris.

Myers caught the movement of his eyes. "The councilwoman has been fully briefed on *'the One'* and my parents' extracurricular activities, as well as yours."

"So much for secrets," Richard thought.

"Ah, yes, the human species and secrets," said Nickelo. *"I sometimes think the only way for a human to keep a secret is to only tell themselves and then pray for amnesia."*

"Don't act so surprised, Rick," said Councilwoman Deloris. "The Commandant and I were close. We had few secrets between us."

"*Hmm,*" said Nickelo. "*I wonder how she can say that without her nose growing longer?*"

Richard understood his battle computer's analogy. He'd read a book of old Earth nursery stories, so he was familiar with the one about a wooden boy who had a nose that grew in length whenever he told a lie. Richard thought it was a good story.

"*Too bad noses don't really grow when someone lies,*" Richard thought. "*As concerned as Councilwoman Deloris is about her looks, I've a feeling she'd speak a lot less.*"

"*No doubt,*" laughed Nickelo.

"Is there a point to all this?" said Sergeant Ron. "I've got a starship to run."

"Uh, yes, Sergeant Ron," said Myers. "The point is during my parents' last mission for '*the One,*' they stowed away on a black dreadnaught. The crew's uniforms had insignias of a black dragon with a red stripe down its side."

Sergeant Ron sat up straight.

Richard noticed the knuckles of Sergeant Ron's fingers turn white as they clinched the edge of the table.

Myers glanced at Richard. "I suspect you're missing the relevance of my last statement."

Richard glanced at Myers. He was curious but refused to give his ex-TAC officer the satisfaction of asking him a question. Councilwoman Deloris came to his rescue.

"Forty years ago, the Commandant and Gaston's mother went on a mission for '*the One,*'" said the councilwoman. "My father and my mother happened to be in the original *Defiant* near the Trecorians' border when they got an encoded message from the central computer. It directed them to pick up survivors in an escape pod a few light years away."

Councilwoman Deloris looked at her father. They exchanged stares for several heartbeats.

Richard was grateful he couldn't read thoughts. From the glare in each of their eyes and the strain on their faces, he figured they were exchanging volumes.

Sergeant Ron was the first to blink. He turned his eyes down to look at the table. Scratching at the table's surface with a fingernail, he took up the story, looking at Richard. "When Sharon.... When my wife and I arrived at the coordinates, we located a strange-looking escape pod that was giving off even stranger energy readings. The pod showed signs of heavy fighting. We tried to make contact but failed to get a reply. Since the original *Defiant* didn't have a tractor beam, I put on a pressurization suit and went over to check it out. Sharon and the rest of the crew remained in our ship. While I was trying to find a way into the pod, a black dreadnaught materialized nearby and began firing at the *Defiant*. The dreadnaught had an insignia of a black dragon with a red stripe down its side."

Sergeant Ron stared up at the ceiling as if lost in his memories. When Councilwoman Deloris cleared her throat, he looked back at the group and continued his story.

"The *Defiant* fought back as best she could," said Sergeant Ron. He shrugged his shoulders. "But she was only a recon ship. Sharon must have decided the only way she could help me was to lead the attackers away. I saw the *Defiant's* hyper-drive activate as Sharon made a run for it. The black dreadnaught followed her. I never saw either starship again." Sergeant Ron's voice broke. He looked back at the ceiling.

Myers took up the tale several seconds later. "My parents told me Sergeant Ron eventually gained entry into the escape pod. My parents were inside, in stasis. Sergeant Ron was able to wake them. Between the three of them, they repaired the pod enough to limp to a shipping lane. After they were rescued, Deloris Armaments mounted the largest search and rescue ever recorded. The searchers never found any sign of the black dreadnaught. However, they did find pieces of the *Defiant's* wreckage. DNA testing confirmed the deaths of the crew, including Sharon Deloris."

Richard had a thousand questions running amok in his mind. He didn't know which one to ask first or even if he should ask any.

"I don't get it," Richard thought into his shared space. *"I've heard Sergeant Ron speak about his wife lots of times. How can she be dead?"*

"Well, I suppose he could have remarried," Nickelo thought back, *"but I calculate less than a four percent probability of that. However, this would explain why you've never seen her. Didn't you think it strange Sergeant Ron left his wife to follow you around for the past year?"*

Richard had thought it strange, but anytime he brought it up, Sergeant Ron always turned his question into some kind of joke about his wife being glad to get him out of the house.

"People deal with grief in different ways," said Nickelo. *"I guess this is Sergeant Ron's way. Based upon information in my databanks, it's not a very healthy way to deal with grief, but there it is."*

"How does all this affect us?" Richard said. "I mean, how does it affect us today?"

"My parents," said Myers, "told me they had stowed away on the black dreadnaught while it was in the magical dimension. They made the mistake of getting locked in a storeroom lined with energized titanium. Somehow, the dreadnaught jumped to the physical dimension. Locked in the storeroom as they were, my parents didn't see how but the Commandant told me they detected a surge of energy before the jump. Eventually, a crewman opened the storeroom, and they made their escape. After sabotaging one of the dreadnaught's engines, they used one of the ship's escape pods to get away. Their pod was damaged by anti-ship fire, but they managed to make it to freedom. 'The One' ordered them to go into the pod's cryogenic chamber until help arrived."

"I still don't get it," Richard admitted. "I don't mean to be unfeeling, but you said this happened forty years ago. How is that pertinent now?"

"The burst of energy sensed by the Commandant and Councilwoman Deluth was similar in frequency to the Power readings from the DNA gas vent at the Academy," said Councilwoman Deloris.

Richard detected excitement in the councilwoman's voice and noticed a strange look in her eyes as well. "So?" he said, still unable to make the connection to current events.

Councilwoman Deloris reached out and grabbed Richard's hand. "The Imperial High Council received word last month that the Trecorians were having problems with pirates in a black dreadnaught."

Richard noticed Sergeant Ron's eyes focus on his daughter as she continued speaking.

"Additionally, our spies, err…the council received word a Trecorian monitoring station on Planet X3321 was picking up an intermittent anomaly nearby registering a frequency that was also similar to the DNA gas vent."

Richard's mind was slow sometimes, but even he could put one plus one together on occasion. The pieces started falling together. "So are you telling me that my mission on Planet X3321 was to obtain information about this anomaly?"

When the councilwoman didn't reply fast enough, Richard said, "I almost got killed. Why the hell didn't you just ask the Trecorians? Why risk my life? And why me?"

"Why you?" said Myers. "Because I told the councilwoman you were the best. And the council didn't ask them directly because there's a spy in our system somewhere. Which I'm guessing is why you walked into a trap."

Richard was growing angrier. He was supposed to be working for the Empire. Now he'd just found out he'd almost lost his life on a private mission for Councilwoman Deloris. He let his feelings be known. When he was done ranting, the room was quiet for several seconds.

"Rick," said Councilwoman Deloris. "I'll admit I have a vested interest in locating a new DNA gas vent, but the benefits would be for everyone. If we could discover a new vent, maybe the Academy could be reopened. Think about it."

"Doubtful," came Nickelo's thought. *"She was trying to close down the Academy last year before the DNA gas vent was even destroyed, if you remember."*

Richard did remember.

"So you think the anomaly is a new DNA gas vent?" Richard said.

"No," answered Myers. When Richard started to speak, his ex-TAC officer held up his hand to stop him. "But we do believe it may be a lead to another vent. That's why the Imperial High Council approved your transfer to Trecor. You failed to get the required information last time. If you're embedded with them, you may be able to find out something pertinent."

"So you do want me to be a spy?" Disgust dripped from Richard's words.

"No, of course not," Councilwoman Deloris assured. "You're there to help with their training. However, if you should happen to find something out about the anomaly, well…"

"What about the black dreadnaught?" Sergeant Ron asked. "How does it fit in?"

"As you well know, Father," said Councilwoman Deloris, "the pirate's black dreadnaught hasn't been spotted for decades. Our informants tell us Trecorian survivors from an ore convoy were attacked by the Balorian pirates. The survivors reported a black dreadnaught with a dragon insignia accompanied their attackers."

"The black dreadnaught gave off energy readings similar to the DNA gas vent as well," said Myers. "If Shepard can't find anything out about the anomaly, perhaps he can discover something about our mysterious black dreadnaught. My battle computer calculates a sixty-seven percent probability it may lead us to another DNA gas vent."

"Why us?" Richard said. "Why not some of your Conglomerate stooges?" Looking directly at Myers, Richard added, "And why me? You're a wizard scout. Why don't you go?"

Myers's eyes flashed anger and his face turned red. Richard noticed Myers bite his lip in an effort to remain silent.

"Rick," said Councilwoman Deloris. "Gaston wanted to go. But you're the best-rounded wizard scout the Empire has. You possess all of the specialized skills. Since we don't know what we're facing, we don't know what skills may be needed."

Richard took the councilwoman's praise with a grain of salt. She was a politician after all.

"And also because of you, Father," said Councilwoman Deloris. "We all know how obsessed you are with that black dreadnaught."

"I don't," Richard said being honest.

"Oh. Well then, let me enlighten you," said Councilwoman Deloris with an evil-looking smile.

"That won't be necessary," said Sergeant Ron glaring at his daughter. "I'll brief him later."

Sergeant Ron directed his attention to Myers. He pointed at the processor chip in Myers's hand. "So this is why the *Defiant* is getting all this new equipment and the Commandant's battle computer. Because you think we can use it to find the dreadnaught?"

"Or the anomaly," said Myers. "That would be our first choice."

Sergeant Ron rubbed the stubble on his chin. He looked at his daughter. "And is that why you're sending Matthew with us? To keep an eye on your investment?"

The councilwoman gave Sergeant Ron a disgusted look. "You think I'd risk my son's life to be a spy for us?"

When it became obvious from Sergeant Ron's expression it was exactly what he thought, the councilwoman said, "Then you don't know me very well, Father."

"Then why?" said Sergeant Ron.

Councilwoman Deloris gave the table an angry slap. Everyone at the table jumped.

"Because, dammit," she said with anger and frustration in her voice, "he's too much like you. He's been talking about running off and joining the mercenaries ever since the battle at the Academy last year. At least I'll know where he's at if he's with you. From the way Matthew talks, Rick's become some fantasy hero of his. I knew Matthew would jump at the chance to go on the *Defiant*."

"So that's why we got the upgrades on our engine and weapons?" Richard said.

"Yes," answered the councilwoman. "If Matthew has to go running off to sow his wild oats, then I want him to do it in the toughest starship credits can buy. And he'll have his grandfather and you to make sure he stays safe. When his two years are up, I expect him to return and take his proper place at Deloris Armaments."

"Then I guess we're decided," said Sergeant Ron. "If that's okay with you, partner," he hastily added with a look at Richard.

Actually, Richard knew he hadn't fully decided yet, but figured it wouldn't do any good to rehash everything again. Besides, he was tired of talking. He was ready for some action, and he'd decided on just the way to get it.

"Fine," Richard said. "Enough talk. Let's get busy."

CHAPTER 19

When Jeena approached the palace proper, she bypassed the main gates and took a lesser path to the right. The path led to the gardens, which were located right behind the Hall of Meetings. The council hall was where the Council of Light conducted its business. Jeena took a risk the hall would be empty this early in the morning.

She passed three sets of guards along the path. They let her by without any questions. Since High Lord Trenadine and his bondmate Lord Reale had taken Ceril and her in as a part of their family after the death of their parents, most of the palace guards were used to Ceril and her entering the palace unannounced.

At the end of the pathway, Jeena opened the door to the palace garden. She felt a flutter of anticipation as she entered the garden grounds. Once inside, Jeena stopped to let the peace and beauty of the garden envelope her. Every tree, flower, statue, fountain, and bench had been artistically arranged to please the eye. Elves with a talent for beauty had spent the last one hundred thousand years making the garden so. Jeena envied the talent of those elves. She could appreciate the beauty they created, but it was not something she excelled at herself.

Forcing herself to move onward, Jeena entered the council chamber proper. There were no doors on the garden side of the chamber. Only a few columns separated the garden from the council hall. A long row of marble tables spanned the front of the meeting hall. Nine high-backed, stone chairs sat behind the tables;

one for each member of the Council of Light.

As Jeena had expected, the chamber was empty. A small side door to the left of the tables led to the private rooms of the council members. A large set of double-doors on the left side of the chamber was Jeena's destination. Walking quickly to the double-doors, Jeena opened them and passed through to the wide hallway beyond.

Long tapestries hung along both sides of the white-stone hallway. Each tapestry denoted a major event in the long history of the elves. Jeena slowed as she neared her favorite tapestry.

The threads of the tapestry formed an image of the ancient battle between High Priestess Remozorz and the undead army of the Northern Mages. The story behind the tapestry was Jeena's favorite. With only a small band of followers, the gnome Remozorz had defeated the necromancer leader of the Northern Mages and prevented the destruction of the elves. Not only did she save the elves but she saved all the civilized nations as well, regardless of their race. For her efforts, the gnome had been declared Elf Friend.

Jeena scanned the tapestry for the controversial figure in black. She spotted a line of red dots and traced it back to its source. There stood a small figure in black. No scholar had ever found mention of the figure in the historical scrolls, but there the figure was nonetheless. The figure in black fought alongside an elf and gnome. All three were beset by an overwhelming force of undead. What part the figure in black played in the battle, Jeena didn't know. But the part was important enough for the original weavers to include the figure in their tapestry. Even some of the other ancient tapestries along the hallway included a figure in black as well. Many elves thought the weavers of old included the black figure in their works as part of a tradition. Jeena wasn't sure. Art wasn't her field of expertise, so she wisely let those specializing in the artistic skills argue the relevance of the figure in black.

As she continued down the hall, Jeena noted the beauty of the other tapestries, but she didn't slow her pace. Tapestries of scenes noting important historical accomplishments whizzed past. The most elaborate tapestries were scenes from the lives of the Elf Friends. In the long history of the elves, there had only been seven known Elf Friends. The giant Elf Friend Amirithoda had come at a time when the entire race of mountain elves were threatened by destruction as the earth shifted. Tremendous earthquakes had rattled the Thandarhar mountain range from one end to the other. It was Elf Friend Amirithoda's ability to work and communicate with stone that had calmed the mountains and bound the earth whole again.

Another tapestry showed a battle in which the unicorn, Swiftmane, and his elven maid, Mendera, had defeated a demon and its army at the very gates of Silverton itself. Jeena noticed the figure in black was included in that tapestry as well. The black figure was barely visible in the upper left-hand corner fighting some type of fire-breathing dragon.

Jeena continued walking. At the end of the hall, she turned left and then took another left. She passed several rooms full of young elves sitting in chairs facing adult elves. As she walked, Jeena listened to the voices from the rooms.

"...art must be appreciated for its own sake before..."

"Your point is logical, but it is incorrect. You must..."

"Infinity is a useful concept if you..."

"...will produce a more powerful spell when accompanied by..."

"...is the reason we must cherish our history. That's why I stress..."

Jeena smiled as the voices took her back to all the years she'd spent in these same classrooms. Jeena enjoyed learning, so the memories of her studies weren't unpleasant.

"Enough reminiscing, Jeena," she whispered. "The high priest is waiting."

Jeena hurried her pace. Before long she came to a stone stairway. She walked down it until the stairs ended two levels below the palace. The stone in this lowest level of the palace was just roughhewn. Priestess Aldriss once told her all the high priests and priestesses kept their office in the lower level to be nearer the roots of the Tree of Light. Jeena thought it was more likely they were there because some of the more politically-minded members of the Council of Light liked to remind the high priests and priestesses they were just humble servants of the council. Unlike the other council members who were elected by popular vote of the elves, the high priest or high priestess was automatically a council member by virtue of their position. And they were not elected as high priest or high priestess. Only the Lady could designate her highest of servants.

All too quickly, Jeena found herself standing in front of a large granite door with a beautiful carving of the Tree of Light etched into its rough surface. No guards stood before the entrance to the high priest's chamber either.

Although Jeena had spent a lot of time in the palace as the adoptive daughter of High Lord Trenadine, she'd never ventured into its subterranean depths. It wasn't that venturing there was forbidden, she'd just never had the need or desire. Of course, Jeena had never been called to a private meeting with the high priest before.

Unsure of the proper protocol, Jeena knocked on the door before giving it a slight push. The massive weight of the stone door moved easily inward on its hinges. Jeena felt pride at the craftsmanship of her ancestors, the Letian elves. They had constructed the palace with the help of dwarves, gnomes, and giants nearly a hundred thousand years ago. They had done their work so well the door before her operated as it had when the door was first installed.

Stepping inside the circular chamber beyond, Jeena immediately became even more nervous. Five chairs were evenly spaced out on the opposite side of the room. The chairs faced the door from whence she'd entered. Three of the chairs held the residing priestesses and priest of the Lady of the Tree; Priestess Aldriss, Priestess Kantaria, and grumpy old Priest Tobias.

The center of the five seats was occupied by an elf who was wrinkled and bent by his years. The old elf held a staff in his left hand. The staff was aged brown from its years, and it was blackened in several spots from previous battles. The old elf was High Priest Questor, and the staff was the Staff of the Lady of the Tree.

Even for an elf, the high priest was ancient in years. He'd lost his sight to old age centuries earlier. However, he was far from decrepit. Jeena sensed his Power blazing like a bright sun. His aura dimmed those of the priest and priestesses sitting around him.

The fifth chair was vacant. It had been vacant since the tragedy. Jeena choked back an involuntary sob at the sight of the empty seat. It had been empty since the death of her mother, Priestess Elysiathoraxen, nearly two hundred years ago. Why the Lady hadn't yet chosen a successor to replace her mother, Jeena didn't know. Never in the history of the elves had a vacancy in the priesthood remained unfilled for so long.

"Ah, Acolyte Jeehanathoraxen," said the high priest. "You're right on time. I expected no less."

The high priest didn't look at Jeena. Instead, he cocked one ear in her direction as if 'seeing' through sound rather than sight.

"High Priest Questor," Jeena said using her most formal voice. She had no doubt if she made any errors in formality, one or all of the priest and priestesses would point out her errors later that day.

"I came as summoned," Jeena continued with the traditional response. "How may I serve the high priest and the Lady of the Tree?"

The high priest smiled. "Oh, how I long for the days past when others spoke to me as a friend and peer instead of as a stodgy-old high priest."

Spreading his hands with a wry smile, the high priest said, "But alas, those days are gone, and they will never come again, I fear."

Jeena was unsure how to respond, so she remained silent. She'd learned long ago it was often best to keep quiet when she didn't know what to say. And she didn't. The words of the high priest were too relaxed for her own comfort. Besides, the scowls on the faces of Priest Tobias and Priestess Kantaria did little to make her relax. Even the forehead of Priestess Aldriss seemed wrinkled from stress, or was it worry?

Jeena heard a sound behind her. She sensed a flare of magic. She spun around. In a chair beside the door through which she'd just entered sat Master Jathar. He was the Master Mage of the mage guild as well as a member of the Council of Light. Jeena detected the remnants of a rapidly dissipating stealth shield.

He must have had an invisibility spell as well, Jeena thought.

As if sensing her discomfort, High Priest Questor distracted her by asking a question. "What can you tell me about this staff?" he asked as he raised the battered Staff of the Lady of the Tree in his left hand.

Jeena was perplexed. *Why is Master Jathar here? And why is the high priest asking me about the Lady's staff? Is this a test?*

"Ah," said High Priest Questor. "You must work on the control of your facial features, Acolyte Jeehanathoraxen. Your thoughts are as plain as if you were holding up a scroll with them written boldly in common. Of course this is a test." The high priest smiled. "All of life is a test, is it not?"

How the high priest could tell what she was thinking from her facial features when he was blind, was beyond Jeena. However, she willed herself to keep her thoughts off her face just the same.

"Yes, High Priest," Jeena admitted. "It's true. I was indeed wondering if this was a test. The appearance of Master Jathar rattled me."

"You didn't sense my presence before you entered?" asked Master Jathar in what Jeena thought was a harsh voice. "Didn't you think to check the area with a detection spell before you entered? If one of my tenth-year mage apprentices had made such an omission, I would have them paying penitence for a week."

"That's not fair, Master Jathar," said Priestess Kantaria interceding on Jeena's behalf. "Your mage apprentices may be taught advanced detection spells by their tenth year, but our acolytes don't learn them until their twelfth year; as you well know."

"My point exactly," said Master Jathar. "This acolyte is too inexperienced for the task at hand. It should be given to one of the current priestesses or Priest Tobias."

"I agree," said Priest Tobias. "The Staff of the Lady of the Tree is too important to—"

"Enough," said High Priest Questor in a weary voice as he held up his right hand. "The decision has already been made. The quest will be given to our young acolyte." The high priest scanned the others in the room. "Unless one of you wishes to take the matter up with the Lady directly?"

A quest? Jeena thought confusedly. *The Lady? What's going on?*

The room remained silent. Apparently, no one was willing to go against the Lady.

"Very well," said High Priest Questor. "We won't rehash old arguments. So I'm back to my original question, Jeehana—err, you don't mind if I call you Jeehana, do you?

Every elf had three names; a common name, a friend name, and a familiar name. Jeehanathoraxen was Jeena's common name, while Jeena was the familiar name reserved for her family members and dearest friends. Jeehana was her friend name. Why the high priest wanted to call her by her friend name was beyond Jeena. She was only an acolyte.

"Uh, of course not," Jeena said still at a loss as to what was happening in the room. "And, err...to answer your question, the Staff of the Lady of the Tree belonged to High Priestess Shandristiathoraxen almost a hundred thousand years ago. It has been passed down from high priestess to high priest ever since. The staff of the Lady used to be very powerful. Legend has it High Priestess Remozorz used the staff to stop an entire army of undead on the Highlamar Plains.

"Yes," said the high priest. "And every elf child knows what you've just told me. I've heard you read a lot. What else do you know?"

"Err...High Priest," Jeena said feeling as if she were treading on thin ice, "the history of the staff is murky in many places. It stopped working forty thousand years ago. Its gem appears to still have abundant Power, but even the high priest is unable to use the Lady's staff anymore. The staff is more ceremonial than functional."

Realizing who she was talking to, Jeena added, "Uh, that's what I've read, anyway."

High Priest Questor smiled. The others in the room remained stony faced.

"You have read correctly for the most part," agreed the high priest. "But while the staff doesn't have the Power or capabilities it once had, it can still be used to perform a few lesser types of magic."

The high priest raised the Lady's staff high and then let go. It floated in the air until it was an arm's length away from Jeena.

"Take it," said High Priest Questor.

Cautiously reaching out, Jeena grasped the aged, dark-brown wood in the middle of the staff with her left hand. Her fingers tingled with the feeling of dormant Power. She was surprised. It must have shown on her face.

Although blind, the high priest registered Jeena's emotion and the reaction of the staff.

"You see," High Priest Questor said tilting his ear in the direction of Priest Tobias. "The staff does not resist her."

Priest Tobias said nothing, but Jeena thought he looked disappointed.

The high priest turned his attention back to her. "You feel the latent Power, don't you? Most do not. In fact, most cannot even grasp the Lady's staff without being attacked."

He nodded his head as if remembering past attempts to handle the staff. "The Staff of the Lady of the Tree has enormous Power, but it is dormant Power. At least no priest or priestess has been able to make use of it in the past forty thousand years."

Jeena barely heard the high priest. The Power of the staff called to her. It yearned to be set free, but she didn't know how. Still, the feeling of holding so much Power in her hand was unnerving. The training staffs her fellow acolytes and she had been issued were like a soft breeze in comparison to a hurricane in the Northern Sea.

"And this brings us to your quest," said High Priest Questor.

The high priest's words brought Jeena back to reality. She sensed danger in the old elf's words. The staff was forgotten as she gave her undivided attention to the high priest.

Priestess Kantaria spoke next. "The Oracle sent word three nights ago that the time was fast approaching when the staff would be needed once more. The Oracle has requested the Staff of the Lady of the Tree be brought to his sanctuary for repair. The Oracle says the assets necessary to return the staff to its former glory are once again available at his location. However, he says the window of opportunity is small. We must act quickly, or the opportunity will be lost.

"I, of course, am too feeble to make the trek," said High Priest Questor. "The task of taking the Lady's staff to the Oracle must fall to a younger elf."

Jeena looked at the others in the room. None of them were young, but with the exception of the high priest, they were all still in the prime of they're lives. The three-week journey to the Oracle's stronghold would be an easy trek for any of them.

"The Lady has chosen you to carry the staff, Jeehana," said the high priest.

Shocked, Jeena barely had the wherewithal to stammer the word, "Me?"

"Yes you," said Priestess Aldriss. "And do not think to argue. Whatever you can say as to why you shouldn't perform this quest has already been said a dozen times by those much more qualified to know."

"For whatever reason," said High Priest Questor, "the Lady has chosen you as her champion."

Forgetting the admonition not to argue, Jeena said, "But I'm only a tenth-year acolyte. Surely one of the Lady's priestesses or Priest Tobias should be given the quest."

No one in the room bothered to agree with her. Not that Jeena got the impression the others didn't agree. She got the impression the topic had already been argued about until they had finally accepted the idea of Jeena taking on the quest through sheer exhaustion.

Grasping at straws, Jeena remembered something she'd read in one of the ancient scrolls at the library. "It's said only one of the Lady's priests or priestesses can wield the Power of the Lady's staff. I'm not of proper rank to perform the quest. The honor should go to another."

"You are correct," agreed High Priest Questor. "Only a priest or priestess may wield the Staff of the Lady of the Tree."

Jeena breathed a sigh of relief. The high priest was finally being reasonable.

"And that's why," said the high priest, "as of this moment, you are no longer an acolyte. You are henceforth Priestess Jeehanathoraxen of the Lady of the Tree."

The word shocked didn't do justice to the feeling that swept over Jeena. Even stunned and overwhelmed were too non-descriptive.

"But I'm a tenth-year acolyte," Jeena insisted. "The path to the priesthood takes centuries. I'm untrained."

"Enough!" said High Priest Questor as he stood and raised his voice for the first time. "The decision has been made. The Lady has decided. It is not the place for you or anyone else in this room to argue. You will leave immediately for the Oracle. You will leave within the hour. You are a priestess now."

With those words, High Priest Questor glared at the others in the room. It was a strange action to have the blind eyes of the high priest lock with hers. However, his actions were effective. Neither the others nor she tried to argue; at least not verbally. But from the looks on Priest Tobias and Master Jathar, Jeena had no doubt they had a multitude of arguments bouncing around inside them.

Although laden with self-doubts, Jeena resigned herself to her unexpected quest.

"Has my escort been prepared?" Jeena said thinking of how much there was to do in so little time. She had to pack. She had to tell her adoptive parents, Lord Reale and High Lord Trenadine, goodbye. And she had to find her brother, Ceril, and let him know where she'd be. Plus she needed to go to the library and find some books on the Oracle as well as maps for her trek. The path to the Oracle's stronghold was an arduous one. Much of the path crossed the lands of the humans. Only a strong guard of elven warriors could guarantee safe passage.

"There will be no escort," said High Priest Questor. "You will travel alone. Priestess Aldriss already has your pack ready along with the necessary maps. Once you leave this room, you will go directly to the city gate and depart."

"But—" Jeena began forgetting the command not to argue. She knew a lone female elf traveling in the lands of the humans was asking for death or worse. Humans, especially human males, were unable to control their emotions. Their lustful thoughts and intense feelings had been known to make emotion-sensitive female elves physically sick. Jeena had no desire to cross paths with any humans. Especially considering what they'd done to her family.

"There are no buts," said High Priest Questor cutting Jeena off. "The Oracle wants you to travel alone. The Lady concurs."

From her readings, Jeena knew the Lady of the Tree used to talk to her priests and priestesses via a form of telepathy. However, those days were long past. She had no doubt when the high priest spoke of the Lady concurring, he was just interpreting the emotions he sensed from the Lady when he prayed for guidance. Although inexperienced in the priestly ways, Jeena was pretty sure the interpretation of emotional responses left a lot of room for interpretation.

He has to be interpreting her emotions wrong, Jeena thought. *I'm not qualified for such a task. I cannot be a priestess. The Lady hasn't even had a selection ceremony.*

Priests and priestesses weren't elected. The Lady chose her

closest disciples during a selection ceremony held around the Tree of Light. Jeena had been chosen as an acolyte during a smaller version of such a ceremony. A branch of the Tree of Light had reached out and placed a circlet of leaves around her head as she'd knelt with a group of other petitioners. Her selection ceremony for acolyte had been ten years ago.

"Actually," said Priestess Aldriss, "you will be escorted by a squad of elven scouts to the edge of Silvertine's lands. After you cross the river Silvore, you will be on your own until you arrive at the Oracle's."

"Upon your return," said Priestess Kantaria, "you will present yourself to the Lady at a selection ceremony. You will receive your priestess staff at that time, assuming the Lady still wants you as her priestess. But until then, for all intents and purposes, you are a priestess now."

"And also upon your return," added Priest Tobias, "you'll begin an accelerated course of training that may make you wish you'd never been promoted early to the position of priestess."

I already wish that, Jeena thought.

"Do you have any questions?" asked High Priest Questor.

Jeena had a thousand questions, but had to deal with the most pressing first. "You say I won't have an escort, High Priest," Jeena said making one last attempt to tactfully point out reasons why she shouldn't go. "Aren't the lands of the humans too dangerous for a lone, female elf to cross on her own? You know the history of my family. Surely I have a reason to be concerned. The first human male I meet is liable to try and have his way with me. Everyone knows how they are."

"You make a valid point, priestess," said High Lord Questor. "And that brings us to why Master Jathar has attended our meeting."

Jeena turned and glanced at the master mage. She didn't like the look in his eyes nor the smirk on his face. Jeena had a feeling she wasn't going to like whatever the mage had up his sleeves for her.

CHAPTER 20

"So you're going to go through with it?" asked Sergeant Ron.

"I'm going to give it a shot," Richard said. "Whether it'll work or not, I have no idea. He may not even come."

Sergeant Ron and Richard were sitting in the control room. A miniature set of buildings were displayed on the holographic table between them.

"Margery?" Richard asked. "You don't mind if I call you Margery, do you?"

"Of course not, wizard scout," said a feminine voice. "Thomas was very fond of you, and you're his son. I'm sure he wouldn't mind. I certainly don't."

The source of Margery's voice was hard for Richard to pinpoint. According to Sergeant Ron, the entire ship had speakers and video equipment embedded throughout most of the *Defiant's* inside bulkheads. With the equipment, Margery could monitor and interact with the ship's crew in almost every part of the ship.

"Good," Richard said. "So where do you think he's located?"

The holograph shifted and zoomed in until it encompassed only one of the buildings. The holograph continued to zoom until the entire table was taken up by a single room. It was a cell.

"Analysis?" Richard said.

"Based upon what data I can glean from the tele-network," said Margery, "your package should be in this room. The cell is composed of energized titanium in the walls, ceiling, and floor to prevent teleportation."

"Is that standard procedure?" asked Sergeant Ron.

"Negative, captain," answered Margery. "The specially processed titanium required to create creallium is too expensive to use in every cell. My databanks indicate only one percent of the cells at Diajor are protected thus. Those cells are reserved for the most dangerous prisoners. Other sensitive areas such as control rooms and the like are also protected by energized titanium."

"What are the odds they'd have Sergeant Hendricks in a cell with that kind of security under normal conditions?" Richard said. "I mean, it's not like he's a desperate criminal."

"The odds are near zero, Rick," came Nickelo's voice over the external speakers of Richard's battle helmet where he'd propped it up on the copilot's seat. "I calculate a seventy-two percent probability Sergeant Hendricks is there because someone suspects you might try something stupid."

"Well then, they're right," Richard said.

Looking at his battle computer, Richard added, "I wish you were going with me, Nick."

"So do I," agreed Nickelo. "But I'm needed here to assist Margery with her integration. The central computer has provided a special security interface to allow us to communicate; at least for now."

"You know," said Sergeant Ron, "even if you get Sergeant Hendricks, you can't bring him back here. The *Defiant* will be the first place they'll look. Once we get off planet, it will be safe, but not here."

Richard nodded. "I know. That's why I'm going to take Sergeant Hendricks directly to Trecor with me. The Empire and Trecor don't have an extradition treaty, or so Nick tells me."

"Your battle computer is correct," said Margery.

"So do you know how you're going to do it?" said Sergeant Ron.

"Not really," Richard admitted.

"Oh, you know our Rick, Sergeant Ron," said Nickelo with a stifled laugh. "He's not much into planning."

Richard ignored his battle computer. "Well, I guess I'll see you guys next month on Trecor. No use wasting time. Once I'm gone, let Myers know I won't need a teleport after all."

"Will do, partner," said Sergeant Ron.

Richard stood and picked up his battle helmet. He shook hands with Sergeant Ron. "Take care of 'em for me, Margery."

"Will comply, wizard scout," said Margery.

Richard went back to his room and changed into a generic soldier's uniform that he pulled out of his dimensional pack. He pulled a camouflage suit out of his pack and put it on over his uniform. Once dressed, Richard left his battle computer, battle helmet, dimensional pack, and the rest of his gear on his bunk.

"I wish you could take your wizard scout gear with you," said Nickelo into their shared space, *"but it would be a dead giveaway if any of your equipment were caught on one of the security cameras on Diajor."*

"Understood," Richard said. *"It won't be my first mission without gear."*

Richard glanced around the room. He felt empty-handed. Nickelo had convinced him not to take any weapons. The guards on Diajor were Empire soldiers. They weren't the enemy. If he was discovered, and the guards started firing, Richard was pretty sure he'd return fire if he had a weapon. Without a weapon, he wouldn't be tempted.

Taking a final look around, Richard activated his best stealth shield as he sent a call for help out into the universe. In the call, Richard pictured a black stallion with glowing-red eyes and claws instead of hoofs.

Richard didn't know if Sheeta, the leader of the dolgar pack, would send him the spirit-horse or not. He could only wait and find out one way or the other.

During his first mission for *'the One'* on the planet Portalis in the magical dimension, Richard had encountered a Master demon who'd linked him up with a pack of wolf-like creatures in the spiritual dimension called dolgars. For some reason, one of the female dolgars, Sheba, had adopted him as one of her pups. Both Sheba and her mate, Sheeta, had since been with him on several missions for *'the One.'* Sheeta had even introduced Richard to a spirit-horse, which Richard thought was really more a demon than it was a horse. However, the spirit-horse could travel between dimensions while carrying a rider, and that's what Richard needed now. Unfortunately, the spirit-horse was not at Richard's beck and call. It only came when Sheeta saw fit to send it. Consequently, all

Richard could do now was wait.

Richard sighed. *I really hate waiting.*

CHAPTER 21

A full two hours passed before a disturbance in the void caught Richard's attention. He recognized the Power frequency of the spirit-horse. The dolgar, Sheeta, was not with the stallion. Richard wasn't concerned. All he needed was the stallion.

Within seconds, Richard sensed the spirit-horse in the void below the floor of his room. After a final glance around the cabin, he wrapped himself in Power and shifted into the void. As soon as he levitated down and mounted the spirit-horse, black tendrils came out of the stallion's back and twisted around his legs and waist securing him in place. Power reached out from the stallion and took over Richard's shift in the void. Once the stallion did that, Richard dropped his own shift to conserve Power.

An emotion from the spirit-horse gave Richard the impression the stallion was asking for directions. From previous experience, Richard knew his mount only condescended to carry him as a favor to Sheeta. The stallion's impatience was obvious.

Wasting no time, Richard sent an image of Diajor's military prison to his mount. The stallion apparently needed no other directions because he immediately did a full shift into another dimension. Richard was shifted along with the stallion. During the next thirty minutes, the stallion shifted through a dozen dimensions before Richard sensed they were back in the void next to the physical dimension. A quick active scan confirmed they were beneath Diajor's military prison.

It was dark in the void, but it didn't matter. Richard's passive scan gave him a lot of information about the section of the physical dimension surrounding him. Richard sent out an active scan to the cell Margery had indicated was the probable holding area of Sergeant Hendricks. Richard hoped for the best. When the active scan returned, he sighed with relief. Not a physical sigh, of course, since he didn't breathe while in the void, but he thought of his reaction as a sigh. In any regard, he was relieved. His active scan confirmed the cell's occupant. Based upon the frequency of the life form, Richard knew the prisoner inside was ex-Sergeant Hendricks.

Now what? Richard thought wishing his battle computer was here to talk things over with. *"Nick? By any chance are you there?"*

No answer was forthcoming. Richard hadn't really expected any. For one thing, Diajor was 40,000 light years from Risors. For another, he was in the void. Since he'd gotten his shared space, he'd discovered he could communicate with his battle computer at a considerable distance. However, based upon the current communication, the max range was either less than 40,000 light years, or it was limited to the same dimension.

Well, he's not here to help, Rick, old buddy, so stop your stalling and get the lead out.

Richard sent an image to the spirit-horse upon which he rode. He imagined them moving to a position underneath the cell. Richard felt the stallion beneath him vibrate as his mount changed positions as requested. Fortunately, the cells around their target were not high-security cells. They weren't composed of energized titanium. If they had been, Richard doubted he would be able to get to Sergeant Hendricks's cell.

Once they were below the sergeant's cell, Richard spent several hours tracking the flows of energy in the area above him. He pinpointed every alarm, video camera, audio sensor, and control panel around the cell as well as the nearby cells and hallways. He also used his passive scan to trace the movement of the guards. When he finished all the preparatory work he thought reasonable, Richard reached out with his mind and began looping energy flows in the alarms back upon themselves.

Disabling the alarms was no big deal. Richard had spent three years on the streets after he'd left the orphanage. During that time, he'd used his skills to bypass a lot of alarms while stealing food. He wasn't proud of the things he'd done while trying to stay alive during that period of his life, but it was what it was. He put those acquired skill sets to good use now.

Once the alarms were deactivated, Richard had the stallion switch positions again until he was in the void directly beneath the hallway floor next to Sergeant Hendricks's cell. Richard waited for the roving guard to make his rounds. As the guard passed overhead, Richard pictured himself getting off the stallion. The long, black tendrils securing Richard to the back of the stallion untwined and retracted back into the stallion's back and sides.

Up until this point, his mount had been keeping him in the void. That needed to change. Wrapping himself in Power, Richard shifted himself in the void just as he felt the stallion remove his Power and move away.

"No," Richard growled using the dolgar's language. "Stay. I return soon."

The stallion sent Richard an emotion letting him know it wasn't happy.

Too bad, Richard thought, making sure he wasn't sending his words to the stallion. *You'll just have to deal with it.*

The stallion and Richard had fought as allies on several missions over the years, but that didn't mean they were friends. As he had come to find out from one of the dolgar pups, the spirit-horse only condescended to carry him as a favor to Sheeta. He had no doubt that if the stallion had its druthers, it would quite happily leave him stranded on Diajor.

As the guard passed overhead, Richard sent out lines of Power to deactivate the prison's video and audio equipment monitoring the hallway. He also disabled all of the monitoring equipment for the hallway's cells as well as that of the nearest control room. Simultaneously, Richard rose through the hallway floor. When his feet were clear, he shifted back into the physical dimension directly behind the guard.

Although the guard was a large, burly man, he went down easily enough with a single hand chop to the side of his neck. Richard grudgingly gave silent thanks to the hundreds of hours his Academy TAC officer had spent training their cadets in hand-to-hand combat. Wasting no time, he grabbed the stun rod on the guard's belt before the unconscious man even hit the floor. In the blink of an eye, Richard was halfway down the hall and running hard for the locked door to the control room for this section of the prison.

Reaching out with his mind, Richard coaxed the locking mechanism's energy to complete the circuit necessary to open the control-room door. Pneumatic pistons started sliding a thick metal panel to one side. Before the door even completed opening, Richard twisted his body sideways and fairly flew into the room beyond. Three guards were inside. Two of them were fiddling with an array of video screens that were currently showing static instead of what Richard assumed would be their normal views of the hallway and cells. The third guard was standing a couple of meters away holding a multi-barreled riot gun. Richard sensed stun rounds inside the magazine of the guard's weapon.

The armed guard raised her riot gun. Richard could tell from the confused look on her face she was having trouble picking out a target. While Richard's camouflage suit didn't make him invisible, from experience, he knew his form would only appear as an indistinct blur against the background behind it.

Before the armed guard could fully react, Richard was on her. A blow to the side of her head with his confiscated stun rod dropped the woman to her knees. The riot gun fell from her limp hands. Scooping up the riot gun, Richard turned toward the remaining guards.

The two guards near the video displays were scrambling to separate. One of the guards grabbed for a hand blaster on his hip. Richard didn't give him time to complete his move. He pulled the trigger on the riot gun. The weapon's six barrels coughed a hand length of fire out its tubes as its stun rounds separated into a hundred and twenty individual pellets of energy. The guard was knocked back into the wall behind. His handgun remained in his holster as he fell to the floor.

The remaining guard didn't try for her weapon. Instead, she dove for a red button on a nearby control panel. Richard intercepted her and threw her against the wall. The guard pulled a stun rod from her belt and swung at Richard's head. Thanks to his camouflage suit, the guard's aim was off. She hit Richard's right collarbone instead of his head. A flash of pain shot up his shoulder as he heard the sound of a snapping bone.

Semi-blinded from the flash of pain, Richard reached out to where his passive scan told him the guard was located and punched her in the solar plexus. He heard a whoosh of air. As his vision returned, he saw the guard bending over holding her stomach. He gave the guard a quick chop to the back of the neck. She joined her two companions on the floor.

Glancing at his passive scan, Richard made sure the three guards weren't seriously injured. They weren't his enemy. From their energy flows, he could tell they were just unconscious. They'd be hurting when they woke, but they'd be alive.

Using his passive scan on the instruments in the control room, Richard let their energy fill his mind. He found what he sought. Moving to a nearby console, he flicked off a switch over a label reading cell 24.

Without wasting any more time, Richard ran back into the hallway. The roving guard was trying to raise himself into a sitting position. Richard put him back on the floor with a half kick to the side of the head.

Without stopping, Richard continued running until he was even with cell 24. He pushed on the door. It was still locked.

Damn, Richard thought.

Reaching out with his mind, Richard spotted the problem. A backup locking mechanism had activated when he'd turned off the primary lock. Although the energy flow in the secondary lock was less complex than many of the locks he'd disabled during his life, Richard didn't think he had the time to mess with it right now. He had no doubt other control stations were even now trying to figure out what was going on with the monitoring equipment in this section of the prison. They were bound to sound the alarm soon.

As if in confirmation of Richard's thought, a loud clanging began reverberating throughout the prison. Ignoring his usual preference for conserving Power, Richard shifted into the void again. He was much more efficient at dimensional shifting than he'd once been, but his shift was still Power hungry nonetheless. Richard could feel his Power reserve draining at a pace much faster than he would like.

While the secondary lock had been activated to secure the door, the titanium in the cell's door and walls was no longer energized.

Consequently, Richard had no problem levitating himself through the door to the cell on the other side. The room's lone prisoner was sitting on his cot looking confusedly at the solid door. The prisoner was Sergeant Hendricks.

Richard shifted back into the physical dimension as he thumbed the off switch for his camouflage suit. The focus of Sergeant Hendricks's eyes shifted to the strips of camouflage cloth covering Richard's face and eyes.

"Who are you?" demanded Sergeant Hendricks as he jumped to his feet and raised his hands into a martial-arts defensive position.

Although Richard had disabled the monitoring equipment in this section of the prison, he had no doubt technicians were even now trying to return all of it to working order. Plus, he figured the prison was probably inundated with tele-bots. Although certain individuals would undoubtedly guess he was the one responsible for the prison break, Richard had no desire to give them physical evidence that could be used during a court martial.

Pulling a card out of a pocket on his camouflage suit, Richard faced the card toward Sergeant Hendricks. The card read: Can't talk; voice recognition. Do you want to be free? Yes or no?

Richard figured Sergeant Hendricks's mind must work faster than his because the ex-Academy armorer didn't hesitate with his answer.

"Hell yeah I want out of this stinkin' place," said Sergeant Hendricks. "How—"

Without giving the sergeant time to start asking questions, Richard wrapped both of them in Power and shifted them into the void. Sergeant Hendricks gave a half-scream, half-expletive, as Richard levitated both of them down into the floor. Richard felt sorry for Sergeant Hendricks. He knew the feeling of being encased in solid material was a terrifying experience. Richard wished he'd had the time to explain, but he hadn't, so there was nothing he could do about it. He just kept levitating both of them downward until their heads disappeared into the cell's floor. They were in the void.

Richard made a desperate call to his spirit-horse. Shifting himself into the void required a lot of Power. Shifting two people effectively doubled the Power requirement. Richard cursed when he realized the stallion had moved. Before he could think of a secondary plan, the stallion appeared next to him. Richard mounted on the spirit-horse as he pulled Sergeant Hendricks in front of him. Black tendrils came out of the stallion and wrapped around his hips and legs securing him to the spirit-horse's back. Richard noticed the stallion didn't bother trying to secure Sergeant Hendricks. Richard clutched the armorer tight and sent the image of Trecor's primary spaceport terminal to the stallion. Richard was thankful Nickelo had made him memorize the image earlier. He dropped his dimensional shift when he felt the Power from the stallion take over. Fortunately, the stallion condescended to shifting Sergeant Hendricks into the void as well as him.

The spirit-horse and its riders vibrated as the stallion shifted completely into a second dimension. Richard saw and felt a blur of landscapes as the spirit-horse jumped from one dimension to another. How it navigated was beyond Richard. But he'd ridden the stallion enough during missions for 'the One' to know it could find its way around multiple galaxies without any problem. Richard had confidence in his mount. Unfortunately, he had no idea how long it would take to reach Trecor.

When the stallion shifted onto a planet with breathable air, Richard took a moment to verbally explain what was happening to Sergeant Hendricks. All things considered, the sergeant took the news relatively well. Their respite didn't last long as the stallion shifted them back into the void and dove into the solid rock below. Everything went black once again.

After another five minutes, Richard sensed the stallion shift into another dimension. This dimension felt familiar. Richard was fairly certain they were back in the physical dimension. Life forms registering on his passive scan told Richard the stallion had stopped a few meters below the surface of whatever world they were at. Richard sent an active scan overhead. He sensed energy flows he associated with starships and other heavy equipment. They'd reached their destination.

Wrapping both Sergeant Hendricks and himself with Power, Richard took over their dimensional shift in the void. He sent a thought of them getting off of the stallion. The tendrils securing him to the spirit-horse's back withdrew as Richard levitated upward. He sent a thought of thanks to the stallion. The ornery spirit-horse didn't bother answering. Richard sensed him shifting into another dimension. Then he was gone.

Yeah, same to you buddy, Richard thought. After several missions with the stallion, he still didn't have a good handle on their relationship.

Shrugging it off, Richard continued levitating Sergeant Hendricks and himself upward. They emerged through thick asphalt into bright sunlight. Richard sensed hundreds if not thousands of life forms around him. Someone screamed in fright. Before long, a score of armed security guards arrived. A few seconds later, both Sergeant Hendricks and he were lying on the ground with their hands secured behind their backs. Richard didn't try to resist.

"Sorry boys," Richard said in Empire standard. "Did we forget to pass through immigration?"

The guards were not amused. One of them gave Richard a kick in the ribs.

Tough audience, Richard thought as he suppressed a groan. He wondered if Nickelo would approve of the way he'd handled the prison break.

Richard doubted it.

CHAPTER 22

The man standing before Richard was tall. He was at least a hands breath taller than Richard. The big man's blond hair and penetrating blue-steel eyes met Richard's as if he were trying to read his mettle.

"Leave us," said the tall man to the two guards standing on either side of Richard.

The guards snapped to attention and saluted. "Yes, sir!"

With a precise movement Richard could appreciate from his years at the Academy, the guards made an about face and left the room.

Two other individuals were in the room as well. One was a female dressed in the uniform of a mechanized soldier. Richard recognized the rank insignia as the Trecorians' version of a colonel. An older man in a naval uniform stood next to her. Richard was pretty sure he was some kind of admiral, but he wasn't sure of the level. The two stood at parade rest in deference to the blond-haired man. The blond-haired man was Duke Bistoria, commander-in-chief of the Trecorian armed forces. According to Nickelo's pre-mission briefing, the duke was also the interim political-leader of the Trecorian Planetary Alliance.

"When we were notified your scheduled teleport had been canceled," said the duke as he continued to eye Richard, "we assumed you weren't coming."

Richard stood at parade rest. The scene felt familiar. It reminded him of all the times he'd stood in front of the

Commandant during his Academy days.

"Sorry, sir. I was inadvertently delayed. I had to make alternate transportation arrangements."

For a moment, Richard thought he saw the corners of the duke's lips twitch as if he wanted to smile, but that he was forcing himself to appear stern.

"And you brought company," said the duke. "Admiral Formida, you look like you want to say something. Spit it out, John. I know you're chomping at the steering levers to speak."

"My duke," said the older man in a voice hinting at years of familiarity. "In answer to our query, the Empire has informed us one of our prisoners is in fact an escaped convict from Diajor. They also hinted this prisoner, err…this wizard scout, is a prime suspect as an accessory to the escape."

"These men are our guests," corrected Duke Bistoria. "They aren't our prisoners."

"Uh, of course, my duke," said Admiral Formida. "But nevertheless, our second…err…guest, broke out of Diajor just a few hours before they showed up here. Our sources in the Empire say our second 'guest' is considered dangerous."

"Hmm," said the duke as he switched his attention back to Richard. "Is your friend dangerous?"

"No, sir," Richard said. "He's just…uh, misunderstood."

This time Richard was sure he saw the corners of the duke's lips twitch. But the duke quickly got his emotions under control. "I suspect you're wondering why we requested your transfer to Trecor, Wizard Scout Shepard."

"Yes, sir," Richard admitted. "I was told it had something to do with training. But…"

"But you think there might be more to it than that," said the duke more as a statement than a question.

"It does seem strange," Richard said.

The duke looked at Richard for several seconds as if struggling with an internal battle. Richard met the duke's gaze straight on. Finally, the duke nodded his head as if coming to a decision.

"The truth is we do want your assistance in training," said the duke.

Richard noticed the female's lips twitch as if she wanted to disagree, but she remained silent. The duke must have noticed the twitch as well.

"This is Colonel Santos," said the duke with a gesture toward the female. "She's in charge of the 147th Mechanized Regiment. They're the personal guard of the Bistoria family. You'll be attached to her unit for the initial part of your assignment on Trecor.

Richard gave the colonel a nod of his head in acknowledgment. She gave a curt nod in return. The colonel gave Richard the impression she didn't consider his assignment to her unit an honor.

"But you're correct," said Duke Bistoria. "That's not the only reason you're here."

The duke turned his attention back to the two officers. "Admiral, Colonel, would you excuse us, please?"

"Sir?" said the admiral.

"I'd like to be alone with our guest."

"Uh, yes. Of course, sir," said the admiral. "I'll send the guards back in."

"That won't be necessary, Admiral," said the duke.

The admiral opened his mouth but immediately closed it. He glared at Richard giving him a non-verbal warning to behave. Then the admiral snapped to attention and saluted the duke. "Yes, sir."

The colonel followed suit. Once the duke returned their salutes, the two officers left the room through a door to their rear. When the door slid shut behind them, the duke seemed to relax.

Sitting down, the duke leaned back in his chair and eyed Richard. "You were outnumbered twelve to one on Planet X3321, but you still took out four of our best crews."

Richard said nothing. He'd been nervous about coming on this assignment in the first place. The two hours of interrogation he'd been subjected to before being brought to the duke's office had done nothing to alleviate his uneasiness. Plus, he was unsure of the whereabouts of Sergeant Hendricks. They'd been separated shortly after their unannounced arrival. Richard figured his best option was to say as little as possible until he got a better lay of the land.

"What was your mission on Planet X3321?" asked the duke. He was apparently not one to waste time beating around the galaxy.

"Uh, sir," Richard said. "I'm sure you know I can neither confirm nor deny missions."

"Naturally," said the duke. "I expected no less."

The duke touched the side of his nose with a finger and then leaned forward as if sharing a confidence. "Then let me hazard a guess. You were sent to Planet X3321 to acquire information about a recent anomaly in our sector."

Richard tried not to give away his surprise, but based upon the half smile on the duke's face, he had a feeling he wasn't succeeding.

"Ah," said the duke. "Based upon your reaction, I'm guessing our information was correct. Would it surprise you to know we were warned someone would be coming? And we knew the exact date and time?"

This time, Richard knew he wasn't doing a very good job of keeping the surprise off his face. "Who gave you that information, sir?"

"Come now, wizard scout. Surely you don't expect me to reveal my sources any more than you're willing to confirm your mission."

The duke gave a slight smile. "But I will tell you we didn't know who was coming, only that someone would be. If I'd known it was going to be the hero of last year's Academy battle, I'd probably have handled things differently."

Richard was confused. Thanks to a few stories on the IEN station, he was not unknown in some parts of the Empire, but he was hardly famous, in his opinion. "Me, sir?"

"My daughter said you were humble," said Duke Bistoria. "I see she was right."

"You mean Captain Bistos, sir?" Richard said knowing full well the duke did. He needed time to think, so was determined to stall for time any way he could.

"Actually, she's Commodore Bistos now," said the duke. "She was promoted two weeks ago."

"I'm impressed," Richard said. "She's moving up the ranks fast."

"Yes, she is," the duke said using a strange tone. "I hazard a guess that's why she volunteered for duty with the Empire instead of opting for Trecor's military."

"To make rank fast?" Richard asked. "Surely she'd have done as well in the Trecorian Navy."

Richard had asked his question without considering he might be delving into the personal lives of the Bistoria family. Fortunately, the duke didn't seem to mind.

"Perhaps," said the duke. "But I'd guess the main reason she chose the Empire was to prove to herself she could do it on her own."

Richard gave the duke a questioning look.

"Oh, come now, wizard scout. Surely you can imagine how difficult it would be living under the shadow of your royal relatives. You'd always wonder whether your achievements were based upon merit or more upon who you were."

Actually, Richard couldn't imagine. He wasn't royalty, and he didn't want to be.

"But I digress," said the duke. "The point I was trying to make was that we thought we were ready for anything. Obviously, we were wrong. Outgunned twelve to one, you destroyed four of our cats and managed to escape unscathed."

"I was hardly unscathed, sir," Richard said. "My Warcat was shot out from underneath me. Not to mention someone put a fist-sized hole through my left shoulder."

"Yes," said the duke. "But only because you insisted on staying and saving the lives of two of Trecoria's finest cat pilots." The duke's voice softened. "You have no idea how much I appreciate what you did. The lives of all my soldiers are precious to me, but some are more precious than others." The duke looked down at his desk for several seconds before looking back at Richard. "I need to know why you did it. I doubt the Empire's standard operating procedures are to save the lives of those who are trying to kill you."

For a second, Richard almost gave a flippant answer. But then he saw the look on the duke's face. It was the look of a man who had a desperate desire to know.

"My orders, sir, were to not kill anyone if it could be helped."

"And was that the only reason you risked your life to stay and rescue those cat pilots?" asked the duke.

Richard contemplated the scene in his memory for a second before answering. "No, sir."

Letting his shields down was something Richard normally avoided, but he decided to take a risk now. After all, the duke was Liz's father.

"The cat was on fire," Richard said, "and the two pilots were trapped. When I saw another pilot trying to beat his way in from the outside...well, sir, I guess I just imagined how I'd feel if it were my friends trapped inside that burning cat." Richard thought of the burning cat and the frantic efforts of the Trecorian pilot to free his companions. "If it had been anything other than fire," Richard said momentarily forgetting who he was talking to, "I...I don't know. Well, I just couldn't leave them to burn."

The duke was silent for several seconds. He seemed to be giving Richard time to compose himself. Richard noticed him pretending to read his computer screen.

"Sir, there were children at the battle. I didn't kill any of them, did I?"

The duke shook his head no.

Richard breathed a sigh of relief. He'd done some bad things during his life, but he'd never killed a child and had no desire to start.

The duke remained silent for a while as if lost in thought. When the duke spoke again, his voice had taken on a hard edge. "Three companies of cadets were on the planet for training. They were under orders to stay well clear of the fight. Their commander made a mistake. That situation has been rectified."

"Sir?" Richard said trying to figure out what the duke was saying.

"Never mind," said the duke. "But then again, their commander thought you were a normal recon soldier, as did we all. He had you outnumbered three hundred to one. Even considering his command was composed of cadets, their commander assumed his infantry would have no trouble preventing you from leaving the kill zone of our trap. The cadet's commander had both armor and air support along with his infantry. But you still managed to break out of what should have been your death trap."

Richard said nothing.

"And that brings us to the second reason why you're here," said the duke with a hint of nervousness.

"Sir?" Richard said, curious about the change in the duke's demeanor but trying not to sound like he was curious.

"You seriously wounded several of our soldiers," said the duke.

Richard nodded. He wasn't sure where the duke was going and

began to get a little nervous.

"Elizabeth and Terrie say you're a healer."

"Yes, sir," Richard said. He wasn't sure who Terrie was, but Liz was certainly familiar with most of his wizard scout abilities.

Is that why he wants me here? Richard wondered. *To heal his soldiers?* He unconsciously shook his head. *He's barking up the wrong tree if he thinks I'm going to heal any more of the soldiers who were trying to kill me.*

"I'm an emp-healer," Richard said. "Surely you have healers of your own."

The duke nodded his head. "We have some of the best in the galaxy. But a few of the injuries continue to resist the combined efforts of our medical teams. Elizabeth thinks you may know why and be able to help."

"How would I know?" Richard asked bewildered. "A wound is a wound."

"Maybe," said the duke sounding unconvinced. "But perhaps you'd take a look before you form an opinion."

CHAPTER 23

The old hag looked back at Jeena in the fading light. Her greasy, gray hair was a tangled mess that hid much of the crone's wrinkled face. The old woman's eyes were a dull gray. She smiled revealing crooked-yellow teeth with large gaps denoting places where a majority of her teeth had rotted away.

Jeena splashed her hand in the water. The ripples momentarily obliterated the reflection of the old hag. But the image quickly returned as the water stilled.

"I'll say one thing for Master Jathar," Jeena told her reflection. "He has one hell of a polymorph spell."

With a final look at her reflection, Jeena finished filling her canteen and retraced her steps along the animal trail in the direction of her camp.

As Priestess Aldriss had said would happen, her escort of elven scouts had left her at the Silvore river. That had been twelve days ago. On the advice of Priestess Kantaria, Jeena had made cold camps ever since she'd entered the lands of the humans. The absence of a fire at night had hidden her from prying eyes, but had also taken a toll on her emotionally and physically.

The first snow of winter had begun falling two days ago and continued still. Both her days and nights had been turned into a continuous series of shivering and sneezing. The kit packed by Priestess Aldriss fell right in line with what one would expect an old crone traveling alone to possess. In other words, she had almost nothing to keep her warm or dry. Priestess Aldriss had assured her if she had nothing to steal, robbers would leave her alone. However, Jeena found scant comfort in her mentor's opinion since she was basically freezing to death.

So far, Priestess Aldriss's plan for avoiding robbers and thieves had worked. No one had tried to steal her meager belongings. But then, she hadn't seen anyone either. While Jeena had spied the smoke of an occasional fire, she'd avoided the isolated farmhouses and camps for fear of what could happen.

Finally, after two days of walking in knee-deep snow and subsisting on cold cheese and semi-frozen grapes, Jeena had come to the end of her vine. She knew if she didn't get a hot meal soon, she'd never make it to the Oracle.

With reluctance, Jeena had set a snare and asked a young rabbit to sacrifice itself for her benefit. With a prayer of thanks and a heartfelt request for forgiveness, Jeena had placed the quartered rabbit in her cooking pot along with some wild onions and a potato she'd been fortunate enough to forage.

As Jeena walked back toward her camp, she could smell the enticing aroma of the rabbit stew as it boiled over her small fire. With liberal use of the fresh water in her canteen, she had high hopes of soon enjoying a plate of warm stew and a hot cup of pine-needle tea. Jeena's stomach rumbled in anticipation of her upcoming feast.

As soon as the sight of her lean-to and small fire came into view, Jeena heard a voice that sent shivers down her spine.

"Well, well," said a deep, gravelly voice. "Didn't I say if we waited long enough someone would return and invite us to stay for supper?"

The sound of laughter from multiple voices came out of the brush on either side of Jeena.

"So you did, Stavis," said a second voice. "But I was hoping for something a little younger to help keep the chill away tonight. It promises to be a cold one again."

A flood of primitive emotions swept over Jeena from all sides, hitting her in the stomach like a balled fist. She bent over and almost fell to her knees, but caught herself with the aid of the Lady's staff. Jeena wracked her brain for any spell that might be of use but came up empty. Tenth-year acolytes weren't trained in offensive spells; at least not any that would be useful in a real fight. And Priestess Aldriss hadn't seen fit to provide her with a wand. The priestess had told her carrying a wand would draw too much attention.

A large, scraggly-bearded man stepped from behind Jeena's lean-to. He eyed her before turning his attention to the pot of stew. "I hope you can cook better than you look, old woman," said the large man. "Otherwise, we may not have a use for you."

"And wouldn't that be a pity," said a voice behind Jeena.

Spinning around, Jeena spied a fat, balding man dressed in rags that were almost as full of holes as her own. However, the dagger in his left hand was top notch. Its blade looked sharp, and there was no sign of rust.

Two other men stepped out onto the trail. One was a human boy not much older than her in human years, but the evil grin on his pockmarked face did nothing to soothe Jeena's fears. Instinct told her the teenager was a born killer. The raw emotions she felt coming from the youth told her he was someone who killed for the sheer joy of killing.

Even from a distance of a half-dozen paces, Jeena could smell the stench of the men. She hadn't had a bath since she'd left the Silvore river, but the smell of the men still overwhelmed her own body odor. Jeena's eyes darted left and right for a path of escape. There was none. The thick brush on both sides of the animal trail would make running difficult. If she'd been in her own elven form, she might have risked a dash for freedom. Unfortunately, Master Jathar's polymorph spell was too good. Her body really was that of an old woman. She had no hope of outrunning the younger humans in her present form.

"You're welcome to what supper and supplies I have," Jeena said trying to stall for time. "What little I have in my pack is yours as well. Take what you want."

"Now, isn't that nice of her," laughed the man with the knife. "She's giving us what we were going to take anyway."

"Well, maybe I want a little more than food," said the teenage boy as he raised a club and walked close enough to grab Jeena's arm. "Come with me, you old hag. We've got some business to take care of."

Jeena jerked her arm free of the boy's grasp.

He was stronger than her current form, but the sudden move

caught him by surprise. His surprise didn't last long. The boy swung his club at her head in a long roundhouse blow.

During her youth, Jeena had spent many afternoons training with the palace guards. Several of them had decided to take her under their wing. Perhaps they felt sorry for the orphaned elf-child. Whatever the reason, they'd taught her well in the arts of self-defense. Their training came to the forefront now as Jeena reacted instinctively.

Striking out with the edge of her foot, Jeena caught the side of the boy's knee. While her body and muscles might have been old and weak, her aim was dead on target. Her blow was rewarded by the clear snap of a breaking bone mingled with a scream of pain and anger.

The sound of running feet accompanied by a feeling of intense hatred warned Jeena of the approach of the boy's companions. The pain in her belly increased as the humans' base emotions took their toll on her senses. However, Jeena managed to duck her head just in time to avoid a swipe by the fat man's knife. Its sharp edge cut a few of her hairs, but that was all.

Swinging her staff with both hands, Jeena aimed for the man's chest. Just before her staff made contact, she felt a blaze of Power. The illusion spell Master Jathar had placed upon the Staff of the Lady of the Tree hid its true form but couldn't diminish the staff's Power.

Jeena traced a flow of Power from the gem at the tip of the staff. The Power struck out as the staff made contact with the man's chest. The air exploded with a blue light so bright it lit the surrounding area for a hundred paces in all directions.

The man was thrown into the air and hit a nearby tree with a resounding crack. Once the man's bloody body fell to the snow-covered ground, it made no further movement.

Without thinking, Jeena pointed the staff at the third human on the trail. He'd drawn a sword, but he hesitated to charge as if unsure of his best course of action. Jeena made the decision for him. She gathered Power from the staff and shot it out at the man. A beam of pure Power hit the man in the chest and blew him into a hundred bloody pieces.

A sound from her rear drew Jeena's attention. The man near her fire who'd spoken first had drawn a bow. It was aimed in her direction. When the man saw her looking at him, he didn't fire. Instead, he threw down his bow and ran through the brush in the opposite direction as fast as his legs could carry him.

Using the Power of the staff, Jeena followed the man's retreat until he was quite a distance away. Somehow, Jeena knew she could still use the Power of the staff to kill the man even at a distance, but allowed the man to continue running.

The sound of nearby groans caused Jeena to turn and face the teenage boy. He was clawing his way down the path while dragging his shattered leg behind him. Jeena allowed him to go free as well. She doubted he'd survive the freezing night that was fast approaching, but gave him the chance. She knew it was more than he'd have given her.

Quickly gathering her meager belongings and stuffing them into her pack, Jeena left her makeshift camp. All thoughts of a hot meal and a warm fire were gone. The sight of the two bodies of the men she'd killed lying in the blood-splattered snow made her sick to the stomach. She'd never killed anyone before. Jeena never wanted to kill anyone again.

CHAPTER 24

Richard had thought the whole situation strange even before his meeting with the duke. It got even stranger as Duke Bistoria personally escorted him to the city's main medical facility. Richard had a thousand questions, but he kept them locked up inside. Duke Bistoria opted not to discuss the situation further either. Instead, the duke became a tour guide of sorts as their hover-car flew toward the city.

The duke pointed at a set of long buildings in the distance. "Those are part of our city's training facilities. Military service is a requirement for every Trecorian who's physically able. There're no exceptions."

Richard doubted the validity of the duke's words. He'd seen too many exceptions made in the Empire for rich kids or sons and daughters with parents who were politically well-connected. He was tempted to argue the point with the duke but decided against it.

"You don't seem convinced, wizard scout. I assure you, every citizen does their duty. The military is considered an honorable profession on Trecor. When our children reach six years of age, they begin their initial military training."

"Why?" Richard asked. "Why start so young? And if you need soldiers so badly, then why allow Trecorians to volunteer for duty with the Empire?"

The duke considered Richard's question before answering. "I suppose the answer lies in our history. You see, Trecor is located near several major folds in the galaxy. Unfortunately for us, this makes our sector a good jumping off point for invading armies trying to pass from one point to another. Also, asteroid belts in several of the Alliance's star systems are rich in critical elements such as brerellium and even titanium. As a result, we've had to defend Trecor and others within the Alliance many times over the years."

"I see," Richard said more because he thought he should rather than due to some great insight on his part.

The duke gave a slight smile as if guessing Richard didn't really see despite his words. "As you know, wizard scout, we're currently at peace with the Empire. But a hundred and twenty-five years ago, our two civilizations fought a major war. It ended in a draw."

Richard nodded his head. He'd read about the Trecorian wars. The conflict had been more a series of large skirmishes fought over a thirty-year period than it had been a full-scale war.

"Now we're being hard pressed by the Balorian pirates and their Crosioian allies," said the duke. "And yes, we could use all our citizens in our own military, but soldiering is in our blood. The military of several other civilizations such as the Empire actively seek our volunteers because they make excellent soldiers. I suppose we allow our volunteers to serve with other militaries as a way of introducing new ideas and concepts into our own armed forces."

"I'd think other militaries would hesitate to have foreign soldiers serving in their units," Richard said. "Aren't they concerned where the volunteer's loyalties lie?"

Richard noticed a strange look cross over the duke's face. It was a cross between anger and hurt.

"We're an honorable race, wizard scout," said the duke. "Trecor has never been the aggressor in an interstellar war. However, when we've been forced to defend ourselves, we have done so with ferocity. And we never quit. But as to loyalty, our word is our bond. Elizabeth tells me the wizard scout corps has a similar code of honor. When one of our volunteers swears to serve in another military, they will do so honorably." The duke caught Richard's eyes and held them for a couple of seconds. "Let me ask you this, wizard scout. Do you think Elizabeth would betray the Empire?"

Richard didn't have to think about the answer. "No, of course not, sir. I'd bet my life on Liz."

The duke smiled approvingly. "And well you could. Elizabeth is an officer of the Empire now. She'll do her duty even if it means waging war against Trecor."

That part of the duke's speech Richard didn't agree with. It seemed to be carrying loyalty a little too far. He couldn't see betraying his own people just because he'd given someone his word. But then, how did anyone know until they faced the situation themselves. The duke had been right on one point. One of the core values of the wizard scout code of honor was that their word was their bond. Richard wondered how far he'd be willing to go to keep his word.

The duke didn't give him time to wonder. "Ah. We've arrived."

The hover-car descended as it made its approach to what appeared to be a large parade field. Richard saw nothing visually. However, his passive scan picked up a blurred mass of life forms below. There were too many to pick out individually.

"Is the hospital underground?" Richard asked.

"Yes," said the duke with an understanding smile. "For a second, I forgot you were a wizard scout. You can sense the staff and patients, can't you?"

Richard nodded his head. "Yes, sir. There appear to be thousands of them."

"Yes, there are," said Duke Bistoria. "But we're only interested in four of them today."

Richard waited for the duke to elaborate, but he didn't. Mentally shrugging his shoulders, he resolved to wait. He hated to ask questions. It made him feel inferior for some reason. Richard supposed his battle computer would chastise him for having such archaic ideas. He had a feeling Nickelo would say, *"How can you learn if you don't ask?"*

While the logical part of Richard's brain agreed, something else inside rebelled against the concept. He supposed it had something to do with the hodgepodge mixture that was his DNA.

Once the hover-car landed, the duke wasted no time in leading Richard to a high-speed elevator. They descended over three hundred meters before the elevator came to a stop. When the door opened, the duke led the way into a crowded room bustling with activity. Without slowing down, Duke Bistoria guided him into a less-crowded corridor.

"The four patients I'd like you to look at are located here," said the duke. "As I said, their injuries have resisted the efforts of our best healers. Neither traditional medicines nor the Power of our healers have been able to counteract the malfeasance that has corrupted their wounds. The best we can do is ease their pain and keep their injuries from getting worse."

"Well, I can certainly take a look, sir," Richard said. "But I doubt I can do anything if other healers have failed, especially if they're any good."

"I can assure you they're the best," said Duke Bistoria. "All I ask is for you to take a look."

Richard was concerned. He was pretty sure the duke hadn't gone to all the trouble to bring him here just to have him take a look. *He's going to want results. I don't care how concerned he is for his troops. It's not standard procedure for a leader of the duke's rank to scrounge up a healer to get a few of his soldiers healed.*

Richard promised himself he wasn't going to take on some stranger's pain without a very good reason.

The duke's healers are just going to have to figure out how to do it on their own.

They continued walking while making enough turns for Richard to get confused. Soon, the portion of the hospital they traversed became nearly empty. Richard saw a sign that read 'Intensive Care Unit' followed by the words 'Contagious Diseases Section.'

Duke Bistoria led Richard past two armed guards who opened a set of double doors at their approach. Richard noticed boxes of bio-suits stacked on shelves near the doors. The duke didn't stop to put on a suit but just kept walking as if contagious diseases were the least worry on his mind.

Richard followed the duke without comment. His self-healing would eliminate any biohazards that might enter his body. During his last mission for *'the One,'* he'd been around enough diseases not to be concerned now. Though he did wonder about the duke's refusal to wear protective gear. *Maybe he's immune to whatever it is*, Richard thought.

Since the crowds had thinned, Richard was able to pick out individual life forms in the nearby rooms and corridors. He drew in a sharp breath. The frequency of one of the life forms was familiar. Very familiar. The life form of interest was with a small group of other life forms heading their way. Richard remained silent but kept a close eye on the intersection of corridors to his front.

Then Richard saw her. Coming around the corner at a brisk walk was a woman with short-blonde hair and blue-steel eyes. She wore a white Empire naval officer's uniform trimmed with gold braid. The woman was Commodore Elizabeth Bistos. He hadn't seen his friend since his graduation from the Academy the previous year. In his opinion, she hadn't changed a bit. She was just as beautiful as ever.

Richard smiled and gave Liz a friendly wave. "Liz!"

Liz was accompanied by an older, blonde-haired woman dressed in the blue jumpsuit of Trecor's mechanized forces. The woman reminded Richard of Liz in both looks and manners. A younger girl in her mid-teens walked next to Liz. Like his friend, the young girl had short-blonde hair and blue-steel eyes. The teenager's right arm was in a sling.

One other individual walked with the group. He was dressed in a black wizard scout jumpsuit. Richard hadn't picked up the man with his passive scan, but as soon as he recognized the man, he understood why. The man had been one of Richard's former TAC officers at the Academy—Wizard Scout Shatstot. His former TAC officer's wizard scout specialization was in healing. Richard remembered his former TAC officer trying unsuccessfully to heal him after a particularly realistic encounter in a holo-square. He had actually liked Wizard Scout Shatstot. Unlike most of his other TAC officers, Shatstot had treated him like a human being most of the time.

What's he doing here? Richard wondered.

Richard didn't wonder about it long. When Liz heard his shout and saw him walking toward her, she had begun running down the hallway in his direction.

Richard picked up his pace and passed Duke Bistoria. Holding out his arms, Richard prepared to give Liz a hug. The scene reminded him of a video he'd once watched where two long-lost lovers had a joyful reunion. Richard didn't care if she was a high-ranking officer or not. He'd missed her.

As soon as Liz drew close, she thrust out her arm and hit his nose hard with the palm of her hand. A white flash of pain took the place of the scenery around him. Richard heard the crunch of cartilage and felt warm liquid splatter across his face as his nose broke.

Power from his self-healing reserve surrounded his nose and immediately began bringing his body back to baseline. Richard's sight started to clear.

Liz had been a pre-Academy cadet for two years with Richard, and she wasn't finished. She didn't give him time to recover.

Richard sensed Liz starting a spin to send a booted foot against the side of his head. He could have dodged, but he didn't. At the last second, he'd seen the angry look on his friend's face. She was pissed. It went against his nature to be someone's punching bag, but he forced himself not to counterattack. He could self-heal. Liz could not.

The kick was well aimed, and Richard felt himself falling to the floor. He spit out a mouthful of blood and part of a tooth when he hit.

"Elizabeth!" shouted a male and female voice in unison.

Richard recognized the male voice as that of Duke Bistoria.

"How dare you?" shouted Liz with pent-up rage hardening her voice. She gave Richard a kick in the ribs. "You're supposed to be my friend. How dare you? They were my family, damn you! How could you?"

Richard had no idea what Liz was talking about. He heard the anger in her voice, but it was outweighed by pain and fear. He'd hurt her somehow. He just didn't know how. Instinctively, he curled up into a tight ball to ride out the storm of his friend's fury.

When the kicks stopped, Richard risked a look between the arms he'd curled around his head. He saw Liz struggling in the arms of Duke Bistoria. The duke had her in a bear hug. The older blonde woman had interposed herself between Liz and Richard. The woman had a finger in front of Liz's face and was moving it in time to words Richard couldn't hear through the ringing in his ears. The teenage girl stood off to one side looking confused.

Wizard Scout Shatstot walked over and helped Richard to his feet. His ex-TAC officer looked like he wanted to laugh.

"Well, 832," said Shatstot, "I see you're still just as skilled at making friends as I remember."

Richard spat another mouthful of blood onto the floor. The bleeding from his nose had stopped and the bone was almost repaired, but it still hurt. He could feel a replacement for his missing tooth starting to form in the empty socket.

Richard was thankful his injuries were minor. He knew they could've been worse. He was well aware Liz had pulled her punches. He'd fought her several times in the combat pit during their pre-Academy days. She was very good. He was thankful she'd only broken his nose. He knew she could just as easily have gouged out both of his eyes if she'd so desired.

"Let me go," said Liz through gritted teeth as she struggled to free herself from the duke's grasp. "I'm fine now. Let me go."

Duke Bistoria reluctantly released his daughter.

Liz twisted her shoulders to speed up the process. She glared at Richard but didn't move to renew her attack.

"I'm sorry," said Duke Bistoria looking at Richard. "I hadn't expected this reaction from my daughter. She's been taught better."

"And you're an Empire officer," said the woman who was an older version of Liz. "I'm ashamed of you, Elizabeth."

"I'm sorry," Richard said as he watched his friend warily. "I don't know what I did, but whatever it was, I'm sorry."

With a glance at the blood and broken tooth on the floor, the duke said, "Are you all right, wizard scout?" Turning to Wizard Scout Shatstot, the duke said, "Terrie, can you help him?"

"He's a wizard scout, sir," said Shatstot. "His Power is already healing him. Besides, he's a resistor. I couldn't heal him even if I tried."

Early in his time at the Academy, Richard had been informed he was a resistor. His Power naturally resisted other forms of Power. While it meant his Power occasionally reacted to prevent or lessen energy attacks on him, it also meant he couldn't be healed by others. The only exception he'd found was some of the dolgars who were healers could heal his wounds.

The older woman turned to Richard. "I apologize for my daughter's actions, wizard scout. Perhaps we should have explained earlier."

The confused look on Richard's face must have more than made up for his lack of words.

"My name is Kristen," said the woman. "You've met my husband and daughter, of course. And I see Wizard Scout Shatstot and you are friends already."

Richard wasn't sure about the friend part. He shrugged his shoulders noncommittally.

Pointing to the teenage blonde-girl, the woman said, "This young lady is my daughter Tianika."

The girl nodded her head a little timidly.

Richard gave her a curt nod in return. He felt as if he were standing on the edge of a deep pit and figured his best bet was to talk very little and listen a lot.

"Before we try to explain further, wizard scout," said the duke, "perhaps you'd like to clean up a bit. Your face is a bloody mess."

Richard thought he caught a sudden look of concern on Liz's face. She still looked angry but gave him the impression of someone who'd just discovered they'd gone further than intended.

"If it's all the same to you, sir," Richard said wiping the worst of the blood off his face with his sleeve, "I'd kinda like to find out what's going on. I've a feeling I'm missing a little information."

The duke nodded his head. "I understand completely. Then let me be blunt. You've met us all before." The duke pointed to his teenage daughter. "Tianika was with the group of cadets you attacked, as were two of my other children. My wife was one of the pilots trapped in the burning Leviathan. I was the pilot who was trying to break the windscreen from the outside when you shoved me to the side and freed them."

Richard's overwhelmed brain tried to catch up. *I attacked the duke and his family. No wonder Liz is pissed. Have they brought me here to kill me in order to get their revenge?*

"We're soldiers," said the duke's wife as if sensing his thoughts. "We all understand you were just doing your duty. We'd have done no less. But you nearly destroyed our entire family. I'm afraid that's why Elizabeth's greeting was less than...uh...cordial."

"You almost killed them all, Rick," broke in Liz. Her voice quivered. Her anger was gone or buried so deep it was undetectable. "You spared their lives, and for that I'm grateful. But that damn phase rod of yours did something to my sisters. They can't even be healed."

Richard stared at Liz and the others. Things were beginning to fall in place. He sent a quick active scan toward the teenage girl, Tianika. He recognized her now. He'd glimpsed her face through her visor when he'd smashed her elbow with his phase rod. His active scan told him all he needed to know. He could sense attempts had been made to heal her elbow, but they were incomplete. Even as he scanned her arm, he sensed something evil inside her arm slowly eating away at the bone. The frequency of the evil was the same as the demon essence that resided in his phase rod. Apparently, a portion of the essence had been transferred to the injury. The demon essence was slowly continuing to eat away at the girl's life force.

Nickelo always said Richard often acted without thinking. He'd proved his battle computer right once again. Without wasting further time on talk, he wrapped Tianika's arm with Power from the reserve he used to heal others. He pictured how the girl's elbow should be and compared it with how it was now. He pulled the difference into himself. Richard sensed the demon essence in the girl's elbow being transferred into him along with the injury.

Since he was looking for it, Richard sensed his own Power isolating the small amount of demon essence. He was a resistor. The action against the demon essence was being done subconsciously. As the girl's injury was pulled into him, his body replicated the injury in his own arm. He heard bone break in his elbow, and he gave a loud scream as he fell to his knees. No matter how often he healed others, the acquired pain hurt just as much. Richard thought it was fortunate for others that he seemed to forget how much it hurt shortly after the healing was complete. As he fell toward the floor screaming in agony, Richard doubted he'd ever heal anyone else if he accurately remembered the pain once the healing was over.

Richard felt Shatstot catch him before his face hit the floor. His ex-TAC officer rolled him onto his back and looked at his arm.

Richard vaguely heard Wizard Scout Shatstot speak. "He's healing Tia's arm."

When the teenager's injury was fully replicated in his own arm, Richard felt the Power from the reserve he used to heal others begin to heal the girl. Within seconds, her arm was whole again. Then the Power began healing his own injury. At the edge of his senses, Richard felt the piece of demon essence struggle against his Power before the essence blinked into oblivion. After a few more seconds, his own elbow was basically healed. The injuries he took while healing others healed much faster than normal injuries to his own body. However, from experience, Richard knew it would be a couple of minutes before his arm was back to normal.

Wizard Scout Shatstot helped Richard to his feet once more. "This is getting to be a habit, Rick."

Richard gave him a wry smile, then glanced to his left. Duke Bistora and his wife were standing by their teenage daughter. Tianika had her arm out of her sling and was twisting it around in an apparent attempt to show her parents she was okay. Richard looked to his right. Liz stood there watching him closely, looking concerned.

When Liz noticed him looking at her, she mouthed the words, "I'm sorry."

"What'd you do differently?" asked Wizard Scout Shatstot. "I've had to re-heal Tianika every day since the battle, and it has never lasted. All I've been able to do is reduce her pain."

"There was something else in the wound," Richard said unsure how to explain it to his fellow wizard scout. "I had to take it into myself. Once I did, my resistor ability handled it from there."

"You're saying because you're an emp-healer, you were able to heal the damage?" said Shatstot.

Richard shrugged his shoulders. "There may be other ways. That's just how I did it."

"Well, are you ready to do it again?" said Shatstot. "Or do you need to recover first?"

"Again?" Richard said.

"Yes, again," said Liz who'd walked closer to them. "Chloe is my youngest sister. She was also hurt. And two of her fellow cadets also have wounds from that phase rod of yours."

The pain from healing Tianika was still fresh in his mind. Richard wasn't sure he was ready to take on another wound so quickly. His thoughts must have appeared on his face. Apparently, Liz noticed his reluctance.

"Chloe's shoulder is crushed, Rick," said Liz in a strained voice. "She's been in extreme pain for the last few days. I only got here on emergency leave last night, but just seeing her suffer tears at my heart. And you broke one of the other cadet's back. He's completely paralyzed and can't even talk, but you can still see the pain in his eyes."

"Now I see why I was brought to Trecor," said Richard. "You expect me to take all the injuries onto myself. That's a lot to ask, Liz. You know I'm an emp-healer."

Liz was silent. Richard knew she wouldn't beg. He didn't want her to. Silence caused him to look to his left. The duke along with his wife and teenage daughter were watching him.

"Fine," Richard said. "Where are they? I'll see what I can do. But...I may not have enough Power. It just depends on their injuries."

"Thank you, wizard scout," said the duke's wife, Kristen.

"I'll take you there," said Wizard Scout Shatstot. "It's not far."

Richard turned to follow his former TAC officer. Before he'd made it two steps, a youthful voice shouted at him.

"Hey, wizard scout!"

Richard turned back around.

Tianika held up her right arm and wriggled it in the air. "Thanks," she said with a half smile.

Richard returned the smile and nodded. He was always amazed by the resiliency of youth. Turning, Richard followed Wizard Scout Shatstot.

As it turned out, he had more than enough guides. The duke, his wife, and both of their daughters accompanied him. Richard's first stop was the duke's other daughter, Chloe. She was a cutie at only eight years old. And Liz had been right. While Chloe tried to be brave in front of her family, Richard sensed her pain. She was in agony. Fortunately, the healing went quickly. Before long, the girl's mother and father were helping her out of bed and giving her all the hugs she could handle.

The next healing was the hardest. Richard had broken a cadet's back, and the demon essence was firmly lodged inside the boy's spine. It took the remaining Power in Richard's healing reserve to heal the boy. The pain was agonizing, and Richard passed out for several minutes after the deed was done. Because his secondary healing reserve was emptied from the healing of the cadet's back, he was forced to use Power from his primary reserve to heal the final cadet. The last cadet he'd hurt with his phase rod had a shattered kneecap. The boy was in bad shape. Richard didn't like using Power from his primary reserve for healing. He'd promised himself long ago to only use it for offense and defense. One look at the demon essence eating away at the cadet had convinced him not to wait until his healing reserve recharged. The boy was in agony. What choice did he have?

When all was finished, Richard had an awkward few minutes while the duke and his family thanked him. It was a strange situation. Yes, he'd healed their wounded, but he'd been the one to harm them in the first place. He supposed his saving grace was that during the heat of battle, he'd taken the time to heal the young boy he'd hit in the side and belly with his phase rod. As he came to find out, the young boy was Duke Bistoria's and Duchess Kristen's son, Daniel.

It came as a shock to Richard when he realized Liz had been right. He really had almost killed her entire family. Fortunately, she forgave him and eventually apologized for breaking his nose. However, Richard sensed a difference in their relationship. He had a feeling it was going to take a while for her to forgive him completely.

"Maybe we can get together later," Richard said to Liz after her parents had left with their youngest daughter. "I've got a lot of things to tell you. A lot has been happening."

"Sorry, Rick," said Liz shaking her head. "There's a war on, remember? I've got to get back. My family emergency is over. My fleet needs me now."

"But—"

"It can't be helped, Rick," said Liz. "Sorry." Liz placed a hand on Richard's shoulder. "But if I hear you harm any of my family again, I swear I'll come back and personally kick your ass from one end of the galaxy to the other. I won't hold my punches next time."

Richard was unsure whether she was joking or not. He'd always had trouble discerning subtle humor.

Finally, Liz smiled. "It's a joke," said Liz. "I keep forgetting you tend to take things too literally."

Richard relaxed a little and smiled. "I would never knowingly harm your family. I swear it."

"I know," said Liz. "But you can be very deadly at times. I'm just glad we're on the same team."

"So am I," Richard said honestly. Liz was a hell of a soldier. No one knew it better than him.

Another awkward silence followed as Liz and Richard looked into each other's eyes. They'd been very close at one time.

"Well, are you guys done saying goodbye?" asked a young, feminine voice. "Or do you want me to find you a room somewhere?"

Richard glanced to his right, learning the voice belonged to Tianika. He felt his face flush.

"Uh, we haven't formally met," Richard said trying to normalize the situation somewhat. "My name's Richard. My friends call me Rick."

"Oh, I know all about you," said Tianika with a mischievous grin. "Liz's holo-mail used to gush with Rick this and Rick that."

Richard was surprised by the girl's playful attitude. Only an hour ago, she'd been in excruciating pain. He decided to ignore that for the moment and concentrate on her comment.

"Used to?" he said with a side glance at Liz.

"Uh, I've been busy, Rick," said Liz.

Richard thought he detected a slight pink on her cheeks.

"I had my hands full as captain of the Raven," Liz said in explanation. "And since my promotion to commodore, I've had even less time. I've been saddled with a hodgepodge of ships damaged from earlier battles. The Imperial High Command has given me one month to retrofit them and get them combat ready. I just don't have any free time anymore."

"Oh, that's not what I hear, big sister," said Tianika. "From what I hear, Admiral Donovan and you—"

"That's enough, Tia," said Liz gritting her teeth in an apparent attempt to control her voice. "You're not so big I can't turn you over my knee and spank you."

"Ha!" said Tianika grinning even wider. "You can try. You've gotten soft in your old age, Sis. I'm still young and agile while you're stuck behind a desk all day growing fat."

Richard found himself forgotten as the two women reverted back to an apparent sibling rivalry. Liz's tone and attitude was no longer that of an Empire fleet commander.

"Well, at least I wasn't taken out of action by a lone foe when I had him outnumbered three hundred to one," said Liz.

Her point struck home. Richard saw the sparkle leave Tianika's eyes. Suddenly, she was no longer smiling.

"That's not fair, Liz," said Tianika. "We didn't know we were up against a wizard scout. Besides, you weren't there. He popped up out of nowhere and took out half my squad before we could react. Even old Cremos was caught by surprise." Tianika looked at Richard. "I don't mind saying you scared the crap out of us, Rick. We're all very aware you could've killed all of us if you'd wanted."

"I'm sorry, Tianika," Richard said. "I—"

"Tia. Please call me Tia."

"All right, Tia," Richard said. "I'm sorry we got pitted against each other."

"Hmm," said Liz. "It looks to me like you're making it a habit of fighting Bistoria women. Heck, you even put poor Chloe out of action. Of course, she's never been much of a fighter."

"I—" Richard started.

"Ignore her, Rick," said Tia getting some of the sparkle back in her eyes. "She's still irritated you got her kicked out of the Academy."

Richard had a feeling Tia meant her comment as a joke until one look at Liz told him she took it seriously.

"No, I'm not, Rick," Liz said very seriously. "I...well..."

"Ahem," came Wizard Scout Shatstot from behind Richard. "Tia, why don't we leave them alone for a minute? Then we can show Rick where he'll be bunking down."

"I think I'd prefer to st—"

"Go!" said Liz in a no-nonsense voice. "For once in your life, don't argue."

Tia got it. So did Wizard Scout Shatstot.

Richard waited as the two walked down the hallway until they were out of earshot.

"Your sister seems to have recovered quickly enough. I gather she's serious about not holding a grudge. Your parents have been more than fair with me as well, all things considered."

"Trecorians are warriors," said Liz. "We always have been. I watched some of the videos from the battle. You fought with honor. My parents respect that." Her voice got quieter. "So do I."

She tentatively raised a hand to touch Richard's face. "I'm sorry about your nose and mouth. My family means a lot to me."

"I didn't even know you were a Trecorian," Richard said. "You never talked about your family. I guess I never pushed because I didn't have a family to talk about."

Liz remained quiet, so Richard tried to lighten the mood. "Heck, I'd probably have been more polite if I'd known you were royalty."

"See?" said Liz pulling her hand back. "That's exactly why I changed my name. And just so you know, I'm not royalty. Things work differently here. My father's a duke. My mother is a duchess. The rest of the family are just regular citizens. We have to earn our way in the world. Nothing's given to us."

From the sound of his friend's voice, Richard guessed he'd hit a raw nerve. He decided to change the subject. "I stand corrected. So who's this Admiral Donovan; a friend?"

Richard thought he noticed Liz turning a light pink again.

"You know, one of these days I'm going to shut Tia's big mouth in a way she won't forget," said Liz.

Realizing he'd probably walked into another sensitive area, Richard beat a hasty retreat. "Sorry. It's none of my business."

Liz looked Richard right in the eye. She'd never been one to walk away from danger. "Tia was talking about Timothy Donovan," said Liz. "He's a rear admiral in the Trecorian Ninth Fleet. We did a lot of training together during our younger years before I volunteered for Empire duty."

Richard was normally not a touchy-feely guy. Emotional situations tended to make him uncomfortable. But in this case, he had a feeling he needed to slog forward. Otherwise, the relationship between Liz and him might never fully recover. At one time, he'd thought he loved her.

Maybe I did at one time, he thought. *But now?* Richard realized while he would always have feelings for Liz, he really considered her a friend more than anything else. And he really wanted to keep her as a friend.

"You know, Liz," Richard said trying to be tactful but realizing he was probably already failing miserably. *The heck with it—once a Marine, always a Marine. I prefer a direct frontal assault anyway.* "Are this admiral and you still close? If so, I just want you to know I'm happy for you. You deserve a good man."

Liz seemed surprised. "Rick. Uh, you've changed since I saw you last year. You're different somehow."

"Well, time changes things. In one respect, it's only been a year since we last saw each other. But if you count my missions for *'the One,'* the battle at the Academy was decades ago."

Liz gave Richard a sympathetic look. "I'm sorry, Rick. I forget what you go through sometimes. Decades, you say?"

"In theory," Richard said shrugging his shoulders. "To be honest, it really doesn't seem that long. Most of my time-commando stuff blurs together. Large parts of it have become more like a half-remembered dream than a reality. Heck, I've got large gaps in my timeline where I don't even have a memory of what I did." Richard leaned back against the wall. He suddenly felt tired. "To be honest, Liz, those gaps scare the hell out of me. I've done some bad things during the missions I remember. Why do I have gaps? Did I do something so horrible *'the One'* purposely erased it from my memory?"

Seconds passed without Liz saying anything. Finally, she spoke in a voice more tender than he'd ever heard her speak. "I can't speak for what you've done elsewhere. But I do know what you've done here today was a good thing." She raised her right hand and touched his cheek. "Hang onto the good. Don't tear yourself apart worrying about bad things you may or may not have done."

Richard nodded his head, knowing she was right but feeling that would be easier said than done.

"Look, Rick," said Liz almost sounding embarrassed. "I'd like to stay and talk more, but I really have to go. A shuttle is waiting to take me to an orbiting transport. They've already delayed their departure for me."

"I understand," Richard said. "Stay careful. I'd hate to lose a good friend."

Liz smiled. "We'll always be friends, Rick. And I'm depending on you to take care of my family while I'm gone. You owe me that for getting me kicked out of the Academy." She followed her comment with a dazzling smile to let him know she wasn't serious. Turning to look down the hallway, Liz raised her voice. "All right you two. He's all yours. I've got a war to fight."

CHAPTER 25

Wizard Scout Shatstot led the way to an underground hover-tram station. They lucked out, and a four-car hover-tram pulled into the station within thirty seconds of their arrival. They entered one of the cars and found an empty cabin. After they were seated, Richard commented on their good timing.

"Oh, it wasn't all that lucky," said Tia. "It's a shift change for the hospital, so hover-trams are pulling in and out every five minutes."

"You know, Tia," Richard said. "It's very kind of you to come with us, but I'm sure Wizard Scout Shatstot could've handled it fine."

"Terrie," said Wizard Scout Shatstot. "Call me Terrie. I'm medically retired from the Empire now, so while I'll always officially be a wizard scout, the title seems a little formal."

Richard was surprised at his former TAC officer's claim to be medically retired. Physically, he seemed fit. Richard momentarily tempted to run a scan of the former TAC officer's Power link and reserve but refrained. It had been his experience that most people with sizeable Power reserves took uninvited scans as a declaration of war.

"You're no longer on active duty, uh, Terrie?" Richard assumed asking would get the same information he could get with an active scan without any of the potentially deadly consequences.

"Does that surprise you?" said Terrie. "I'm sure Chief Instructor Winslow pounded it in your head when you were a cadet that the life expectancy of a wizard scout is five years. I was on active duty for fifteen years, so I beat the law of averages."

"What happened?" Richard asked more than a little curious. "You look fit enough."

"Humph," said Terrie with a snort of disgust. "That's what I tried to tell the medical review board, but they wouldn't listen to reason. I was too close to a nuke when it went off. My Power reserve was damaged. All I'm good for now is healing others. Offensive and defensive actions put too much of a strain on my reserve."

"So how did—"

"Have you two about caught up on old times?" Tia said frowning. "I'm here too, you know."

Terrie caught Richard's eyes and gave a wink. "Oh, Tia, you know we couldn't ignore you for long. Why don't you explain to our friend here what I'm doing on Trecor? I'll bet he's curious."

It was exactly the question Richard was going to ask before he'd been interrupted.

"Fine," said Tia losing her frown. "Terrie's a Trecorian. Where else do you think he'd go after he retired?"

Richard shrugged his shoulders. He hadn't really thought much about his former TAC officer's background. He supposed his battle computer would tell him he should take more interest in people.

"Before he volunteered as a wizard scout," said Tia, "Terrie was assigned to the 147th Mechanized Regiment. That's my unit as well. That's also the unit where you've been assigned. All unmarried personnel live at the barracks. It's an unwritten law."

"Oh," Richard said suddenly understanding why the duke's daughter was with them. "So you live there too? I just assumed you lived at the palace."

Both Tia and Terrie laughed.

They were friendly laughs, so Richard forced himself not to be insulted. A part of him had never liked being laughed at, but he'd gotten a lot better over the years at controlling that part of his ego.

"What did I say?" Richard said. "Why are you laughing?"

"Well," said Tia. "I'm laughing because I'm trying to figure out what palace you're talking about. Didn't you read up on Trecor before you came here?"

"Uh, only a little," Richard admitted. "I was a little busy for too much in-depth research."

"So we heard," laughed Terrie. "Between preventing Councilwoman Deloris's assassination and breaking Sergeant Hendricks out of Diajor, I suppose you had a pretty full schedule."

"You did what?" said Tia.

Richard got the impression she was more impressed than shocked. "Now wait a minute," Richard said confused how he'd gotten put on the defensive so quickly. "Don't go making accusations you can't prove. I'm not admitting to anything."

"I doubt you'll have to," Terrie said still laughing. "Half the galaxy saw the IEN videos of you coming out of the ground last year on that demon horse of yours. I don't think it's going to take an astral physicist to determine who broke Hendricks out of prison."

"What videos?" demanded Tia. "I didn't get to see any videos. Mother and Father never let me see anything good."

Terrie laughed playfully. "I'll let you take a look at them tonight. I was deployed off planet at the time of the attack on Velos, so I didn't personally see it happen. I've talked to a couple of the other wizard scout instructors who were there, though. Between the dimensional-shifting wolves and the demon horse, I think some of the Conglomerate soldiers probably had to put on clean underwear afterward."

Tia giggled. Her blue-steel eyes sparkled and the freckles on her nose became darker. Richard realized she looked a lot like her older sister.

"Whatever," Richard said. "What about my question? Why'd you guys laugh?"

"Because if my parents have a palace tucked away somewhere, they forgot to tell me about it," Tia said grinning. "I grew up in a six-room bungalow. Mother and Father live there now with my younger sister, Chloe, and my brother, Daniel. When I lived there, I had to share a bedroom with Liz until she left to join the Empire. Then I got stuck with Chloe. I've got a lot more room at the barracks than I ever had at home."

"Trecor doesn't have royalty in the sense you're thinking, Rick," said Terrie. "Duke Bistoria was voted into office twenty-two years ago. He can be voted out just as easily. I guess you could think of him more as a CEO than royalty."

Scratching his head, Richard said, "So he's a duke? Is there a king?"

"No," answered Tia. "We Trecorians only elect kings in time of full-scale war. We haven't had a war-king in over a hundred years."

"But you're fighting Balorian pirates, aren't you?" Richard said.

"Ha!" said Tia. "We're always fighting pirates of one kind or another. It's been more of a century-long skirmish than an actual war. We haven't needed a war-king to unite the various Trecorian systems in recent memory."

"I thought the systems in this part of the galaxy were all in the Trecorian Planetary Alliance," Richard said.

Richard normally didn't like politics, and he was already starting to lose interest in the direction of the conversation. But he forced himself to understand at least a little more while he had Tia and Terrie with him. He wasn't sure when or if he'd see them again.

Tia and Terrie looked at each other. They seemed to exchange unheard words.

Finally, Terrie nodded. "All right, Rick. You asked for it, so here it goes. The Trecorian Planetary Alliance consists of twenty-two permanently inhabited star systems with Trecor being the most populated. Each of those twenty-two star systems has their own autonomous governments, and each of those governments is loosely headed by a duke or duchess. You noticed I said *loosely*. Things can get plenty rowdy on some planets during their political meetings. Do you understand so far?"

Richard nodded his head affirmatively.

Terrie gave a nod of his own and proceeded with his explanation. "The Alliance also consists of a hundred and twenty-six planets that have light or temporary populations. A lot of them are mining planets where the population increases or decreases dramatically depending on shift changes. We also have between eight hundred and eleven hundred asteroids with mines or outposts of various types. Each of those mines and outposts consider themselves autonomous. The majority of the Alliance is of Trecorian stock, and we're a pretty independent bunch."

"Then how—"

"How do we operate?" said Tia. "We may be independent, but

we make allowances for the common good. We have elected commissions to handle the details of trade, mutual defense, and various legal whatnot."

"Sounds confusing," Richard said. He liked the Empire's way of doing business. The Imperial High Council could be a little heavy-handed at times, but all in all, they did a good job of running the 4,300 plus star systems that formed the Empire.

"Confusing?" laughed Terrie. "You can't begin to imagine. But in times of war, things change."

"That's right," said Tia. "Such a loose organization of governments would be easily defeated by a determined enemy. Fortunately, whenever a war looms, the Alliance votes for a war-king or war-queen. Gender doesn't matter. In times of war, the best leader as determined by a majority vote of the various governments takes absolute control of the Trecorian Planetary Alliance for the duration of the crisis."

"And when the crisis is over?" Richard said. "Then what? Sometimes it's harder to get someone out of Power than it is to get them in."

Both Tia and Terrie laughed.

"You really don't know Trecorians very well," said Terrie. "We're simple people for the most part. Who in their right mind would want the job? It would be a thankless task trying to control eighty billion cantankerous Trecorians. If you ever get a chance to read some of our history, I think you'll see most of our war-kings couldn't wait to get rid of the job."

Richard wasn't convinced but nodded his head in what he hoped might be construed as a sign of agreement.

The three of them made small talk for the next ten minutes. As they did, Richard sensed the hover-tram gradually making its way upward. Before long, the windows of their car were flooded with bright sunlight as the hover-tram exited its tunnel. Shortly thereafter, the hover-tram pulled into a station teeming with life forms. Most were humans of Trecorian stock, but about ten percent were other species. Richard recognized many of the races, but a few were unfamiliar.

If Nick was here, he'd have them cataloged and identified in nothing flat, Richard thought. *But he ain't, so I'm not going to worry about it.*

Not for the first time, Richard had a momentary regret about leaving his battle computer and dimensional pack on the *Defiant*. But logic told him he'd made the right decision. Margery needed Nickelo to help with her indoctrination to the *Defiant*. Besides, carrying his dimensional pack would have positively identified him as the culprit in the prison break.

No, the best thing was to leave my equipment behind, Richard thought. *And if it wasn't, then it's too late to change it anyway. What's done is done.*

When the hover-tram came to a complete stop, Tia and Terrie jumped to their feet and rushed out the cabin door. Richard followed in their wake. The corridor was crowded, and Richard lost sight of his two guides. He wasn't concerned. In wizard scout jargon, he had both of their scents by their unique frequency of Power. Richard had both Tia and Terrie marked on his passive scan and could easily track either one of them out to a distance of several kilometers.

Once he was off the hover-tram, Richard elbowed his way through the crowd of people trying to get onboard the car he'd just exited. As he made his way forward, the crowd thinned somewhat. He found Tia and Terrie waiting for him near one of the station's exits.

"Are we catching a cab?" Richard asked.

"Nope," said Terrie with a contagious grin. "We're hoofing it. The barracks is only four kilometers away. The exercise will do you good." Terrie gave him a wink.

Richard gave a subdued smile back. They were both wizard scouts. Their self-heal kept their bodies at whatever condition they were when their DNA baselines were taken. No amount of exercise would ever change that. They were what they were. Tia, on the other hand, was a cadet in the Trecorian's military. Richard had a feeling Terrie had been a TAC officer so long he just naturally assumed Tia would benefit from the exercise.

Just as well, Richard thought. *I don't have any credits on me anyway.*

The three of them exited the station onto a busy street beyond. As far as Richard could tell, they were near the city's center. He noticed the sidewalks were divided into lanes. One lane was full of people walking. The second lane was less crowded. The people on it were jogging or even running in some cases. Most of the people in the running lane wore various versions of military uniforms. While the street did sport a variety of vehicular traffic, Richard noticed the number of pedestrians far outnumbered the vehicle occupants.

Tia and Terrie stepped into the running lane and took up a fast jog. Richard fell in behind. He'd never been all that fond of running. As a wizard scout, running wasn't physically demanding since his self-heal considered any fatigue as an injury and healed it appropriately. Besides, running was boring, and Richard got bored easily. It was one of his faults.

"Hey," Richard said. "Can I use my Empire credits here? Until the *Defiant* gets here next month, I don't have any extra clothes. And I'm a little hungry. I wouldn't mind buying a snack."

"Sure," said Tia who was starting to breathe hard at the pace Terrie had set. "The Trecorian's main computer is tied into the Empire's financial network via the tele-network. It's not like our governments are at war with each other or anything."

"But I doubt you'll need to use any of your credits," said Terrie. "You'll be issued gear when we get to the barracks. You're already on the regimental roster. You can grab something at the mess hall if you get hungry. It's open twenty-four seven."

"Plus, I heard Father say you've been set up in the computer system with an expense account," said Tia. "My understanding is you're on temporary assignment. Trecor has to pay you. It's not the other way around." By this time, Tia was beginning to pant even heavier. "Hey, you guys, how about slowing the pace a little? I'm a normal Trecorian. I actually get tired, you know."

Terrie gave Richard a knowing smile as he slowed his pace.

They ran for several more minutes. By the time they arrived at their regimental barracks, Tia was sweating profusely. Neither Terrie nor Richard had broken a sweat. Tia gave them both a nasty look before muttering something about needing a shower.

Tia ran ahead and entered the building.

Richard sensed her turning left. The barracks was huge. Richard sensed several thousand life forms in the nearby buildings. When Terrie and he entered their building, they passed some guards who waved them through. Terrie turned right at the first intersection.

"Tia turned left," Richard said. "Is that the female section?"

"Nope," Terrie said. "We're co-ed. However, Tia stays in the fighter pilot's section. You'll be in the part of the barracks designated for cat pilots. I'll show you around before I leave you to the wolves."

True to his word, Richard's ex-TAC officer gave him the grand tour of his part of the barracks. Once Terrie was satisfied Richard knew his way around, he left. After a small meal in the regimental mess hall, Richard made his way back toward the small room where he'd been assigned. The room contained four bunks, but Terrie had told him he'd be the lone occupant. Richard was glad. He hated trying to get to know new people. For the most part, he preferred being left alone.

Even before Richard got to his room, he sensed he wasn't going to be left alone. Three life forms were already in his living quarters. Richard recognized one of them. It was Colonel Santos of the 147th Mechanized Regiment.

CHAPTER 26

The door to Richard's room was already open. As expected, he found Colonel Santos inside conferring with two other soldiers dressed in the blue jumpsuits of Trecor's mechanized forces. Richard noticed an insignia of a comet with a large 147 emblazoned on its tail over the left-chest pockets of all three jumpsuits. One of the soldiers with the colonel was a male with master sergeant chevrons pinned to his collar. The other soldier, a dark-skinned female with penetrating black eyes, wore officer bars on her jumpsuit. The female reminded him of his friend Tam a little.

As soon as Richard entered the room, his three uninvited guests immediately stopped talking. He didn't have to guess too hard who they'd been talking about.

"Glad to see you finally decided to show up, Shepard," said the colonel.

Richard immediately stiffened and went into defensive mode. He didn't have to be an empath to detect the hostility in the colonel's voice. "I just came from the mess hall," Richard explained fairly certain no one in the room really wanted to hear his reason. *Why does everyone always act like they hate my guts?*

He knew that wasn't really true. Most people treated him fairly. But he was a soldier, and as such, he liked to complain at times. Richard was pretty sure it was an unwritten-law of soldiers the galaxy over.

"Well, while you were lollygagging around," said the colonel, "we've been wasting our valuable time waiting on you. I'm not sure how you're used to operating in the Empire, but you'll soon find out we expect a little more discipline. Maybe you're used to getting special treatment in the Empire because you're a wizard scout. However, you're just another soldier to us. You'll get no special treatment here. Do I make myself clear?"

"Perfectly, sir," Richard said. *This is just great*, Richard thought. *I'm stuck with a female version of Myers.*

A trace of a smile must have crossed his lips because Colonel Santos stood up and said, "Have I said something to amuse you?"

"No, sir," Richard said. "On the contrary, I'm just trying to figure out why I'm still on Trecor. I've healed the duke's soldiers. I doubt there's much I can do here training wise."

Instead of being angry, the colonel nodded her head. "Well, in that we're in agreement. The 147th is the personal guard of Duke Bistoria. Every one of our soldiers is handpicked. From the newest mechanic to the most-experienced cat pilot, they're the best the Alliance has to offer."

Richard didn't argue. If the 147th was who he'd fought on Planet X3321, he had no complaints about their proficiency. They hadn't made many mistakes. They just hadn't been prepared to deal with a wizard scout.

When Richard said nothing, the colonel pointed to the man. "This is Master Sergeant Stover. He'll be your chief trainer during your indoctrination into the unit." The colonel pointed to the woman. "This is Commander Leander. She'll be your squadron leader. From what I understand, you're being temporarily assigned to Trecor for the next six months. I don't know if you'll be with the 147th the whole time. However, while you're assigned to us, I'll expect you to conform to our rules and standards the same as every other member of the 147th. Do I make myself clear, Shepard?"

"Yes, sir," Richard said. *Hmm. Definitely a female version of Myers.*

"Very well," said Colonel Santos. "Then I'll leave you in their capable hands. The duke wants a demonstration in the near future to ascertain our progress. I don't intend for you to mar the 147th's reputation. Master Sergeant Stover and Commander Leander are going to personally see to your training."

The colonel gave a smile that was anything but friendly. "Maybe you thought your training at the Empire's vaunted Academy was hard, but by the time these two get done with you, you'll think the Academy was a five-star vacation resort."

Looking at the others, Colonel Santos said, "Carry on!" Then she left the room.

Richard said nothing, but he thought plenty. *My life sucks.*

* * *

As it turned out, the 147th did train hard. About twenty-five percent of the unit was cadets in training while the other seventy-five percent were experienced soldiers. Most of the unit, including the cadets, had seen at least some combat. From what Richard gathered, about a third of the unit was deployed to fight the Balorian pirates at any one time.

Master Sergeant Santos soon learned physical training came relatively easy to Richard. Since wizard scouts didn't get fatigued, the sergeant decided to switch Richard's training emphasis to cats. Consequently, Richard spent most of his time training in medium and heavy cats. They were the mainstay of the Trecorian military, and Richard was impressed with the unit's cat pilots. They were good. Unfortunately, he was not.

While he'd been in the larger cats a few times, Richard normally depended on his battle computer to do the heavy lifting. He'd only received introductory training to the larger cats during his junior year at the Academy. The advanced training in cats that should have happened during his senior year never came to pass thanks to the Crosioian's surprise attack on the Academy. He'd been forced to graduate as a wizard scout a year ahead of schedule. As a result, a lot of advanced training had been missed.

Richard didn't mind the additional training in the medium and heavy cats. He knew he might need it in the future. But the training regimen confused him. He'd been told he was supposed to be training the Trecorians. Instead, he was the one being trained. However, Richard didn't complain. He assumed the cat training was just make-work. He'd already done the duke's primary mission. He'd healed the duke's children. Richard took it for granted when the *Defiant* arrived in a few weeks, the duke would release him from his assignment and send him packing for home. In the meantime, life wasn't too bad. At least *'the One'* hadn't sent him on any more clandestine missions.

At 0600 on the morning of the fifth day, Richard found himself inside a Leviathan training simulator with Tia. The simulator was just two cat-pilot chairs in the middle of a small room embedded with holographic equipment and force-beam generators. Once Tia and Richard strapped themselves into their seats and plugged in their armor, the techs flipped a switch. The walls of the room disappeared to be replaced by the inside of a Leviathan cockpit.

Richard glanced out the cockpit window at an alien scene. They were at an undisclosed mining camp located on some twenty kilometer-wide asteroid. Except for a couple of airlock doors in a wall to the cat's right, Richard saw only bare rock.

"What now?" Richard said into the microphone of his cat-pilot helmet. He was wearing the 147th's standard-blue, cat-pilot armor. He would have preferred his battle suit instead, but it was what it was.

"Don't ask me, Rick," said Tia sounding very serious. "You're the pilot. I'm just the copilot. It was made very clear to me I was to take my orders from you."

"Hmm," Richard said. "Who'd you piss off to get stuck with me this early in the morning?"

"Nobody," said Tia. "I volunteered. I was curious what a wizard scout could do. We don't interact with your kind much out here fighting pirates. Terrie's the only wizard scout I've ever met until you."

"Volunteered, huh?" Richard laughed. "Didn't anyone ever tell you never to volunteer in the military? I thought that was a required class in basic training."

"Not on Trecor," said Tia apparently missing his attempt at humor.

Richard swept his eyes over the large amount of computer readouts, levers, and flashing lights on the Leviathan's control console. It was a little overwhelming without Nickelo there to help him make sense of everything. Richard concentrated on moving the Leviathan's six legs to advance forward.

"So how come you're in a cat simulator with me?" Richard asked more to make conversation than anything else. "I thought you were a fighter pilot."

"I am," said Tia. "But we're required to cross-train. I can pilot a cat, but I'm much better in fighters. By the way, it looks like you're drifting to the left. I think you're overcompensating on the right-side hydraulics."

Richard tried to lessen the pressure on the Leviathan's right-side legs, but the hydraulic pressure on leg number five continued to climb. The cat drifted even farther left.

"It's not responding correctly," Richard said. "The number five hydraulics is acting screwy."

At that moment, a red light on the console began flashing accompanied by the sound of an alarm in Richard's helmet.

"We've got a fire in number five hydraulics," said Tia. "Master circuit breaker out. Activate number-five fire suppressor. Recycle hydraulic switch. Master circuit breaker in."

With each statement, Richard saw Tia's hands do the appropriate action of the emergency procedure. The flashing light went out, and the alarm bell ended. Richard noticed the hydraulic pressure on the number five leg return to normal.

"That was good, Cadet Bistoria," said the voice of Master Sergeant Stover over the intercom. "But we're here to train Shepard, not you. I'm well aware you know your emergency procedures. Let him handle it next time."

"Yes, Sergeant," said Tia as she looked at Richard and gave a shrug. "It's all yours, Rick."

The remainder of the training scenario didn't go well. Richard had tried to memorize a few of the Leviathan's emergency procedures, but the sheer number of them overwhelmed his overworked mind. Plus, while he was above average in intelligence, he didn't think fast. He preferred doing things where he could just react.

By the end of the day, Richard had gone from bad to worse. After six hours in simulators with three different copilots, Master Sergeant Stover pronounced him hopeless and advanced him to the real thing out of sheer frustration. Richard didn't complain. He actually had fun at the cat's live-fire gunnery ranges. He'd never had the opportunity to fire all the weapons on a Leviathan before. After only a few minutes, he was blowing targets apart left and right. However, the master sergeant wasn't impressed.

"It's one thing to shoot stationary targets that don't shoot back," said Master Sergeant Stover after Richard used a salvo-fire sequence of every weapon on the Leviathan to obliterate a target.

Richard had no doubt the sheer number of weapons on the Leviathan made it difficult to operate during active combat. Still, Richard chose to enjoy the moment. During a skirmish a few days before the battle at the Academy's airfield, Richard had seen the firepower of a Leviathan overwhelm the defenses of two magic users. True, he'd helped a little by dimensional shifting a missile through their defensive shield, but the Leviathan's weapons had basically disintegrated the two magic users. Richard had no doubt the large cat was a dangerous weapon in the hands of a skilled pilot.

* * *

After the day's training ended, Richard ate a quick meal, showered, and hit the sack. In theory, his body didn't need sleep, but after the day's training, Richard's overworked mind needed the rest. Besides, anytime he could save Power in any of his reserves, he liked to do so. By sleeping a couple of hours, his body wouldn't have to be healed back to baseline as much.

Richard had only been asleep an hour or so when a disturbance in the flows of energy around him brought him out of his slumber. More specifically, it was a change in the flows of Power. Someone nearby was using Power. Richard became instantly alert and immediately activated his best stealth shield.

The sound of distant laughter drifted through the door to Richard's room. From his passive scan, he could tell the laughter and Power fluctuations were coming from the same general location. The Power flows didn't seem dangerous. He let his mind drift along with the Power around him until his mind was deep in the midst of the concentrated flows of energy. He sensed the Power was coming from multiple sources. Most of the sources were small, but several sources came from medium to large Power reserves.

Lines of energy from some of the larger Power reserves appeared to be opposing each other. But even so, they didn't appear hostile to one another. First one flow would push against the other as if attempting to gain the advantage, and then the other flow would shift position to gain the advantage and push back. Each time one of the flows of Power shifted position to gain the advantage, Richard heard a surge of laughter and cheers from down the hall.

Curious, Richard pulled on his jumpsuit and boots. After dressing, he went out into the hallway and followed the sound of laughter. It appeared to be coming from the mess hall. When he entered, he noticed all of the tables had been pushed to one side to clear an area in the center of the room. A crowd of about four hundred soldiers in various stages of dress were gathered around a twenty-meter long rectangle marked on the floor with white tape.

Four soldiers from the cat squadrons stood at one end of the rectangle. Four other soldiers from the fighter squadrons stood at the other end. Richard noticed Tia among the four fighter squadron soldiers. All eight of the soldiers were concentrating intently on a small red ball rolling around on the floor of the rectangle. Richard's passive scan picked up lines of Power from each of the eight soldiers reaching out to the ball and attempting to move it around.

Realization came to Richard. *They're playing a game. Cool.*

"All right," shouted a familiar voice from the other side of the rectangle. "I'm giving double or nothing on the cats."

Richard looked over at Sergeant Hendricks. He was surrounded by several soldiers who were handing him slips of paper. Richard noticed the three shooting-stars insignia of the 147th's fighter squadron on the soldiers' left chest pockets.

Hmm, Richard thought. *I hope he's got the credits to back up his talk.*

Actually, Richard wasn't all that concerned about Sergeant Hendricks. Unlike himself, the armorer had fit right in with the 147th. Richard could easily understand why. As far as he was concerned, Sergeant Hendricks was the best armorer in the Empire. Richard doubted there was a ground or ship-based weapon the armorer couldn't repair and make better than it had been when it rolled off the assembly line. In just the few days they'd been on Trecor, Richard had seen Sergeant Hendricks find his niche as a well-respected member of the 147th.

Since Richard was wearing the comet insignia of the 147th's cat squadrons, he wisely chose to make his way around the left side of the rectangle. There were too many shooting-star insignias for his liking on the right side of the rectangle. And the crowd on that end was getting a little uh…spirited, to say the least.

As Richard made his way over toward his armorer, he monitored the flows of Power from the two teams. The four members of each team seemed to cooperate by combining their Power flows to push the ball toward a net on the opposite end of the rectangle. Every so often, one of the participants would suddenly remove their Power from their teammates and try to hit the ball from a different angle in an attempt to gain control. Whenever the other team didn't react fast enough, the ball went shooting toward the opposite goal. That normally seemed to cause the four opposing team members to separate their Power flows and set up defensive positions as they tried to slow or stop the ball's advance. Richard could tell the defensive team normally had an advantage. From what he could tell, it was very difficult for the offensive team to advance and score.

As Richard watched, one of the flows of Power from the shooting-stars' team separated and hit the ball from the right side. Richard traced the flow back to Tia. As the cat team separated into four defensive lines of Power, Tia moved the ball in a zigzag motion to keep the ball out of the cat team's clutches. When two Power flows from the cat team appeared to have Tia trapped, she suddenly switched the direction of the ball back toward her own goal. One of her fighter teammates was waiting and intercepted the ball. From the precision of the hit and catch, Richard could tell the maneuver had been practiced many times. The fighter team knocked the ball from one teammate to another until they suddenly combined their Power into a single flow and forced the ball down the court. One cat pilot formed a defensive position with her Power in an attempt to stop the ball, but the combined strength of the four soldiers overwhelmed the cat soldier's defenses. The ball shot into the net before the other cat pilots could react.

The right side of the rectangle erupted in cheers. Several soldiers with comet insignias unfortunate enough to be standing nearby suddenly had glasses of some foamy liquid dumped over their heads by the members of the shooting-star squadrons. Richard thanked his lucky stars for having the sense to be on the left side of the rectangle instead of the right.

By the time Richard made it to Sergeant Hendricks, a crowd of shooting-star soldiers had been paid their winnings and were walking back toward their side of the rectangle.

"I see you've found yourself a home," Richard told Sergeant Hendricks. "I'm surprised you have any credits left."

"Hey, Rick," said Sergeant Hendricks with an infectious grin. "It's easy come, easy go. Our cat squadrons aren't doing too hot today, but that's okay. We pretty much cleaned out the shooting-star squadrons' bank accounts two days ago. They're just earning some of their credits back."

"I don't remember hearing any of this noise two days ago," Richard said gesturing toward the enthusiastic crowd on the fighter squadrons' side of the rectangle.

"Oh, there's an actual bongo field a kilometer south of here," explained Sergeant Hendricks. "But it's raining outside today, so we moved the game into the mess hall. These Trecorians take their bongo seriously."

"Bongo?" Richard said. "I've never heard of it."

"Well, you'll hear about it if you stay here long enough," said Sergeant Hendricks. "Our cat squadron happens to be the reigning regimental champs."

Smiling, Richard pointed at the cheering shooting-star soldiers. "I guess someone forgot to tell them."

"Uh, yeah," said Sergeant Hendricks returning the smile. "We were doing great until that little wildcat over there showed up. She's very aggressive."

Following the finger Sergeant Hendricks was using to point out the fighter soldier in question, Richard wasn't surprised to see it led to Tia. "You mean, Tia? She's Liz's sister. That alone would tell me she's probably pretty good at whatever she does. They both share the same Power reserve, and it's a pretty sizeable affair."

"Commodore Bistos's sister?" said Sergeant Hendricks. "Heck, if I'd known that, I wouldn't have been offering no double or nothing bet." With a grin and a wink of his eye, he added, "I think I've been hoodwinked."

"Live and learn, buddy," Richard said. "Live and learn."

"Tell me about it," said Sergeant Hendricks.

Richard noticed his armorer's brow wrinkle as if he was in deep thought.

Suddenly, the soldiers on the fighter squadron's end of the rectangle began chanting, "Fighters! Fighters! Fighters!"

A response of "Cats! Cats! Cats!" came from the opposite end of the rectangle.

"Hey, Rick," said Sergeant Hendricks with a devious smile. "You're a member of one of our regiment's cat squadrons now. How about giving us a hand?"

"Uh, no thanks," Richard said hurriedly. "I'm quite happy watching. Besides, it wouldn't be fair. I'm a wizard scout, in case you've forgotten."

"Yeah, I know," said Sergeant Hendricks. "That's the beauty of it. Trecorians don't seem to be as impressed with wizard scouts as a lot of the other parts of the galaxy. I think it's high time they learned some respect. Besides, I need to earn some of our cat squadrons' credits back."

Richard shook his head no, but Sergeant Hendricks ignored him and pulled his arm until they were both standing in the middle of the rectangle.

"I have a challenge if there are any fighters brave enough to take it!" shouted Sergeant Hendricks. He had to repeat his yell several times until the raucous crowd quieted enough for him to be heard.

"One lone cat pilot against four of your best," yelled Sergeant Hendricks. "We'll give four-to-one odds."

That got the attention of everyone in the room. Richard saw a group of soldiers from the fighter squadrons talking to the team who had scored the last point. A vocal group of cat soldiers descended on Sergeant Hendricks and began questioning his sanity.

"Hey," Richard shouted at Sergeant Hendricks. "I told you I wasn't going to play."

One of the shooting-star soldiers overheard Richard and yelled, "Then it's a forfeit. Pay up cats. Your guy's too much of a coward to play."

"He'll play," said Sergeant Hendricks. "Won't you, Rick?"

One thing Richard hated was being called a coward. It just irked him to no end. He gave his armorer a nod. "Fine. I'll play."

Several of the cat soldiers cheered. Not many, but some. More of the fighter-squadrons' soldiers cheered. Richard had a feeling they were anticipating how they were going to spend their credits.

It took a few minutes for the crowd to settle down and for the teams to take their place. Sergeant Hendricks announced all bets were made and the game could start. Tia and her three teammates positioned themselves at the fighter end of the rectangle. Richard walked to the cat end.

The referee shouted the command to begin.

Richard reached out with his mind and put kinks in the Power links of each member of the opposing team. He'd had a feeling their links to their Power reserves wouldn't be protected, and he'd been right.

As the crowd watched, the red ball slowly rolled from the center of the rectangle toward the net of the shooting stars.

Richard noticed a strain on the faces of Tia and her teammates as they desperately tried to stop the ball. But with their Power links disabled, they were unable to summon up even a wisp of telekinesis. The red ball continued rolling slowly until it made its way into the net.

The crowd on the cat's side of the rectangle went wild. Anyone foolish enough to be wearing a shooting-star insignia on the left side of the rectangle got a sudden drenching with glasses of foamy liquid.

Richard hazarded a glance at Tia.

Her glare was hard to miss.

Hmm, Richard thought. *I don't think she likes to lose any more than her sister.*

* * *

As it turned out, all bets were deemed null and void. While the referees couldn't find any rules against disabling an opponent's Power link, the coaches for the fighter squadrons objected on principle. And the coaches on the cat side were kind enough to concur. Richard had a feeling the bongo regulation book would soon have an additional rule added to it.

Richard hadn't delayed restoring the Power links for the fighter squadrons' team. Even before the red ball had stopped rolling in the net, he had removed the kinks in their links.

After all, he thought. *It's just a game.*

But from the look on Tia's face, he had a feeling she was already plotting her revenge.

The only person in the room who looked unhappier than Tia was Sergeant Hendricks.

When Sergeant Hendricks accompanied Richard back to his room, the armorer half-jokingly said, "Heck. I could've retired to a life of luxury with my winnings."

"You know it was a little on the cheating side," Richard said. "I'm a wizard scout, after all."

Sergeant Hendricks laughed. "Yes you are. And now everyone in the regiment knows it as well."

"Fat lot of good that'll do," Richard said with a hint of bitterness.

Based upon previous experience, he'd found it rarely did any good to flaunt his wizard scout abilities. *But damn it, they made me mad with that coward talk.*

Richard knew his line of thinking was childish. He also knew his battle computer would be lecturing him about it even now if he were here. Richard shrugged the thought off. He was what he was. Any further conversation was interrupted by a knock on the door.

"Come on in," said Sergeant Hendricks in a friendly voice. "My casa is your casa."

Richard thought his armorer was awfully free with his invitation considering it wasn't his room. But Richard actually didn't mind all that much. His passive scan had already told him there were two people outside. From their Power frequencies, he knew who one of the visitors was. And he had a good hunch about the identity of the second visitor based upon similarities in frequencies.

The door to the room opened. Tia walked in followed by a young boy of about twelve years of age. He was dressed in a blue mechanic's uniform with the comet insignia of the cat squadron on his chest.

"Oh, you already have a visitor," said Tia looking a little embarrassed. "We'll come back another time."

"Hold on there," said Sergeant Hendricks as Tia and the boy turned to leave. "I'm just a fly on the wall. Don't mind me."

"Well," said Tia looking at Richard. "It wasn't all that important. I just wanted to introduce my brother to you. This is

Daniel."

Looking at her brother, Tia said, "Daniel, this is Wizard Scout Richard Shepard."

"Hello, Daniel," Richard said trying his best to sound unintimidating.

The boy looked down at the floor. Richard didn't blame the young lad for being a little hesitant. The last time they'd met, Richard had scrambled half of the boy's intestines with his phase rod.

No one said anything for several seconds.

In an attempt to break the ice, Richard said, "Daniel, I'd be honored if you'd call me Rick. All my friends do, don't they Tia?"

"Yes," said Tia. "And even some people who aren't all that friendly with you. I don't think it was fair what you did to my teammates and me. I haven't quite decided whether we're friends or not."

"Well, I think of you as a friend, Tia," Richard said trying to mend any fences before they were totally broken down. "And, Daniel, I'm sorry I hurt you before. I really am. If it's any consolation, your sister broke my nose and knocked out one of my teeth."

The boy looked up at Richard's remark. "Liz told me about it. She said you're lucky she wasn't really mad."

Richard gave a slight smile. He was grateful for being lucky as well. He knew Liz could be extremely vicious if she were of a mind. Daniel returned Richard's smile with a tight-lipped one of his own. Richard had a feeling all was forgiven.

"I'm sure you two know this old space-dog," Richard said pointing at Sergeant Hendricks.

"Oh, yes," said Daniel in a voice Richard took as semi-controlled excitement. "You're the famous, crazed, escaped-convict from Diajor. My father says you're the only person to ever escape from the prison. Did you know the Empire has set a two hundred thousand credit bounty for your return dead or alive?"

Sergeant Hendricks laughed. "That much, huh? If that's the case, then heck, I'm tempted to turn myself in just to collect the reward."

Tia and Daniel looked at Sergeant Hendricks as if trying to figure out whether he was serious. When the armorer smiled, Tia and Daniel broke out in laughter. Sergeant Hendricks and Richard joined in. Richard gave a sigh of relief. He was pretty sure the fences were mended.

"I'm glad you're here, Tia," Richard said. "How proficient at Power usage are you, if you don't mind my asking? You've got access to a large Power reserve." Looking at her brother, he added, "And you do too, Daniel. You're both linked to the same Power reserve as Liz."

"Proficient?" said Tia. "I'm good at bongo, if that's what you mean. So is Daniel, and so was Liz."

"Is bongo all you use your telekinesis for?" Richard asked.

Richard had noticed earlier a high percentage of the regiment had access to Power reserves, but he hadn't pursued the matter. He'd figured it had nothing to do with his mission. But after watching the game of bongo, he wasn't so sure. Richard wished he'd gotten the chance to talk to Liz about it before she'd left. Liz had been a wizard scout cadet the same as he until she'd been forced to D.F.R. out of the Academy. He was certain Liz could give him the information he needed much better than her siblings. But she was already gone.

"What else would we use it for?" said Tia with a questioning look on her face. "All it's good for is moving around a bongo ball."

"Why?" asked Daniel who seemed more interested in the subject than his sister. "Is something wrong?"

Richard shook his head no.

"Of course not. I was just curious. I'm just surprised the Empire hasn't tried to recruit more of you. They pretty much stripped everyone in the Empire with even a meager Power reserve during the last couple of years."

Richard remembered the battle at the Velos spaceport the previous year. When the Crosioian dreadnaught had crashed into the spaceport, part of it had broken off and landed on the barrack's complex used by the pre-Academy cadets. The loss of life had been horrendous. Only a few of the pre-Academy cadets had survived.

"Most of the Empire's potential recruits for the wizard scout corps were killed last year," Richard explained. "Quite a few of the soldiers in the 147th could easily qualify for wizard scout training."

"We're Trecorians," said Tia a little harshly. "We're not some breeding ground for the Empire. Your government tries often enough to lure our best soldiers away. Most of us tell them to stick their head in a supernova."

Considering her sister was a commodore with the Empire's navy, Richard was surprised at Tia's response. He'd assumed Tia would consider it an honor to be thought good enough to become a wizard scout. Apparently, he was wrong.

"Why do you mention it, uh…Rick?" said Daniel. "There isn't even an Academy anymore. Everyone knows the era of the wizard scout is over."

Not everybody, Richard thought. *I don't think that.* "True, there's no Academy now," Richard admitted. "However, there could be again in the future. We just need to find another source of DNA gas."

"Why?" said Daniel sounding surprisingly bitter. "So wizard scouts can continue to keep the secret of eternal youth to themselves?"

"What?" Richard said taken aback by Daniel's response. "The average life expectancy of a wizard scout is five years after graduation. That's hardly a perk."

"Yeah," said Tia getting back into the conversation. "But for the ones who do make it past those five years, they might stay young for another eighty years. Terrie is forty-two years old, but he still looks like he's in his twenties. He once told me he might live another sixty or seventy years." Holding up her hand before Richard could speak, Tia said, "Don't get me wrong. I like Terrie. But when I'm an old lady forced to get around in a hover-chair, Terrie will still be running around in the body of a twenty-eight-year-old. That's a hard pill for a lot of people to swallow."

"Terrie's disabled," Richard said. "His Power reserve was damaged last year. He can never be an active-duty wizard scout again, you know."

"So?" said Daniel. "A lot of people would risk dying in five years if they had a chance to stay young for the next seventy or eighty years. Isn't that why you volunteered?"

The double attack from the children was a little daunting to Richard. He'd often suspected a lot of strangers were at least unconsciously jealous of the seeming Fountain of Youth reserved for wizard scouts during the last eight hundred years. Richard wished Terrie was here to help him navigate through the treacherous asteroid belt he suddenly found himself in.

"Actually," Richard said in answer to the boy's question. "I didn't volunteer. I was escorted to a starship by armed guards and sent to Velos for training, no questions asked."

"You could have left," Tia pointed out. "Don't tell me avoiding the ordeal of old age didn't play some part in your staying."

Richard had a sudden, burning desire for his battle computer. Participating in philosophical discussions on the good and bad points of youthful longevity was not something he enjoyed or was good at. Richard wasn't entirely sure of his motives for remaining at the Academy. However, he was pretty sure semi-eternal youth hadn't played a major role in his decision.

"Actually, Tia, I'm not sure I had a choice," Richard said. "My life is…complicated. But I don't think a long life was a deciding factor in not trying to leave. You can either believe that or not."

Neither of the children seemed convinced.

"Well, anyway," Richard said in an attempt to get the conversation back on track. "That's not my original point. I was curious about the extent of your abilities with Power. Haven't you tried training them? Heck, as far as I can tell, a lot of the soldiers in our regiment have access to Power reserves a whole lot larger than mine."

Tia looked at the floor as if seeking the right words before answering.

Richard waited patiently, which even he had to admit was unusual.

After a few seconds, Tia spoke. "You should probably talk to Terrie about it. He's a wizard scout after all. I can't speak for everyone, but my abilities are limited to bongo. I've tried moving objects heavier than a bongo ball, but it never works."

Richard was well aware most people with Power reserves required training to fully use their abilities. He'd been a rare exception in that he'd been able to levitate objects and work with energy flows as an untrained child. He'd always assumed at least some others could as well. Now he wasn't so sure.

"Surely some people do more with their Power than use it to

play some silly game," Richard insisted. The reddening faces of Tia and Daniel let Richard know he'd used a poor choice of words.

"What's wrong with bongo?" said Daniel sounding more than a little affronted. "It has an important role in the Alliance. Wars between Alliance members have been averted due to bongo."

"Wars?" Richard said amused at the exaggeration of children.

"He's not kidding, Rick," said Sergeant Hendricks apparently jumping to the children's defense. "Once I found out about the...uh...financial possibilities of bongo, I did some research. The politics of the Alliance is a strange beast. Without a war-king, the member planets are free to ignore directions of the Alliance's governing body of dukes and duchesses. When major disputes arise between planets in the Alliance, they are sometimes settled by a game of bongo."

"You're kidding," Richard said. "What kind of silly system is that?"

The glares from Tia and Daniel told Richard he'd made another poor choice of words.

I really wish Nick was here, Richard thought.

"Actually," said Sergeant Hendricks, "I think it beats the hell out of blowing each other to bits. A lot of people would say settling differences with war is a silly system."

Richard shrugged his shoulders and admitted defeat. He couldn't argue against all three of them. Besides, he hated conversations that required a lot of thinking on his part. He much preferred action to words.

"Fine," Richard said. "I stand corrected. And I think I'll take your advice, Tia. I will talk to Terrie about it."

CHAPTER 27

The twenty-second day after Jeena left Silverton found her standing in front of a shimmering wall of energy. It was unlike any magic she'd ever encountered. The energy felt alien to her. A hundred paces beyond the wall of energy, Jeena saw the dark entrance to the Oracle's compound.

"So how am I supposed to get in?" Jeena wondered aloud. "No one bothered to give me a word of passage."

Reaching out with her hand, Jeena touched the shimmering wall of energy. It looked like magic, but it didn't feel like magic. Jeena frowned. She pondered its source.

"It seems similar to the frequency of the Power in the gem on the Lady's staff," Jeena said.

On impulse, Jeena touched the tip of the Lady's staff to the wall of energy. Blue ripples of Power shot out in all directions along the length of the energy-wall as it responded to the touch of the staff. Jeena drew the staff back and waited. She didn't have to wait long.

Within five minutes, a small figure walked through the entrance of the Oracle's compound in her direction. As the figure drew closer, Jeena realized the figure was a human boy. If he'd been a high elf, Jeena would have guessed his age at about 140. After doing a rough calculation in her head, she estimated the boy was about seven in human years.

"Hello," said the boy as he stopped on the other side of the wall of energy.

"Hello," Jeena replied politely.

Unlike the other humans Jeena had encountered on her journey, the boy didn't give off waves of emotion. She could sense his aura, but his emotions weren't unfettered; they were controlled.

"I'm here to see the Oracle," Jeena said trying to prod the young boy into fetching someone in authority. "It's urgent I see him."

"I know," replied the boy with an infectious smile. "The Oracle sent me to meet you."

The boy pulled a mask of some kind out of a bag at his waist and put it over his eyes. The device reminded Jeena of the goggles some elves put over their eyes to protect them when they were swimming.

"Oh," said the boy sounding surprised. "You're an elf. That's a very good spell you have. Did you do it? Can you do it to others? Can you teach me how to do it? I'd like to turn Dren into an old woman. I think that'd be funny. Wouldn't it, Omar?"

"Whatever you say, captain," said a strange sounding voice.

Jeena looked around. She saw no one besides the small boy.

"Uh, who's Dren?" Jeena asked ignoring the disembodied voice for the moment.

"Dren's my sister," said the boy. "She used to be fun, but not anymore. All she wants to do is work."

As Jeena tried to process the boy's words, he suddenly lost his boyish attitude and spoke in a manner well beyond his years.

"My name is Brachia, fair maiden," said the boy. "It's an honor to meet you."

The boy looked at Jeena for a moment, and then he switched back to his boyish mannerism.

"You're beautiful," said Brachia. "What's your name? Are you married?"

Although she was in a hurry to meet the Oracle, Jeena didn't want to hurt the inquisitive boy's feelings. Because elves had so few children, all children were precious to them, even children of other races. For that reason, in addition to the innocent smile on the boy's face, Jeena took the time to reply patiently.

"Thank you, Captain Brachia," Jeena said as she performed the best curtsy her old body could handle. "My name is Jeehanathoraxen. I'm a priestess of the Lady of the Tree. And no, I'm not what you humans would call married."

"Good," said Brachia grinning. "I'm not married either,

err…Jehan…err…"

Jeena returned Brachia's smile. "It is a rather large name for someone so small. Perhaps it would be better if you called me, Jeehana. That's my friend name."

"Jeehana," said Brachia as if mulling the name over. "Yes, I like that name much better. And you're not married. That's good."

"Oh?" Jeena said with a smile. "Are you looking for a wife, Brachia? Perhaps you should consider waiting a few years before making such a drastic move."

"Oh, not me," laughed Brachia. "I'm only seven, silly. But I was thinking of—"

The disembodied voice that had spoken earlier interrupted the boy. "Your sister says less talk and more walk, my captain. She said the Oracle is waiting."

"Oh," said Brachia sounding a little embarrassed. He flashed a grin at Jeena.

"Watch this, Jeehana. This is cool."

Straightening up and speaking in a formal voice, Brachia said, "You may enter the home of the Oracle, fair Jeehana, as long as your intentions are pure."

The shield in front of Jeena shimmered slightly, and she sensed a change in the flow of energy. When the boy waved his hand to beckon her forward, Jeena stepped through the energized wall. As she did so, a warm tingle passed through her body. With the tingle, Jeena felt her back straighten. She looked at her left hand where she grasped the staff. Her wrinkles were gone. She was young again. The polymorph spell was broken. Jeena noticed the illusion spell Master Jathar had placed on the Staff of the Lady of the Tree was gone as well.

Once Jeena was past the wall of energy, Brachia removed his goggles. Jeena noticed the boy's eyes widen as he looked at her true form for the first time. The boy smiled shyly.

"Uh, I could tell you were beautiful," said Brachia. "But I had no idea how beautiful. Everything was a little blurred through the true-form goggles. You're only the second elf I've ever met. The other elf was a male. He was mean. He tried to kill my sister and me."

The boy looked closely at Jeena as if evaluating her. "I think you're a nice elf."

Without warning, the boy's manner switched back to that of a young child. "Are all elves pretty? How old are you? My uncle's in his twenties. Well, he was. I'm not sure how old he is now. Time works strange for him. Do you like older men? I think he'd like you."

The thought of a human male liking her made Jeena's stomach churn. However, she kept her feelings hidden since she was talking to a little boy. Still, Jeena didn't have time for an endless supply of questions from the child. Because she wanted to remain patient, Jeena made another stab at getting the boy to take her to the Oracle.

"I'll tell you what, Captain Brachia," Jeena said. "I'll answer some of your questions if we start walking to our destination. Does that sound fair?"

The boy pursed his lips as if considering the idea.

"I guess so," replied Brachia as he walked toward the compound's entrance. "Most of the lights no longer work inside. You're not scared of the dark, are you?"

Jeena smiled. In her opinion, children were so innocent. She enjoyed talking to them most of the time.

"Actually," Jeena explained, "I can see in the dark, so it's not all that scary. Besides, you'll protect me, won't you?"

Brachia giggled. "Yes, fair maiden. Omar and I will protect you."

Jeena smiled back. "Good. Now, I promised to answer your questions, so I will do my best. You asked if all elves were beautiful. Some elves are more beautiful than others. However, I was raised to believe beauty is more than just an elf's physical appearance. Someone can appear beautiful on the outside and be quite ugly on the inside."

Jeena looked at Brachia. "Now let me ask you a question. Which type of beauty do you think is more important?"

By this time, Brachia had led them into the entrance tunnel. He reached into a cabinet on the side wall and extracted a metal bar with a small globe of light attached, then continued walking.

"I'd say being beautiful on the inside is more important," said Brachia. "I think some pirates can be ugly on the outside, but they can be nice on the inside. Is that what you mean?"

"Yes, it is," Jeena said. "You're a very smart boy."

"Yes, I am," agreed Brachia matter-of-factly.

Jeena smiled again. She could tell the boy wasn't bragging. He was just innocently agreeing with her.

"And to answer your other questions," Jeena said. "I'm three hundred and twenty-two years old. That would be about sixteen in human years. And no, I don't think I'd be interested in an older man. I'm an elf. One day, I'll find the elf who is the other part of my soul, and then we'll pledge bonds. Once we do that, we'll be bondmates."

"Bondmates?" asked Brachia.

"Uh," Jeena said trying to think of a way to put the intense feelings of a bonding pledge into a form the young boy could understand. "Being bondmates is sort of like what you humans would call marriage. But at the same time, it's much different."

Jeena spread her hands and shrugged her shoulders at the hopelessness of trying to explain bondmates to a non-elf. "I'm sorry. I can't explain it any better. I think you'd have to be an elf to understand."

The young boy continued asking questions as they walked. Jeena did her best to answer. She didn't mind his questions for the most part. He was quite likable and had a sharp mind for one so young. As they talked, she took in her surroundings. She'd never been to the Oracle's before but had heard so many stories growing up about the glory of the Oracle's compound. What she saw now left her disappointed. At one time, the Oracle's subterranean compound might have been grand, but those days were obviously long past. Broken pieces of aged marble tile from the walls and floor littered the hallway. Several of the side corridors showed signs of cave-ins. The evidence of extreme neglect was everywhere.

While the complex was quite extensive, they met no other inhabitants on their way to the Oracle's quarters. Jeena mentioned the lack of residents to the boy.

"Yeah," said Brachia. "It can occasionally be a little depressing. The last time Dren and I were here, there were hundreds of guards and servants. The place was in a lot better shape then."

Brachia pointed overhead at some broken panes of quartz in the ceiling. They were about half the length of a tall elf.

"Those used to work," said Brachia. "The gnomes made them.

When we were here before, the entire compound was lit up day and night by those lights. Now only a few of the rooms have working lights. Dren and I have to carry these light-globes with us wherever we go."

The boy lifted his rod with the attached light-globe for emphasis.

"What do the others use?" Jeena asked.

"There aren't any others," said Brachia with a sigh. "The Oracle says he's been alone for almost four hundred years."

"Oh," Jeena said. "I didn't know. Don't your sister and you get lonely? Why don't you leave? Surely you have relatives."

The boy had just started down some rough-hewn steps. At her question, he stopped and faced her. "We can't leave. All our equipment is here. Besides, our uncle is going to come and get us. The Oracle says our uncle is probably just waiting until it's safe back home."

"Safe from what?" Jeena asked. "And how long have you been waiting?"

The boy thought for a second. "We've been here a little over a year. We had to come here to escape Kreathin. He's the only other elf I've ever met. He's not nice like you."

Jeena was unsure how much of the boy's story was true. She couldn't imagine an elf threatening a child. But Jeena said nothing. Instead, she pondered the name used by the boy; Kreathin. It wasn't a common elf name. Jeena wondered at the coincidence of the boy speaking the name she'd been reading about in the diary of High Priestess Remozorz.

When Jeena said nothing, the boy turned and continued walking down the stairs. Soon, they were standing in front of two massive wooden doors. The wood on the doors was so old it had turned black. The doors had intricate carvings of events long past. The figures in the carvings flickered in the glow of Brachia's light as if trying to relive events of the past.

"The Oracle is waiting for you inside, Priestess Jeehana," said Brachia.

Nodding her head to her young escort, Jeena said, "Thank you, Brachia. You've been very helpful. Will you be escorting me back after my meeting?"

With a shake of his head, Brachia said, "No, Jeehana. I was told to return to my duties after bringing you here. Do you want me to leave my light-globe?"

A thin smile crossed Jeena's lips. "No, that won't be necessary. I can see in the dark, remember? But thank you anyway."

Brachia gave a deep bow from the waist as if he was a well-trained courtesan. "Then I'll take my leave, Priestess Jeehana."

Without skipping a beat, the boy slipped back into his world of childish imagination. "You're more than welcome on my ship anytime. You'd make a great pirate." Brachia paused for a second before adding, "Oh, and I hope your meeting with the Oracle is productive."

With another bow, the boy turned and left.

Once the boy was out of earshot, Jeena whispered, "So do I, Brachia; so do I."

When the footsteps of her young escort faded into the stillness of the Oracle's compound, Jeena returned to the task at hand. With a light shove, she pushed the massive doors inward to reveal a brightly-lit room beyond.

The end of my quest is near, Jeena thought.

With the thought still bouncing around in her head, Jeena stepped inside to find what fate had in store for her.

CHAPTER 28

A few days after his talk with Tia and Daniel, Richard was jogging back to the barracks. He'd just finished a grueling day of training in heavy cats under the watchful eye of Colonel Santos. The regimental commander had taken it upon herself to act as his copilot during an urban-area training scenario. The two hours of simulated combat had turned into a constant stream of snide remarks from the colonel as she pointed out everything he was doing wrong. As far as Richard was concerned, it was life as a lowly cadet under the watch care of TAC Officer Gaston Myers all over again.

Richard considered revolting and telling the smug colonel what she could do with her comments, but he refrained. The truth was he knew everything she said was correct. Without his battle computer, he was only a mediocre, heavy-cat pilot. Richard was fairly certain he'd never be more than a mediocre pilot. He supposed part of the problem was that he just didn't like operating heavy cats. Plus, the Trecorian's tactics were significantly different from the Empire's.

When push came to shove, Richard figured it didn't really matter. He was a wizard scout, not a heavy-cat pilot. Besides, his particular skills were tailored toward one-man missions deep behind enemy lines. The odds he'd ever need to pilot a Leviathan as part of a multi-cat unit was nil to none.

It was with little enthusiasm Richard found himself heading back to the barracks. He had no doubt in just a few hours he'd be back in a heavy cat getting lectured by either the colonel, Master

Sergeant Stover, or Commander Leander as to why he'd be dead in real combat.

"Hey, soldier," shouted a friendly-sounding voice from a hover-cycle approaching from his rear. "Need a ride?"

Richard turned and looked at the hover-cycle. The driver was Terrie Shatstot.

With a wave of his hand, Richard said, "Hey, Terrie. I thought you said I needed to run wherever I went."

Terrie grinned. "Yeah, you do. But I'm a poor-old, disabled wizard scout living on a government-disability pension, remember? How else do you think I can afford this deluxe-model, genuine hover-cycle?"

Richard laughed. During his Academy days, he'd never have guessed his ex-TAC officer had such a laid-back personality. Nothing seemed to upset him.

"Well," Richard said. "I guess I've got something to look forward to if I ever get disabled."

"That's the spirit," laughed Terrie. "I can see both of us banding with other disabled wizard scouts and forming our own hover-cycle gang. We'd be the terror of Trecor."

"I'm sure," Richard said still smiling.

Getting serious, Richard said, "I'm glad you happened by. I wanted to talk to you about something."

"Well, whatever it is can wait," said Terrie. "I'm on a high-priority mission from the highest-possible level. And I didn't happen by. I was ordered to find you and bring you back to my superior."

Suspicious, Richard asked, "And who might that be?"

"By my wife," said Terrie smiling. "She outranks everybody as far as I'm concerned. And believe me, she doesn't take no for an answer."

Shocked was too mild a word to describe Richard's feelings. His mother and the Commandant were the only two wizard scouts he'd ever met who were married. He'd been told often enough marriage and wizard scouts didn't mix. Although he had to admit, he did have high hopes for his friends Jerad and Trinity.

"Your wife?" Richard said. "When did this happen? Is she a wizard scout? Do I know her?"

Terrie gave a wry smile. "No, she's not a wizard scout. We got hitched last year after I got disabled. My last mission as a wizard scout was to rescue a group of settlers from a mining asteroid near the Trecorian's boundary line. The miners were under attack by some pirates. Angela, my wife, was one of the miners. I was able to get everyone off the planet before the pirates started bombarding their camp. However, my shuttle was caught in the blast from the initial wave of missiles. My Power reserve was damaged, and I was in a coma for two weeks. Thankfully, my battle computer was able to get my shuttle back to our mother-ship. Angela took care of me until I recovered. To make a long story short, we've been together ever since."

Richard didn't know what to say. He had lots of questions but hesitated to ask. He and Terrie seemed to be getting along okay lately, but Richard didn't believe for one instant he was close enough to his ex-TAC officer to ask personal questions.

"Don't bother asking," said Terrie as if reading Richard's mind. "Believe me, I know. Whatever reasons you can think of why someone shouldn't become involved with a wizard scout are the same reasons I brought up to Angela. But she's a stubborn woman. She really doesn't take no for an answer."

At a loss for words on the subject, Richard decided to try a different line of questioning. "It must have been a heck of an explosion to affect your Power reserve. I've heard of some wizard scouts being a little too close to nukes and still making it out alive with their Power reserves intact."

"Well, I've heard that too, but I'm not sure I believe it," said Terrie with a grin. "However, in my case, it wasn't a nuke. I'm not sure what kind of explosives were in those missiles, but they did a number on my reserve. I've never seen anything like them before."

Richard tried to sort the information out in his head but wasn't fast enough for Terrie.

"Enough dilly-dallying, cadet," said Terrie pointing to the back of his hover-cycle. "Slide on. I'll guarantee you a home-cooked meal that beats anything they're serving at the mess hall."

Unsure if he was doing the right thing, Richard slid onto the hover-cycle's seat behind his ex-TAC officer. He snapped the seat belt around his waist and placed his hands on Terrie's shoulders for support. The truth was he didn't have anything to do back at the barracks. He was mentally tired, but a short nap would fix that. To be honest, Richard was more interested in meeting Terrie's wife than he was in eating.

"All set when you are," Richard said. "By the way, I'm not a cadet anymore, in case you've forgotten."

"Ha!" laughed Terrie. "You'll always be a wet-nosed cadet to me."

Without any warning, the hover-cycle's engine roared to life. Richard was thrown back as he hastily tried to wrap his arms around Terrie's waist. If not for the seat belt and liberal use of his telekinesis, Richard was sure he would've fallen off the back of the cycle. By the time he recovered, Terrie had the hover-cycle at fifty meters above the ground and accelerating at a high rate of speed.

"If I'd known you were going to drive like a maniac," Richard yelled into Terrie's ear, "I would've worn a helmet."

"Ha!" Terrie laughed back as he revved the engine and accelerated even faster. "We're wizard scouts. We don't need no stinking helmets."

"Says you," Richard shouted. "I'd probably be more apt to value your opinion on safety-related items if you weren't already disabled. Besides, even though I can heal my injuries, it still freaking hurts."

Laughing, Terrie said, "I'm glad to see you're finally developing a sense of humor. If you can't laugh at this old world every once in a while, it will eventually beat you down."

Richard didn't bother telling his ex-TAC officer he hadn't been joking.

The next ten minutes was a wild ride zooming around, down, or over the heavy traffic on the city's sky-lanes. Richard had to admit Terrie was an excellent driver. The hover-cycle obeyed his every command with nary a problem. However, despite Terrie's obvious skill, he was pretty sure they were breaking a plethora of traffic laws.

Fortunately, before any blue lights announced the presence of irate law-enforcement personnel, Richard felt the hover-cycle beginning a tight turn toward a group of tall buildings sporting windows every few meters. He estimated the tallest of the buildings was over two hundred stories in height. As the hover-cycle completed its turn, he decided the tallest of the buildings was their destination.

Surprisingly, Terrie didn't make for the top of the building. The hover-cycle leveled off about three-quarters of the way up the building and made for one of the windows. When it became obvious Terrie wasn't slowing the hover-cycle down fast enough to avoid a collision, Richard wrapped both Terrie and himself in Power in preparation for shifting them into the void.

"Relax," shouted Terrie. "Trust me."

Richard decided to trust his former TAC officer enough not to shift into the void. However, he didn't relax. Just prior to the hover-cycle ramming into the window, he squeezed Terrie's shoulders tight enough to cause the man to yelp.

They sped straight through the window. Only it wasn't a window. It was a semi-clear force field. Richard felt a tingle as the field's energy slowed the hover-cycle and its riders to a smooth stop. The hover-cycle's engine automatically shut off.

"Geesh, Rick," said Terrie rubbing his left shoulder. "Haven't you ever parked in a high rise before?"

"No," Richard admitted. "I was raised in a two-story orphanage. We didn't get out much."

"No, kidding," said Terrie. With a grin, he added, "Now, off with you so I can park this sucker."

After they'd both gotten off the cycle, a panel in the ceiling opened up and two mechanical arms came down to grab the cycle.

Swoosh!

The hover-cycle was lifted out of sight and the panel closed behind it.

"This way," said Terrie. "We're just down the hall. It's nothing fancy, but we call it home."

Giving Richard a wink, his ex-TAC officer said, "Heck. Nothing on Trecor's fancy. We tend to go more for functionality than looks."

"Yeah," Richard said, "Tia told me the duke doesn't even have a palace."

"Well, that's not quite true," said Terrie as he led the way down the hall. "Duke Bistoria has a palace for official functions. He just doesn't live there. It's more for entertaining visiting dignitaries and such."

When they'd walked a few more steps, Terrie stopped in front of a green door with a large 'S' painted on it. "Here we are. By the way, the duke and duchess are having a formal ball in two weeks. Angela and I are going. I assume you've been invited."

"Uh, no," Richard said smiling as he tried to picture himself on the floor of some ballroom. "It's just as well since I don't know how to dance."

Grinning, Terrie said, "Oh, I guess you must've been on extra duty the day they had that class at the Academy. My, my, what are they teaching you cadets nowadays?"

As Richard was trying to think of some wisecrack response, the green door opened to reveal a tall, broad-shouldered woman with fiery-red hair and sparkling green eyes. Richard guessed the woman was nineteen or twenty standard years in age. From the light in her eyes when she looked at Terrie, he didn't need to be told this was Angela.

"Well, it's about time you two showed up," said Angela in a mock-scolding voice. "I was beginning to think you'd gone to some bar to ogle the girls and swap wizard scout lies all night long."

"Oh, now, Angela," said Terrie as he grabbed his wife and gave her a hug. "You know you're the only girl I ever want to ogle."

"Yes, I do," said Angela as she forced her way out of Terrie's grip. "But it doesn't hurt to remind you every once in a while."

Terrie gave Richard a wink. "See what I have to put up with. My only hope is she'll get better as she matures."

"Ha!" snorted Angela. "And look at the pot calling the kettle black. I was more mature than you when I was five years old."

For the next hour, Richard was in continuous amazement at the banter between his ex-TAC officer and Angela. As Terrie had said, she was a strong force of nature and didn't mind letting her opinions be known. Richard had met a few miners during his time with the mercenaries, and they all seemed to have a no-nonsense attitude. Richard supposed it was just part of being in a profession where they laid their lives on the line every single day. Mining was definitely a dangerous lifestyle. Of course, Richard couldn't say anything. Being a wizard scout wasn't the safest job in the galaxy either.

After a delicious home-cooked meal, Angela got up from the table and stepped into the small alcove they used for a kitchen. She came back carrying a tray with three steaming bowls of fruit cobbler adorned with a dab of cinnamon ice cream on top, which was just beginning to melt.

"Now, I know you wizard scouts don't need to eat to survive," Angela said with a wink. "But I dare you to take a bite of this without licking the bowl clean. It's my grandma's own recipe, and I'm sworn to secrecy on pain of horrible death should I ever reveal the O'Reilly clan's secret ingredients."

Terrie gave Richard an elbow in the side. "The thing is, I think she's only half joking. I met a few of the O'Reilly clan at our wedding. They're a rough lot, if you ask me."

"Hush, now," said Angela as she gave her husband a playful punch on the arm. "Don't be feeding Rick any of your blarney."

"Blarney?" Richard once again found himself missing his battle computer. Sometimes Nickelo came in handy for interpreting.

"In other words, bald-faced lies," said Angela with a laugh. "Some of the stories he tells me about you wizard scouts make me think he's feeding me a lot of blarney."

"Well, could be," Richard laughed. "But I've done and seen a lot of strange things since I've been a wizard scout."

"See, Angela," laughed Terrie. "Not everything I tell you is a lie." Terrie winked at Richard. "At least fifty percent of what I tell you has a grain of truth to it."

They ate their dessert with very little talking. Richard had to admit it was one of the most delicious things he'd ever eaten. When he complimented Angela, he could swear she blushed. Richard had a feeling she might look hard on the outside but was a kind soul on the inside where it counted.

During the course of some after-dinner small talk, Richard said, "Terrie told me how you two met. I'll bet it was frightening having those space pirates bombing you."

"Ha! Weren't no space pirates," said Angela with a wave of her hand. "I don't give a hoot for space pirates. My momma told me I killed my first space pirate when I was three. The O'Reilly clan doesn't need help handling space pirates."

Puzzled, Richard glanced at Terrie. "I thought you said—"

"Oh, don't go looking to him for answers," said Angela. "He's just going by what his official orders said. I was there, and I saw them up close. It wasn't no space pirate ship, and those four-armed goons in them weren't no pirates I've ever seen."

"Then who were they?" Richard asked.

"I don't know," admitted Angela. "But their destroyer had a black dragon with a red stripe painted on its bow."

"You mean a dreadnaught," Richard corrected her. He was always amazed how civilians could mix up the various starships.

"Don't you be telling me what I mean, Mr. I-know-everything Wizard Scout," said Angela sounding affronted. "My uncle served in the navy. I know the difference between a dreadnaught and a destroyer. It had four missile tubes on the stern and bow. It also had double main batteries fore and aft. But they didn't look like normal plasma cannons to me."

Richard tried to play back Sergeant Ron's tale of his encounter with the black starship. He was sure Sergeant Ron had said it was a dreadnaught.

"Angela's right, Rick," said Terrie. "I wasn't as close to the ship as Angela, but it was about the size of one of the Empire's M-class destroyers. And the weapons were strange. They weren't plasma weapons."

"You said they used nukes," Richard said.

"Well, I said that because I didn't know what else to call them," said Terrie with a shrug of his shoulders. "They had a hell of a wallop. I definitely know that. And the radiation or energy or whatever the hell they released did a number on my Power reserve. I've never experienced anything like it."

"Angela," Richard said. "You said something about the pri—uh, the attackers having four arms. We're they Sterilians?"

Angela shook her head. "No way. They were in armored suits, so I didn't get a good look at their faces, but they weren't Sterilians. However, they all had the same red-striped, black dragon insignia painted on their armor."

Richard sensed Terrie looking at him. When he turned his attention, sure enough, he saw he was being watched. "What?" Richard said feeling a little self-conscious.

"You know something, don't you, Rick?" said Terrie. "Why'd you say it was a dreadnaught?"

Richard weighed his mission. It had been given by Councilwoman Deloris, not the Imperial High Command. And he hadn't been briefed on any security requirements. He was just supposed to find something out about the black dreadnaught or a possible source of DNA gas. He had a feeling he'd been thrust into a situation where everything was falling into place a little too readily. He smelled the stink of *'the One'* all over everything.

"All right, Terrie," Richard conceded. "I know a little more. I'll share what I know. But let me ask you something first. Who gave you your orders to go rescue these miners? Did the orders come verbally from the Imperial High Command? Or were they encrypted orders transmitted through the central computer?"

With a little hesitancy, Terrie said, "I was in a shuttle in deep space. So no, they weren't verbal orders. They were sent through the central computer but encrypted with the Imperial High Command's security code. They couldn't have been forged if that's what you're getting at."

Again Richard wished he had his battle computer with him. His brain was going a hundred kilometers an hour trying to sort things out. He didn't believe for one second Terrie's orders had come from the Imperial High Command. The central computer was part of *'the One.'* The question was why was *'the One'* interested in the black-dragon starship, and why had he been sent to Trecor. Richard had a funny feeling even Councilwoman Deloris was unwittingly being used as a tool for *'the One.'*

"Well?" Terrie said interrupting Richard's thoughts. "I answered your question, now how about you answering mine."

Richard explained about Sergeant Ron's encounter with the dreadnaught with the red-striped dragon insignia and the death of his wife and crew.

"That was forty or fifty years ago," Terrie pointed out. "Maybe those four-armed creatures Angela saw replaced their ship."

"Maybe," Richard said.

Turning to Angela, Richard said, "If you don't mind my asking, what were you mining when the black ship attacked?"

Angela looked down at her empty bowl and played with the spoon for a few seconds, then raised her head to look at her husband as if seeking advice.

"Angela," said Terrie in a soft voice. "Do you know something you haven't told me?"

Richard saw Angela give a nod so slight it was barely noticeable.

"I know you haven't known Rick long," said Terrie keeping his voice gentle. "But he's been involved in some pretty heavy-duty stuff over the years. He's probably one of the best, if not *the* best, wizard scout in the galaxy. If you know something, I think you should tell him."

Angela looked down at her bowl again. Finally, she turned to Richard and looked him dead in the eyes. "All right, Rick," she said in a cold voice that was deadly serious. "But this stays here in Trecor. It's not Empire business. Agreed?"

Richard had no idea what the young woman knew, but it was obvious she wasn't going to tell him if he didn't agree to her terms. "Very well, Angela. I give you my word of honor as a wizard scout that I won't relay whatever you tell me to the Empire. Is that good enough?"

"Fine," said Angela. "I'll trust you because Terrie trusts you." She took a deep breath as if seeking the resolve to tell something important. "My clan was ordered to the outer belt by Trecor's primary computer to locate the source of an anomaly."

Terrie must have seen the confusion in Richard's eyes because he broke in to explain. "The efforts of the Trecorian miners are coordinated through Trecor's primary computer. The O'Reilly clan are some of the best miners in the Trecorian Planetary Alliance."

"We *are* the best," said Angela sounding indignant.

"All right, they're the best," said Terrie rolling his eyes. "Anyway, they were ordered to a dense gathering of asteroids located near Trecor's boundary with the Empire. They call it the outer belt. It's near Planet X3321."

"All right," Richard said. "I understand. Go on, Angela."

"Well, it was a typical exploration and mining expedition for the first few months. Then we found something."

Richard waited several seconds for Angela to expound on the subject. When she didn't, he urged her onward. "Okay. I give up. What'd you find?"

"We found three...uh...spheres," Angela said as if seeing the objects in her mind. "I don't know how else to explain them. They...ah...seemed to hypnotize anyone who looked at them."

Alarm bells went off in Richard's mind. During his freshman year at the Academy, he'd been sent on a mission by '*the One*' to help the elf, Shandria, retrieve three spheres. They had been guarded by a powerful demon. They had barely escaped with their lives. Shandria had told him the spheres were parts of a seed. According to the elf, the seed was needed to guard a gate between dimensions. The only other things he remembered about the spheres were that there was one of each primary color and looking directly at one of the spheres put the viewer in a trance.

"Uh, were the spheres about the size of a man's head?" Richard asked. "And were they red, blue, and yellow?"

"No," said Angela.

Richard felt his muscles relax. He hadn't realized it, but just the thought that his current mission might involve demons had started to stress him out.

"I mean, the size is right," said Angela. "But the colors were green, orange, and purple."

"What's wrong, Rick?" said Terrie. "You look like you've seen a ghost. Have you seen those spheres before?"

Richard shook his head no.

"Oh," Terrie said. "I just thought—"

"I saw three spheres of primary colors," Richard said slowly. "Angela's spheres are the three secondary colors."

Richard noticed Angela and Terrie exchange glances.

"Do you know what they do, Rick?" said Angela.

Without hesitating, Richard said, "No, not really. The primary-colored spheres were very powerful, and they were well-guarded. I was told they had something to do with keeping some kind of interdimensional gate closed."

For the next fifteen minutes, Richard related his adventure with the elf, Shandria. He wasn't sure whether his two listeners believed him or not, but all he could do was tell them the truth as he knew it. When he finished, the three of them sat in silence for several seconds.

Terrie's wizard scout training kicked in, and he recovered first. "That's a lot to take in all at once, Rick."

Angela nodded her head in agreement.

"So," Terrie said, "you've been going on missions for this *'the One'* character and doing your wizard scout missions as well. Must suck."

"Tell me about it," Richard said. "But don't get me started. I only mentioned it because of those spheres." Turning to Angela, he said, "Where are the spheres now? Did you guys take them somewhere? Does the duke have them?"

"Slow down," said Angela holding up her hands. "The O'Reilly clan is beholden to the duke, but he doesn't have any say over us. So, no, we didn't give them to the duke. And no, we didn't move them. We tried, but they wouldn't budge. They're right where we found them."

"Oh," was all Richard could think to say. He didn't know whether the spheres not being moved was good news or bad news.

"Uh, do you want to know something strange, Rick?" Angela said leaning close as if not wanting to speak too loud.

Richard found himself leaning close as well. So did Terrie.

"I think they're some kind of teleportation device," said Angela.

"Why?" said Terrie.

"Because I was in the mine with the green sphere when the black ship showed up," said Angela. "I was wearing special protective goggles while trying to move the sphere. It started glowing bright enough that the light hurt even with my protective gear. Shortly afterward, the communication channel was flooded with reports that we were under attack."

Richard took a moment to ponder the information. He did his best to merge it with what Shandria had told him. When his brain started hurting from the effort, he gave up.

The three of them talked for another hour trading information. The high point of the information was that the miners hadn't told the Trecor government about the spheres. They'd only told them they'd found an anomaly. Also, as far as Angela knew, the spheres were still on the asteroid. And finally, Richard learned Angela thought the black ship and its crew had sensed the spheres were being tampered with and come to protect them.

When it became obvious to Richard he could discover no additional information, he excused himself by feigning a need to return to the barracks. Terrie let him drive the hover-cycle back. Richard thought the gesture was brave on the part of his ex-TAC officer. Although Richard was better at driving a hover-cycle than he was at piloting a Leviathan cat, that wasn't saying much. He did manage to land in front of the barracks without any major mishaps.

As Terrie was settling himself back in the pilot's seat in preparation for leaving, Richard remembered the original reason why he'd wanted to see his old TAC officer.

"Before you go, Terrie, I'd like to ask you a question."

"Shoot," said Terrie.

"I noticed a significant number of Trecorians are connected to Power reserves," Richard said. "Some of them were using it the other night to play some game called bingo."

"Bongo," Terrie said, grinning at Richard. "You'd better learn to say it right. It's the main pastime of Trecorians. Some of the more diehard fans can get downright sensitive on the subject."

"Okay," Richard said. "Bongo. The players were using telekinesis to move the ball around. It seemed kind of a waste of time to use Power for a game. Don't they use their Power for military applications? It seems like a waste of potential."

Terrie shook his finger at Richard. "And that's why it was a mistake graduating you cadets early from the Academy. You missed out on some of the more advanced-concept classes reserved for senior-year students."

"We didn't have much choice in the matter," Richard said defensively. "The Crosioians destroyed the Academy, if you remember."

"I do," said Terrie. "Still, you missed out on a lot of the information you're going to need in the years ahead."

"For instance?" Richard said, trying to prod his ex-TAC officer for information.

"Well, for one thing, why most Trecorians aren't trained in their use of Power other than the little telekinesis they use for bongo."

Richard hated it when people refused to just come right out with the information he needed. His battle computer said he was too impatient. Richard thought other people were just too patient for their own good.

"Okay, Terrie," Richard said, trying his best to keep his impatience out of his voice. "Why aren't they trained?"

"Because except for a few rare instances, it takes a diviner to unlock a person's Power."

"No one helped me," Richard responded.

"What can I say?" Terrie replied. "You're one of the exceptions. Besides, you're a diviner."

"Okay, then why don't the Trecorian diviners train your soldiers?"

Terrie gave a laugh. "Because, Rick, old buddy. Trecor doesn't have any diviners. The only Trecorians who've been fully trained in their Power usage were trained while they served in the Empire. The Empire isn't too keen on training potential enemies. And you know diviners are pretty rare. Only one in a thousand wizard scout cadets are diviners.

Richard had been told often enough diviners were rare. But he'd always assumed there were plenty of diviners to go around.

"It seemed like there were plenty of diviners at the Academy," Richard pointed out. "I was tested by five diviners during my freshman year. And I know the Commandant, Myers, Stella, and I were also diviners. That makes nine I know of."

"Yeah, well," said Terrie, "the Commandant and Gaston were assigned to the Academy as instructors specifically because they were diviners. And having Stella and you both as diviners in the same cohort was a rarity. Believe me, diviners are rare. And only a diviner can train another diviner to use their Power properly. That's why Trecor doesn't have diviners of their own."

"Nobody trained me," Richard stubbornly insisted. "I've been able to use my Power reserve as long as I can remember."

Terrie shrugged his shoulders. "As I said, you're a rarity."

If he was anything, Richard was persistent. He refused to give up on his point. "Okay, fine. But it seems like a big waste of potential. Why hasn't Trecor tried to get diviners of their own? Or, why haven't they at least tried to get one of the Empire's diviners to train their soldiers?"

The look Terrie gave Richard cut off any further thoughts of being stubborn. His old TAC officer looked as if he was surprised Richard couldn't answer his own questions for himself. If he'd still been a cadet, he would've assumed he was on the verge of getting extra duty.

"Trecor has tried," said Terrie. "But until now, we haven't been able to persuade the Empire to loan us one of their diviners. We've never had anything the Empire wanted bad enough to make that trade."

Richard's confusion must have shown on his face because Terrie explained without requiring additional prodding.

"You, Rick," said Terrie. "Why do you think I worked so hard to convince the duke he needed to pressure the Empire into assigning you to us?"

"Uh, I didn't know you did," Richard said genuinely surprised.

Richard liked Terrie but wasn't sure he liked him meddling in his life. "Are you saying I have you to thank for this assignment?"

"Only partially," Terrie answered with a shrug. "The duke needed you to heal his soldiers. The fact some of them were his own children motivated him even more. My battle computer, Taylor, told me the Empire was interested in obtaining information about the anomaly. I wanted you here to help train Trecorians. So…"

"So you put the pieces together and got me assigned here." Richard thought he was finally starting to see the behind-the-scenes manipulations that had gotten him where he was. "So why didn't you just flat out tell me, Terrie? Why all this subterfuge? Was this meal invitation just a ploy to get Angela and me together?"

Terrie's face reddened a little. "A little. But Angela wasn't in on the plan. She really did want to meet you. I just figured the two of you would eventually get around to talking about the anomalies. And just so you know, I haven't told the duke everything. Taylor actually suggested I go about it this way."

Richard had a distinct feeling that he knew who made the original suggestion to Terrie's battle computer. He could smell the manipulations of *'the One.'*

"Well, not to burst your bubble," Richard said, "but no one's said anything about me training anyone to use their Power reserves."

Terrie grinned. "No, I don't suppose they have. Like I mentioned before, we Trecorians are a proud and independent lot. We don't like admitting we need help. But I've a feeling that's going to change tomorrow."

"Tomorrow?" His interest was piqued. "Why tomorrow?"

Terrie gave a knowing laugh. "Because, my friend, tomorrow Colonel Santos is going to show off all she's taught you about heavy cats to the duke. And to be quite frank, Rick old buddy, you suck at piloting heavy cats."

Richard didn't disagree.

CHAPTER 29

The next morning found Richard in the pilot seat of a Leviathan cat. His copilot was Colonel Santos. His two tail gunners were none other than Commander Leander and Master Sergeant Stover.

A glance at the computer readout on his pilot's console confirmed the positions of the other Leviathan and the two Long Cats in his quad. As of yet, he didn't know the positions of his opponents. Colonel Santos had ordered him to only use the cat's electronics for the training exercise. She'd told him if she detected any indication he was using his wizard scout abilities, she'd consider it cheating and automatically fail him for the exercise. Richard's initial reaction was he didn't care. Besides, he seriously doubted the colonel could detect one of his active scans unless he let her. But in the end, he decided to play by her rules. The end result was that even though the regiment's intelligence officer had indicated his quad would be opposed by four aggressor quads totaling sixteen cats, none of his cat's electronics were picking them up.

"Do you have any suggestions?" Richard asked.

"The duke's here to observe you, Shepard, not me," said Colonel Santos in a tone Richard thought was a little too smug. "I'm just here to act as your copilot. So what are your…err…orders?"

Richard forced himself to swallow the anger welling up inside him. He hated things that weren't fair. And this whole test scenario wasn't fair as far as he was concerned. Richard supposed he should be used to it after all his years with Myers riding his back, but he wasn't.

The whole testing scenario had turned out to be a much larger affair than he'd anticipated. The duke was in the control tower along with Admiral Formida and a dozen other high-ranking officers.

To make matters worse, while Sergeant Hendricks had been hooking Richard's armor into the Leviathan's computer system, his armorer mentioned Admiral Donovan was in the control tower with the duke as well. Having Liz's current love interest watching did nothing to quell Richard's sense of pending doom.

"Fine," Richard said as he moved the two hand levers to start the Leviathan forward.

"Leviathan two," Richard ordered into his communicator. "Take both Long Cats and sweep around to the right. I'll try and smoke our targets out by drawing their fire."

"Roger," replied a voice over the cockpit's intercom.

"Quads are meant to support each other," said Colonel Santos. "I told you that before. You should keep—"

"I asked for suggestions, and you wouldn't give any," Richard said without attempting to hide his irritation with the colonel. "You want to be a copilot? Fine, be a copilot. You want to be in charge, that's okay too. Just say the word, and you can have the controls."

The colonel's face turned red. Through her visor, Richard noticed she was biting her lip. However, she didn't say anything further. The colonel just folded her arms and stared stoically ahead.

Richard hadn't moved the Leviathan more than a hundred meters when an excited voice came over the intercom.

"Contact," said the voice of Leviathan two's pilot. "Long Cat one is down."

"Roger," Richard said as he made an awkward turn toward the position of the other cats in his quad.

"You're too tight on your turn," said Colonel Santos. "You're going to tangle your legs if you're not careful."

"Then take the controls and get us over there," Richard said irritably.

The colonel kept her arms folded across her chest. "It's not my test. You should've kept the quad together. You obviously left their flank exposed."

Before Richard could respond, a voice over the cockpit speaker said, "Leviathan two is down." Richard recognized the voice as one of the Long Cat pilots. "What are your orders, Leviathan one?"

"Hold fast," Richard said. "We're on our way."

"See what happens when you separate your quad," said Colonel Santos. "This is a classic example of why—"

"Incoming," came the voice of Master Sergeant Stover over the cockpit intercom. "Four missiles are coming from our six o'clock. Another four is inbound from our eight."

"Activate countermeasures," Richard ordered.

"Activating," replied Colonel Santos as she slapped a button in the middle of her copilot's console.

Richard picked up eight energy readings on his passive scan tracking inbound. He had a momentary thought he might be cheating, but he didn't care.

"Can you take them out?" Richard said using the dedicated channel for his tail gunners.

A series of shudders from the rear of the Leviathan told Richard his tail gunners were responding to the attack. He saw four of the energy readings blink out. However, four of the energy readings continued tracking toward his Leviathan.

Richard pulled back hard on the levers for the Leviathan's rear legs in an attempt to kick the cat out of the missiles' paths.

"No!" said Colonel Santos in a high-pitched voice. "That's non-standard. You'll tangle—"

The colonel's warning came a little too late. Richard felt the Leviathan lean to the left. Before he could do anything to compensate, Colonel Santos made a grab for the levers controlling the Leviathan's legs.

"I've got the controls," shouted the colonel.

"You've got the controls," Richard said as he willingly released the levers. He hadn't wanted to pilot the Leviathan in the first place.

The colonel's hands moved deftly over the controls. Richard felt their cat slowly right itself. While he didn't especially like the colonel, Richard was forced to admit she was one heck of a cat pilot.

Before the colonel could do more than get the Leviathan stabilized, the cat shook several times. The vibrations were accompanied by the sound of four loud bangs.

"We're hit," said Master Sergeant Stover. "The commander and I are dead."

No sooner were the sergeant's words out than Richard sensed a score of energy readings heading his way. A warning alarm sounded. The alarm was followed by a computerized voice saying, "Missiles inbound from nine, eleven, one, and three o'clock positions."

The distance was short, and before either Colonel Santos or Richard could react, the Leviathan shuddered as missile after missile hit. The lights in the Leviathan's cockpit went out and all was silent.

"Well, I hope you're satisfied, Shepard," said Colonel Santos in an angry tone. "Thanks to you, we're—"

The animal which was Richard's temper broke out of its cage. Richard slammed his hand down on the control panel. "Enough!" he said between gritted teeth.

The colonel's initial shock at Richard's outburst quickly gave way to anger. She started to speak, but Richard beat her to the punch.

"No!" Richard said. Anger flooded through him. "I've had enough of your crap. I'm a wizard scout, not a damn cat pilot. And I'm certainly not a heavy-cat pilot. You wanted me to do this exercise as a cat pilot. Fine. I gave it my best shot. But if this was real combat instead of a training exercise, there'd be sixteen smoking cats out there. And none of them would be ours."

The colonel's mouth remained shut as she struggled for words.

"I'm tired of playing games, Colonel," Richard said. "I'm a highly-trained killer. I don't appreciate being treated like some wet-nosed cadet. You want to send a hundred cats against me with no limitations on my part to keep their crews alive? Fine. I'll destroy every one of them given enough time. And there wouldn't be a damn thing they or you could do about it."

Richard knew that wasn't exactly true, but he was too angry to care.

The colonel and Richard glared at each other. Where things would have went from there, Richard didn't know. As it was, he wasn't given a chance to find out.

The lights in the cockpit lit back up as the control tower

returned the Leviathan to full functionality.

"Leviathan one," said an authoritative voice over the cockpit intercom. "Pilot and copilot are to report to Duke Bistoria in the control tower immediately."

"Roger," said Colonel Santos.

Without asking Richard's permission, the colonel took over control of the cat and moved it at a double-quick pace in the direction of the distant control tower.

Neither the colonel nor Richard said anything further. Richard thought it was the quietest five minutes he'd ever experienced.

* * *

Admirals Formida and Donovan stood at stiff attention in front of Duke Bistoria. Colonel Santos and Richard stood next to them at attention as well. Except for the five of them, the control tower was devoid of life. Duke Bistoria had ordered everyone else out. Richard had never seen twenty soldiers including senior officers clear a room faster.

The duke was angry. He was a big man, and his size only added to the intimidation factor of his anger. Richard began wishing he'd tried a little harder to cooperate with Colonel Santos. Not that it would have mattered. No one knew better than Richard his skills in heavy cats were less than desirable.

The duke faced the four of them. He let his eyes wander down the line. They stopped on Colonel Santos.

"Report," ordered the duke.

"Sir," said Colonel Santos. "It's as I said before. Shepard's not a cat pilot. He can't even grasp simple quad maneuvers. I can teach him nothing."

The duke looked at Colonel Santos for several seconds. "You teach him? Is that why you think he's here?"

"Uh, sir?" said Colonel Santos sounding less confident. "I assumed—"

"You assumed?" said the duke.

Richard thought the duke's voice had lost a lot of its anger, but his displeasure still came through loud and clear.

"Sir," said the colonel. "I'm not sure what value you thought this outsider could bring to our forces. Our regiment has a five to one kill ratio over our enemies. The Trecorian-wide average is three to one. Our cat pilots are the best, sir."

The duke looked at Colonel Santos for a few seconds before glancing at the others.

"Is that what the rest of you think as well?" asked the duke.

The two admirals remained silent. Richard wisely chose to follow their lead.

When no one responded, the duke said, "Well, let me tell you what I think. The Trecorian Planetary Alliance has 22,000 cats. How many cats do the Balorian pirates have at their disposal?"

Admiral Donovan answered for the rest of them. "Approximately 15,000, sir."

"That's right," said the duke. "And how many do the Crosioians have?"

"Uh, sir," said Admiral Donovan less confidently. "No one knows for sure. Our latest estimates are about 140,000 cats of various models. We think many of them are older models though."

"Your numbers are a little off, Admiral," said Duke Bistoria. "What I'm going to tell you now is classified, and it stays in this room. Is that understood?"

The three Trecorians immediately answered yes. The duke looked at Richard.

"Uh, understood, sir," Richard said.

"Very well, I'm going to hold you to that, wizard scout," said Duke Bistoria. "Three weeks ago, we received word the Crosioians had signed treaties with the Balorian pirates along with the Katlan and Namidian federations. Their forces now have a total of nearly a half a million cats, not to mention a combined naval force of 180,000 starships and an army of eighteen billion."

"Uh, but sir," said Admiral Formida speaking for the first time. "We're not at war with the Crosioians. Neither are we at war with the Katlan or Namidian federations for that matter. The Crosioians have their hands full with the Empire. As long as the Empire stands, we have little to fear from the Crosioians."

In what might have been an attempt to support his superior, Admiral Donovan added, "Admiral Formida is right, sir. The Balorian pirates may harass us with a few raids now and then as the Crosioians' proxies, but we've never had direct combat with those bat creatures."

The duke stared at all four of them for a few seconds before turning his back to look at a star map on the wall.

"Wizard scout," said the duke. "How many cats can the Empire muster?"

"Uh, sir," Richard said unsure of his footing. "I'm not sure I should—"

"Oh, come now," said the duke turning back around. "It's not like it's a great military secret. But let me save you the trouble. On a good day, the Empire can muster 90,000 cats and about 35,000 combat starships. And what's the size of your army? About two billion?"

"Uh, sir," Richard said amazed at the accuracy of the duke's numbers. "Maybe. That's not counting the reserve forces like the Conglomerate though. I think the Conglomerate actually has more combat ships and cats than our regular forces."

"Yes, they do," agreed the duke. "And as long as the Empire can count on the Conglomerate's continued support, the Empire will continue to be a buffer between us and the Crosioians."

The way the duke put it worried Richard. It was as if the duke knew or suspected something.

"What are you saying, sir?" Richard asked.

"What am I saying?" said the duke. "I think I'll let you all figure that out on your own. In the meantime, I'm telling all of you a kill ratio of five to one isn't good enough. I'm not even sure a kill ratio of twenty to one would be enough. But by the Creator, it's a hell of a lot better than we can do now."

The duke paced the room a couple of times.

"I have no one to blame but myself for today's fiasco," said the duke as he turned and pounded his fist on a nearby desk. "But by the Creator, heads will roll if it happens again."

Pointing his finger at Colonel Santos, Duke Bistoria said, "Can you or can you not take orders from Wizard Scout Shepard?"

"Uh, orders, sir?" said the colonel sounding confused. "But...he's not one of us. He's a wizard scout. He doesn't even have a rank. Uh, sir."

The duke spun on his heel and pointed at Richard. "As of this moment, you are promoted to the rank of brigadier general in the Trecorian Army. For the next five and a half months, I expect you to conduct yourself as such."

Spinning back to Colonel Santos, the duke said, "Now, these little turf wars end here and now. You will give General Shepard your full cooperation, or so help me I'll make you wish you'd never been born. Do you understand?"

"Yes, sir!" said Colonel Santos hitting a stiff brace.

Turning back to Richard, the duke said, "And don't for one minute think I hold you blameless for what happened here today. I don't believe you thought I brought you here to be trained as a normal cat pilot. You should've contacted me before now if things weren't going the way you thought they should."

As he spoke, the duke's voice took on a heated emotion that was a cross between anger and pleading. "The continued existence of Trecor and your Empire may well depend on what we do here. Wizard Scout Shatstot told me you were the best. Now prove it."

"Yes, sir," was all Richard could think to say as he hit the stiff brace he hadn't used since he'd left the Academy.

If Richard thought the duke was finished, he was wrong. Turning to the two admirals, Duke Bistoria said, "Can I expect the Navy to give their full cooperation to General Shepard? Or do I need to promote him to fleet admiral as well?"

"I have nothing but respect for wizard scouts," said Admiral Donovan. He looked directly at Richard. "If there's anything you need where I can help, just let me know. Liz would never forgive me if she thought I wasn't giving you my full support."

"And you, Admiral Formida?" asked the duke.

"Of course, sir. Wizard...uh...General Shepard can expect the full cooperation of my staff and me."

"Good," said the duke. "Then we all understand each other."

Facing Richard, the duke said, "General Shepard. I'll give you another three weeks. If I'm satisfied with your progress at that time, I'll provide you with the information requested by your Imperial High Council."

Without another word, Duke Bistoria turned and left.

After the duke departed, Admiral Donovan turned to Richard. "On the surface, it sounds as if the duke has given you an impossible task, general. I hope you're as good as Liz thinks you are."

After a short pause, Admiral Donovan gave Richard a sympathetic smile. "So what are your orders, General?"

For once, Richard wasn't at a loss for words. He'd been the unofficial trainer for his cohort at the Academy. Since viewing that first bongo game, he'd been kicking some ideas around in his head. After his talk with Terrie the previous night, Richard had spent a lot of time thinking about what would be needed to train the Trecorians in how to better use their Power. Richard knew his plan would be better if his battle computer was here to help, but he wasn't. He'd just have to do the best he could on his own. However, Richard was confident he could come up with something, especially if he could get Terrie to convince his own battle computer, Taylor, to help.

"My orders?" Richard said. "Let's call them strong suggestions more than orders. But I do have a few ideas. Colonel Santos, I'll need your six best cat pilots, and two of your best fighter pilots. I happen to believe a twenty to one kill ratio is a distinct possibility if we work together. That is, if you're interested."

"I may be a stubborn fool, uh...General," said Colonel Santos, "but I'm not a complete idiot. If you know how to save my soldiers' lives, then I'm in. What do you have in mind?"

CHAPTER 30

Three weeks later, the control tower was devoid of any talking. All eyes watched the movement of the holographic images on a table in the center of the room. A sextant of cats composed of two Leviathans, two Long Cats, and two Warcats were advancing toward the center of the urban-training area. All six cats gave off a white glow. The holographic images of two fighters highlighted with white halos circled to the cats' rear.

From his seat in the control tower, Richard counted the number of orange-haloed cats advancing from the other side of the training area. The count hadn't changed. It was still twenty-four. The 147th's sextant was opposed by a full six quads of aggressor cats. An additional twelve orange-haloed fighters circled over the aggressor's side of the training area.

"I'm surprised their fighters haven't started making strafing runs yet," whispered Richard to Colonel Santos.

The colonel happened to be sitting in the seat next to him.

Responding out the side of her mouth, Colonel Santos whispered, "The 23rd Mech's commander is no fool. She'll suspect a trick. It's common knowledge we're going to be trying something new. She's just being cautious."

Richard continued sitting in his seat while waiting for something to happen. He was just a spectator at this point. Duke Bistoria, Admiral Formida, and Admiral Donovan stood near the holograph table. The two admirals were whispering in the duke's ear as they pointed at the moving holograms.

"They're confused because our cats are so spread out," whispered Colonel Santos.

"Do you think it'll work?" Richard asked getting nervous.

Richard preferred action to waiting. He'd never had children, but he imagined he was feeling something similar to an expectant father in a hospital waiting room.

"Don't go second guessing our plan now, General," said Colonel Santos. "Commander Leander knows what she's doing. She's our best. If anyone can pull this off, she can."

The lead Warcat of the 147th's sextant reached the designated line. The holographic images on the table blinked out for a split second before the computer system compensated for what Richard knew was a surge of electromagnetic energy from the pulse generator that had been hastily attached to the Warcat.

"What just happened?" said the duke to a technician sitting at the control panel nearest him.

"Uh...I, uh," stammered the technician. "I'm not quite sure, sir. I think the lead Warcat set off an electromagnetic-pulse device. The electromagnetic radiation has disrupted all sensors."

"Then why are we still seeing things?" asked Admiral Formida.

A nearby major dressed in the orange jumpsuit of the technical corps came to the enlisted technician's aid. "Our computer system is using visual data from tele-bots located throughout the training area in order to create the holographic images. We can still see, but every cat and fighter within a five-kilometer radius of that pulse generator has lost their electronic sensors. They'll only know what they can visually see until the disruption clears."

Before the technician could explain further, a score of missiles left each of the sextant's Leviathans. The missiles spread out in all directions, and at a height of three hundred meters, they exploded into a dense cloud of haze.

"We can't see," said Admiral Formida. "Do something."

The major and his technician fiddled with some controls. The haze cleared.

"We can see now," said the technician, "but most of the exercise's participants are in dense smoke. It looks like those were R22 military-grade smoke dispensers. Without their electronics, the cats will be basically blind. Even the fighters will be unable to see if they enter the smoked part of the training area."

"Should I abort the training scenario?" asked the major.

"Negative," answered Duke Bistoria.

The duke turned to look at Colonel Santos and Richard. "I'm assuming whatever you've got up your sleeves is safe."

Richard shrugged his shoulders. He wished Nickelo was here to calculate probabilities.

"I wouldn't have approved the plan if it wasn't within standard-safety guidelines, sir," said Colonel Santos.

The worry lines on the duke's forehead lessened, but Richard noticed they didn't disappear completely.

At that moment, the two fighter's supporting the sextant dove in for strafing runs. Their course stayed steady even when they entered the dense haze.

"How?" asked Admiral Donovan. "Their sensors should be out of commission."

"Passive and active scans," Richard explained. "The pilots can 'see' well enough if they don't get too fancy."

Two of the smaller orange-haloed cats winked out on the holograph table.

"Our fighters are taking out the enemy scouts first," said Colonel Santos for both the admirals' and duke's benefit. "General Shepard thinks their advanced electronics would be the first to recover."

More missiles left the sextant's two heavy and two medium cats. The missiles tracked unerringly toward orange-haloed targets. Four more orange-haloed holographs disappeared off the table.

"How are the missiles locating their targets?" asked the duke.

From the confused looks on the faces of the admirals and other VIPs in the room, the duke wasn't the only one seeking the answer to the question.

"Bongo," Richard said.

The duke gave Richard a look that seemed to say, '*What the hell are you talking about?*'

"Our cat pilots are using telekinesis to guide the missiles to their targets," Richard explained. "Sergeant Hendricks figured out a way to put receivers in the missile warheads, which are sensitive to telekinesis. Both our cat and fighter pilots are basically guiding the missiles the same way bongo players guide the ball into an opponent's net."

When the duke looked unconvinced, Colonel Santos spoke up. "He's correct, sir. As long as our pilots can sense their opponents with their passive and active scans, they can guide the missiles to their targets. Our heavy cats are doing most of the firing. Our two Warcats and our fighters are piloted by the regiment's best bongo players. Those pilots are the ones guiding the missiles to the enemy cats."

Colonel Santos shrugged her shoulders as she waved her hand at the holograph table. "I know it sounds strange, sir, but you can see the results."

Half of the orange-haloed cats were no longer on the holograph table. As the duke and the two admirals stared at the table, two missiles from the 147th's fighters shot out through the haze and struck two aggressor fighters circling outside the smoke cloud. The two orange-haloed fighters disappeared from the table.

"You're lucky there is very little wind today," observed Admiral Formida. "A gale would have made your plan useless."

"Then we'd have done something different," Richard said getting a little defensive. He had never liked having people criticize his plans with imaginary *what if's*, especially when they didn't provide a better alternative.

"Well, I think—" started Admiral Formida.

"Well, I think it's brilliant," cut in Admiral Donovan with a loud laugh. Turning to Richard, he asked, "How many pilots have you trained? Do you think the technique can be applied to naval vessels? What about—"

"Gentlemen," said the duke holding up his hands. "Let's save the questions until we've had time to analyze what just happened."

Turning to the major, the duke said, "Stop the training scenario. I've seen enough."

Richard thought it was just as well. Only six of the orange-haloed cats and eight of their fighters remained. All of the white-haloed cats and their two fighters continued to shine brightly on the holograph table.

"Congratulations, General, Colonel," said Duke Bistoria as he shook each of their hands. "I expect a full report by tomorrow morning. Colonel Santos, I want the 147th to take the lead on expanding this methodology into other units as soon as possible."

"Yes, sir," said Colonel Santos. "You know you can count on

the 147th."

"Yes, I do," said the duke smiling. "And as for you, General, I owe you some information. The duchess is having a ball in honor of a visit by a member of the Empire's Imperial High Council tomorrow night. You'll get your official invitation later today. However, my wife gave me strict orders to invite you personally. You'll come, of course?"

"Uh, yes, sir," Richard said.

A ball? Richard thought. *I can't even dance.* Another thought suddenly occurred to him. *And what the hell am I supposed to wear?*

CHAPTER 31

As it turned out, Richard didn't have to worry about finding something to wear. Late that afternoon, he heard a familiar voice in his shared space.

"Rick, are you there?"

"Nick," Richard replied more relieved than he cared to admit. *"You're a week late."*

"So we are, but who's counting," said Nickelo. *"Did you miss me?"*

"Maybe a little," Richard grudgingly admitted. *"Now hush, I've got a lot to tell you."*

Before he started the tale of the last five weeks, Richard had a thought. *"By the way, where are you?"*

"Margery brought us out of our hyper-jump just outside Trecor's system," said Nickelo. *"The* Defiant *should be landing at the spaceport in two hours and thirty-seven minutes."*

"Good," Richard said. *"I need my dimensional pack. I've gotta go to a ball tomorrow night."*

"Ooh! Aren't we enjoying the Trecorian nightlife?" said Nickelo with a laugh. *"The rest of us have been working our fingers to the bone trying to get the* Defiant *ready, and you've apparently been kicking back taking it easy."*

"Yeah, right," said Richard. *"First off, you don't have any fingers, so I'm not impressed. Now, listen up. I've got some things to tell you."*

For the next thirty minutes, Richard explained what he'd been doing and what he'd discovered over the last five weeks. The whole story should have taken only a few seconds to relay in their shared space. However, Nickelo insisted on having Sergeant Ron, Charlie, and Matthew hear the tale at the same time. Even feeding the battle helmet's video and audio readouts from the others into Richard's shared space took time. To top it off, Sergeant Ron kept interrupting him to ask questions about the black ship.

"I don't know, Sergeant Ron," Richard said for the tenth time. "Maybe the duke will tell me more about it tomorrow night."

Richard waited a few seconds for Nickelo to relay the information to the others before he received their replies through the battle helmet's communication array.

In the end, Richard cut the question-and-answer session short. While he waited for the *Defiant* to make landfall, Richard held another training class with a dozen of Colonel Santos's soldiers. He'd originally thought the Trecorians had a greater than normal share of people with sizeable Power reserves. As it turned out, the 147th just attracted a lot of those people. Early in his training at the 147th, Richard had come to realize it would take a significant amount of time to train enough soldiers to make a difference. He was just one man. He had other things to do. He couldn't spend all of his time training bongo players on how to use passive and active scans.

"We need more diviners," Richard thought.

"Well, they're pretty rare you know," said Nickelo intruding on Richard's thoughts.

"Yeah, so I've been told a zillion times," Richard said. *"Now, stop reading my mind."*

"Then stop thinking in your shared space," said Nickelo ignoring Richard's order. *"My point is still valid. Diviners are rare. Only one wizard scout cadet out of a thousand is a diviner. And only one out of eight cadets become wizard scouts. So, statistically, you may have to train eight thousand people before you find a single diviner. How many have you trained so far?"*

"About twelve hundred," Richard said. He wasn't looking forward to training another 6,800 before he found a replacement diviner.

"Hey, look at the bright side," said Nickelo. *"You might have a diviner in the very next group you train."*

"We can only hope," Richard said accompanying his answer with a silent prayer.

An hour later, Richard knew there wasn't a diviner in the new group. Colonel Santos's soldiers were motivated. The 147th tended to attract good bongo players as well as good soldiers. For the most part, they picked up the basic skills for passive and active scans fast enough. But since none of them were diviners, they couldn't train others themselves. The training was hard and frustrating work for Richard. By the time the *Defiant* landed, he was ready for a break.

Upon his promotion to general, the duke had provided Richard with a staff car. However, Richard preferred riding a hover-cycle whenever he could. He'd had to buy one on credit, but it was worth it as far as he was concerned. When Richard got word the *Defiant* was on final approach, he hopped on his hover-cycle and made for the spaceport. The gate guards waved him through without questions.

Being a general does have its perks, I guess, Richard thought.

"It has its responsibilities too," replied Nickelo in their shared space.

"I know," Richard said as he guided his hover-cycle down a taxiway to the berth assigned to the *Defiant*.

When Richard parked his cycle near the *Defiant's* open gangway, he gave a whistle. The Conglomerate had gone all out on the overhaul. The outside of the ship was buffed to a high shine, and even the *Defiant's* name was emblazoned boldly across the bow in fresh paint.

As Richard marveled at the changes in the *Defiant's* looks, a slim figure walked down the gangplank at a quick pace. It was Matthew Deloris.

"Rick!" yelled Matthew.

The teenager gave a laugh when he saw Richard's ride. "Sergeant Ron said you'd been promoted. I hadn't realized it was to the rank of leader of a Trecorian cycle-gang."

Richard smiled back. "One does what one does best."

When Matthew drew close, Richard reached out to shake the teenager's outstretched hand. But Matthew had other ideas. The teenager not only grasped Richard's hand but gave him a big hug as well.

Richard was a little taken aback. Other than hugs from his nephew and niece, he wasn't used to signs of affection.

"Get used to it," came a thought from Nickelo. *"You're all the kid's talked about for the past month. Apparently, he thought you were a big hero even before you saved his mother's life."*

"Whatever," Richard thought back. But in truth, he was touched.

Attempting to avoid any additional awkwardness, Richard whistled and pointed at the *Defiant*.

"What the hell did your mother do to our ship?" Richard asked. "It looks more like a mini-destroyer than a recon ship now."

"Ha!" laughed Matthew. "I told Mother she was overdoing it. Grandfather and she have been at each other's throats non-stop for the last month. I was glad to finally get off planet."

Richard smiled. He had a feeling he might have gotten the better part of the deal by arriving on Trecor five weeks early.

As Matthew and Richard looked the *Defiant* over from the outside, a hover-truck pulled up and came to a stop. The passenger door swung open and out jumped Sergeant Hendricks.

"Hoo-wee," said Sergeant Hendricks. "You said the *Defiant* was getting spiffed up a bit, Rick, but geesh, you didn't tell me you'd turned it into a miniature dreadnaught. Are those main guns Deloris model 200 plasma cannons?"

"Hell if I know," Richard admitted. He'd never had to deal with the larger ship armaments of the Empire.

Richard pointed at Matthew. "You'd have to ask this guy here. He's our resident weapon's expert. Sergeant Hendricks, this is Matthew Deloris. Matt, this is my old armorer from the Academy. There isn't a weapon made he doesn't know how to fix."

The two shook hands.

"Well, I don't know about the old part," said Sergeant Hendricks grinning. "But I've certainly gotten a lot of experience fixing all the weapons Rick has broken over the years."

Matthew laughed.

In a more serious tone, Sergeant Hendricks said, "It's a pleasure to know you, Matt. I can certainly see advantages to serving on the same starship as the future owner of Deloris Armaments."

"Well, don't get your hopes up too much," said Matthew. "There's about fifty relatives all vying for control of the company.

I'll probably be lucky if I get to clean the company bathrooms by the time I'm old enough to move into management."

"I'll take the risk," laughed Sergeant Hendricks. "In the meantime, how about showing me around? I'm anxious to get the lowdown on our weapon systems."

After Sergeant Hendricks and Matthew left, Richard was left to his own devices. He made his way back to his quarters on the *Defiant*. He found his battle helmet and dimensional pack stacked neatly on his bunk.

"Hey, Nick," Richard said out loud. "It's good to see you again."

"Same to you, buddy," replied Nickelo using the helmet's external speakers. "Anything I can do for you?"

"Actually, yes," Richard said. "I need my dress uniform for a ball tomorrow. How about sending me the specs?"

"Your wish is my command, oh greatest of wizard scouts," Nickelo said laughing while still using the battle helmet's speakers. The sound of his laugh echoed off the starship's bulkheads. "And see? I told you it would be smart to store your extra gear in your dimensional pack. I've no doubt whoever maintains clothing on Storage will have made sure it's already cleaned and pressed just in the off chance you'd need it."

"You did tell me that," Richard agreed. "I hope you're right about the pressed part." After a pause, Richard said, "I'm glad we're together again. I hated trying to figure everything out on my own. I think I like it better when I can just sit back and complain."

"Well, from what I can tell," said Nickelo sounding serious, "you've done very well. I knew you were trainable." Starting to laugh again, Nickelo said, "You're turning out to be quite the little wizard scout."

"Not funny," Richard said. He laughed in spite of himself. It was good to just have his friend back.

CHAPTER 32

The staff hover-car with the single star of a brigadier general pulled up in front of the palace steps. Once the honor guard opened the hover-car's door, Richard stepped out followed by Matthew Deloris.

Richard was in his wizard scout dress uniform. It had been made special for him to wear to the Fleet Admiral's Ball on Velos the previous year. Although he'd never gotten a chance to wear it, his friend, Telsa, had told him the creator of his dress uniform, Monsieur Geraldo, was one of the finest tailors in the Empire. Richard believed it. Even he had to admit he looked resplendent in the black and silver-trimmed uniform. The golden-dragon insignia of the wizard scout corps on his collar drew curious stares from those around him.

Although non-standard for dress uniforms, Richard had strapped his black utility-belt around his waist. Of course, he'd stripped everything off the belt except for his phase rod. He had a feeling wearing a pistol and carrying live grenades wouldn't go over too well at the duchess's high-society event.

"Are you sure it's all right for me to be here?" said Matthew trying to straighten out the tuxedo Richard had summoned for him. "I mean, I wasn't officially invited."

"Nonsense," Richard said smiling at the young man's obvious nervousness. "My invitation said General Shepard plus one. You're the one. Besides, there's someone I want you to meet."

As they walked up the stairs, Matthew stumbled. Richard

caught him by the elbow to keep him steady.

"Relax, Matt," Richard said. "Why so nervous? I thought being in the Deloris family, you'd be used to going to balls and big-wig parties."

"Then you thought wrong," said Matthew sounding a little affronted. "Mother tends to keep me in a pretty protected environment most of the time." With a slightly embarrassed sound to his voice, Matthew added, "Heck, I don't even know how to dance."

"Well, join the club," said Richard as he laughed and gave the teenager a slap on the back. "I don't know how to dance either. Maybe we should both keep score of how many female toes we step on tonight. The loser with the most toes has to cook supper for the *Defiant's* crew tomorrow."

Matthew seemed to relax noticeably with Richard's jest. "It's a deal. But just so you know, I don't know how to cook either."

Once they were inside, Richard introduced his young charge to several of the people he'd gotten to know over the last month. Despite the teenager's protest to the contrary, Richard thought he presented himself with well-practiced grace. Richard was pretty sure the young man had spent a lot of time observing Councilwoman Deloris over the years.

After introducing Matthew to Colonel Santos and Admiral Donovan, Richard found who he'd really been seeking.

"Tia," Richard said as he approached the duke's daughter.

The teenager was only dressed in a standard fighter-pilot's dress uniform. However, she made it look like the finest ball gown as far as Richard was concerned. From the stares of the young men around her, he wasn't the only one who thought so. In Richard's opinion, Tia was every bit as beautiful as her older sister.

Tia turned away from the three young naval officers who were vying for her attention. When they saw Richard approaching in his wizard scout uniform, they beat a hasty retreat.

"Rick," said Tia with a dazzling smile that reminded Richard of her sister. "You look good enough to eat. I'm beginning to think my sister was a fool for letting you slip through her fingers."

Richard felt himself blush.

"Uh, well," Richard stammered. "Anyway, Tia, I'd like to introduce you to my friend, Matthew Deloris. Matt this is Tianika

Bistoria. She's been a big help to me over the past month. She is by far the best fighter pilot I've ever seen. You should've watched her making mincemeat out of a bunch of cats yesterday."

To Richard's amazement, Matthew bent low at the waist in a formal bow.

"The pleasure is all mine, Miss Tianika."

This time it was Tia who blushed. "Uh, thank you, uh…Matthew," said Tia. "I think you'll find we Trecorians are a lot less formal than you may be used to, Mr. Deloris. My family's mostly soldiers. They're not diplomats."

"Please call me Matt," said Matthew. "And you're the most beautiful soldier, uh…I mean, ah…" Matthew blushed.

Richard watched the two trade compliments and blushes for a couple of minutes before deciding his self-imposed mission was complete. He'd been sure the two would hit it off together. When he got the chance, he excused himself. He left the two teenagers in a deep discussion over the best weapon system for a Zip fighter.

"Ah. Rick, the matchmaker," commented Nickelo in their shared space. *"You missed you're calling, buddy."*

Richard mentally shrugged. *"I had a feeling they'd get along. I think they're both good kids."*

"I calculate a hundred and ten percent probability you're correct," said Nickelo. *"They are good kids."*

"You didn't calculate that," Richard said. *"It's not possible to have more than a hundred percent."*

"Sure it is," laughed Nickelo. *"I gave both of them bonus points."*

* * *

Richard roamed around a little and spoke to a couple of people he knew, but for the most part, he stayed to himself. About thirty minutes later, Richard became bored with what he thought was all the nonsense of a ball. After loading down a small plate with appetizers he rescued from a passing waiter, Richard made for a less crowded hallway leading away from the main ballroom. Once clear of the crowd, Richard felt a little more comfortable.

I don't think I'll ever get used to this kind of fancy stuff, Richard thought.

"Probably not," answered Nickelo. *"We're going to have to work on your diplomatic skills anyway. Not all wars are won on the battlefield. You can accomplish a lot during diplomatic affairs like this."*

"Well, I think I'll leave it to the politicians," Richard said. *"I prefer action to words."*

"Hmm," said Nickelo with a chuckle. *"I see we've got a lot of training to do."*

Still bored, Richard headed for an open set of double doors where he heard the sound of laughter. The laughter was combined with a lot of cheering. Once inside, he saw a group of twenty or so well-dressed military personnel along with a similar number of people in tuxedos. Most of them were gathered around a small rectangle marked on the carpeted floor with white tape. As Richard watched, he saw a miniature red-ball scooting across the floor.

"Bongo," Richard thought. *"They really are serious about the game."*

"Well, lucky thing for you they are," replied Nickelo. *"At least you have a ready-made batch of personnel with sizeable Power reserves to test and train."*

"Yeah," Richard said. *"Tell me about it. Most of them are connected to Power reserves a whole lot larger than mine."*

Richard spotted the duke's son, Daniel, standing near the circle. He wasn't one of the current players, but he was cheering enthusiastically for those who were. When Daniel spotted Richard, the boy gave a wave and went back to watching the game.

"Yep, they're definitely addicted," Richard thought.

Richard noticed a miniature version of Tia sitting on a sofa in the far corner of the room. It was Chloe. She was dressed in a light-blue ball gown. She didn't look like she was having fun.

Richard made his way over and sat down beside the child.

"You're supposed to ask permission before you sit down next to a young lady," said Nickelo. *"Where'd you learn your manners?"*

Richard was tempted to say, "in an orphanage," but resisted the urge. He was well aware his manners could be atrocious on occasion. Trying to make up for his mistake, he held his plate out to the young girl. "Want one? I don't know what those yellow and green things are, but they're delicious."

The few times Richard had met Chloe, she'd been pretty timid and shy. This time she actually gave him a slight smile.

"They're fargo eggs," said Chloe. "You shouldn't eat more than two at a time. They tend to give you bad breath."

"Oops!" Richard said covering his mouth with his hand. "I think I've had six already."

"You've had seven," Nickelo said correcting Richard's count, *"and your breath won't stink. Your self-heal will identify the chemicals in the eggs as poison and negate them in order to return your body to baseline."*

"Sometimes you're silly, Rick," said Chloe using his nickname for the first time Richard could remember. "Tia says I shouldn't be afraid of you."

"Well, of course you shouldn't," Richard assured her.

"That's probably easier said than done considering you almost killed her," Nickelo pointed out.

"Hush, Nick," Richard said. *"I apologized. What more can I do?"*

"Uh, your brother sure is into bongo," Richard said. "How come you're not over there with him?"

The young girl frowned and gave a sigh.

"Because my mother made me wear this," she said lifting up part of her ball gown. "Mother said I had to be ladylike tonight. Besides, I'm not really a big fan of bongo."

"Oh?" Richard said surprised. He was intrigued. The young girl was the first Trecorian he'd met who wasn't an enthusiastic supporter of the game. "I was beginning to think it was an unwritten law every Trecorian had to be a head-over-heels fan of bongo. Your brother and sister certainly are."

"Yes. Well, they're good at it," said Chloe.

Something in the child's voice sounded strange to Richard. She sounded sensitive about the subject.

"And you're not?" Richard asked. Something told him he should probably leave the matter alone, but his classes at the Academy hadn't included sensitivity training, so he pressed onward.

"Not really," said Chloe.

Richard noticed the young girl seemed to be concentrating very hard on her shoes.

"I once heard our family's bongo trainer tell my parents I had a strange Power reserve," said Chloe. "He said I'd never be very good at bongo. He told them it was a waste of time to continue training me."

"Oh, sorry," Richard said detecting the obvious sadness in the little girl's voice. Personally, he thought bongo was a silly game anyway. But then, he wasn't a Trecorian.

"You know, Ric," said Nickelo, *"she's connected to a pretty large Power reserve."*

"Yeah, I know," Richard said. *"I'm picking up her reserve with my passive scan. So?"*

"Oh, I don't know," said Nickelo. *"I just think it's curious her bongo trainer thought her Power reserve was strange. I calculate a one hundred percent probability a Trecorian bongo trainer is nowhere near the skill level of one of the Academy's diviners."*

Richard thought about it a few minutes. He'd been concentrating on working with the bongo players Colonel Santos had recommended to him. As the Trecorians' lone diviner, he was kept too busy to test other people. For reasons that were now obvious, Chloe hadn't been referred to him by the local bongo experts.

Being a little bored anyway, Richard said, "Chloe, I don't know if you know this, but I'm a diviner."

"Yes, I know," said Chloe. "That's all Daniel and Tia have talked about lately. Mother and Father have made a big deal about your training of the bongo players in passive and active scans."

"Oh, okay," Richard said. "Well, I was just wondering if you'd mind if I checked your Power reserve for myself. It might be good to get a second opinion."

"That's fine," said Chloe. "Go ahead if you want. But why ask? You're a wizard scout. You can pretty much do whatever you want, can't you?"

Richard laughed. "Uh, not hardly. Besides, sometimes people with large Power reserves get perturbed if they discover someone inspecting their Power reserve or link without permission. A lot of wizard scouts and magic, uh, I mean other people, might consider it an act of war."

"Oh," Chloe said sounding surprised. "Well, I won't consider it an act of war if you want to try. But Mother and Father had me tested by several bongo trainers."

"Well, let's just have a looksee," Richard said.

"Will it hurt?" Chloe asked.

"No. You probably won't even know I'm scanning you," Richard said trying to give the little girl a reassuring smile. "My battle computer tells me I'm getting very good at doing active scans without being detected."

While Richard talked, he formed an active scan. In spite of what he told the girl, he knew Nickelo was a lot better at scans than he was.

"*Nick?*" Richard said.

"*Understood, Rick,*" replied Nickelo taking the hint. "*Give me control of your active scan. We'll see what we can find out. I'm a little bored anyway. Oh, and make sure you follow along with the scan. Sometimes you sense things I don't.*"

Richard took his battle computer's advice and followed along as Nickelo traced a thin link between Chloe and her Power reserve. She had a large reserve, and there were no other links coming off of her reserve.

"*Hmm, that's interesting,*" said Nickelo. "*She's got a solitary Power reserve. But look how flimsy the link to her reserve is. No wonder her testers thought it was strange. She's barely connected to her Power reserve. Heck, if she sneezes too hard, it'll probably break.*"

"*Doubtful,*" Richard said as he analyzed the data from the active scan being fed into his shared space by Nickelo.

"*I was joking,*" said Nickelo. "*You still take things too literally sometimes.*"

"*Whatever,*" Richard said concentrating on the scan results too much to waste time bantering with his battle computer.

"What is it?" said Chloe sounding alarmed.

"Oh, I'm sorry," Richard apologized. He'd been concentrating so hard he'd forgotten his test subject was a little girl. "I think you've got a lot of potential. I'm just trying to figure out the dynamics of your Power reserve. It is a little different."

"Oh," said Chloe casting down her eyes and concentrating on her shoes again. "So they were right? I'll never be a good bongo player."

"Does that really matter?" Richard asked as he continued to probe the girl's link. He was really just trying to take the girl's mind off the scan more than he was truly interested in her answer.

Richard was jerked out of his concentration by what sounded like a sob. One look at Chloe's downcast head and jerking shoulders told him the source of the sound.

"Great job," said Nickelo. *"Mr. Sensitivity strikes again. Will you ever learn to consider other people's feelings before you open your mouth?"*

Richard wanted to tell his battle computer where he could put his advice but refrained. Nickelo wasn't the problem. While Richard could handle fighting off a line of plasma-firing UHAAVs without fear, a crying little girl left him petrified.

"Uh, I'm sorry," Richard said. "Really. Whatever I said, I'm sorry."

Chloe just shook her head and stood up. Without looking at Richard, she hurriedly walked away until she disappeared through the open double doors.

"Well, that went well," said Nickelo.

"Just be quiet, Nick," Richard said. *"For once in your life, just be quiet."*

When Richard finally made his way back into the main ballroom, he wasn't in a good mood.

"When will I learn to just mind my own business?" Richard thought. *"Life would be a lot simpler."*

"Maybe," said Nickelo intruding on Richard's thoughts, *"but maybe not. Take a look at my latest calculations from the data we obtained from the scan on Chloe."*

Richard let his mind absorb the data his battle computer released into their shared space.

"Hmm," Richard finally said. *"Are you sure?"*

"Need you ask?" said Nickelo sounding indignant. *"I'm the most advanced prototype computer the Empire has ever produced. I think at nanosecond speed on my slow days. I—"*

"Fine," Richard said admitting defeat. *"I'm sorry I questioned you."*

"Wizard Scout Shepard," said a voice from Richard's rear.

Turning, Richard saw a squat, bald man in a tuxedo. His oversized belly made him look like one of the Earth penguins Richard had once seen at a zoo during an outing at the orphanage.

The man was Councilman Jenkins, the Empire's current

representative on Trecor. Richard hadn't previously met the man, but he'd seen him from a distance.

"May I have a word, if you don't mind?" said Councilman Jenkins making it obvious he expected Richard to take the time to talk whether he minded or not.

"What is it, sir?" Richard said forcing himself to be polite.

"If you don't mind," said the councilman, "perhaps we can find a place a bit more, uh, private."

Richard shrugged his shoulders. "Fine by me."

The councilman led Richard through several hallways until they arrived at the door to a small room. The books stored neatly on shelves along the walls identified the room as the palace's library. The room was empty.

Councilman Jenkins shut the door behind them. Richard heard a click and noticed the councilman drop something into his pocket.

Did he just lock the door? Richard thought. *Is he kidding?*

Richard made a quick active scan of the walls, floor, and ceiling just to make sure the room wasn't lined with creallium. It wasn't. His momentary concern he'd somehow walked into a trap disappeared.

"I received a high-priority communique this morning from the Imperial High Council," said the councilman. "They're extremely disappointed you haven't been providing them with detailed reports on your progress."

Richard stared at the potbellied politician.

"Is he serious, Nick?" asked Richard.

"Uh, are you?" laughed Nickelo. *"He's a politician. Does he look like a comedian?"*

"Uh, sir," Richard said trying his best to be tactful. "I think we both know your communique came from Councilwoman Deloris and not the council itself."

The councilman glared at Richard. "I don't think you realize who you're dealing with. Councilwoman Deloris speaks for the Imperial High Council."

Richard gave a little smile. "I've a feeling Councilwoman Deluth might disagree."

At Richard's words, Councilman Jenkins gave a tight-lipped smile of his own. Red warning lights began to go off in Richard's mind.

"Nick?" Richard thought.

"I don't know," answered Nickelo. *"I'm not connected to the tele-network."*

"Ah," said the councilman. "It's as I suspected. Wizard scouts aren't the all-knowing, mystical warriors some of the less educated citizens in the Empire seem to believe."

Richard had initially been ambivalent toward the councilman. That was quickly changing. He suddenly felt his ambivalence turning into a definite dislike.

"I seriously doubt any wizard scout told you they were all-knowing," Richard said. "What's your point, sir?"

If anything, the councilman's smile widened. "My point is you should be as concerned about Empire affairs as you are with Trecorian politics, uh…General."

The councilman had a smirk on his face while waiting for Richard to react.

Richard wanted to wipe the smirk off the fat man's chubby face, but with a self-control he didn't know he possessed, resisted the urge.

"Very good, Rick," said Nickelo approvingly. *"He's just trying to bait you."*

The councilman waited a good five seconds for Richard to say something. When he didn't, the councilman's smirk faded and was replaced by irritation.

"I was told you were stubborn," said the councilman, "but no matter. As you would know if you weren't so involved with Trecorian affairs, Janice Deluth is no longer a member of the Imperial High Council. She resigned last week. Councilwoman Deloris and her allies now hold the majority votes on the council."

Richard's mind raced. He hated politics and tried to stay out of them. However, even he knew the councilman's news didn't bode well for either the Empire or what remained of the wizard scout corps.

"Stay calm, Rick," warned Nickelo.

"I'll be calm as a cucumber," Richard answered. He'd never actually seen a real cucumber, but it was one of his battle computer's sayings. Richard figured it was a good time to throw it back in his face.

"Does all this have some bearing on me?" Richard asked

knowing full well it did. However, he refused to give the councilman the satisfaction of snapping at his bait.

"What? Are you that obtuse?" said Councilman Jenkins sounding flustered for the first time. "It means when Councilwoman Deloris orders you to do something, you'd best do it without questions. The winds of power in the Empire are changing. If what remains of your precious wizard scout corps doesn't wish to be blown to the wayside, you'd best get on the right side."

"Hmm, really?" said Richard slowly giving way to the anger rising inside him.

He'd always hated it when people who had no authority over him tried to order him around. Richard was a good soldier, and he obeyed legal orders to the best of his ability. However, pompous, backstabbing diplomats who assumed they had power over him pissed him off to no end.

"Yes, really," replied the councilman. "The Imperial High Council didn't invest all those credits on your starship for nothing. They expect something in return. So that bedraggled excuse for a ship's captain and you had better start obeying orders. Otherwise, you may find yourself in serious trouble."

As he spoke, the councilman's face took on a deep red. Richard noticed a drop of spittle drip down a corner of the fat man's mouth.

"And believe me, I don't make idle threats," said Councilman Jenkins as he poked Richard in the chest with a pointed index finger. "So watch your step, wizard scout. You don't impress me."

The councilman started to pull his finger back, but his hand didn't move. With a growing look of concern on his face, the councilman struggled to free his finger. Instead of coming free, the finger continued to sink slowly into Richard's chest. The more the councilman struggled, the deeper his fingers and hand disappeared into the black and silver of Richard's dress uniform.

Between gritted teeth, Richard said, "Never...ever...threaten a wizard scout, Councilman. We don't take threats well, idle or otherwise."

Richard continued using his telekinesis to hold the fat man's hand inside his chest for a few more seconds. Since he'd only shifted the man's hand and fingers into the void, it cost very little Power to maintain the shift. Once the fear in the bald man's eyes grew to a satisfying size, Richard pushed on the councilman's hand with his telekinesis until the man's chubby fingers were again in open air. At that point, Richard dropped the Power he'd placed around the councilman's hand. The hand shifted out of the void and back into the physical dimension.

"Let me tell you what I think, councilman," Richard said in a voice so icy it surprised even him. "I think the Conglomerate paid for the upgrades to the *Defiant*, not the Imperial High Council. The *Defiant* is a privately-owned starship. Neither Captain Ronald Deloris nor I take our orders from the Conglomerate. And I take my orders from the Imperial High Command, not the council. I definitely don't take orders from Councilwoman Deloris or any other individual member of the council."

Richard poked the councilman in the chest with his index finger. But unlike during the councilman's attempt at intimidation, Richard's hand was not shifted into the void. The councilman winced with pain when Richard's finger struck home.

"So don't you or the councilwoman ever presume you've got any influence over me," Richard said letting his anger fill every word. "Neither of you have any idea who or what you're dealing with. If you ever try to threaten me again, one of my dolgar friends is liable to visit you some night while you're sleeping in your cozy little bed. If they do, the last thing you'll feel will be their fangs sinking into that piece of flab you call a body as they suck out your life force. Then they'll drag you down to the center of the planet and leave you with the rest of the refuse where you belong."

Richard had more to say, but he forced himself to keep his mouth shut. He knew he'd said way more than he should have.

"That's for sure," said Nickelo in their shared space. *"We've got to get you enrolled in some anger-management classes."*

Richard chose not to reply to his battle computer. He just turned and made for the library's door. Richard didn't give the councilman the satisfaction of seeing him struggle with the lock. He just wrapped himself in Power and shifted into the void as he walked through the ornately-carved woodwork of the door.

"That was a waste of Power," said Nickelo. *"You could've picked the lock with your Power a lot more efficiently."*

"I don't care," Richard thought back. *"Walking through the door was a hell of a lot more satisfying."*

CHAPTER 33

"Well, that could have gone better," said Nickelo.

The anger was slowly leaving Richard, but he wasn't quite ready to make his way back to the main ballroom. He knew he still needed to see the duke, but he had something else to do first.

"Find me an empty room, Nick."

"Compliance. I'm having Margery download the specs for the palace to me."

"She's got them?" Richard asked. *"I figured they'd be a Trecorian state secret or something."*

"Not hardly," replied Nickelo. *"If you know where to look, anything paid for with government taxes leaves a paper trail. By the way, since I'm still on the* Defiant, *I can't use the battle helmet's electronic sensors. You'll need to feed the results of your passive scan to our shared space."*

"I'll do you one better," Richard said as he held out his hand and summoned his battle helmet to him. When it appeared in the air, he caught it and swung it up on his head. Somewhere between the point where he caught it and his head, the battle helmet changed shape to three quarter's mode.

"What'd you do that for?" asked Nickelo. *"I could've used the info from your passive scan to find an empty room. Besides, you'll look strange trying to dance with a battle helmet stuck on your head, don't you think?"*

"I'm not in the mood for jokes," Richard said. *"I want you to contact Councilwoman Deluth's battle helmet. Then I want the two*

of you to set up a holograph communication between us. I need to talk to my mother."

In rather quick time, Nickelo found a small linen room. The only occupants were two young people trying to get to know each other a whole lot better. They hurriedly left the room when Richard entered. He locked the door behind them.

"Ready," said Nickelo. *"Margery has the councilwoman on standby."*

"Fine," Richard said. *"Activate the hologram."*

The room shimmered and shifted into two visions overlaid over each other. Richard still saw the contents of the linen room through the sensors of his visor. At the same time, he also saw the holographic image of a dimly lit room with a cushioned chair near a lit fireplace.

Councilwoman Deluth sat in the chair. Although her body appeared to be that of a woman in her late twenties, Richard got the impression of extreme fatigue from her. Perhaps it was the weak smile, or maybe it was the way she seemed to struggle to sit upright in her chair.

"Ah, Richard," said the councilwoman. "I expected you to contact me last week. I assume you've heard."

"That you've resigned from the council?" Richard said. "Councilman Jenkins just told me. I guess he told me the truth. You have resigned."

"Yes, it's true," said his mother.

"Why?" Richard asked. "The Empire needs you now more than ever. Only you can stop Councilwoman Deloris and her cronies."

Richard's mother smiled. "You overvalue my importance, Richard. But it doesn't matter. I no longer have the strength to fight. It's time for someone else to take up the battle flag. My time has come and gone."

"No," Richard said. "You've got many years ahead of you yet. Don't give up now. I...we...uh, I mean, I have a lot of things I want to talk to you about."

"I'm sorry, Richard," said the former councilwoman. "I'm much older than Thomas was when he passed. Some of my missions for *'the One'* lasted more years than I care to remember."

"But—" Richard started to argue.

His mother held up her hand to stop Richard before he got

started.

"There is no but, Richard. However, I promise you, we'll meet again. In the meantime, Wizard Scout Shatstot has kept me updated on your progress. You've done well. I'm proud of you. The Trecorians are valiant fighters. They'd make good allies should the need ever arise. And I fear it might."

"What do you mean?" Richard asked as he struggled to assimilate everything he'd been told during the last couple of hours.

"It doesn't matter, Richard," replied his mother. "Just keep doing what you do best; shaking things up. But I'll give you a word of warning. Be cautious around Councilman Jenkins. He may look like a fool, but he's intelligent and deadly. Try not to make an enemy of him. I'd recommend steering clear of the councilman if possible. And for the Creator's sake, watch what you say to him. He's definitely one to hold a grudge."

"Oops!" said Nickelo in Richard's shared space. *"That advice is a day late and a dollar short."*

"What's a dollar?" Richard asked absentmindedly.

"It's another word for a credit," said Nickelo. *"The point is you screwed up."*

"You know what, Nick?" Richard thought back. *"At this point, I really don't care."*

Shifting back to his conversation with his mother, Richard said, "I'm going to see if I can get back to Risors. We can talk more then. I'll help take care of you. Maybe we can—"

Again his mother held up her hand to stop Richard.

"No," she said. "What you're doing on Trecor is more important than anything you could do here. Besides, Gaston is here if I need anything."

"You need someone besides Myers to—" Richard started to say.

"Richard, please," came a weak protest from his mother. The obvious weaknesses of his mother stopped Richard's rebuttal quicker than any words could.

"I've lived a good life, Richard," said his mother. "My only regret is we didn't have more time together. For my sake, I wish you'd try to get along with Gaston. He's your brother after all. His life hasn't been easy either. Please try to understand."

Richard didn't say a word. When it came to Myers, he'd make

no promises.

"I grow tired, Richard," said his mother. "It's time to say goodbye."

A sense of dread told Richard his mother's goodbye was intended for more than their current conversation.

"May...may I call you, Mother?" Richard said surprising even himself.

His mother smiled. "I'd be honored...Son."

"Goodbye, Mother," Richard said.

"Goodbye, Son," she replied. "May the Creator watch over you always."

CHAPTER 34

By the time Richard finally got back to the main ballroom, he was emotionally spent. All he wanted to do was go back to the *Defiant* and lie down. As far as he was concerned, the duke could wait. However, when Richard saw Tia and Matthew dancing together and obviously having a good time, he decided to suck it up and stay.

"I think you're starting to turn into an old softy," said Nickelo.

"Don't start," Richard said. *"I'm really not up to it."*

Richard watched the two teenagers dance for several minutes. As he watched, he felt himself beginning to relax.

"General Shepard?" said a young man in a lieutenant's naval uniform. "If it's convenient, the duke would like to see you now."

"Will this night ever end?" Richard wondered.

"Yes, it will," said Nickelo with a barely hidden laugh. *"Sunrise is in eight hours and twenty-seven minutes. I calculate a one hundred percent probability this night will end then."*

"Grow up, Nick."

Richard followed the duke's orderly through a series of hallways. They eventually entered a comfortable looking room with several cushioned chairs and sofas. When Richard entered the room, Duke Bistoria rose.

"Ah, General Shepard. I hope you're enjoying my wife's party. The duchess doesn't get a chance to entertain much."

"It's been interesting," Richard said trying his best to be truthful.

The duke either took Richard's answer as an affirmative, or he was just making small talk and didn't really care. Whatever his reason, he motioned to a chair across from him and took a seat.

Richard sat down.

Besides the duke, Admiral Donovan, Admiral Formida, and Colonel Santos were in the room. So was Wizard Scout Shatstot. Surprisingly, Sergeant Ron sat in one of the seats as well.

The duke didn't speak again until the orderly had left the room. Once the door shut behind the lieutenant, Duke Bistoria nodded his head at Sergeant Ron.

The captain of the *Defiant* lifted a small, rod-like device and swept it across the room. Richard noticed several quick flashes similar to static electricity in the corners of the room.

"We're clear now," said Sergeant Ron replacing the rod in a pocket on his uniform. "There were five tele-bots in the room. They're destroyed now. We can talk securely."

"What about static tele-bots?" Admiral Donovan asked.

"Nothing I can do about them if there are any here," confessed Sergeant Ron. "But if they aren't activated, they can't observe us anyway. We're safe enough."

"You can detect tele-bots, Sergeant Ron?" Richard asked. Even Nickelo couldn't detect them as far as he knew.

"Me?" said Sergeant Ron. "Heck, no. But I swiped this handy little gadget from my daughter."

With a mischievous smile, the old man added, "I felt it was my civic duty to ensure the openness of the Empire's elected officials. Now why would a member of the Imperial High Council need one of these? Surely Diane doesn't have anything to hide."

The twinkle in Sergeant Ron's eyes told Richard the captain of the *Defiant* knew full well Councilwoman Diane Deloris had many things she wished to keep hidden from others.

"Well, my duke, I for one," said Admiral Formida, "think it's shameful the Empire stoops so low as to spy on you in your own palace."

"Admiral," said Duke Bistoria with the hint of a smile. "I seriously doubt all five of those tele-bots belonged to the Empire. Also, I don't for one minute doubt more than a few Trecorian tele-bots are haunting the halls of the Aloran planetary administration building on Risors. It's called politics, gentlemen. It's just the way the game's played."

"Well, I don't like it," said Admiral Formida.

"Of course you don't," said the duke. "Nor do I. But we must do what needs to be done for the survival of our people."

The duke turned to Richard. With the tips of his fingers, he pushed a small disk across the top of the small end-table separating Richard and him.

"And now, General Shepard," said the duke. "Here is my part of our bargain. I'm a man of my word."

"Sir?" Richard said picking up the small disk and turning it over. "A data disk?"

"Ah, not just any data disk," replied the duke. "That disk contains all available information my government has on the anomaly. Also, it contains all recorded sightings of the black-dragon ships."

"Ships?" Richard asked. "I thought it was a single ship."

"Not hardly, my friend," said Admiral Donovan. "These black-dragon pirates or whatever they are have been making raids in warships ranging in size from recon shuttles to a massive dreadnaught. They—"

"When was the dreadnaught last seen?" interrupted Sergeant Ron. "And where?"

"It's all on the disk, captain," said the duke. "But I don't think you'll find what you're seeking. The black dreadnaught with the red-striped dragon insignia hasn't been spotted since your last encounter forty-two years ago."

Sergeant Ron sat back in his seat with a look of disappointment. He took the disk from Richard and stared at it lost in thought.

"You said the black ships have been making raids," Richard said. "So they're pirates after all."

"Doubtful," said Admiral Donovan. "They're raids are too selective. Almost all recorded attacks have been on supply ships or mining facilities carrying titanium or processed creallium. They seem interested in nothing else."

"Oh," Richard said. "Have you captured prisoners? What have they told you?"

"Uh, actually," said Admiral Donovan sounding slightly embarrassed. "The truth is we haven't taken any prisoners."

"We've disabled a few of their warships from time to time,"

said Admiral Formida. "But they've always self-destructed before our soldiers have been able to board."

"The shields on their ships are tough, and their weapons are even tougher," said Admiral Donovan. "I've lost several good ships in two of my squadrons over the last few months."

"Which is another reason Trecor is grateful for your efforts in our training program," said Duke Bistoria. "I won't say those black ships are better than ours, but they're different. Their energy sources are strange, to say the least, and their ship-to-ship weapons have been able to wear our shields down much quicker than normal weapons."

"So," Richard said stalling to give his brain time to catch up. "Are you asking Sergeant Ron and me to snoop around and see what we can find out about those black ships?"

"Uh, not you, Rick," said Sergeant Ron.

"You're needed here, General," said Colonel Santos speaking for the first time. "I know I was resistant at first, but we don't have near enough of our cat and fighter pilots trained in the new procedures yet. To be honest, I doubt we'll have enough pilots tested and trained in active and passive scans by the time your six-month assignment is completed."

"You're the only diviner Trecor has access to at the present," said Terrie. "Sergeant Ron and the *Defiant* will have to investigate the black ships without you. And," Terrie said while motioning a hand in the duke's direction, "Angela and I have been temporarily assigned as part of the *Defiant's* crew, so your crewmates will still have a wizard scout with them. I may be disabled, but I'm not exactly helpless."

"They're right, Rick," said Sergeant Ron. "You'll be more effective here. I'll ferret out the base for those black ships, or I'll die trying."

Unfortunately, that was exactly what Richard feared. He remembered a story Nickelo had once read to him about a white whale and a captain whose obsession destroyed his ship and crew.

Richard removed his battle helmet from his hip and set it on the table to his front. The helmet changed shaped until it was level.

Reaching out, Richard plucked the data disk from Sergeant Ron's hand.

"No disrespect to Margery," Richard said as he inserted the disk into a slot that appeared on the side of the battle helmet.

"Nick," Richard said in command voice. "Analysis."

"The data's been through a complete analysis by Trecor's main computer," said Admiral Formida. "I doubt a mere battle computer can—"

"No battle computer is mere, Admiral," interrupted Duke Bistoria. "But Terrie has told me the general's battle computer is exceptional."

"As it so happens," said Nickelo over the battle helmet's external speakers, "I'm an advanced prototype."

"Don't brag, Nick," warned Richard only half in jest. *"Haven't you heard what they say about pride and a fall?"*

"Yes, I've heard," replied Nickelo. *"It's not bragging if you're just stating a fact."*

Whatever, Richard thought doing his best to roll his eyes in his mind.

"Analysis is complete," said Nickelo out loud.

Richard noticed Admiral Formida start to open his mouth as if to protest, but a look from the duke stopped him.

"Report," Richard said.

"Are you sure, Rick?" said Nickelo privately. *"Perhaps we should discuss my findings in private."*

"Negative," Richard said. *"Full report. I hate secrets. Either we trust these Trecorians or we don't."*

Without further protest, Nickelo gave his report over the battle helmet's speaker for all to hear.

"Based upon analysis of every battle with the black-dragon ships, I calculate an eighty-two percent probability the warships' offensive and defensive systems are magic based."

Richard wasn't too surprised by his battle computer's revelation. The thought had been kicking around in his head ever since Angela told him about the three secondary-colored spheres discovered by the O'Reilly clan. However, others in the room weren't so willing to accept Nickelo's analysis.

"What nonsense is this?" said Admiral Formida. "Is this why I was called here tonight? To hear fairytales?"

Admiral Formida rose from his seat.

"Sit, Admiral," said Duke Bistoria. Then as if to soften the sting of his command, he added, "Please."

Richard noticed Admiral Donovan looking at him. "Liz told me she helped you fight a magic user at the Academy's spaceport last year. Is that what you're talking about?"

"I've no idea," Richard admitted. "I've fought creatures that used magic before, but I'll admit I don't see how it would apply to starships."

"That's because you were born in the physical dimension," said Nickelo. "You're used to everything being based on physics. If you'd been born and raised in the magical dimension, you'd just accept everything as being based on magic."

"But starships based off magic?" Richard said. "Do you have information on that in your databanks?"

"No," admitted Nickelo. "But it seems like I should."

"This is nonsense," said Admiral Formida. "I know the theory of alternate dimensions, but it's never been proven."

"True," said Admiral Donovan. "But there are a few planets such as Measta Minor in the Empire's District 6 where magic works. Some scientists theorize those planets are somehow connected to a magic-based dimension."

"That's all very interesting," said Admiral Formida. "But I think—"

"Gentlemen," said Duke Bistoria. "It doesn't matter. Unless one of you has additional information, I've made my decision. As Trecor's only diviner, General Shepard will remain here to test and train additional bongo players in scans. Captain Deloris along with Wizard Scout Shatstot and his wife will leave with the *Defiant* to further investigate the anomaly and the black ships."

It took a moment for Richard to figure out when the duke said Captain Deloris, he was talking about Sergeant Ron.

Looking at the *Defiant's* captain, the Duke said, "If you need anything, let either Admiral Formida or Admiral Donovan know. I'm sure they can accommodate any reasonable request." The duke scanned the room. "Are there any questions?" he asked more as a closing statement than an actual question.

"Ah, sir," said Terrie without elaborating. He just pointed at Richard. All eyes in the room shifted toward Richard.

"General?" asked Duke Bistoria.

Richard jerked up in his seat. He'd been in deep conversation with Nickelo. When he realized everyone was looking at him, he quickly had Nickelo play back what had just been said.

"Oh, uh, sorry, sir," Richard said. "I think I have an alternate suggestion. I'm ninety-five percent sure I'm not the only diviner on Trecor. Based upon what I've seen of her Power reserve, your daughter is also a diviner."

"Tia?" asked the duke a little incredulously. "Why didn't you say something before now? She completed your testing weeks ago."

"No, sir," Richard answered looking the duke in the eyes. "Not Tia. I mean Chloe."

"Chloe!" exclaimed the duke. "Impossible. She failed all her bongo testing. I love her, but she isn't even a good soldier."

"Nevertheless, sir," Richard said. "I had a chance to run an active scan on her Power reserve and link earlier this evening. She's the real deal. It's no wonder she failed the tests with your trainers. Power reserves for diviners are, uh…different."

Richard watched the duke bite his lip.

"Are you sure?" asked the duke.

"I concur," chimed in Nickelo over the battle helmet's speakers. "With a couple of weeks training, Rick and I could teach your daughter enough to begin testing and training others in scans."

"So we'd have two diviners training our pilots?" asked Colonel Santos. "That would definitely speed things up."

"Actually," Richard said. "I think you'd have more. I'd recommend assembling anyone who failed their bongo testing due to a strange Power reserve. If we can train a few more diviners, then I could accompany Sergeant Ron on the *Defiant*."

"Out of the question," said the duke. "We need every diviner we can get. I don't know how much time we have before…"

The duke stopped talking.

"Before what, sir?" Richard asked. He hated secrets and any other kind of political wheeling and dealing.

"Nothing," said the duke. "I still need you here. I can't take any chances."

Richard and the duke stared at each other for a few seconds.

"Well, sir," Richard finally said to break the silence. "Then let me put it this way. I've fulfilled the initial part of our bargain. I healed your wounded, which was very painful, by the way. Additionally, I'll probably take some heat from my chain of command for conducting unauthorized scan training for non-Empire personnel. And who knows what kind of trouble I'll be in if I actually train diviners for you."

The duke said nothing. Richard wasn't sure whether the look in the big man's eyes was slowly building anger or another emotion.

"According to my orders, sir," Richard said, "which were sketchy since they didn't come directly from the Imperial High Command, I have less than five months left here. I can either spend a couple of weeks training a half dozen Trecorians as diviners and then go with the *Defiant* to search for the source of those black ships. Or, I can spend the next five months cleaning latrines or some other kind of menial work. But either way, I'm done training pilots."

Richard noticed the blood vessel on the side of the duke's neck budge out. As the seconds passed, the artery slowly returned to a more normal size.

"Very well," said the duke.

Richard relaxed.

"If," the duke continued. "If you're able to find and train six diviners before you leave. Otherwise, you stay here and continue to train additional pilots with Colonel Santos in our new tactics."

Richard thought for a moment. The fact was, he had a feeling the duke could register a protest with the Imperial High Command. Depending on how much the Empire wanted additional information, they might modify his orders.

He was an Empire soldier. His personal code of honor required him to obey any legal commands from his authorized chain of command.

"Fine, sir," Richard said. "But we'll need a couple of additional crew members on the *Defiant*."

"Very well," said the duke who was obviously ready to end the discussion. "Get with Colonel Santos. Take your pick from her regiment. You can have anyone you want as long as they're not one of the new diviners."

"Agreed," Richard said.

"Agreed," replied Duke Bistoria.

The duke rose and headed for the door. The two admirals and Colonel Santos followed. Before the duke reached the door, he turned back around. Richard half expected an angry outburst.

Instead, the duke smiled.

"Councilman Jenkins warned me you were a troublemaker," said the duke. "I'm glad to see he was right. I think we're going to need a lot of troublemakers in the days ahead."

The duke laughed. Then he departed. When the door closed behind them, Sergeant Ron looked at Richard.

"And I thought I caused waves," laughed Sergeant Ron. "I've a feeling I've finally met my match."

CHAPTER 35

Jeena stopped inside the doorway of the brightly-lit room to give her eyes time to adjust. The room was a large chamber fifty paces across and a hundred more in length.

The floor of the chamber was highly-polished marble of various colors. Unlike the rest of the compound Jeena had seen, this room was meticulously maintained. The colored stone formed complex patterns that were pleasing to the eye. Jeena recognized the handiwork of her ancestors, the Letian elves. No living hand could match their artistry.

Bright lights from the ceiling fifty paces overhead lit the entire audience hall. The overhead lighting was a pleasant glow. Except for a lone man sitting on a cushion at the far end of the chamber, the room was empty.

Jeena walked toward the man. She walked with great dignity as she'd been taught by Priestess Aldriss. She didn't need to be told the man was the Oracle. When she got close, Jeena gave him a dignified nod.

"Oracle," Jeena said. "I am Priestess Jeehanathoraxen of the Lady of the Tree. High Priest Questor sends his regrets he was unable to come himself. He asks your forgiveness. The high priest bids me to say the years have been long since he first appeared before your predecessor. He wishes he could have talked to you in person, but he is no longer able to make the trek from Silverton."

"Yes," replied the Oracle in a voice that was soft but carried to the entire audience hall. "I remember the day High Priest Questor presented himself to my earlier form. It has been long indeed."

Motioning to a second cushion placed nearby, the Oracle said, "Please, sit down, Priestess Jeehanathoraxen."

With great dignity, Jeena lowered herself onto the cushion. Once down, she straightened out the rags that served as her clothing before placing the Staff of the Lady of the Tree across her lap. She folded her hands over the staff and looked at the Oracle. He was a human, of course. Every Oracle had been a human since before the Tree of Light was planted. Like the boy, Brachia, Jeena didn't sense any hint of the uncontrolled emotions that were normally given off by humans. In fact, Jeena sensed nothing at all from the Oracle. Even his aura was invisible to her. She could only wonder at the skill it took to completely hide an aura. Neither High Priest Questor nor even Master Jathar could accomplish such a feat.

The current form of the Oracle was ancient for a human. Jeena thought he must be over a hundred years in age. A thought came to her that this version of the Oracle probably wouldn't live much longer. She wondered who'd replace him.

Does he even now have an apprentice somewhere in the complex preparing to assume the duties of Oracle? Jeena wondered. *Brachia said besides his sister and he, there's no one else here.*

"You honor me, Oracle," Jeena said brushing her thoughts to the side. "How may the elves of Silvertine serve you?"

"Ah, yes," said the Oracle with a trace of a smile. "My information was correct. You are one to come directly to the point. But," he said as he spread his hands, "I am an old man, so perhaps you will indulge me if I meander a bit."

Jeena said nothing. She wasn't sure what to say. Her classes at the priest guild hadn't covered conversations with semi-mystical beings.

"What is the purpose of the Tree of Light?" asked the Oracle.

The Oracle's tone reminded Jeena of one of her teachers at the priest guild drilling her on a previous day's assignment. Jeena was unsure where the Oracle was headed, but she could think of no reason not to follow along. Besides, the answer to his question wasn't a secret. Every elf child of school age knew the answer.

"The Tree of Light grew from a seed planted by High Priestess Shandristiathoraxen," Jeena answered. "The Power of the Tree of Light protects a gate hidden beneath the city of Silverton. Without the protection of the tree, our world would be invaded and destroyed."

"By whom?" asked the Oracle.

"Uh," Jeena said trying to give herself time to think. This was where the information from the ancient Letian elves grew sketchy. Filtering fact from myths was a task many a scholar had tried and failed to do over the years.

"Uh," Jeena said again. "Some say the gate is a doorway to a dimension of demons. Others say there is no doorway. They say the gate is not a gate at all. Rather, they say, the gate is a source of energy that must be contained else it would destroy all we know."

The Oracle nodded his head. "Ah yes, the eternal question of trying to separate valid input from corrupted data. The information has been convoluted by a hundred thousand years of half-truths and lies."

After a pause, the Oracle asked another question. "What do you believe, Priestess Jeehanathoraxen?"

Jeena knew what she believed. Two centuries of hounding the Silverton librarians for information on the ancient Letians had given her a solid basis upon which to form an opinion. It was an opinion that wasn't shared by many scholars, but she didn't care. She believed what she believed.

"In my opinion, Oracle, the children's tales are true," Jeena said in a confident voice. "I believe the Tree of Light closes a gate to a place of demons and other creatures of great evil."

The Oracle considered Jeena's answer for a few seconds. Finally, he said, "Based upon my information, I cannot disagree with you. However, would it surprise you to know the gate is both a doorway to other dimensions as well as a source of great energy?"

Jeena said nothing. After a short wait, the Oracle asked a third question.

"Is there more than one gate?" asked the Oracle.

Pausing before answering, Jeena looked at the Oracle closely for any hint of a smile. He seemed serious. While a few scholars over the years had theorized the existence of an additional gate, their theories were basically laughed at by mainstream scholars. No evidence of a second gate existed.

Taking a risk of being ridiculed, Jeena decided to answer the Oracle's question as honestly as she could.

"No one has ever found hard evidence of a second gate. However, from my readings, I believe such a gate does exist. I believe High Priestess Remozorz closed a second gate to stop the undead armies of the Northern Mages."

The Oracle smiled. Jeena stiffened and mentally prepared herself to be laughed at. But the Oracle didn't laugh.

"Yes, Elf Friend Remozorz," said the Oracle as he nodded his head. "I remember when she came here asking for advice as if it were yesterday. Like you, she believed there was a second gate. I concurred. How do you think the Elf Friend was able to close the gate?"

"Uh, I'm not sure," Jeena admitted.

"Then let me answer my question for you," said the Oracle. "She closed it with the aid of the staff you now hold in your hand."

Jeena involuntarily looked down at the blackened and brown-stained length of wood. The blue gem at its tip gave off a soft glow even in the brightly-lit room. Jeena could feel the Power of the staff pulsing through her hands. She knew the staff had Power. However, since the fight with the human bandits, she hadn't been able to call upon the staff's Power again.

"Would it surprise you to know a third gate exists on Portalis?" asked the Oracle. "Or rather I should say a third gate used to exist a hundred thousand years ago."

Jeena didn't answer, but her surprise must have registered on her face.

"Don't feel bad," said the Oracle in a kind voice. "The gate existed before the Letians even began storing their writings in a sleepy little village called Silver."

Jeena thought back to her history lessons as a child. The city of Silverton had once been a village called Silver. As the population grew, its name was changed to Silver Town. Eventually, it became the city of Silverton, the capital city of Silvertine, the land of the high elves.

"Pardon my impatience, Oracle," Jeena said attempting to be

tactful, "but I've spent the last three weeks traveling here at great peril. Is there a reason you're telling me about a gate from the past?"

This time the Oracle did laugh. But Jeena sensed he was not laughing at her. It was almost as if he found her impertinence refreshing.

"Yes, there's nothing quite like youth to make an old man stick to the point," said the Oracle. "I mention the third gate because it's the purpose of your visit."

Jeena became instantly alert.

"Ah," smiled the Oracle. "I see I have your attention again. The third gate was on a continent located on the other side of Portalis. I say was, because the gate was brought into existence by a race of beings called Dragars a hundred thousand years ago. However, their gate was, and is, much more than a gate. It's also a time-bubble."

"A time-bubble?" Jeena asked. The term was only faintly familiar to her. She'd once come across the term while reading an ancient scroll discussing the rescue of the seed parts by High Priestess Shandristiathoraxen. Unfortunately, the writer must have assumed the readers of the scroll would be familiar with the term because no explanation was given.

"Yes, a time-bubble," said the Oracle speaking in a very soft and patient voice. "A time-bubble exists in all time at the same time. The Dragars use their combination gate and time-bubble to acquire sources of energy from the future in the physical dimension."

"You say use," Jeena said. "Don't you mean used? And while I'll admit I enjoy hearing and reading about historical events, I'm having difficulty understanding how it affects us here today."

Jeena was beginning to wonder if High Priest Questor had sent her on a wild-unicorn chase.

The Oracle smiled as if guessing her thoughts. "Bear with me but a moment longer, priestess. We have almost reached the purpose of your quest."

Jeena composed herself. This was the Oracle after all. Despite her title of priestess, Jeena was well aware she was a mere tenth-year acolyte.

"Because the third gate is also a time-bubble," explained the

Oracle, "it exists both a hundred thousand years in the past as well as today. It also exists in the future. The Dragars are hiding in the past while they acquire energy from the future to fuel their armies. One day the Dragars will attempt to use their gate to bring their armies to our world in our time. It will precede a time of a great battle when the fate of three galaxies will hang in the balance."

"But—" Jeena started to say while feeling overwhelmed. She still had no idea where the Oracle was headed. She wasn't even sure she wanted to know.

I'm a tenth-year acolyte, she thought. *This is beyond the scope of my abilities.*

"But," said the Oracle raising his hand to stop Jeena's protest. "But nothing. You were created as a variable in the algorithm."

Jeena had no idea what a variable or an algorithm was, but the Oracle gave her no chance to ask. He continued talking in a voice that brooked no interruption.

"Your silver hair and silver eyes declare you as an heir of High Priestess Shandristiathoraxen," said the Oracle. "The staff you hold was her staff when she rescued the seed parts from the demon Efrestra. The high priestess used her staff to merge the three seed parts together and by doing so created the Tree of Light. Because of her efforts, the first gate has remained closed for nigh-on a hundred thousand years. You must do the same to protect our world."

Confused, Jeena blurted out, "Do what? I'm just an acolyte. I'm not a high priestess."

The Oracle smiled sympathetically. "What is a high priestess other than a name? You have been chosen, Priestess Jeehanathoraxen. You must travel to the place and time appointed for you, and you must close the third gate before the Dragars gather their full supply of energy."

"Close the gate how?" Jeena said.

"By using the Staff of the Lady of the Tree," said the Oracle as if the answer should have been obvious.

"But, the staff hasn't worked in thousands of years," Jeena protested. "It's broken."

"Nonsense," said the Oracle. "I watched you use it against the robbers who accosted you. The staff knows you. It recognizes the part of its original owner that resides in you. And the blue gem on the staff is attuned to something that was placed inside you before you were born. The Lady's staff has much Power. You can wield it if you will only try. You must use it to close the gate before it's too late."

"But it's broken," Jeena repeated. She didn't understand why the Oracle failed to grasp the concept.

"Yes," agreed the Oracle. "The staff is broken."

Finally, Jeena thought as a sense of relief washed over her. *He finally understands. Now we can set this foolishness of closing gates to the side.*

"But," said the Oracle raising a hand and pointing a finger toward the ceiling. "But...the staff is not broken in the manner you probably think. In addition, the assets needed to repair the Staff of the Lady of the Tree back to its full Power are even now in a room above us. You will take the Lady's staff to them. Once it's repaired, the assets will send you where you need to go. It's all part of the algorithm. But we must hurry. The time is short."

"When? Now?" Jeena asked stalling for time.

Surely he can't mean now, Jeena thought. *Something this important needs to be planned. I need time to prepare.*

But even as she thought the words, Jeena had a feeling that months or even years would not be enough time to prepare for the Oracle's task.

"Yes, now," said the Oracle. "The time is now. The assets will help you. Give them the Lady's staff. When they finish repairing it, you will be sent to the three who are one. You will use the staff to merge them together just as your forebear did with the seed parts."

"The three who are one?" said Jeena trying her best to grasp the situation. "I don't understand. Are they seed parts? Are you telling me to plant another Tree of Light?"

"No," said the Oracle. "They are...different. You will understand when the time comes. You must bring them together and end their misery."

"How?" said Jeena. "I'm a tenth-year acolyte. I can't use the staff. I don't know any spells to merge things together. I can't do this by myself."

"I will teach you the spell you need," said the Oracle. "Also, another variable will help you. He will come when you need him. You will help each other. You must help each other. You are a part of each other. It is only logical."

"What are you talking about?" asked Jeena. "Are you mad? Your words make no sense, Oracle. What is an algorithm?"

"Enough," said the Oracle as he clapped his hands together. "Go! The assets are waiting."

Jeena felt a tingling throughout her body. The room and the Oracle moved in and out of focus. Then everything turned black.

CHAPTER 36

"Margery, take us in," said Sergeant Ron.

"Compliance, captain," replied Margery.

The counter-thrusters shook the *Defiant* as the ship's computer slowed the rate of descent.

"I thought this was a mining camp," Richard said as he watched the details of the built-up area come into focus. "Geesh. This piece of rock is more like a small planet than it is an asteroid."

"Actually," said the voice of Margery over the cockpit's intercom, "most star maps do classify it as a small planet. It's large enough to maintain an atmosphere of sorts, but I wouldn't suggest trying to breathe the air unless you enjoy having ammonia in your lungs."

Richard got the impression Margery was making a joke. Richard had always thought Nickelo was the only computer with a sense of humor. However, after spending the last five weeks on the *Defiant*, Richard knew he was wrong. The Commandant's old battle computer had a well-defined sense of humor. Richard enjoyed talking to Margery. In a strange way, Richard felt a connection to his late father just by being around the Commandant's battle computer.

"Tia," Richard said. "Are Matthew and you in the Zip fighters?"

"Affirmative, Rick," answered Tia. "We'll launch as soon as the *Defiant* hits the atmosphere. Once we're clear, you can exit. We'll cover you on the way down."

"Understood," Richard said. "I want the two of you to be careful. We're not picking up any signs of life, but that doesn't mean anything. For all we know, there's a whole regiment down there hidden by stealth shields."

"We'll be careful, Rick," promised Tia. "You've made it plain our job is recon, not fighting."

"Well, I promised both of your parents I'd keep you safe," Richard said. "Uh, just be careful."

"The town below appears to have been hit pretty hard," said Nickelo using the battle helmet's external speakers. "But I calculate the Warcats will have no trouble maneuvering through the streets as long as they're careful."

"The town looks like it's in pretty good shape to have been hit by a nuke," Richard said over the ship-wide intercom.

"I only used the word nuke because I didn't know how else to describe it," said Terrie over the intercom. "I told you it was strange energy. It was similar to a neutron bomb. It did very little physical damage compared to the released energy."

"Roger that," Richard said. "Don't get defensive on me. I was just making a comment. Are Charlie and you ready in the Warcats? I want both of both of you out as soon as the *Defiant* touches down."

"Two minutes out, Rick," said Sergeant Ron. "If you're going, you better get to the ejection tube."

"On my way now," Richard said as he unbuckled from his seat and headed toward the exit.

"And Rick," said Sergeant Ron.

Richard turned back around.

"Be careful," said Sergeant Ron with a cockeyed grin. "I'd hate to have to break in a new partner."

Richard nodded his head. "Take care of yourself as well. I'd hate to have to break in a new ship's captain."

Wasting no further time, Richard ran down the steps toward the cargo bay. As he passed by one of the side doors, he saw Angela at the control panel for the *Defiant's* primary cannons.

"Give em hell, Rick," she shouted as he passed. "And take care of my husband."

Without replying, Richard jumped from the top of the steps

onto the cargo bay's steel floor.

"Seal me up, Nick," Richard thought.

The battle helmet's force field lowered to meet the bottom part of the helmet. The familiar tubes forced their way into his mouth and other body openings. Richard barely noticed. His thoughts were on the possible problems ahead.

True to his word, the duke had released Richard to full duty on the *Defiant* once Richard had trained six diviners. Finding potential diviners hadn't been a problem. Due to the abundance of bongo testing on Trecor, Richard had a ready list of Trecorians with strange Power reserves. Two weeks had been plenty of time to train Chloe and another five diviners in how to manipulate the links of pilots so they could perform passive and active scans.

Once the diviners were trained, Richard spent the following three weeks helping Sergeant Ron and Charlie integrate the new crew members into the routine of the *Defiant*. Much to the duke's chagrin, Richard had selected Tia and her brother Daniel as the *Defiant's* newest crew members.

If truth be told, Richard would have to admit he'd picked Tia and Daniel partially to get back at the duke for making him come to Trecor in the first place. At the same time, Tia and Daniel were excellent additions to the crew. Although both were young, they'd been training as soldiers since they were basically old enough to walk.

Tia really was a hotshot fighter-pilot. Whether she was as good as her sister, Liz, Richard didn't know. But he did know the teenager was very good. Tia was also an excellent instructor. Once she'd picked up the finer points of flying the Zip fighters assigned to the *Defiant*, Tia had spent hours training Matthew Deloris in them as well.

Tia also spent a significant amount of time trying to train Richard in Zip fighters as well. Unfortunately, Richard's skills at flying the little zippers weren't much better than his skills at piloting heavy cats.

Matthew, on the other hand, had easily transitioned his cat piloting skills to piloting the little Zip fighters. Matthew was a dedicated student when it came to learning to fly the zippers. Richard had a feeling the fact Matthew's instructor was a beautiful and highly intelligent girl contributed to his motivation to learn as well.

While the crew was training and finalizing their places in the *Defiant's* routine, Nickelo and Margery analyzed the data disk supplied by Duke Bistoria. The results of the analysis were why the *Defiant* was even now approaching the mining camp.

When Richard reached the cargo bay, he headed straight for the ejection tube. He immediately lowered himself into the top of the long cylinder.

Using the ship's intercom, Richard said, "You do realize, Sergeant Ron, this tube's original purpose was to eject garbage and waste material out into space, don't you?"

Richard heard Nickelo laugh over his shared space. *"What makes you think it's not being used for that right now?"*

"Yuk, yuk," Richard thought back. *"I keep telling you you're not as funny as you think you are."*

"Sure I am," said Nickelo. *"According to my calculations, I'm the funniest prototype battle computer on this starship."*

Richard chose to ignore his battle computer. He'd learned from experience he couldn't win the argument anyway.

"Relax, Rick," came Sergeant Ron's reply over the intercom. "The Deloris Armaments' technicians modified it for bombs, missiles, and the occasional crazy-as-all-hell wizard scout."

"It's fine, Rick," yelled Daniel from across the cargo bay. "Charlie and I checked it out this morning. It'll serve your purpose."

Richard glanced to the other side of the cargo bay. Daniel was busy helping Charlie and Terrie get strapped into their Warcats. The two cats were top-of-the-line Deloris models. Richard had a momentary regret he wasn't piloting one of them for the insertion mission instead of using just his battle suit. The newer Warcats were heavier armed than the standard models issued to active line battalions, and Richard was a little envious.

"No time for regrets now," said Nickelo. *"Besides, Warcats aren't air droppable without additional gear. The extra equipment would nullify their stealth capabilities. You, on the other hand, can go in without being detected if you're just wearing your battle suit."*

"I know," Richard admitted. *"Can't I even complain just a little once in a while? Sometimes it makes me feel better even if it*

doesn't do any good."

"Fine then," said Nickelo. *"Complain away. By the way, we're twenty seconds from the drop point."*

"Twenty seconds," said Margery over the intercom.

"Thanks, Margery," Richard said.

"Hey, that's what I told you," said Nickelo with a mock hurt-feelings tone. *"How come you didn't thank me? I have feelings too, you know."*

"Whatever," Richard said.

Just before Richard's head dropped below the lip of the ejection tube, he noticed Daniel and Terrie give him a thumb's up. Charlie gave him a thumb's up with both of his right hands.

"You ready, Rick?" asked Sergeant Ron from the bridge.

"All set," Richard replied as he tried to relax. No matter how often he did them, he always got nervous right before a high-altitude drop.

"Are you sure you don't want us to just land?" said Sergeant Ron. "It would be safer if you had the Warcats backing you up right off the bat."

"Negative on that," Richard replied. "Tia and Matthew will cover me with the zippers until I give you the all clear. Based upon their analysis, Margery and Nick are sixty percent certain warning sensors were left on this chunk of rock. I don't want anyone touching down until I give the okay."

"All right, Rick," said Sergeant Ron. "You're the wizard scout."

"Drop in five seconds," said Margery. "Four...three...two...one...execute."

The bottom of the tube opened up below Richard's feet. At the same time, compressed air forced him out of the blackness of the tube and into the emptiness of space. Bright sunlight reflected off of the small planet's surface below him. Everything was in red since the battle helmet's visor was down. Richard preferred the red light to the pitch black of the ejection tube. The truth was, he was a little on the claustrophobic side.

At 6,000 meters, he was on the edge of the planet's thin atmosphere. Wrapping himself in Power, Richard gave a series of intermittent taps to slow down.

"Good job, Rick," said Nickelo in rare praise. *"Very efficient use of your Power."*

Richard waited a second for his battle computer's invariable but. However, none came.

"Miracles do happen," Richard thought.

"Of course, I could have done it better if you'd given me control," said Nickelo. *"Still, it wasn't half bad for a human."*

"I should've known," Richard thought. *"So much for miracles."*

As Richard descended through the planet's atmosphere, his battle suit heated up. When he'd done drops as a cadet, he'd used a personal force field to protect himself from the heat of entry. As a full wizard scout, he had better methods of protecting himself at his disposal. And unlike a personal force field, his wizard scout methods were practically non-detectable.

Wrapping himself in Power once again, Richard caused himself to shimmer in and out of the void. Using a technique the Commandant had shown him, Richard barely entered the void before shifting back into the physical dimension. Although sub-second in duration, the intermittent dimensional shifts were enough to dissipate the heat buildup.

"Margery says the zippers are out, Rick," said Nickelo.

Richard picked up the locations of the two Zip fighters with his passive scan. They were flying in stealth mode. However, he'd tagged both Tia and Matthew earlier that morning, so he had a trace on them. He was positive he could easily locate them anywhere on the small planet as long as he kept the trace active. He'd also put a trace on the rest of the crew. If anything went wrong, Richard didn't plan on wasting time trying to figure out his friend's locations.

"I've marked the two zippers and the location of the Defiant *on your heads-up display using the information from your passive scan,"* said Nickelo. *"The zippers are in white, and the* Defiant *is in green."*

"I see them," Richard said when he noticed the dots appear on the display of his battle helmet.

"You're drifting to the left of your most efficient course," said Nickelo. *"That is, assuming you still want to head to the mine's entrance."*

"I do," Richard said. *"I've given you control of the battle suit if you need to make adjustments. Believe me; I wouldn't be offended*

if you gave me a hand. That is if you get bored."

"Oh, I rarely get bored when I'm with you," said Nickelo accompanying his comment with a half-hidden laugh. *"It's always entertaining to calculate all the ways I could do things better than you. It's amazing how many mistakes you make."*

"Ha, ha," Richard said while trying to concentrate on keeping his body position aligned to keep him on track to the mine's entrance. Unfortunately, the planet's thin atmosphere was making it more difficult than he'd anticipated.

Richard felt the arms of his battle suit move slightly to take better advantage of what little air was available.

"Thanks, Nick."

"No problem," said Nickelo. *"You're still falling too fast. I recommend using your telekinesis to slow down."*

"No can do, buddy," Richard said. *"I want to keep a higher speed than normal. I don't want to be out here falling through the air like a sitting duck longer than necessary."*

"Well, if you don't slow down, you'll wish you had when you smack into the rock this planet calls for topsoil," admonished Nickelo. *"You'll have to waste a lot of Power to stop on the surface at this speed."*

"Actually, I'm not going to stop on the surface," Richard replied. *"I'm going to shift into the void just before I make contact with the ground and use my momentum to carry me directly into one of the mine tunnels below the surface."*

"When were you going to tell me your little plan?" said Nickelo sounding alarmed. *"Are you sure you're good enough to get your timing right?"*

"Actually, no," Richard answered being honest with both his battle computer and himself. *"I know I'm not good enough. That's why I have you. You're the most advanced battle computer in the galaxy, remember? The timing shouldn't be a problem for a big, bad, battle computer like yourself."*

"How true, how true," answered Nickelo ignoring Richard's obvious sarcasm. *"I'm glad after all these years you're finally starting to appreciate my obvious abilities."*

Richard ignored his battle computer in order to concentrate on the planet's surface as the ground continued approaching at a rapid rate. He doubted he'd ever get used to his eyes telling him he was falling to certain death while his logic told him his wizard scout abilities would keep him alive. He didn't mind admitting he was a little skittish during every jump. But of course, he jumped anyway, skittish or not. That's what wizard scouts did.

The mine's entrance came into focus. It was located in the wall of a quarry on the east side of town. Richard expanded the range of his passive scan in order to pick up readings from the three anomalies located below the planet's surface. One of the anomalies was located about five hundred meters below the surface almost directly below the mine's entrance. The other two anomalies were located twenty kilometers away at sixty-degree angles.

"The three anomalies form a triangle," said Nickelo in their shared space. *"I believe the anomalies are similar to the spheres you helped the elf recover from the demon. I can sense links connecting the three spheres together. It's strange that you're picking them up so easily with your scan."*

"Roger that," Richard said. *"I see them. Are you saying they're seed parts?"*

"Negative," said Nickelo. *"They're spheres, but I don't believe they're seed parts. I calculate they're something else. It appears the spheres and their links are designed to form a gate. The gate's not active at the moment, but there's enough latent energy being released to allow you to sense them. By the way, you only have six seconds until you splatter on the ground."*

"I'm getting ready to shift into the void now," Richard said. *"I'll give you control of the dimensional shift as soon as it's formed. I'm hoping it will be just like when we shifted that missile through those magic users' shield at the airfield last year."*

"Roger that," replied Nickelo. *"I'll take control. By the way, you do realize it was only last year as far as the Empire is concerned. It was many years ago if you count the years you've spent doing missions for* 'the One.' *I worry about you sometimes, Rick. I think your brain has trouble keeping the time differences straight. Good thing you have me around to help."*

"Whatever," Richard said dismissively. However, he had to admit, he really did have trouble keeping time straight in his head.

The increasing details of the sharp rocks below jerked Richard's thoughts back to reality. Wrapping himself in Power, Richard shifted into the void when he was a mere fifty meters above the ground. He caught a glimpse of a few vehicles parked near the black entrance of the mine. Then everything went dark as he plunged through the rocky surface.

"We're off target," said Nickelo in their shared space. *"Set up telekinesis on yourself and give me control."*

Richard didn't bother answering. He just did as asked and gave control to his battle computer. Richard sensed the Power in his reserve begin to deplete. Although he was significantly more efficient at dimensional shifts and telekinesis than he'd been while a cadet, both abilities were still very Power hungry.

Suddenly, Richard caught a glimpse of light. In a maneuver too fast for Richard to have accomplished by himself, he came to a stop with the soles of his boots only a few millimeters above the floor of a dimly-lit tunnel. Richard immediately dropped his Power to shift back into the physical dimension. He barely noticed the drop to the tunnel floor as he released his telekinesis.

"Power?" Richard asked.

"Eighty-seven percent," said Nickelo. *"You're sitting pretty good all things considered."*

"Rick," said the voice of Tia over the battle helmet's intercom. "We lost track of you. Are you all right?"

"I'm fine, Tia," Richard replied. "I did a dimensional shift. I'm in one of the tunnels now. I'm going to try and locate the first anomaly."

"Crap, Rick," said Terrie. "How about giving us a heads up next time? I'm a disabled wizard scout, remember? Your unannounced disappearance nearly gave me a heart attack. I thought you'd splattered on the ground."

"Sorry, guys," Richard apologized. He wasn't sure what else to say. "Uh, I should have said something, but I didn't think of the plan until the last second. I forgot to tell you. I guess I'm used to working alone."

"Hey, what about me?" said Nickelo over the communication network for all to hear. "What am I, chopped pactar?"

"You know want I meant, Nick," Richard thought.

Reaching over his shoulder, Richard pulled his M63 out of his dimensional pack. No Power left his reserve. The weapon was one of his freebies.

After making sure the weapon's isotopic battery was fully

charged, Richard clicked off the safety and trotted down the tunnel. He didn't sense any life forms in the immediate area. However, he wasn't going to take any chances.

"Keep an eye out for booby-traps, Nick," Richard thought.

"Roger that, oh wizard scout extraordinaire," said Nickelo with a short laugh. *"I'd hate to get a perfectly good battle helmet blown up."*

CHAPTER 37

The Oracle's teleport deposited Jeena on a circular, knee-high dais. The dais was five paces across, and it was located in the center of a large room filled with strange-looking boxes. The boxes were adorned with flashing lights of every color of the rainbow. Two children were in the room.

One of the children was Brachia. The other was his sister, Dren. Jeena knew at fourteen, Dren was physically only a little younger than herself. However, the girl had an air of maturity far beyond her years. Once the introductions were over, Dren took Jeena aside and told her the boxes with the flashing lights were computers.

After only a few minutes interacting with the children, Jeena began to understand the children's mysterious computers played a large part in their 'magic.' The children had a name for their magic. It was a strange word called technology. They also used an alternate word called science. Jeena didn't like either of the words. They sounded harsh.

"Well," said Dren. "I guess you'd better let me see Rem's staff. It looks in worse shape than it did the last time we saw it."

Jeena clutched the Lady's staff closer to her chest. She wasn't sure she wanted to trust a child with the Staff of the Lady of the Tree.

Noticing her action, Dren said, "We're going to fix the staff. Didn't the Oracle tell you?"

"The Oracle said many things," Jeena said. "Much of what he said made no sense. The Lady's staff is too valuable to risk being damaged."

"Okay," said Dren as if used to people not taking her seriously. "Then how about this? What if I tell you what to do and you do it? I won't even have to touch the staff."

Slightly mollified, Jeena nodded her head. "Very well."

"Good," said Dren turning all businesslike again. "You see the five white dots near the top of the staff?"

Jeena nodded her head. She'd noticed the dots during her journey to see the Oracle. They appeared to be discolorations in the darkened wood. When pressed, they moved slightly inward. When the pressure was released, the dots moved back to their original position.

"Imagine those dots are numbered one through five from top to bottom," said Dren. "I want you to press them in this order: 1, 5, 3, 3, 2, 5, 1, and 3."

Unsure what the girl hoped to accomplish, but seeing no harm, Jeena pressed the dots as requested. When she pressed the third dot for the last time, she heard a click. Without warning, the blue gem on the top of the staff popped off and fell onto the stone floor.

"No!" Jeena shouted. "What've you done?"

"Relax, Jeehana," said Brachia who had walked over while Jeena was pressing the dots. "Those blue gems are the hardest substance I've ever dealt with. It takes a type III plasma cutting-torch to even scratch one. I should know. I had to cut some smaller gems made out of the same material to put in my uncle's armor."

Jeena stared at Brachia as he reached down and picked up the blue gem. He handed the gem to her.

"See?" said Brachia. "Not a mark on it."

Reaching out, Jeena snatched the gem from the boy's hand and held it up to the light. She spent the next minute verifying the blue gem was undamaged.

Holding the blue gem in one hand and the Lady's staff in the other, Jeena said, "The high priest will kill me if I've let two children destroy something that has survived for a hundred thousand years."

"Humph," snorted Brachia. "I'll be glad when I grow up. I'm tired of people always thinking I don't know what I'm doing just because I'm a child."

"They'd probably trust you more if you didn't go off playing pirate so often," said Dren.

Turning to Jeena and holding out her hands, Dren said, "Please give me the staff, Jeehana."

When Jeena hesitated, the girl said, "It's already broke, right? Obviously, you can't take the staff back to your high priest this way. We can fix it. We may be young, but we do know what we're doing."

"Actually, it's not really broken," said Brachia. "The gem had to come off in order for us to check out the internal electronics. I suspect one of the circuit boards just needs adjusting."

"I know it's not broken," said Dren. "I'm just trying to get Jeehana to give the staff to me so we can run a diagnostic's check."

Facing Jeena, Dren said, "Won't you trust us, Jeehana. We're on the same side, remember? I'm sure the Oracle told you we'd fix it."

With little choice in the matter, Jeena passed the Lady's staff to the girl.

After all, Jeena reasoned, *it's already broken. What further harm can she do?*

Once Dren had the staff in her hand, Jeena noticed the girl give the staff a hard twist in the middle. After a loud click, the staff split into two halves with the girl holding a half in each hand.

"No!" Jeena said aghast.

Jeena was almost ready to take the two halves out of Dren's hands when the girl turned the bottom half downward. A long piece of quartz-looking material with dozens of flashing lights inside began sliding out.

Brachia reached past Jeena and caught the quartz tube in his hands.

Jeena stared at the tube of quartz. So did Dren and Brachia. The flashing lights were hypnotic in a pleasant way.

"Our parents made this," said Dren in a near whisper as she gestured at the quartz-tube. "They died protecting it. Brachia, Sam, and I placed it in the staff. Rem used it to close the gate before the necromancer's army could destroy everything."

"Rem? Sam?" Jeena said. "You mentioned Rem before. Who are Rem and Sam?"

"Rem and Sam are gnomes," said Brachia. "Or, I guess I should say they were gnomes. They died a long time ago." After a pause, he said, "I like gnomes."

"Rem was a high priestess for the elves," said Dren ignoring her brother. "I never could pronounce her name. She let us call her Rem. Sam was a mage. He helped our Uncle Rick hold off the undead army long enough for Rem to use the staff."

"We were told Rem was an Elf Friend," said Brachia looking at Jeena. "You're an elf. Have you ever heard of her?"

"Are you talking about Elf Friend Remozorz?" Jeena asked.

"That's her," said Brachia smiling. "Why do gnomes and elves have such hard names?"

Ignoring her brother, Dren said, "Yes. That's her. Our uncle brought us the blue gem. It's the primary Power source for the device Brachia holds in his hands. Sam, Brachia, and I put the device in the staff and hooked it up to the gem. By combining the energy of the device and the staff, they can close gates."

"If what you say is true," Jeena said doubtfully, "then you'd have to be almost eighty-nine thousand years old."

"No," said Brachia. "I'm just seven."

"We're time travelers," said Dren as if that explained it. She awaited a reply, when none came quickly, she continued. "I've read some of the history scrolls in the Oracle's library. Brachia, Uncle Rick, and I were here about eighty-nine thousand years ago. And we're here now. I think we were brought here so we could repair your staff."

Placing the two halves of the staff on a table, Dren reached out and placed both of her hands on Jeena's.

"The Oracle says you have a purpose as well," said Dren. "He says we need to repair the staff and give it back to you so you can fulfill your purpose. Won't you let us help you?"

Both Brachia and Dren looked at Jeena. She saw only honesty in their eyes. They were humans. She knew she should probably hate them after what their kind had done to her family. But she didn't. They weren't evil. They hadn't harmed her parents.

With a nod of her head, Jeena handed the blue gem to Dren. The girl smiled in thanks before holding out the gem to Brachia.

"Get it done, Brachia," said Dren. "Our window's closing. We need to finish this before Jeehana loses her chance. The Oracle says the fate of three galaxies hang in the balance."

"The equipment's all ready," said Brachia as he grabbed the blue gem from his sister. "Just give me a few minutes."

Jeena watched the boy run over to a corner full of equipment while carrying the gem and the quartz-tube along with the staff. Once there, he began arguing with the disembodied Omar.

Jeena shook her head. She had a feeling nothing would ever be simple in her life again.

CHAPTER 38

As Richard ran down the tunnel, he kept a close watch for any signs of life forms. He sensed nothing.

"This doesn't make sense," Richard said. *"There should be something alive down here, but there's nothing. I'm not even picking up rodents or snakes or spiders."*

"Well, I suppose those kinds of creatures could be around but are just out of range," said Nickelo. *"Even so, I'm with you. The lack of life isn't logical. Do you want me to do a sweep with the battle helmet's electronics?"*

Richard weighed the options; risk versus reward. Finally, he shook his head.

"No. Not until we've done an initial sweep I've got my best stealth shield up. Still, I don't want to risk an active scan at this point."

The tunnel floor where Richard was walking was relatively smooth. However, he could see a buckling in the floor about fifty meters ahead. When he got there, Richard's advance was stopped by a large crack in the tunnel.

"Actually, the crack works to our advantage," said Nickelo. *"Down will save us some steps."*

Without hesitating, Richard did a quick bunny-hop into the crack. The fall was short; only about fifteen meters. For such a short distance, Richard didn't even bother using telekinesis to slow down. Once the battle suit's legs took the initial shock, he tucked and rolled to dissipate the momentum. He was up on both feet almost at once.

Glancing around, Richard noticed this part of the tunnel was different. He noticed marks on the walls that resembled claw marks more than they did marks left by tools.

"The tunnel above appeared to have been cut by standard plasma drills," Richard said. *"This part looks like a bunch of kids were clawing in mud, which has turned into stone."*

"Hmm," said Nickelo. *"I've a feeling your analogy may be closer to the truth than you might think. Based upon what readings I can get with my electronics, this part of the tunnel is ancient. I'd say those marks were made tens of thousands of years ago; possibly hundreds of thousands of years."*

Richard sensed a large source of Power ahead. The frequency reminded him a little of the seed parts he'd helped the elf Shandria find. Those seed parts had given off an aura of good. This Power source did not. While not evil per se, the Power source didn't register as good either.

"If this Power source is a seed part," Richard said, *"remind me not to look directly at it without a filter. I've got a feeling it wouldn't take my mind to a very nice place."*

"I hear you, brother," replied Nickelo.

While his battle computer was replying, Richard turned the next corner of the tunnel. The source of the Power came into view. The Power was in the shape of a round sphere about half the size of a human head. Due to the visor on his battle helmet, the sphere looked red. Although he couldn't tell the sphere's true color, he did recognize the swirling molten-lava look he'd seen before. The sphere ahead looked the same as the seed parts he'd seen on his first mission for *'the One.'*

"Color?" Richard asked.

"Green," answered Nickelo.

Richard stopped about twenty meters from the sphere. It was hanging in midair in the middle of the tunnel.

"Green?" Richard said. *"The three seed parts we encountered before were red, blue, and yellow. I wonder why this seed part isn't a primary color."*

"Well, for starters," said Nickelo. *"I calculate the sphere*

ahead isn't a seed part. It's something different."

"*What?*" Richard asked.

"*I'm not sure,*" said Nickelo. "*I need additional information before I can even hazard a guess.*"

Continuing to hold his distance from the green sphere, Richard looked closer at the tunnel near the sphere. The tunnel was littered with broken pieces of stone.

"*Look at those stones,*" Richard said. "*It looks to me like they were cut with a plasma drill.*"

"*I calculate you're correct,*" said Nickelo. "*In fact, there's a discarded plasma drill to your rear. According to Angela, all three anomalies were embedded in solid rock when they arrived. The O'Reilly miners were trying to free the anomalies when the black ship attacked.*"

"*Well, looks like they freed this one at least,*" Richard said. "*The sphere's floating in midair. I wonder why the miners didn't remove the sphere when they got it free.*"

"*Hmm, I'm not so sure it's free, Rick.*"

"*What do you mean?*" Richard asked. "*I can see it with my own eyes. If you know something I don't, just spit it out. It would save us a lot of time.*"

"*Fine,*" replied Nickelo who sounded like he was getting perturbed at Richard's impatience. "*If you look with your senses and not your eyes, you'll see the sphere isn't really here. It's somewhere else. Based upon the data we acquired on our mission with the elf, Shandria, I calculate a seventy-two percent probability the sphere is in a time-bubble. The sphere's here, but it's not here, if that makes any sense. Or to make it even more confusing, it's in a point in space in all times at the same time.*"

Richard didn't like what his battle computer was saying. He'd nearly died the last time he'd messed with time-bubbles. Plus, he'd made an enemy of a powerful demon to boot. He'd come to this mine in the hopes of finding a gate to the magical dimension. Anything to do with time-bubbles was useless to him.

When Richard didn't reply, Nickelo said, "*If you think I'm wrong, then check for yourself.*"

Richard decided to do just that. He moved closer to the green sphere until it was only an arm's length away. He sensed the same type of Power he'd sensed from Shandria's spheres. He also felt an odd sensation he'd felt once before. During the battle to acquire Shandria's spheres, Richard had grabbed onto a demon-dog. The demon had created a time-bubble around both of them. The sensation he was feeling now reminded him of the demon-dog's time-bubble.

"See what I mean?" said Nickelo.

"Yeah, I see it," Richard admitted albeit grudgingly.

"Hey, what's going on down there?" said Sergeant Ron over the communication channel Margery had set up for the *Defiant's* crew. "I'm getting tired of circling this chunk of rock. I'm coming in for landing on my next orbit."

"Negative," Richard said in a tone he hoped indicated the subject wasn't up for discussion. "Not yet. Something's strange about this anomaly."

"No kidding," said Sergeant Ron. "That's why they called it an anomaly. I don't like you being down there all by your lonesome."

"I'm not by my lonesome," Richard said. "Tia and Daniel are covering me. Aren't you kids?"

"Roger that," came Tia's voice. "We're circling over the mine's entrance at five hundred meters. And we're not kids. I can do things in this zipper people twice my age can't do."

"Touchy, isn't she?" said Nickelo. *"Reminds me of you."*

"Understood, Tia," Richard said while choosing to ignore his battle computer. "Climb to one thousand meters and keep circling. This anomaly is a sphere. I've dealt with something like it before. I'm going to take a few minutes to check it out. Once Nick and I are sure everything's safe, the *Defiant* can land."

"But—" started Sergeant Ron.

Richard was ready for his old maintenance officer. "No buts. You're the *Defiant's* captain, but I'm the wizard scout. No one lands until I give the word. Got it?"

"Yeah, I've got it," said Sergeant Ron. "But I don't have to like it."

"Anybody else want to argue?" Richard asked. "Or can I get on with the task at hand?"

No one else said anything.

"Well, that went over better than I would have calculated," said Nickelo in their shared space. *"So, oh wizard scout extraordinaire, what do we do now?"*

"Now?" Richard said. *"Now we get down to business. I'm setting up an active scan, and I'm giving you control. I want you to scan this bad boy. Make me proud, little buddy."*

"Don't I always?" laughed Nickelo. *"Wrap the scan with a stealth shield, please. The sphere may not appreciate being probed. Oh, and follow along with your mind. You may sense something I don't."*

In short order, Richard intermeshed a stealth shield with the active scan. Once completed, he followed along as his battle computer used the active scan to delicately probe the area around the green sphere. Although Richard knew he could've handled the scan himself, he also knew he could never do the scan as well as his battle computer. To be honest, Richard knew he would never be as patient as Nickelo.

"Well," Richard said five minutes into the scan. *"You were right. It's definitely a time-bubble. At the same time, this sphere is linked to two other spheres. Why? Shandria said she was going to merge her seed parts together. But these anomalies are linked together at a distance. Big question, buddy. Are they forming a gate into the magical dimension? Or, are they forming an entrance into a time-bubble?"*

"In all honesty," said Nickelo, *"I'm not sure. However, I've compared the results of our active scan against the data we gathered when we were in the other time-bubble. My best guess is the three spheres the miners found are forming a gate that gives access into the magical dimension. The gate also happens to be a time-bubble. You can see for yourself."*

A stream of data flooded the shared space in Richard's mind. He ignored it for the most part. While he could catch the gist of the information since he shared some of his battle computer's processing power, he couldn't assimilate the data fast enough to make a full analysis.

"You said guess," Richard said. *"What do you mean by that? You're always telling me computers don't guess."*

"You're always telling me to make a guess," said Nickelo sounding defensive. *"I used the word guess to please you. But if you must know, I calculate a twenty-eight percent probability the three spheres are forming an entrance into a time-bubble."*

Richard let his senses reach out to the sphere.

"*Careful,*" said Nickelo. "*I've already sent you all the data from the scan.*"

"*I know,*" Richard said, "*but that's data. I'm trying to sense feelings and emotions.*"

"*Oh,*" said Nickelo. "*You do realize these spheres aren't living things, don't you?*"

"*How do we know?*" Richard said. "*Plus, I doubt they just magically appeared in these three points in space at the beginning of time. Someone put them here. If so, maybe they left some kind of emotional residue.*"

When his battle computer didn't try arguing further, Richard proceeded with his scan. He ignored the spots his battle computer had already touched. Instead, he concentrated on the overall feel of the sphere. He sensed nothing.

"*Uh, I'm just a computer,*" said Nickelo, "*but I think you'll have to open your mind up more. You've got too many defenses up.*"

Richard hesitated. He knew what his battle computer meant. The problem was, if he lowered the defenses he'd carefully crafted around his mind over the years, he'd be making himself vulnerable.

"*I'm not sure I'm ready to do that, Nick.*"

"*Then don't,*" said Nickelo. "*Call Sergeant Ron to come pick us up so we can leave. Maybe these spheres aren't important anyway.*"

Richard almost took his battle computer's words at face value; almost, but not quite.

"*You know they're important,*" Richard said after thinking about it. "*You know as well as I having anomalies similar to those seed parts popup in our lives is too much of a coincidence to be anything other than the handiwork of* 'the One.' *We're supposed to be here. This is important. My only question is whether it's important to us or just to* 'the One.'"

"*You hate* 'the One,' " said Nickelo. "*Normally, you're fighting against any hint of manipulations by him. Why are you going along with him now if that's what you believe?*"

"*Because, old buddy, if this gate does simultaneously go to both the magical dimension and a time-bubble, maybe we can use it to travel back in time.*"

"Ah, I see," said Nickelo. *"You're hoping to find a way to rescue your niece and nephew. I think you're wrong on this. I calculate less than a one percent chance you'd be able to use a time-bubble with the degree of control necessary to travel a hundred and fifty-eight years back in time to find Brachia and Dren."*

"You mean a hundred and fifty-seven years," Richard said correcting his battle computer. *"Are you getting forgetful in your old age?"*

"Not hardly," said Nickelo sounding not at all amused. *"The children traveled back in time a hundred and fifty-seven years, but that was a year ago in our time. Consequently, you need to add a year if you want to get them at the same moment they arrived in the magical dimension."*

Richard had forgotten to add the extra year, but he didn't like having his mistake pointed out to him.

"It doesn't matter," Richard said. *"If we can figure out how to control time-bubbles, maybe we can travel to anywhere in time we want."*

"Don't get your hopes up," said Nickelo.

"Stop reading my mind."

"Then stop thinking in our shared space," said Nickelo. *"Now, get busy if you're going to do something. Otherwise, I calculate a ninety-seven percent probability Sergeant Ron will do something foolish."*

"Fine," Richard said.

Forcing himself to relax, Richard gently lifted part of the shield he'd created around his mind until a miniscule opening appeared. Tentatively, Richard reached out through the opening toward the green sphere. As his mind drew close, Richard sensed…something.

"Help us," said a voice. Only it wasn't a voice. It was more of a feeling.

The words reminded Richard of the way the dolgars communicated through emotions. He wondered if what he was sensing were really words, or whether he was possibly misinterpreting his own emotions.

"What?" Richard said startled. *"Was that you, Nick?"*

"Was what me?" asked Nickelo. *"Your heartrate and blood pressure are going up. What's wrong?"*

348

As soon as Richard heard the voice, he'd reflexively pulled his mind back behind his shield. Very carefully, he let his mind move back through the opening he'd made toward the green sphere.

"Who are you?" Richard asked trying to send the thought as an emotion. He felt foolish doing so. The sphere was only an object.

"It's not a living thing. Is it?" Richard wondered.

"You can hear us?" said a voice. *"Help us,"* said the voice once again.

This time the emotions were distinct and crisp. Richard could tell they were most definitely not coming from within himself.

"What's going on, Rick?" said Nickelo. *"Talk to me."*

"Can't you hear them?" Richard said. *"They're asking for help."*

"Hear who?" asked Nickelo.

Richard thought his battle computer's voice was taking on a definite tone of concern.

A light came on in Richard's mind. His battle computer had trouble with emotions. When Nickelo needed to communicate with the dolgars, Richard had to interpret for his battle computer. Richard did so now as well by doing his best to turn the voice's emotions into words that he sent into his shared space.

"Help you?" Richard said. *"Help you how? Who are you?"*

"They enslaved us," said the voice. *"They murder others of our kind. Please, help us."*

"Who are you?" Richard asked again.

A brief image of a golden-winged reptile flashed into Richard's mind. He'd only seen a dragon once before in his life, but he recognized the distinct form. He reacted instinctively. The last time he'd encountered a dragon, it had nearly killed him.

"You're a dragon," Richard said as he pulled his mind back.

"No, don't go," pleaded the voice. *"You're the first to contact us in more years than we care to remember."*

If the words had been spoken in a physical voice, Richard would have ignored the entity. But the words weren't spoken. They were sent as pure emotions. Richard felt a mixture of fear and hopelessness in the words. Whoever or whatever was speaking was desperate beyond anything Richard had ever experienced himself.

A bit reluctantly, Richard kept his mind in contact with the green sphere. At the same time, he prepared himself to pull his mind back and close off the hole in his shield at the first sign of treachery.

"One of your kind tried to kill me," Richard said remaining vigilant. *"Why should I help you?"*

"It was not us," said the voice of the dragon, which apparently was also the green sphere.

At the emotion for the word 'us,' Richard sensed an image of a golden dragon with three heads. One head was green, one was purple, and the other head was orange.

"No, it wasn't you," Richard admitted. *"How can I help? Why should I help?"*

The voice of the dragon didn't answer at once. Richard sensed a flood of emotions as if the dragon was having difficulty finding an answer.

Finally, an emotion came to Richard. He interpreted the emotion as *'Because you are one of us.'*

The words were accompanied by a flood of images. Richard felt his mind being drawn toward the green sphere. He heard a warning shout from Nickelo, but try as he might there was nothing Richard could do. He was inexorably drawn toward the desperation that was the dragon.

Something inside Richard responded to the dragon's plight. He sensed three spheres. The spheres were the three anomalies. Each of the spheres was a part of the dragon. The three entities were separate living beings, but at the same time, they were one life form. Memories flooded into Richard's mind. He was an egg. He was captured. As the egg, he was placed in a container with other eggs. He sensed life forms inside the other eggs. The life forms in the eggs were his kind. They were dragons, but yet they were not exactly his kind. The container in which he was placed was sealed. An unknown amount of time passed.

An image of a city flashed into Richard's mind. The city was alien. The city was on a planet in the magical dimension. The planet seemed familiar to Richard. It was Portalis. However, he didn't recognize the city. Richard saw starships with insignias of a black dragon emblazoned on their hulls. The dragon insignias had red stripes down their sides.

The city's spaceport was busy. A starship landed. Richard sensed magic coming from the starship. The memory forcing itself into Richard's mind showed huge, furry, four-armed humanoids unloading dozens of large containers full of dragon eggs. A convoy of vehicles pulled up. The vehicles seemed to be using magical energy the same way Empire vehicles used the energy in isotopic batteries. The containers of eggs were loaded onto the vehicles.

The vehicles took off at a high speed. They were joined by several armored vehicles full of the large, hairy, four-armed humanoids. The convoy soon approached a domed-shaped building several hundred meters high.

Richard sensed residual energy being released from the building. He grew excited when he recognized the energy frequency. The same energy had flowed out of the DNA gas vent at the Academy's spaceport on Velos.

"Nick, are you seeing this?" Richard asked in his shared space.

"I see it," said Nickelo. *"Traces of DNA gas are coming from that building."*

"This is it," Richard said excitedly. *"It's another source of DNA gas. If we can harness it, the Academy can be started up again. The Empire can train more wizard scouts."*

"I don't know, Rick," said Nickelo dubiously. *"Something about the energy coming from the dome seems strange."*

"But that's DNA gas," Richard said barely able to control his excitement. *"We need to find the location of this building on Portalis. If we can get to it, we may be able to get all the DNA gas the Empire will ever need. We just need to acquire it here at its source."*

"Rick, I—"

"I'm telling you this is it," Richard said doing his best to ignore his battle computer's less than enthusiastic response.

Richard was on a roll. The possibilities for the new source of DNA gas seemed endless. The Commandant's legacy at the Academy would continue. For the first time in over a year, Richard felt as if his father hadn't died in vain. If he could only get access to this seemingly abundant source of DNA gas, then all would be well.

"Maybe the Empire won't even have to fight for it," Richard reasoned. *"Maybe we can buy it or set up some kind of trade system with these creatures. They're obviously intelligent. They have starships for Creator's sake. Heck, maybe we can trade our*

technology from the physical dimension for their magic-based technology. This could be a win-win scenario."

Although he thought it odd his battle computer didn't respond to his thoughts, Richard let it slide. As far as he was concerned, he was finally thinking and planning ahead for a change instead of rushing headlong into battle. He was sure his father would be proud of him if he were still alive.

At that moment, Richard's point of view changed. He was once again the dragon embryo inside the egg. As the egg, his point of view was limited to the inside of the container. Several other eggs were in his container as well. Richard felt the emotions from the life forms in the other eggs. He sensed fear. As the egg, his mind was merged with the mind of the three-headed dragon occupying his egg. Richard felt the fear of the three-headed dragon along with the fear of the others. He also felt a feeling of helplessness. He sensed the three-headed dragon scratching furiously at the inside of the egg, but its claws didn't even scratch the surface of the shell. It wasn't time to hatch. The shell was too hard, and the dragon's claws were still too soft.

Without warning, the lid of the container opened. Large, hairy hands reached inside and began removing eggs.

"Careful," said a reptilian voice in a language Richard shouldn't have been able to understand but did. "Every egg is precious."

Richard wondered why the dragons in the eggs were so frightened. Based upon the reptilian voice's words, the creatures apparently intended the eggs no harm.

Two hairy hands reached into the container and pulled out his own egg. Somehow, Richard could see through the eggshell even though it was solid in color. The bright light hurt his eyes after so long in the darkness of the container. Once his eyes adjusted to the light, Richard saw a large, open space underneath a massive dome. He was inside the building. Thousands of creatures of every shape and size were standing alongside hundreds of conveyor belts. Most of the creatures were of a species unknown to Richard, but he did see some who appeared familiar. He spotted a few humans. Others appeared to be of gnome, elf, and dwarf stock. Richard even saw a group of orcs lined up alongside one of the conveyor belts. The orcs were taller than the ones Richard was used to seeing, but there was no doubting their heritage.

Richard heard a cracking sound. He shifted his gaze in the direction of the noise. The sound repeated itself. He saw one of the hairy, four-armed creatures raising a wicked-looking whip. It struck the back of a nearby human. The human screamed. Two more of the four-armed creatures joined the first one. All three began swinging their whips. The human fell to the floor. Richard heard a sound he associated with laughter come from the four-armed humanoids. They continued to beat the withering body on the ground until sprays of blood spattered on nearby workers. The other workers ignored the blood. They seemed to concentrate even harder on whatever tasks they were performing.

Richard looked at the vast expanse around him. He noticed hundreds of the hairy, four-armed creatures walking around carrying whips. As he watched, they frequently swung their whips at the backs of the workers. If the workers screamed, the four-armed guards appeared to whip them even harder.

"What the hell is going on?" Richard thought into his shared space.

"It looks like slave labor," replied Nickelo. *"Stick with this memory. We need to know exactly what's happening."*

Richard felt his egg being moved toward a nearby conveyor belt. The other eggs that had been in his container were already spaced out on the belt. They were secured in place by metal clamps.

The guard holding Richard's egg started to place it on an empty spot on the belt. Richard sensed the fear from the dragons in the other eggs continuing to grow.

"No," said a reptilian voice. "This one is special. Give it to me."

The speaker wasn't one of the hairy creatures. Instead, it was a man-sized humanoid with scaly skin. It had an elongated head with small spikes spaced out along two ridges running from its forehead to the back of its neck.

"This one reminds me a little of a dragon," Richard said.

The word 'Dragar' popped into Richard's head.

"Did you say that, Nick?" Richard asked.

"Not me," answered Nickelo. *"It came as an emotion. You interpreted it in our shared spaced. Otherwise, I wouldn't have known what it meant."*

The conveyor belt began moving in the direction of a pyramid-looking tower located at the center of the building. Richard had trouble estimating heights from his position in the egg, but he guessed the tip of the pyramid was about a hundred-meters high. The Dragar carrying the egg which was Richard walked alongside the belt while keeping pace with the other eggs.

As the conveyor belt drew closer to the pyramid, Richard sensed an increasing amount of energy being released from the tip of the pyramid. Richard noticed thin tubes stretching out from the pyramid to points situated near the various workers. Smaller lines branched off of the primary tubes. Each workstation appeared to have one of the branches with a nozzle at the end.

"What is this place, Nick?" Richard asked.

"How would I know?" said Nickelo. *"If I had to hazard a guess, I'd say it's a factory of some type."*

Richard looked closer at some of the nearby workers. He zeroed in on an old gnome. When a conveyor belt brought a round globe to the gnome's workstation, she took her workstation's line and attached the nozzle to the globe. A reddish gas began filling the globe. Richard heard the gnome muttering words that he quickly forgot. The red gas in the globe converted to energy.

"That's a spell," Richard said. *"The gnome's changing the red gas to magic energy."*

"So it seems," agreed Nickelo. *"Just guessing, I'd say the globe is a type of storage device similar to the Empire's isotopic batteries."*

Richard glanced around the factory floor. Everywhere he looked he saw globes of various sizes being transported by the conveyor belts to various workstations. There were tens of thousands of globes. They ranged in size from the tip of his little finger to a massive globe the size of a large hover-truck.

As Richard observed the scene around him, he realized each of the slaves were magic users.

"I don't get it," Richard said. *"Why aren't the slaves and spellcasters revolting?"*

As Richard spoke, he saw two of the hairy, four-armed humanoids begin whipping another one of the slaves.

"You can't tell?" asked Nickelo. *"Look closer."*

Richard did. Then he saw the reason. Each slave had a thin collar around their neck. Richard sensed energy flowing through the collars. A line of energy from each collar reached out to the spellcasters' links to their Power reserves.

"The collar must be some type of filter," Richard said. *"It's limiting what spells the spellcasters can do."*

By the time Richard finished analyzing the slaves' collars, the Dragar carrying his egg finished climbing the stairs to the top of the pyramid. From his new vantage point, Richard could see the entire expanse of the factory floor. The sight of dozens of workers being whipped at any one time was depressing enough. However, the feeling of fear and hopelessness from the slaves was even worse. A part of Richard wished he could help. But another part pushed the thought aside. He could do nothing for the poor souls. His mission was to find a way to access the DNA gas that was apparently stored in the pyramid.

"Where does the DNA gas come from?" Richard asked his battle computer. *"Is this pyramid on a vent of some kind? I can sense some residual gas escaping out of the pyramid. Do you think this is the source of the DNA gas vent that was at the Velos spaceport?"*

"I can't be sure," said Nickelo.

The way his battle computer answered disturbed Richard. His intuition told him Nickelo knew more than he was saying. Before he could pursue the matter further, a wave of absolute fear swept over Richard.

The fear came from the direction of the tip of the pyramid. The first of the eggs had arrived on the conveyor belt. As Richard watched, four of the reptile-looking Dragars grabbed the egg and positioned it on the tip of the pyramid. They pressed downward until the tip penetrated the shell of the egg.

An intense emotion that Richard could only interpret as a scream of agonizing pain echoed off every wall inside the dome. Richard sensed Power flowing out of the egg into the pyramid. The scream intensified into an emotion of absolute agony. Richard tried to cover his ears, but he had no hands. He was still sharing the form of the dragon inside the egg. Logic told him it wouldn't do any good anyway. The scream was composed of pure emotion, not sound.

The screams of the tortured, unborn dragon inside the egg continued for a full five minutes. Eventually, the intensity of the screams diminished until they disappeared altogether. One of the Dragars removed the egg from the pyramid's tip and threw it down. The lifeless egg bounced along the sides of the pyramid as it made its way ever downward. At each bounce, pieces of the shell broke off. By the time the egg reached the base of the pyramid, the broken body of a bloody, miniature dragon lay sprawled among the shell fragments. Richard could see tens of thousands of partially-decayed, miniature dragons discarded at the base of the pyramid.

"What is this place?" Richard thought. After the tortured screams, his mind was barely able to comprehend his surroundings. *"What's happening?"*

"Don't you know?" said Nickelo. *"I calculate a ninety-seven percent probability these four Dragars are priests. They're sacrificing those unborn dragons to get their Power. Based upon information in my databanks, dragons don't have reserves. Their Power is a part of their DNA makeup. The priest's spells combined with this pyramid somehow extracts the Power and converts it to DNA gas. The gas then appears to be converted into magic energy by those poor workers and stored in the globe-batteries. I can only surmise the magical batteries are somehow used to supply energy to devices the same way as our isotopic batteries."*

Richard only caught about half of his battle computer's explanation. Another egg had been brought to the top of the pyramid by the conveyor belt. Once again, the priests took the egg and shoved it onto the tip of the pyramid. If anything, the emotional screams from the second egg were louder than the first.

"I can't take this anymore," Richard yelled in an attempt to stop the flow of memories entering his mind. *"Get me out of here."*

"Not yet," came the emotion from the creature that was both the green sphere and part of the three-headed dragon. *"Watch."*

The memory skipped forward. The last of the eggs on the conveyor belt had been sacrificed. The egg of which Richard was a part was brought to the priests. Richard sensed fear on the verge of panic overcome the three-headed dragon inside the egg.

"No!" the dragon screamed in a burst of emotion. But there was no one there to hear other than Richard, and he was helpless to do more than watch.

"This one is special," said the reptile holding the egg. "Those fool Thargs were going to send it onto the conveyor as a normal sacrifice."

Richard's dragon-memory gave him the knowledge that the Thargs were the hairy, four-armed humanoids.

"Yes," hissed one of the reptilian priests as it took the egg. "You did well. This one is indeed special. It can be separated to form a time-gate. Our ships can use it to raid the physical dimension. We must have more of the holy metal. Our conquests depend on it."

A second priest took the egg and inspected it. "Ah. This one is a gold dragon. It is strong. If we are careful, its Power can hold a gate for many years."

"Yes, if we are careful," agreed a third priest. "But we must use the energy in this egg wisely."

The first priest took the egg of which Richard was a part and placed it onto the tip of the pyramid. But the priest didn't shove the egg downward. When the outer shell of the egg touched the pyramid's tip, Richard felt an ocean of pain, fear, and agony that was contained in the pyramid. The sacrificed dragons were dead, but their last agonizing emotions appeared to be the energy that formed the DNA gas.

As the four priests began chanting, energy from the pyramid rose upward and wrapped around the three parts of the three-headed dragon inside the egg. Richard remembered more than felt pain beyond measure as he shared the memory of the dragon's life force being split into three separate parts. When the deed was done, Richard felt loneliness beyond compare.

Richard realized the egg was now gone. In its place were three spheres; one green, one orange; and one purple. With that realization, Richard's mind was released from the memory. He was back in the tunnel. His legs gave out, and he fell to the floor.

"They're coming," said the green sphere. *"We were not careful enough. I'm sorry. They know someone is here."*

The green sphere started glowing brighter. Richard sensed lines of energy reaching out to the orange and purple spheres. The connecting lines enlarged until a triangle 20,000 meters to a side began twisting the very fabric of time and space.

"What's going on?" said the voice of a panicking Sergeant Ron "My instruments are going haywire."

"Pick up the kids and go," Richard said hoping the *Defiant's* captain wouldn't argue. "They're coming. Get out of here now."

"Not without you," said Sergeant Ron. "I'm coming in for landing."

"Negative," Richard yelled back. "Do not land. Save the kids. That's an order."

Before Richard could argue further, the space between the physical and magical dimension was torn asunder. Something was trying to come through. The something was big.

CHAPTER 39

When the tingling from the teleport stopped, Jeena found herself in a dark tunnel. Even without the dim glow of the blue gem at the end of the Lady's staff, Jeena would've been able to see with her night vision. But she needed more than the greys and whites of her night vision for the task at hand. Calling to the blue gem, Jeena coaxed it to use some of its Power to brighten until the tunnel was illuminated.

True to his word, Brachia had repaired the Lady's staff in short order. Since the repair, the Staff of the Lady of the Tree seemed more willing to respond to her requests.

Jeena walked along the tunnel. Using the Power of the Lady's staff to aid her, she reached out with her mind seeking those she had been sent to find. After a time, she sensed something. In fact, she sensed three somethings.

"Hello," said a voice in her mind. But it was not a word. It was more an emotion of greeting than it was a word. Along with the emotion, Jeena sensed the color green.

"Are you the helper?" said the voice using another emotion. *"You were foretold."*

"I've been sent to save you," Jeena thought back. *"Where are you?"*

"My brothers and I have been waiting for you," said the green voice. *"We are all here. The hated ones are coming. Please help*

us. We have been used far too long aiding them in their evil. Please release us."

"I'm here to save you," Jeena thought trying to assure the green voice. *"I can't do it alone."*

"You will not be alone," said the green voice. *"A dragon-friend, the Elf Friend, is here as well. He will help you. But you must be strong. You must do what needs to be done when the time comes."*

Jeena felt the desperation in the green voice. The voice was in agony, and it had been for a very long time. She sensed all the green voice wanted was peace. Something in Jeena yearned to help the green voice.

"I will save you," Jeena promised. *"You're no longer alone. I will save you."*

Jeena felt another emotion from the green voice. It was hope. The emotion of hope spread and touched two other colors; purple and orange. Jeena sensed their hope as well.

The location of the green voice appeared closest. Jeena ran toward it. She had to help the voices. Somehow, she would use the Lady's staff to bring them together. She would give them peace.

I will save them, Jeena thought. *I must save them.*

CHAPTER 40

The last thirty minutes had been quiet. Tia continued to lead Matthew in a circling path above the quarry while providing cover for their wizard scout as best they could. Other than the anomaly Rick was recovering, nothing registered on her instruments. Even Rick didn't show up. That didn't surprise Tia. After all, Rick was a wizard scout.

Suddenly, things changed without warning. All three anomalies appeared on her instruments as they began sending out high levels of strange energy. A glance at her rear video cameras showed Tia what she feared. The triangular land mass between the three anomalies was starting to shimmer in and out of focus. Intermittently, she saw flashes of blackness with pinpoints of white light.

"Stars," Tia said. "Margery, give me an analysis."

The voice of the Commandant's old battle computer immediately came over the zipper's intercom. Although Margery's primary processor was embedded within the *Defiant's* computer system, she was also serving as the primary computer for both of the zippers as well as the two Warcats.

"Energy readings indicate the anomalies are forming a gate," said Margery. "The energy being released is magical in nature. Recommend you climb to at least twenty thousand meters. I would highly recommend you not be caught in the gate's energy."

"I hear you," Tia said as she thought the command to increase the zipper's speed. A surge of plasma energy shot out the back of the fighter. She was pressed into her seat. Tia could only hope Matthew was continuing to follow her lead.

Tia pulled hard on the controls of her Zip fighter. The agile craft readily responded. Tia was pushed back into the thick cushion of her seat.

"Climb, Matt," Tia said over her intercom.

"I'm right on your tail," said Matthew. "You don't have to tell me twice."

"Tia," said Sergeant Ron over the communication channel the *Defiant's* team was using. "My sensors are picking up something behind you. Evasive maneuvers."

Tia didn't ask questions. She kicked the controls of the Zip fighter hard to the left.

Several beams of multicolored energy passed through the point in space where she'd been.

"Matt!" Tia said concerned her friend hadn't dodged in time.

"I'm still here," said Matthew. "You can't lose me that easily."

"Analysis indicates the energy beams are magic based," said Margery. "I calculate your fighter's shields will be thirty to fifty percent less effective against magic. I've fought against magic before. I'm modifying the shield frequencies for both fighters to compensate."

A blue beam of energy passed close to Tia's left side. She was buffeted back and forth several times as her zipper was thrown to the right by the force of the beam.

"Shields are at eighty-five percent," said Margery. "That was a glancing blow. Recommend you not allow a beam to hit you straight on."

"I'll take that under consideration," Tia said as she moved her hands furiously across the zipper's control panel. "Matt, are you still with me?"

"Affirmative," replied Matthew. "My shields are only at thirty-five percent. Some kind of green ball of energy hit me dead on. I activated my zipper's electronic countermeasures, but they had no effect."

"They won't," said Margery. "The enemy ship isn't using electronics. It's using magic. I'm trying to modify your countermeasures to affect magic. Recommend you descend to get closer to the enemy ship. I calculate its gunners will be attempting to lock onto you with their primary weapons within the next twenty seconds. The current fire appears to be the ship's smaller anti-fighter weapons."

Tia was about to ask, "What ships?" when she glanced at her rear videos and saw two black starships behind her; a small one and a larger one. She noticed both ships had a black dragon with a red stripe down its side painted on their hulls. The smaller of the two black ships appeared to be about the size of the *Defiant*. The larger ship reminded her of one of the navy's destroyers. Only the bow of the black destroyer was currently through the gate. Colored beams of energy were shooting out from her bow guns. The smaller ship was several thousand meters ahead of the destroyer. Tia got the impression the smaller of the two starships was a recon ship. The black recon ship was completely through the gate and heading their way.

"Recommend you expedite your descent to a lower altitude," said Margery. "The black destroyer is only partially through the gate. If you can get close to the destroyer, their larger weapons may not be able to target you."

Tia moved the zipper's controls to initiate a high-speed descending turn to the right.

"By the Creator," said Matthew. "Those are the pirate ships we've been looking for."

Blackness filled Tia's windscreen as she closed the distance to the destroyer. Her maneuver had caught the smaller recon ship by surprise. It was just now starting a turn back toward them.

As Tia flew her zipper alongside the black destroyer's portside, she made out the details of over twenty gun turrets along its length. The design of the gun batteries was alien to her, but the purpose of the beams of blue, green, and red energy shooting out of them weren't. They were designed to kill.

As she passed the image of the black dragon on the destroyer's bow, Tia hit her decelerators and made a hard turn to the left. She was too close to the gate, and she had no desire to go through. From her current vantage point, she could make out a third starship behind the destroyer. The third ship was an immense mass of black metal that could only be a dreadnaught. Like its two smaller companions, the dreadnaught had a black dragon with a red stripe down its side painted on its bow. The dreadnaught hadn't yet entered the gate, but Tia had no doubt it would as soon as the destroyer cleared.

"What are you doing?" said Matthew over the communication channel. He sounded concerned. "We're going to be in range of the destroyer's main guns again."

"Look through the gate," Tia said. "Would you rather be in range of that thing's guns?"

Matthew must have seen the dreadnaught because he said, "No. I think I like the destroyer better."

"Uh, not that I'm complaining, Margery," Tia said, "but how come we didn't disintegrate on the destroyer's shields. Surely she has a force field of some type."

"I calculate a fifty-seven percent probability the destroyer had to lower any shields before it could pass through the gate," said Margery. "However, she'll be clear of the gate in twenty-two seconds. I would advise making sure you're not inside her shields when they come back online. Otherwise, you'll be trapped inside. I calculate you need to be at least five hundred meters away to be safe."

Tia made a quick calculation. As far as she could tell, the only reason the two zippers hadn't been blown out of the sky already was because they were too close to the destroyer for its larger weapons to be brought to bear. But at five hundred meters, she doubted that would continue to be the case. On the other hand, according to Margery, if she stayed where Matt and she were currently located, they'd be trapped inside the destroyer's shields.

A sudden thought crossed Tia's mind that a starship the size of the destroyer was bound to have fighters of some type. Magic based or not, she had no doubt enemy fighters could destroy both zippers at their leisure once they were trapped inside the destroyer's shields.

"Tia! Matthew!" said Sergeant Ron over the com-link. "I'm on the far side of the planet. I'll be at your location in two minutes. Hold on!"

Tia was about to tell her captain she wouldn't be alive in two minutes when someone else beat her to the punch.

"They haven't got two minutes," said Richard over the com-link. "Tia, I've got you on my passive scan. Your best bet is to engage the recon ship. You need to alternate fire between your plasma, phase, and 30mm chain guns. Matthew, stay at a distance and fire your torpedoes. Tia can guide them in with her telekinesis just like a bongo ball. Do it just like we practiced."

"My chain guns are for use against ground-based armor, Rick," Tia protested. "We're in space."

"Trust me, Tia," said Richard. "The recon ship's shields are magic based. If you can confuse it by alternating attack forms, you may be able to get some fire through."

Without arguing further, Tia turned her zipper in the direction of the black recon ship. It had almost completed its turn. Surprisingly, Tia noticed the fire from the destroyer slacken considerably as she lined up on the smaller ship.

"The destroyer's gunners must not want to risk hitting their recon ship," observed Margery. "I recommend disabling the recon ship's guns before it completes its turn."

Tia turned toward the black recon ship even though instinct told her it was a bad idea. But she trusted both Rick and Margery. Tia only hoped her trust was warranted. She had a feeling the next few minutes would prove her trust one way or another.

With a silent prayer to the Creator, Tia began her attack run.

CHAPTER 41

Sergeant Ron stared at the holograph. The images for the two Zip fighters were turning to attack the black recon ship. A sense of fear for his grandson rose up in his mind, but he forced it back. He'd been in enough battles to know a little fear was good, but too much could make a soldier indecisive. Hatred for anything sporting the black-dragon insignia took the place of his fear. Sergeant Ron forced it out of his mind as well. Too much hatred would cloud his judgement. He needed a clear mind if he was to save his grandson and Tia.

If you hurt them, I'll kill every one of you, Sergeant Ron swore. *I'll kill you if it's the last think I do.*

"Margery!" Sergeant Ron said. "Time to target?"

"The *Defiant's* primary weapon systems will be within range in one minute and twenty-one seconds," said Margery over the cockpit's intercom system. "The destroyer's shields will probably be up by then. I highly recommend you abort your attack run and activate your hyper-drive to make your escape."

"Well, you know what you can do with your recommendation," Sergeant Ron said. He increased the *Defiant's* speed to the maximum velocity it could take while continuing to stay in orbit.

"Terrie! Charlie!" Sergeant Ron said. "Get out of those Warcats and man the portside weapons. Daniel, you handle the rear weapons. Angela, you take the starboard-side guns. I'll handle the forward guns and torpedoes. We're going in with everything blasting at that destroyer."

"No!" came Richard's voice over the com-link. "Don't be a fool. The kids aren't dead yet. But they will be if you don't use your head."

Sergeant Ron barely heard his friend's words. His hatred for anyone with the black-dragon insignia was rising again and pushing all thoughts out of the way except those of revenge.

"One minute and ten seconds," Margery said over the *Defiant's* ship-wide intercom. "The destroyer has activated her shields. I calculate only a twenty-seven percent chance you can penetrate her force fields with the *Defiant's* weapons. The destruction of the *Defiant* is near one hundred percent given your current course of action.

"Sergeant Ron!" said Richard. "Abort your attack run. The destroyer is through the gate. Help the kids with the recon ship."

* * *

Richard was growing desperate. Although he was only an arm's length from the green sphere, the connecting lines of energy to the other two spheres and the resulting gate was located on the other side of the green sphere. While Richard's feet were on solid rock on his side of the sphere, just two meters away on the other side was the blackness of deep space. It was very disconcerting.

Richard could see the hull of the black destroyer as it continued to exit the gate. Its front half was already through, but the ship was large enough its back part was still in the magical dimension.

"Help me," Richard said to the part of the dragon that was the green sphere.

"I cannot," said the green sphere. *"We are the gate, but we cannot control the gate. The Dragars control the activation of the gate. They won't close it until their starships are through."*

Richard sensed a strange emotion from the green sphere. The closest word Richard could find for the emotion was the word perhaps.

"Perhaps what?" Richard said.

"Perhaps you could close the gate before all the ships get through," said the green sphere.

Desperate for anything, Richard said, *"How?"*

A thought came into Richard's mind. The thought was alien in nature. It was a dragon thought. But somehow Richard understood. He now knew how to open and close the gate. There was only one problem.

"I don't have the kind of Power necessary," Richard said losing hope. *"It would take a hundred times more Power than is in my reserve to do what's needed."*

"Yes, it would," replied the green sphere. *"But you won't have to do it alone. There is another. She is an ally. She has the Power to close the gate, but she doesn't have the knowledge or skill."*

Richard looked around. He saw no one. But what he did see was that only a small portion of the tail of the destroyer was still within the gate. Even worse, the immense form of a black dreadnaught loomed behind the destroyer. Richard had no doubt the dreadnaught would enter the gate as soon as the destroyer was completely clear.

"I'd say that's a reasonable expectation," said Nickelo in their shared space. *"By the way, I've made an analysis of the gate and compared it with the information from your first mission with the elf Shandria. This anomaly is not just a gate. It is also a time-bubble."*

Richard looked at the edge of the gate, which was only a couple of steps away.

"A time-bubble?" Richard asked trying to make sense of the mass of information he was receiving.

Richard had a thought. *"If the gate is also a time-bubble, where in time are these starships from? Do you think they're from a hundred and fifty-seven years in the past?"*

"No," said Nickelo. *"I think they're from a lot earlier than that; a lot earlier."*

"You spoke of an ally," Richard said to the green sphere. *"Where? How?"*

"I will help you contact her," said the green sphere. *"First you must make me a promise.*

Richard was pretty sure he knew what the sphere wanted. It's what he would have wanted.

Fine, Richard said. *"I promise I'll free you somehow. Now, contact your ally."*

The sphere surprised Richard. *"No. It's too late for us. Our Power, our life force, is nearly drained. Our death is near, but we do not fear it."*

Richard wanted to scream in frustration. He never understood why some people, and apparently some spheres, wasted time by talking about things that didn't matter.

"Why can't they just get to the point?" he wondered.

Even though the emotion-driven language of the dragons was fast, precious seconds were passing way too quickly.

"Then what do you want?" Richard demanded. *"Either get on with it, or I'll try to do something on my own."*

"The black ships operate from a base a hundred thousand years in the past," said the green sphere. *"They use my brothers and me to create a gate and time-bubble combination to raid the physical dimension during your time for the holy element. They use the life force of dragon eggs to energize the holy element."*

An image of the holy element flashed into Richard's mind. It was titanium. With the image, Richard understood more of what he'd seen in his vision at the pyramid. The sacrificed dragon eggs were being used to charge batteries made out of titanium. Or rather, out of the energized titanium that Richard knew better as creallium.

A flash of colored beams and projectiles lashing out from the black destroyer drew Richard's attention. The destroyer was completely clear of the gate. It was now fully in the physical dimension. Richard saw it move to join the fight against the two zippers. Richard noticed the black dreadnaught begin to maneuver into position to enter the gate. Time was getting short.

"Fine," Richard said. *"Whatever you want done, I'll do it. Just tell me how to close this gate."*

"First you must promise me," said the green sphere. *"You must promise me you will destroy the Dragars' temple. You must stop them from sacrificing more of the dragon eggs."*

"Fine, I'll do it," Richard said.

Richard had no idea how the sphere thought he was supposed to travel back in time a hundred thousand years, but at the moment, he didn't care. The sight of the black destroyer firing at Matthew and Tia spurred Richard on to promise anything. He'd worry about how to keep his promise later.

"Promise," said the sphere.

"I promise," Richard said. *"I give you my word as a wizard scout."*

"You are one of us," said the green sphere. *"We will trust you. I am contacting your helper now. When she sends you the Power, you must start the cycle to close the gate. And then you must run, or you will be destroyed."*

"Wait," Richard said. *"How am I supposed to destroy the temple? I can't time travel."*

An image of a dragon egg flashed into Richard's mind. With the image came a location. The egg was located only a hundred meters away.

"Go," said the green sphere. *"The egg is special. Take it. Save it. When the egg hatches, the dragon will take you where you need to be. Go now. You don't have much time."*

* * *

"Hurry," said the green sphere. *"You don't have much time."*

"I'm doing my best," Jeena said as she tried to control her temper. She didn't like being ordered around, especially by a green ball of energy.

"I am in contact with the helper," said the green sphere. *"Can you sense him?"*

Jeena reached out with her mind through the green sphere as she attempted to locate her supposed helper. She sensed nothing. She told the sphere as much.

"He is using a stealth shield," said the green sphere. *"You will not be able to sense his aura. Try to sense his Power."*

Jeena reached out once again and tried to locate the sphere's helper. She concentrated her senses for any hint of good or evil Power. Again she sensed nothing.

"I tell you there's nothing there," Jeena said growing increasingly frustrated. *"I checked for both good and evil Power. There is nothing. Nothing exists at the end of the path you've given me."*

"This helper is neither good nor evil," said the green sphere. *"He is neutral. Look for an absence of good and evil. Look for nothing. You can do it, but please hurry. The existence of my*

species, the existence of your world, depends upon you closing the gate."

Jeena wanted to scream. She was just an acolyte. What did she know of gates and time-bubbles? In desperation, Jeena shouted a prayer to the Lady.

"Please help me, Lady. I lack the skill. Please show me the way."

A heartbeat passed, then another. Jeena sensed nothing. But on the third beat, she felt a tickle at the back of her mind. It was accompanied by a sense of peace and tranquility. The fear and tenseness that had been building up in Jeena departed. Her mind cleared, and she could hear in a way she'd never heard before.

"Seek with your heart," said a voice in her mind.

"What?" Jeena thought. *"Who?"*

The voice was not the gravelly voice of the green sphere. This voice was soft and comforting.

"Lady?" Jeena asked as she was suddenly filled with hope. *"Is that you, Lady?"*

No reply came. However, Jeena was certain the voice had been that of the Lady. Jeena was just as sure the Lady was gone back to whence she'd come.

"Seek with my heart," Jeena said out loud. Her voice echoed off the wall of the cavern and came back like a command.

With nothing to lose, Jeena dropped her scan. The thoughts of the green sphere faded away. Jeena sought a place in her heart that had always felt empty. For as long as she could remember, Jeena had felt as if the part of her heart that was missing existed somewhere; in some time. She only needed to find it. Jeena reached inside herself; not into the physical heart she felt beating inside her chest, but into the heart that was her eternal soul.

Jeena found the empty spot and let her mind enter. The way was dark, and the path appeared to be dangerous. Jeena pressed onward. The stakes were too high to turn away now.

CHAPTER 42

Richard ran to a point in the tunnel closest to the location of the 'special' egg. He reached out with an active scan and found a source of Power. It was indeed a dragon egg. Even though the egg was protected by a stealth shield, Richard found it easily enough. It was almost as if a part of him was drawn naturally to the egg.

Reaching out with his mind, Richard wrapped the egg with Power and made it shimmer. He shifted the egg into the void and drew it to him with his telekinesis. When the egg cleared the tunnel wall, Richard shutoff his Power and caught the egg before it could fall.

"Okay," Richard said using his emotions. *"I've got the egg. Now what?"*

"She is coming," said the sphere. *"You must meet her halfway. Follow your heart. You will find her."*

"What are you talking about?" Richard said. *"What do you mean by follow my heart?"*

"I don't think the sphere means it literally, Rick," said Nickelo. *"Reach inside yourself with your mind. I calculate that will have the greatest chance of success."*

Even though he was still in the tunnel, Richard could still see the gate intertwined with the physical dimension surrounding it. The black destroyer was almost in position to add its firepower against the two zippers that were hounding the black recon ship.

And the black dreadnaught was growing ever larger as it drew closer to the gate. Richard knew full well if something didn't change soon, the kids would be dead for sure.

"You will be too if you don't stop stalling," said Nickelo sounding increasingly impatient. *"You're a wizard scout. Do something."*

"Easy for you to say," Richard replied a little angrily.

Doing his best to reach inside himself, Richard tried to sense anything different. All seemed as it was before. That is, all was the same except for a spot inside him that he'd always tried to avoid. The spot had always seemed too empty, too lonely. But for some reason, it seemed different now. It was still empty and lonely, but less so. Forcing his inhibitions aside, Richard reached out with his mind and entered the emptiness. His friends were near death. He had no other choice.

CHAPTER 43

"Hang on, kids," Sergeant Ron said over the *Defiant's* com-link. "We're twenty seconds out."

"Hurry," said Tia. "The destroyer's lining up for the kill. Our shields are almost gone."

Sergeant Ron eyeballed the *Defiant's* track toward the black destroyer. From the console's holograph display, he could tell the destroyer was preparing to clear the planet's thin atmosphere. From what he could tell, while the black destroyer was inside the atmosphere, it was forced to use its maneuvering thrusters. That limitation reduced the destroyer's speed to a crawl. But Sergeant Ron had no doubt once the destroyer cleared the atmosphere, the ship's captain would switch to the destroyer's hyper-drive or whatever it used for propulsion. Once it did so, the children's zip fighters would be caught between the destroyer and the black recon ship.

"Margery," Sergeant Ron said. "Give me a short burst from our hyper-drive."

"I highly advise against that, captain," said Margery. "We're heading straight for the planet. If our timing is off, we'll crash."

"Do it," Sergeant Ron ordered.

While he respected Margery, he didn't need an ex-battle computer to tell him it was a dangerous maneuver. But based upon previous experience, Sergeant Ron didn't think it was as dangerous as it seemed. The *Defiant* was as much a part of him as was his own skin. He was confident he could close the distance to the black destroyer quickly and still avoid crashing into the planet.

The hyper-drive kicked on for a sub-second burst. The distance to the destroyer closed rapidly. Sergeant Ron's hands flew across the control panel without conscious thought. His mind knew what needed to be done. His body automatically followed his mind's intent.

"Gunners!" Sergeant Ron yelled over the *Defiant's* com-link. "Fire as you bear. Aim for the destroyer's engines. If we can cripple her while she's still in the atmosphere, we've got a chance."

The *Defiant's* crew didn't waste time answering with words. Instead, the *Defiant* vibrated violently as all of its gun and missile batteries fired at the same time.

Warning lights flashed all across the control console as the *Defiant's* sensors detected return fire from the destroyer. Dozens of balls of energy along with beams of every color of the rainbow were heading straight for the *Defiant*.

"Margery," Sergeant Ron said. "Handle the shields. I'll control the ship."

"Compliance," said Margery. "Impact with the planet's surface will be in three seconds."

Sergeant Ron kicked the *Defiant* to the left with the ship's side thrusters. At the same time, he activated the electronic countermeasures. The ship shuddered again as dozens of fist-sized decoys ejected outward from the *Defiant* in all directions. The countermeasures had previously been adjusted by Margery to react to magic. Sergeant Ron had a feeling the next few seconds would tell if Margery's modifications had been successful.

The area around the *Defiant* was lit up by flashes of bright light as dozens of the black destroyer's missiles and energy rounds were fooled by the decoys. The *Defiant's* sudden movement to the left also caused a sizeable chunk of missiles and energy weapons to miss. However, others locked onto the *Defiant* and slammed into her shields.

The *Defiant* rocked crazily from side to side. Loose pieces of equipment were thrown around the cockpit. While he was jostled violently back and forth, Sergeant Ron remained in his seat. He'd been in too many ship-to-ship battles during his life not to be prepared. At the first sign of danger, he'd automatically strapped himself in with the command-seat's shoulder harness.

"Shields are holding at seventy-six percent, captain," said Margery.

Sergeant Ron said a silent thank you to his daughter. He knew Diane could be a hard-headed 'B' sometimes, but by golly, she hadn't skimped when it came to equipping the *Defiant* with the best the Empire had to offer. He was certain the *Defiant's* normal shields would have been overwhelmed by the destroyer's initial onslaught.

"Keep firing," Sergeant Ron ordered.

He could've saved his breath. The *Defiant's* crew needed no urging. The sight of the black destroyer bearing down on Matthew's and Tia's zippers was all the motivation they needed. The *Defiant* bucked as another volley of missiles shot out of her portside torpedo tubes and headed toward the destroyer. Beams of plasma energy from the *Defiant's* two massive 200-gigawatt plasma cannons followed close behind.

Reaching out with his left hand, Sergeant Ron pressed the lever for the front torpedo tubes. Eight of the newly installed Alpha 5 torpedoes shot out toward the destroyer's rear area.

"Tia," Sergeant Ron said over the *Defiant's* com-link. "The Alpha 5's are inbound. Guide them to the destroyer's engines."

No reply came over the network, but Sergeant Ron saw the track of the torpedoes deviate toward the rear of the destroyer. The Alpha 5's guidance systems had been modified by Sergeant Hendricks to take mental commands from any of the *Defiant's* bongo players. Six of the torpedoes were knocked out by the destroyer's anti-fighter weapons and countermeasures. However, two of the torpedoes zigged and zagged in such an erratic fashion the enemy's gunners were unable to hit their targets. First one torpedo then the other exploded against the shield protecting the destroyer's engines.

"Their rear, portside shield is down to thirty-eight percent," said Margery. "I calculate another salvo has a forty-two percent probability of hitting their engines."

"Then we'll hit them again," Sergeant Ron shouted anxiously. He lost all pretense of command dignity as he lined the *Defiant* up for another salvo of torpedoes.

"Reload will be complete in five seconds," said Margery.

The *Defiant* shuddered again as another round of return fire hit the *Defiant's* shields. The *Defiant* was briefly thrown off course, but Sergeant Ron quickly got her back under control. From the *Defiant's* new position, Sergeant Ron got a better glimpse of the gate behind the black destroyer. What he saw caused him to draw in a sharp breath.

Through the gate, Sergeant Ron saw the immense form of a dreadnaught. It wasn't registering on any of the *Defiant's* instruments, but there it was nevertheless. Even after over four decades, Sergeant Ron recognized the ship. She was all black except for lights coming from thousands of portholes and dozens of open bay doors. A large black dragon with a red stripe down its side was painted on the dreadnaught's hull.

Hatred blazed inside Sergeant Ron. A rage he hadn't felt in decades consumed him.

"You bastards!" Sergeant Ron shouted as he changed the *Defiant's* course from the destroyer to a straight line toward the dreadnaught. "You killed her! I'll kill you all if it's the last thing I do. I'll kill you all."

Sergeant Ron fired the *Defiant's* newly loaded torpedoes in the direction of the dreadnaught. The black destroyer was forgotten in the red haze of his hate. Only the destruction of the black dreadnaught mattered. For the first time in decades, he had an opportunity to exact revenge. Sergeant Ron swore he wouldn't let the chance slip away. Nothing was more important than destroying those who'd killed his wife.

CHAPTER 44

"Sergeant Ron," Terrie said over the ship's intercom. "What are you doing? We need to attack the destroyer. We've almost got them. Line back up so we can fire."

No reply came from the cockpit. The *Defiant* didn't alter course.

Although he was medically retired, Terrie was still a wizard scout. As such, he'd been in too many battles to panic when things went awry.

"Margery, take command," Terrie said in command voice.

"Unable to comply, wizard scout," said Margery. "The captain has turned the ship's override off. He is in full control."

Terrie fired a final salvo from the portside plasma batteries. He didn't need to look at his gunner station's holograph to know the situation. His passive scan told him everything he needed to know.

The black destroyer was seconds away from clearing the atmosphere. The black recon ship had turned back and was engaging Tia and Matthew's zippers in an attempt to drive them toward the destroyer. Although still on the other side of the gate, Terrie sensed the thousands of life forms on the black dreadnaught. The huge starship would soon be entering the gate. Terrie figured in less than two minutes, it would be entering the fray as well.

Making a decision, Terrie unhooked from his gunner's chair and ran into the cargo bay. He took a hard left straight toward the stairs leading to the crew compartments. Aided by the strength of his battle suit, Terrie made the leap to the top of the stairs in a single bound. The leap took him through the hatch and into the dining room.

As Terrie passed an open door to his right, he glanced in. Angela was hunched over her gunner's console pulling levers and pushing buttons in a blur of motion. A pang of regret and longing swept through Terrie.

Will this be the last time I see her? Terrie wondered.

Until this moment, Terrie had only thought he loved his wife. But now he knew beyond a shadow of a doubt he loved her. Someone had once told him a person never really appreciated what they had until they lost it. Terrie swore if they made it out of the battle alive, he'd spend the rest of his life appreciating the woman who possessed his heart.

Then the door was past, and Terrie lost sight of Angela. He ran straight for the short stairs leading to the cockpit. At the same time, he drew his phase rod and activated it in destructive mode.

"Margery," Terrie yelled. "Open the door."

"Noncompliance, wizard scout," said Margery. "The door is locked from the inside."

Terrie hit the cockpit door with the full force of his battle suit. At the same time, he swung his phase rod at the door's locking mechanism. Both he and the phase rod bounced off. Terrie hit the steel planking of the crew's dining area with a loud thump.

"The cockpit is encased in titanium," said his battle computer. "The captain has energized it. The cockpit is now protected by a creallium shield."

Terrie jumped up and began pounding on the cockpit's door with both fists. "Sergeant Ron! You're going to kill the kids. You're going to kill your grandchild. The Commandant wouldn't like this. You know he wouldn't."

* * *

Tia didn't understand what was happening. The *Defiant* was no longer heading toward the destroyer. After guiding the two torpedoes through the destroyer's rear shields, she had fully expected the *Defiant* to fire another salvo. But the *Defiant* had suddenly changed course toward the gate behind the destroyer. And the *Defiant's* portside plasma batteries were firing at a significantly reduced rate. The destroyer was using the lull to concentrate its fire on the two zippers.

"Tia," said Matthew. "The black recon ship is on my tail. My shields are at twelve percent. I'm not going to last much longer."

Tia twisted her Zip fighter in a hard, hundred and eighty-degree turn. A dozen energy beams and lightning blasts came within meters of her ship, but none hit. As she straightened out her turn, Tia lined up on Matthew's zipper. The black recon ship was directly behind her friend's Zip fighter lining up for the kill.

"Dodge right when I tell you," Tia ordered.

Without waiting for a reply, Tia slammed the button for the remaining two anti-ship missiles still under her left wing. Her Zip fighter vibrated as the missiles' engines activated and sped them toward Matthew's zipper. Tia reached out with her mind and grabbed hold of both missiles' guidance systems.

Stay calm, she thought. *It's just like playing bongo.*

"Dodge! Now!" Tia shouted.

At the same time, Tia pulled the trigger for her zipper's forward-plasma guns. She knew they were too light to penetrate the black recon ship's shields, but she fired them just the same. Sometimes it just helped to shoot something.

Matthew's Zip fighter dodged to the right just before the two anti-ship missiles passed through the point in space where he'd been a split second earlier. Guided by her telekinesis, the missiles sped toward the center point of the black recon ship's cockpit. Anti-missile missiles shot out from the recon ship. Before they could strike Tia's missiles, her salvo of plasma rounds hit the leading missiles of the recon ship's return fire. Bright explosions lit the area in white and yellow flashes of light. One of Tia's anti-ship missiles was destroyed. The other missile struck the shield protecting the black recon ship's cockpit.

A flash so bright it momentarily activated the sun-filter on the windscreen of Tia's zipper lit the area. The windscreen cleared almost immediately as the explosion dissipated. In spite of the ferocity of the explosion, Tia could tell the black recon ship was unharmed.

"The recon ship's forward shield is down to eighteen percent," said Margery. "Too bad your second missile was destroyed. I calculate it would have been able to break through."

Tia didn't have to look at her heads-up display to know she was out of missiles. She was young, but she'd learned early on to keep a running total of expended ammo in her head. Failure of a pilot to do so usually meant death.

Streaks of energy shot out from the recon ship in her direction. Other streaks made their way to her left in the direction of Matthew's zipper. Tia dodged her Zip fighter to the right. Most of the energy streaked past without hitting their target. However, two beams of energy along with a solid chunk of metal hit her forward shield. Her zipper shuddered so violently Tia's head hit the control panel in spite of the fact she was wearing her shoulder harness.

"And that's why fighter pilots wear helmets," said Margery. "By the way, you're on a collision course with the recon ship. Recommend you take evasive maneuvers."

Before Tia could respond, Matthew called from his zipper. To Tia, her friend's voice sounded steady, but even so, she detected a sense of panic behind his calm exterior.

"I'm hit," said Matthew. "My shields are down to two percent. I'm sorry, Tia. Tell my mother and grandfather I love them."

A wave of emotion swept over Tia. She replied without thinking. "Tell them yourself."

Without giving her logic time to overcome the desires of her heart, Tia shoved the hyper-drive's acceleration lever to maximum velocity. She was immediately pushed back in her seat as the Zip fighter jumped forward. Tia struggled to move her hand to the eject button. It was only a handbreadth away on the armrest of her pilot's chair. But the g-forces were too much. Her gloved hand remained pinned at her side. Memories of Tia's family flashed through her mind. Her thoughts were overridden by an image of Matthew. The black recon ship grew in size until it took up her entire windscreen. Tia was overcome with a deep sense of regret. She knew she would never see Matthew again.

* * *

Matthew struggled to dodge the incoming balls of energy from the recon ship. The destroyer had stopped firing, apparently out of fear of hitting their own recon ship. But the destroyer's lack of fire mattered little to Matthew. With only two percent shields remaining, he had no doubt the next volley from the black recon ship would destroy his little zipper. He had little doubt his death was imminent. Matthew resolved to give his death meaning.

Pulling his zipper into a hundred and eighty-degree turn, Matthew headed straight for the black recon ship. He fired his last remaining anti-ship missile and pulled the trigger of his plasma cannon. If he was going to die, he'd go down fighting. Matthew only hoped his mother would be proud of his final moments.

"I'm hit," Matthew said over the *Defiant's* com-link. "My shields are down to two percent. I'm sorry, Tia. Tell my mother and grandfather I love them."

The com-link was silent for a second. Then it crackled.

"Tell them yourself," said Tia.

A shudder of fear swept over Matthew. Something in his friend's voice scared him. Without warning, a streak of bright-blue energy lit the sky to Matthew's right. A part of Matthew's mind registered the energy as the exhaust of a hyper-drive. Logic told him it could only be from Tia's zipper. The streak of blue headed straight for the black recon ship. The energy made contact with the recon ship's shield. A violent blast erupted from the front of the recon ship.

"Their forward shield is down," said Margery. "Your anti-ship missile will make contact in one second."

As soon as Margery finished speaking, another explosion erupted to Matthew's front. It was followed by a larger and even more violent secondary explosion.

"The black recon ship has been destroyed," said Margery. "Recommend you decelerate immediately to avoid colliding with the debris."

Matthew reacted instinctively and pulled back on the zipper's thrusters. The agile Zip fighter responded immediately as its forward movement slowed to a near stop.

"Tia," Matthew said. "We got it."

There was no reply.

"Tia," Matthew said growing fearful.

The streak of hyper-drive exhaust from a zipper and the resulting explosion on the black recon ship's shield flashed through his mind.

"Tia!" Matthew said more forcefully. "Answer me!"

No answer.

"Margery," Matthew said. "Plot me a course to Tia's zipper."

"The other zipper was vaporized when it hit the recon ship's shield," said Margery. "Tia's zipper destroyed the shield. That's why your missile was able to get through."

Matthew's belly gave a spasm. He felt as if someone had punched him in the stomach. Tia's face flashed in his mind. In that moment, he suddenly realized how much he cared for the feisty fighter pilot. He realized how much he loved her.

She can't be dead, Matthew thought. *Life can't be that unfair.*

"Now that the black recon ship is out of action, I calculate the destroyer will be turning its weapons back on you," said Margery. "Recommend you pick up Tia and exit the area post haste."

"Wha...what? Matthew said trying to make sense of the computer's words.

"I said you need to pick up Tia," Margery repeated. "I'm sending her coordinates to your nav-computer."

"She...she's not dead?" Matthew said as the image of the blue streak and the resulting explosion flashed back into his mind.

"No, of course not," said Margery. "What kind of battle computer do you think I am? I activated the Zip fighter's ejection seat before her zipper hit the black recon ship's shield. But if you don't hurry and pick her up, the destroyer is going to start bombarding this whole area. Then you'll both be dead, and there won't be a thing I can do about it."

Matthew wasted no time in turning his zipper in the direction of the blinking light on the hologram. He had to get Tia before anything happened to her.

Alarm bells interrupted Matthew's thoughts.

"Too late," said Margery. "The destroyer has got a lock on you. Your shields are still only at two percent."

"Recommendations?" Matthew said desperate for any kind of plan.

"Sorry," said Margery sounding as apologetic as a computer could sound. "I have none.

Unfortunately, neither do I, Matthew thought.

CHAPTER 45

The area in Jeena's soul that had been empty all her life seemed less empty. She let her mind drift. Neither thoughts from the green sphere nor the thoughts of the Lady intruded into the quietness around her. Jeena felt a sense of peace. The empty spot in her soul had always frightened her a little when she'd been a child. The spot didn't frighten her now. In fact, the sense of peace she now felt made her smile.

How could I have been so foolish? she wondered. *There's nothing here to be frightened of.*

Nevertheless, doubts began to surface. Jeena started to worry she might be wrong. She sensed something ahead. Whatever it was, the something was getting closer. Jeena stopped the movement of her mind. The something stopped as well. Tentatively, Jeena stretched out her thoughts toward the something. It reached out toward her also.

Jeena drew Power from her reserve and silently said a spell to protect her mind. The Power converted to magical energy. She finished thinking the words of the spell. The magic energy transformed into a shield between the something and her. Jeena sensed the something forming its own shield. The something's shield wasn't magical. It seemed to be composed of pure Power.

How? Jeena wondered.

Jeena sensed an emotion from the something. The emotion

seemed to be a question or perhaps a request.

"This one is the helper," came a thought from the green sphere. *"You can trust this one. He has the knowledge to close the gate. You have the Power and skill. Do it now. There is little time."*

Jeena hesitated. After all, what did she really know about the spheres?

"Don't you trust me?" asked the green sphere.

"I'm not sure," Jeena answered honestly, *"but I promised I would help, and I always keep my word. Tell me what I need to do."*

A memory from the green sphere gave Jeena the idea of sending out a line of Power toward the something; toward the helper. As soon as she conceived the idea, Jeena drew Power from her reserve and began transforming it into magical energy.

"No," said the green sphere. *"This one cannot use magic. You must use your Power to create a link between your staff and the helper. Allow the staff's Power to flow to the helper."*

"Why?" Jeena said. She was worried. There were too many unknowns. *"How do I know this so-called helper won't use the Power of the staff against me? I'll be defenseless."*

"He won't harm you," said the green sphere. *"This helper is one of us. He can be trusted."*

Jeena still hesitated.

The oracle said I could trust the spheres, Jeena thought, *but how do I really know for sure? For that matter, how do I even know I can trust the oracle? He is from the old legends. But does that mean he's trustworthy? What if everything I've experienced up until now is a ruse?*

"You said the helper is one of you," Jeena said to the green sphere in an attempt to probe for more information. *"Do you mean he's a dragon?"*

"This helper is...different," said the green sphere. *"But he can be trusted."* After a pause, the sphere added, *"He is an elf friend."*

That caught Jeena by surprise.

"An elf friend?" Jeena said unsure whether to believe the green sphere. *"The dragon Rasianate was declared an elf friend by High Lord Skyfall. But Elf Friend Rasianate died in the battle of the Algosa Seas. Your helper can't be Elf Friend Rasianate."*

"No, he cannot," said the green sphere.

"What is this elf friend's name?" Jeena demanded. *"Who declared him such?"*

"I did," said a voice in Jeena's mind. It was the voice of the Lady again.

"Lady? Lady?" Jeena said unable to believe what she was hearing.

In all of Jeena's 320 years of life, the Lady had never spoken to her. Jeena wondered if she were being tricked. Only High Priest Questor could speak to the Lady, and then only through emotions and feelings

Who am I that the Lady speaks to me with words? Jeena wondered. She shook her head to clear it. *This must be a trick.*

"It is no trick," said the green sphere. *"The High Priestess Shandria and the High Lord Carndador declared this helper as elf friend. He was the first."*

Before Jeena could ask further questions, the green sphere spoke in a voice tinged with fear. *"The time of decision is now. Either trust the helper or don't. But decide now. In a few more heartbeats, it will be too late."*

Jeena heard no further words from the Lady. However, she did feel a sense of calm assurance pass over her. Jeena made her decision.

Reaching out with her mind, Jeena removed Power from her reserve and created a link. She attached one end of the link to the Power in the Staff of the Lady of the Tree. Jeena moved the other end of the link toward the something; toward the helper; toward the one who she prayed was indeed an elf friend as the green sphere said.

Without warning, the link was snatched out of her control. She sensed Power from the blue gem in the staff being drawn toward the helper; toward the elf friend. Jeena tried to stop the flow of Power, but the link to the staff was no longer responding to her commands. Even worse, because the link to the staff was formed with Power from her reserve, the helper had a direct line to her Power reserve as well. The realization hit Jeena that if this was all a well-laid trap, she'd soon be dead.

"What have I done?" Jeena thought.

CHAPTER 46

The other life form, the green sphere's supposed helper, sent a line of Power at Richard. The frequency of the Power seemed strangely familiar. The Power was intermixed with another Power frequency he didn't recognize.

The line of Power tried to form a link to Richard's reserve, but he knocked it aside before it could lock into place. He wrapped the end of the link with his own Power and held the link at a safe distance.

"Nick," Richard said. *"Analysis?"*

"Create an active scan and give me control," said Nickelo.

Richard did so.

After a few nanoseconds, data rushed into Richard's shared space.

"This can't be right," Richard said. *"The Power inside the link is the same frequency as High Priestess Remozorz's staff. Is it her? Is Rem the presence I sense? Is she the helper?"*

"No, it's not the gnome," said Nickelo. *"She died almost 90,000 years ago. However, the Power inside the link appears to be from her staff. Your active scan is picking up the frequency of the blue gem the kids mounted at the top of the staff."*

"I sense another frequency as well," Richard said. *"What is it from?"*

"Unknown," said Nickelo. *"The other frequency you're sensing is from the Power that formed the link. It is from the helper."*

"I know this sounds strange, but I almost feel as if the second frequency is familiar as well," Richard said. He was perplexed by the whole situation.

"It should be," replied Nickelo. *"The frequency is similar to the frequency of the elf you were with on your first mission for 'the One.'"*

"Shandria?" Richard said excitedly. *"Are you saying Shandria is alive?"*

"Negative," said Nickelo dashing Richard's budding hopes. *"I'm saying the frequency is similar. I calculate the creature is linked to the same Power reserve the elf Shandria used. However, it isn't her."*

"Then who?" Richard asked.

"Insufficient data to speculate," said Nickelo sounding a little defensive. *"I'm a computer, not a psychic."*

"Hurry," interrupted a thought from the green sphere. *"The dreadnaught will be entering the gate. If the gate does not start closing within the next few seconds, it will be too late. All your friends will die, and your galaxy will soon follow."*

Still thinking at nanosecond speed in his shared space Richard took stock of the situation. The black destroyer was almost free of the atmosphere. It was turning its main gun batteries toward a target just outside the atmosphere. Richard followed the track of the guns. He mentally drew in a deep breath when he saw where the tracks intersected. A lone Zip fighter was floating in space. The hatch was open, and a person in a fighter-pilot's environmental-suit appeared to be trying to pull in a second pilot who was also in an environmental suit. A quick calculation from Nickelo confirmed the two pilots wouldn't complete their maneuver before the black destroyer blasted them into nothingness.

Richard also sensed the location of the *Defiant*. Instead of engaging the black destroyer as Richard expected, the *Defiant* seemed to be heading straight for the black dreadnaught on the other side of the gate.

"What the heck?" Richard said into his shared space.

A voice that was neither his battle computer nor the green sphere answered his query.

"I've overridden my security protocol, wizard scout," said Margery. *"I'm passing information through your battle computer*

directly to you. I have no algorithm to prevent the destruction of the Defiant. *What are your orders?"*

A flood of data from Margery flowed into Richard's shared space. The data showed Sergeant Ron hunched over the controls in the *Defiant's* cockpit with a wild look on his face. Richard rewound the video back a few minutes. He immediately understood Sergeant Ron's fixation. Richard had no doubt the *Defiant's* captain assumed the black dreadnaught was the one that had killed his wife so many years ago.

The video dump also showed Terrie in his battle suit beating on the door of the *Defiant's* cockpit in a vain attempt to reason with Sergeant Ron. When there was no response, Richard sensed Terrie sending out a line of Power and wrapping it around Sergeant Ron's heart. Richard didn't need his battle computer to tell him the retired wizard scout would kill Sergeant Ron before he would allow the *Defiant's* captain to fly the ship into certain doom.

The scene changed. Richard saw the massive bulk of the black dreadnaught lining up to enter the gate. The green sphere was right. He had only seconds to act.

The continuing onslaught of information would've been too much for a normal human mind to take. Fortunately, Richard wasn't normal. He was a wizard scout, and he had Nickelo to help him make sense of the information flowing into his shared space. Thankfully, it was all being done in the space of a few nanoseconds.

Richard made a decision. He wasn't sure if it was the right decision, but he was a battle-hardened Marine at heart. He knew from experience even a mediocre plan was better than no plan. Richard gave his orders to the two battle computers using command voice. Nickelo and Margery didn't argue. Their wizard scout had given an order. They had a mission. They would obey.

Once his orders were given, Richard turned his attention back to the link attached to the high priestess's staff. From his previous contact with the staff, Richard knew its Power was immense. He didn't profess to know all of the staff's capabilities, but he did know its Power. He'd found the blue gem in the first place, after all.

Using the knowledge of gates and time-bubbles given to him by the green sphere, Richard siphoned Power from the staff through the link created by the other life form; the so-called helper. Richard made sure not to allow the link to connect to him or his Power reserve. He just drew the necessary amount of Power out of the link and formed it into a ball. Still thinking at nanosecond speed in his shared space, Richard sensed the changes required to transform the Power into something that could pull the green, orange, and purple spheres together. Richard was positive doing so would close the time-bubble and its corresponding gate.

"I would highly advise you hurry, Rick," said Nickelo. *"If any part of the dreadnaught gets in the gate, I calculate a sixty-four percent probability the gate won't close until the dreadnaught has passed through."*

Richard twisted the flows of Power from the link into what was needed. Once he was done, he sent the modified Power back down the helper's link.

"What can I do now?" Richard said.

"You can pray," answered Nickelo.

Richard seldom prayed. But he did so now. Sometimes even battle-hardened marines needed help.

CHAPTER 47

When Jeena felt her link jerked out of her control, she struggled to free it from the helper's grasp. But for some reason she didn't understand, the Staff of the Lady of the Tree didn't aid her. If anything, the staff willingly allowed its Power to be pulled down the link. It was almost as if the staff was familiar with the helper and was willing to sacrifice itself if necessary. Panic swept over Jeena. Her own Power reserve was intimately linked to the staff.

"The helper can drain me dry if he wants," Jeena thought.

"Do not worry," said the green sphere as if reading her thoughts. *"Stop struggling. He is a dragon friend. He is an elf friend. He is trying to help us."*

"No he isn't," Jeena said. *"He's stealing the staff's Power."*

Jeena increased her efforts to free her link. The helper's grasp remained firm.

A large amount of Power was transferred from the staff to the helper before the flow stopped. A few heartbeats later, the flow of Power reversed itself. Jeena sensed Power returning down her link. To what purpose, she didn't know. When the Power drew close, Jeena braced herself as best she could. She expected the worst, but she wouldn't go down without a fight.

The worst didn't happen. The Power filled her link and halted as if awaiting her command. Jeena tentatively touched the Power with her mind. It had been changed. She recognized the Power as that from the blue gem adorning the Staff of the Lady of the Tree. However, the Power was different in a subtle way. The flows of energy twisted upon and around itself in ways that seemed familiar to Jeena.

Is that a spell? Jeena wondered. But she knew it wasn't. It couldn't be. The flows of energy were pure Power. The flows weren't magical in nature.

"*Use the spell,*" said the green sphere. "*The time is growing short. Use it now.*"

"*What spell?*" Jeena said. "*That's Power, not a spell. It isn't magic.*"

"*The helper cannot use magic,*" said the green sphere, "*but he understands it. He helped write some of the spells in your spell book.*"

"*What nonsense is this?*" Jeena snorted. "*No new spell has been written in over twenty thousand years.*"

"*There is no time for this,*" said the green sphere in growing desperation. "*Convert the Power to magic. Use the spell. Use it now, or all is lost.*"

Jeena had a thousand questions. But one look at the massive black object with the image of the red-striped dragon floating near the gate overrode her curiosity. She didn't know the helper. She didn't know the green sphere. She didn't know the black object. But she did know the image of the black dragon with the red stripe down its side. And what she knew of the red-striped dragon from her readings was bad; very bad. The Oracle had told her she could trust the spheres. The green sphere said she could trust the creature it called the helper.

Making her decision, Jeena reached out with her mind and pulled the modified Power toward her. She changed the Power into magic energy using the words taught her by the Oracle. When the last word of the Oracle's spell was completed, Jeena transferred the ball of magic energy into the Staff of the Lady of the Tree. Using the staff, Jeena sent the spell toward the center of the gate.

Lines of magic leaped out and connected to the three spheres. The magic of her spell drew the spheres toward the center of the gate. As the spheres drew closer to each other, the gate began to shrink. It shrank slowly at first, but it picked up speed as the green, orange, and purple spheres quickly closed the distance between them.

Jeena saw lines of energy jet out the front of the black object with the black dragon image. The jets of energy slowed the black object's forward momentum. Soon it was no longer moving toward the gate.

The gate is closing, Jeena thought. *Whatever the black beast is, it knows it's in danger.*

Jeena watched with fascination at the scene laid out before her. Even though she was in a tunnel deep underneath the world's surface, she could see all around. The second image before her was overlaid onto the real world.

"This time-bubble will cease to exist when the gate is closed," said the green sphere. *'You must leave before that happens. Otherwise, you will be destroyed as well."*

"What about you?" Jeena asked. *"How will your brothers and you get free?"*

"When the gate closes," said the green sphere, *"Then we will be free. After all this time, we will finally be free. Now go. Go now!"*

Something in the sphere's voice frightened Jeena. Somehow, she knew the freedom of which the green sphere spoke was its death. She also sensed her death was assured as well if she remained.

"Goodbye," Jeena said. *"May the Creator bless your brothers and you, and may you find happiness and peace wherever you travel next."*

Without waiting for a reply, Jeena touched the runes on the staff in the order taught her by the human child, Dren. The blue gem atop the Staff of the High Priestess glowed brightly. Everything zoomed in and out of focus. Then all turned black.

CHAPTER 48

Within seconds of Richard sending the modified Power back to the helper, lines of energy jumped out of the green sphere in the direction of the other two spheres 20,000 meters away. When the lines of energy made contact with the other spheres, they moved in the direction of the green sphere's location.

"It has started," said the green sphere. *"The gate is closing. My brothers are coming to join me. You must leave now. Take our egg with you. Promise me you will care for it. Do not allow the Dragars to get their hands on our egg. They will sacrifice it and use its Power to open another gate."*

"You can make sure the egg is safe yourself," Richard said still using the dragon's emotion-speak. *"Once the gate is closed, I'll take you and the other two spheres back to the* Defiant. *I'm sure Sergeant Ron will take you wherever you want to go."*

An emotion of intense sadness flowed outward from the green sphere and into Richard.

"No, wizard scout," said the green sphere in an emotion forceful enough to echo off the tunnel walls. *"I wish it could be so, but it cannot. Once my brothers and I converge, the gate will be closed by our destruction. You must take the egg and flee. You must leave now, or you will also be destroyed."*

Richard was momentarily shocked. *"You didn't say anything about being destroyed before. Maybe we can think of a different way to close the gate. We—"*

"No," said the green sphere. *"There is no other way. We were doomed the moment the Dragars split us apart at their temple. Only death can set us free. We have been tortured by the Dragars far too long. We have been forced to help them too many times by opening the gate. Finally, we will be free. After all we have been through, we do not fear death. It will be a blessing. It will be a release."*

"But—," Richard started to argue.

"Go! Now!" said the green sphere with a burst of emotion. *"Your time is short. Save the egg. Save yourself. Save your friends. Go!"*

"Rick—," began Nickelo.

Richard didn't wait to hear what his battle computer had to say. He just turned and ran for all he was worth.

As Richard ran, he heard one final burst of emotion from the green sphere. It was a plea from the deepest part of the sphere's soul. A memory accompanied the plea. The memory showed a vast host of dragons. Somehow, Richard knew the memory was a species' memory from millions of years in the past. The dragons were on the planet Portalis in the magical realm. In the memory, Richard watched the dragons rule the land for many generations. Occasionally, some of the dragons teleported to a small planet. The planet was more a ball of super-heated mud than it was a planet. The dragons burrowed deep into the mud and laid their eggs.

Over time, millions of dragon eggs were buried in the hot mud. Eventually, the mud cooled until it formed a soft rock. More time passed. A black starship appeared and landed on the planet. Dragon-looking humanoids accompanied by hairy, four-armed creatures exited the starship. Other creatures, some humanoid, some not, were driven out of the starship. They were chained together in long lines of fifty each. Richard recognized some of the races in the chain gangs. There were gnomes, elves, dwarves, orcs, and even an occasional troll. Other unfamiliar races also adorned the lines. However, humans were by far the largest majority of the prisoners. Richard had no doubt the chained prisoners were slaves.

The Dragars and their four-armed lackeys forced the slaves to dig in the soft rock. The slaves tunneled deep below the planet's surface. More often than not, the slaves were forced to dig with their bare hands. Occasionally, Richard saw one of the slaves uncover an oblong rock.

No, not a rock, Richard thought. *Those are dragon eggs.*

The dragon eggs were loaded onto the black starship. Eventually, the cargo holds of the starship were filled with dragon eggs. At that point, the Dragars lined up the slaves along the side of the quarry near the mine's entrance. There weren't many slaves left. What few slaves hadn't died from the hard work and constant beatings were nearly skeletons. Richard noticed one of the Dragars nod to a group of their four-armed helpers. The hairy creatures turned their weapons on the slaves and the slaughter began. Afterwards, the guards loaded on their starship and departed.

More time passed. Another black starship arrived and the cycle began anew. After a blur of starships, mining, and killings flashed through Richard's mind, the memory faded.

While he'd been in the memory, Richard had continued running. When the memory finally ended, he stopped.

"Nick," Richard said. *"How much time? Can we make it?"*

"On foot?" said Nickelo. *"Doubtful. I'm sorry to say my calculations indicate you need something a lot faster than your battle suit."*

Richard had been coming to the same conclusion while experiencing the memory. The tunnels kept zigging and zagging as they made their way toward the surface. There was too much distance and too little time.

Drawing together his strongest emotions, Richard sent out a call for help. He didn't wait for a response. Whether any dolgars would answer his call, Richard didn't know. But he wasn't going to sit around waiting to find out. He pulled off his dimensional pack and shoved the dragon egg inside.

"Rick," said Nickelo. *"What are you doing? You need to keep running. Maybe you'll get lucky."*

No, Richard said as he closed the flap of his pack. *This time I'm not going to rely on luck. I'm going to try and be smart.*

After closing the flap of his pack, Richard opened it again to make sure the egg was gone. It was. He let the flap fall back shut.

"You're always telling me to use my brain instead of rushing into things, right?" Richard said. *"So that's what I'm trying to do."*

"*After all these years of rushing into things you decide to change your tactics today?*" said Nickelo. "*For once, I calculate rushing is your best course of action. Besides, I fail to see any wisdom in stopping.*"

Richard decided to add to his battle computer's confusion even more.

"*Pull me up the specs for a hover-cycle,*" Richard said. "*Make it the same model as the one I have back on Trecor. It's fast, but it's small enough to maneuver in these tunnels.*"

An image appeared in Richard's mind accompanied by a long list of technical specifications.

"*There it is, oh greatest but most foolish of wizard scouts,*" said Nickelo. "*However, I doubt* 'the One' *will let you summon it. It's a high-tech item. You know* 'the One' *tries to limit you to older technology for the most part. The more technically advanced the item, the more Power it requires to summon. Your Power reserve's too small. I calculate a ninety-two percent probability you're wasting your time.*"

"*Maybe,*" Richard said, "*but I've got a hunch you're wrong this time. You know* 'the One' *is occasionally flexible on the rules. Besides, either* 'the One' *lets me summon the hover-cycle, or I'm dead. Either he wants to keep me alive, or he doesn't. It's his choice.*"

With those words, Richard imagined the hover-cycle. The merest drop of Power left his reserve. With only a little hope, Richard lifted the flap of his dimensional pack. He saw a piece of olive-drab metal.

"*Hmm,*" said Nickelo. "*I guess I was wrong. What are the odds?*"

"*About eight percent,*" Richard said throwing logic at his battle computer.

"*Ha,*" said Nickelo sounding unamused.

Wasting no time, Richard pulled the opening of his dimensional pack around the piece of metal. It was the front fender of a hover-cycle. Richard gave a hard jerk on the pack. The pack's opening elongated and slid around the metal until a complete hover-cycle was sitting on the tunnel floor.

He didn't waste time trying to figure out why *'the One'* allowed him to summon an advanced piece of equipment for so little

Power. Richard just threw his dimensional pack over his shoulders and mounted the hover-cycle. With the click of a switch, the engine roared into life. A second later, he was blazing down the dark tunnels at breakneck speed.

Slowing down for a hairpin turn, Richard miscalculated. His knee made a grove in the rock wall before he was able to complete the turn.

"You're lucky the rock here is soft," said Nickelo. *"If it was granite, you'd have wrecked your cycle."*

"I'm doing the best I can," Richard said.

"Well, it's not going to be good enough," said Nickelo. *"Based upon your current rate of speed, I calculate it'll take you three minutes and twelve seconds to reach the surface and get to a safe distance from the mine entrance. Unfortunately, I'm currently estimating the spheres will come together in only two minutes and forty-seven seconds."*

The tunnel narrowed suddenly. Richard scraped a metal beam on one side of the wall with his rear bumper. The hover-cycle wavered back and forth for a few tense gyrations. Somehow, Richard managed to recover and keep going. He heard a loud crash behind him. Switching a part of his battle helmet's visor to its rear visuals, Richard saw the tunnel roof collapsing behind him.

"Geesh," said Nickelo. *"You need to do better than that."*

"Well, if you think you can do a better job then be my guest," Richard said. *"Believe me, you won't hurt my feelings."*

His battle computer didn't give a verbal reply. However, Richard felt the right glove of his battle suit twist the cycle's throttle full open. The hover-cycle leaped forward with a loud roar as the rear anti-gravity fan kicked into high gear. The tunnel walls became a blur as Richard felt the battle suit lean into turns on its own volition.

Glancing at the green path to the exit on his heads-up display, Richard noticed it had changed.

"You've switched our route," Richard said.

"Affirmative," said Nickelo while giving a crazy-sounding laugh. *"The previous path was based upon your skill level. You're riding with the big boys now. So hang on, because I was born to be wild."*

Richard was tempted to ask his battle computer if he was on

drugs. However, since they were traveling down the tunnel at a hundred and fifty kilometers an hour, Richard decided to remain silent.

A glance ahead made Richard begin to regret he'd given control to his battle computer. The roof of the tunnel was starting to slant downward. Just a hundred meters ahead, the tunnel roof appeared to be lower than the height of the hover-cycle.

"Nick?" Richard shouted.

"I see it," said Nickelo. *"Hang on."*

With those words, Richard felt the battle suit twist violently. The hover-cycle fell on its side and slid along the tunnel floor. It passed beneath the low point in the tunnel at more than a hundred kilometers an hour. Once past the low point, the battle suit's left leg kicked out and straightened the hover-cycle upright again.

Once the cycle was back in its normal position, Richard felt a little better. But his relief was short-lived. Without warning, the tunnel floor gave way to a deep cavern. The cavern's ceiling towered overhead. Its floor was lost in darkness so intense even the battle helmet's night vision couldn't penetrate it. The hover-cycle fell several meters before its anti-gravity fans caught hold. With a hard lurch, the cycle rose rapidly.

Richard risked a glance at his heads-up display. He looked at the green path that was his battle computer's intended path. The ceiling of the cavern was only five hundred meters below the surface. The green path went almost to the ceiling before it cutoff to a side tunnel near the cavern roof. From there, the path was another five thousand meters of hairpin turns before it arrived at the mine entrance.

"Are we going to make it?" Richard asked.

Nickelo didn't hesitate with his reply.

"Negative. We're going to be a few seconds too late. Sorry, Rick."

"Then why bother?" Richard said.

"You know why," answered Nickelo.

Richard did know. He'd been a Marine. Marines never gave up, no matter the odds.

"Can I shift us into the void and get through the ceiling," Richard said knowing the answer before he'd even completed his question.

"Negative. Your Power reserve's too small. You'd never make the five hundred meters. Your Power would give out before we made it halfway to the surface."

Richard shuddered. The thought of coming out of the void and being entombed in solid rock scared him. He didn't mind admitting he was claustrophobic. If he had to choose between being blown up and being buried alive, he'd choose an explosion every time.

Sending scans out in all directions, Richard tried to sense anything that might help. He sensed the link to the staff. It was still dangling where he held it locked in place with his Power. The helper at the other end was jerking the link in an attempt to free it. Her efforts were to no avail. His grip was too strong.

Richard sensed the Power radiating from the staff. The potential energy from the blue gem his niece and nephew had placed on the staff was enormous. But Richard knew instinctively he couldn't access the blue gem's Power directly for his own use.

Another link caught Richard's attention. It was the link the elf Shandria had attached to him during his first mission for *'the One.'* She'd used the link to train him in creating and protecting Power links. Shandria's link was a dead-end since she'd died thousands of years ago, but her link was still attached to him.

Richard sensed the frequency of Shandria's link. It was the same as the frequency of the staff.

"That makes sense," said Nickelo. *"The staff was originally Shandria's. A part of it's connected to her old Power reserve."*

Gambling the staff wouldn't rebel against its original owner, Richard took the end of the helper's link and connected it to Shandria's link.

Power from the staff surged into Shandria's link. Richard pulled the Power from the link into himself and made both the hover-cycle and him shimmer. He shifted into the void while taking the hover-cycle with him. Using telekinesis, Richard lifted the cycle upward straight into the cavern roof.

Twenty seconds later, Richard's head popped through the rocky surface of the planet. As soon as the hover-cycle was in the clear, Richard dropped his dimensional shift. Then Nickelo took control of the battle suit again. The hover-cycle's anti-gravity fans roared as Nickelo headed for the rim of the quarry at max speed.

"Go!" Richard urged.

The link from the creature twisted and jerked with increasing intensity. Richard had a feeling the helper at the other end was redoubling her efforts to free her link. Guessing it was only a matter of time before she tore her link free, Richard drew enough Power from the staff to recharge his Power reserve to one hundred percent. Then he released the link to the staff. As soon as he did, he felt the helper jerk the link away into the nothingness from which it had come.

With the link's departure, Richard no longer sensed the helper. Whoever or whatever she was Richard didn't know. Even so, Richard felt a pang of regret the helper was gone. In spite of the situation, her presence had given him comfort.

Nickelo jerked Richard out of his thoughts. The hover-cycle was just topping the lip of the quarry.

"It's going to be close," said Nickelo. *"I'm going to try to get us a little more distance before the gate implodes. Brace yourself."*

Using his passive scan, Richard sensed the three spheres coming closer together. He realized his battle computer was right. It wouldn't be long now.

CHAPTER 49

Terrie beat on the door to the cockpit one last time. He knew he couldn't delay any longer. His passive scan showed their danger all too well. The children were drifting in space. The black destroyer's weapons were zeroing in for the kill. The three points of energy forming the gate were drawing closer together. The gate was shrinking correspondingly.

The *Defiant* was also drawing closer to the gate with each passing second. The *Defiant* bucked as Sergeant Ron released another volley of missiles toward the black dreadnaught on the other side of the gate.

"Sergeant Ron," Terrie shouted. "This is your last chance. Turn around now. Don't make me kill you."

Terrie concentrated on the Power he'd wrapped around the old sergeant's heart. With a thought, Terrie knew he could kill the *Defiant's* captain. He didn't want to, but what else could he do? He had to kill Sergeant Ron.

Then what? Terrie thought.

He wasn't even sure Margery could regain control of the *Defiant* after the death of its captain. But Terrie could think of no alternative. He had to try something.

Just before Terrie tightened the Power wrapping around Sergeant Ron's heart, a thought from his battle computer stopped him. A surge of data entered his shared space. The data was orders.

They were orders from Wizard Scout Richard Shepard. The orders came from his friend through Nickelo to Margery and on to Taylor. Despite the orders convoluted path, Terrie had no doubt they were from his fellow wizard scout.

Terrie didn't understand the reason for the orders, but he didn't hesitate. He trusted his friend. With a final look at the cockpit door, Terrie turned and made for the cargo bay as fast as his battle suit's legs would take him.

"Charlie," Terrie said over the *Defiant's* com-link. "Turn control of the portside weapons over to Angela. Then strap into your Warcat. We're going for a ride."

* * *

Sergeant Ron fired another salvo of torpedoes toward his enemy. The black dreadnaught seemed to float there on the other side of the gate taunting him.

It killed my wife, Sergeant Ron thought. *It's going to pay. It's going to pay today.*

A flicker of light from the direction of the copilot's chair caught Sergeant Ron's attention. He took his eyes off of the black dreadnaught long enough to look to his right at the copilot's position. He drew in a deep breath as a shiver ran down his spine. Sitting in the cushioned chair dressed in a black and silver wizard scout uniform was the Commandant.

"Sir?" Sergeant Ron said as he fumbled for words. "But…but you're dead."

"Yes, I am," said the figure of the Commandant. "And so will your entire crew and you be if you don't stop what you're doing."

Sergeant Ron shook his head. *This can't be happening*, he thought. *The dead can't come back to life. I wish they could so I could see my wife one more time, but they can't. This can't be happening.*

"You're breaking your promise to me," said the Commandant with a look in his eyes Sergeant Ron had seen a hundred times before. The Commandant was disappointed. "You swore you'd take care of Rick for me. You swore you'd protect him. But you're abandoning him on that planet and throwing your life away as well."

"They killed my wife," Sergeant Ron protested. He needed time to think.

"I know," said the Commandant. "Janice and I were there, remember? You saved our lives. I know it cost you dearly with the deaths of your crew and your wife. That's why I've tried to watch over you these last fifty years. I tried to watch over you when you left the Conglomerate and joined the military. I tried to watch over you when you fought on Ashton Minor. I tried to watch over you when you left for years at a time in your pursuit of that accursed black dreadnaught. And that's why I'm trying to watch over you now and help you keep your promise. You promised to take care of Rick. You know how important he is to our cause."

"But you promised to help me destroy the ones who killed my wife," Sergeant Ron said grasping at straws. "You didn't. Now you're dead."

"Yes, the Commandant is dead," said the figure of the Commandant. "But I'm not."

The figure of the Commandant shimmered. It morphed into the figure of Wizard Scout Richard Shepard.

Realization came to Sergeant Ron. "You're a hologram. Margery, I know it's you."

"Yes, I am creating the holograms," admitted Margery over the cockpit's intercom. "But my words are those the Commandant would have spoken if he was here. I was his battle helmet. I knew him better than any living person ever could. I calculate the Commandant would be ashamed of you, Sergeant Ron. And my next words are those of Wizard Scout Shepard. He told me to tell you he's counting on you."

As Sergeant Ron looked at the holographic image of Richard, the figure spoke. Even knowing it was a hologram, Sergeant Ron was drawn to the words of the *Defiant's* co-owner.

"I don't claim to understand how you feel, Sergeant Ron," said Richard's image. "But what you're doing is wrong. Your grandson is dead if you don't save him. So is Tia. So is your crew. And so am I for that matter. We need you, Sergeant Ron. Margery says you promised. The Sergeant Ron I know doesn't break promises."

"They killed my wife," Sergeant Ron said weakly. The images of the Commandant and Richard might be holograms, but in his heart, Sergeant Ron knew their words were true.

"I know," said Richard's image. "And I give you my word as a wizard scout, I will help you destroy that black dreadnaught and anyone else responsible for your wife's death. But we can't do it today. The *Defiant* will be destroyed, and the dreadnaught you hate so much will go free. Keep your promise, Sergeant Ron. Keep it, and I'll keep mine. That's wizard scout honor."

The insanity that had overcome Sergeant Ron's mind slowly withdrew. He became more aware of his surroundings than he'd been in years. He could've been a wizard scout, but his pursuit of the dreadnaught had taken priority. But he still had his Power reserve, and the Commandant had taught him many tricks with his Power over the years.

Sergeant Ron reached out around him with his passive scan. He sensed his grandson and Tia floating helplessly in space. Lines of energy from the black destroyer was zeroing in on their stationary forms. Sergeant Ron sensed Charlie and Terrie in the cargo hold strapping into their Warcats. He sensed his friend, Richard, moving quickly along the surface of the planet away from the mine entrance.

Most of all, Sergeant Ron sensed the dots of energy that were the three spheres drawing closer together. The gate was being drawn closed as the distance between the spheres shrunk.

Sergeant Ron could tell the black dreadnaught was no longer trying to get through the gate. With a clarity he didn't know he possessed, Sergeant Ron realized the *Defiant* would never make it through the gate either. His ship would be destroyed as the gate shut around it.

The last of Sergeant Ron's insanity departed. He looked at Richard's image. "All right, I'm back. What do you want me to do?"

"Just listen to Margery," said Richard's hologram as it faded out of view.

With the disappearance of the hologram, Margery spoke over the ship's intercom informing everyone onboard of Rick's plan. When she was done, Sergeant Ron spoke.

"And I thought I did stupid things," said Sergeant Ron. "Rick's even crazier than I am."

With those words, Sergeant Ron turned the ship's overrides back on in order to let Margery assist with the required maneuvers.

Then he hit the *Defiant's* reverse thrusters as he turned it away from the closing gate toward the black destroyer.

"Let me know when the last of our torpedoes have reloaded, Margery," Sergeant Ron said. "We're going in. They took my wife, but they sure as hell aren't going to get my grandson. Not if I can help it."

CHAPTER 50

Just as Richard crossed the crest of the hill overlooking the quarry, he sensed the three spheres come together.

"Remember your promise," came a final emotion from the green sphere.

A bright flash lit the air around Richard. A wave of air and debris caught him from behind and knock him off the hover-cycle. Both Richard and the cycle went tumbling end over end along the rocky ground. The hover-cycle broke into pieces as it bounced along the sharp rocks.

Richard kept tumbling as well, but his battle suit was the best the Empire's technicians could devise. It was tough. As he rolled, Richard wrapped himself in Power and used telekinesis to slow down. Once he rolled to a stop, he stood up and looked toward the mine entrance in the distance. The entrance was gone. In a strange illusion caused by the fading time bubble, Richard saw a large explosion overlaid on the reality of the planet's surface in the physical dimension. However, the explosion wasn't destroying the buildings and equipment around it. The explosion was in the time-bubble. Richard pitied anyone who might still be in the collapsing time-bubble. From what he knew, their torturous death could take eons.

The gate that was also the time-bubble flickered in and out of focus a few times. Richard caught glimpses of the black dreadnaught getting smaller as its engines strained to get a safe distance from the gate. The dreadnaught disappeared completely as the gate closed. Its energy dissipated. Only the quarry in the physical dimension remained.

"Nick," Richard said. *"Get me into the destroyer's computer."*

"It's going to be different, Rick," said Nickelo. *"It's magic based."*

"I'm depending on it," Richard said.

"Compliance," said Nickelo. *"Give me control of an active scan."*

Drawing Power from his reserve, Richard formed it into an active scan. He wrapped it with a stealth shield and gave control to his battle computer.

"Follow along," said Nickelo. *"I can handle the logic, but you'll have to take care of the magic part."*

Richard sensed the active scan stretch outward and upward. It reached out farther than Richard had ever attempted to scan before. The end of the active scan touched a flow of energy. Richard recognized the flow. It was magic. The magic was familiar. It was as if he'd come home to an old friend.

"We're there," said Nickelo. *"I'm not sure what we're looking at. The flows of energy keep shifting."*

"I know," Richard said. *"We just have to anticipate the shifts. Magic has rules. It's logical in its own way."* Richard wasn't sure how he knew those things, but he had the knowledge, and he was going to use it.

"I'm taking control of the scan," Richard said. *"Follow along."*

"Compliance," said Nickelo.

Richard took control of the active scan and continued probing. He picked a flow of magic and followed along as it twisted and twirled. Somehow Richard anticipated its every move. The flow of magic reminded Richard of how the spells in Shandria's spell book kept moving as if attempting to keep their secrets. He remembered how he'd helped Nickelo and Jonathan hack into the Crosioians' master computer by unlocking the secrets of its magic-based security.

Richard used those experiences to trace the flows of magic protecting the black destroyer. He sensed a line of magic that seemed more logical than the other flows around it. Richard traced the line of magic to its source. He touched the source with his active scan. Massive amounts of data flowed into Richard's mind.

"Nick," Richard thought. *"A little help would be nice."*

"I'm on it, buddy," said Nickelo. *"Stay with the magic. I'll handle the data."*

The flood of information continued, but it became less overwhelming. Richard sensed his battle computer sorting through the data and presenting him with the most important information.

Security protocols swirled around the flows of magic as if seeking an intruder. Richard deftly moved his active scan to avoid detection. The flood of data continued uninhibited.

Finally, Richard saw the information he sought. He found the flow of magic controlling the destroyer's shields. Richard let his mind merge with the flow of magic. He became part of it. He twisted the flow of magic back on itself. The magic flared outward before collapsing back on itself. The magic controlling the destroyer's shields dissipated back into the universe from which it had come.

"Tell Margery to inform Sergeant Ron the shields are down, Richard ordered. *And have her tell Terrie I'll be there as soon as I can."*

"Compliance," said Nickelo. *"In case you haven't noticed, we've got company.*

Richard drew his mind back and dropped his active scan. Once again, he saw the world around him. Three life forms registered on his passive scan. They were still a distance away, but they were drawing nearer. They were coming. Richard recognized their frequencies. He drew his phase rod and waited for their arrival.

Richard gave a tight-lipped smile as he thought, *It's payback time.*

CHAPTER 51

Terrie finished plugging the Warcat's flight harness to his battle suit. The inside of his cat began filling with the translucent sensory-gel that would transmit his movements to the Warcat's hydraulics.

As Terrie made the final steps of his preflight check, he used his passive scan to pick up the Power sources of the three spheres. He sensed them touch. A blaze of Power flashed on his heads-up display. Then it dissipated into nothing. The yellow dot Terrie had been using to track Richard on his heads-up display disappeared as well.

"*Taylor,*" Terrie said. "*I've lost track of Rick. Is he—*"

"*Your fellow wizard scout is fine,*" answered Taylor before Terrie could even complete his question. "*I'm in contact with Margery. She's in contact with your friend's battle computer. Wizard Scout Shepard is fine.*"

"*Are you sure?*" Terrie said not completely satisfied with his battle computer's answer. "*Maybe you should contact Nickelo directly. I was tracking Rick on my passive scan, and he's no longer there.*"

"*You know I can't communicate directly with his battle computer,*" said Taylor. "*I've no desire to be corrupted. But your friend is fine. You weren't tracking him. You were tracking his hover-cycle. It was destroyed in the blast when the gate collapsed.*"

Wizard Scout Shepard has his stealth shield up. You can't detect him. He's too good. However, Margery is in direct contact with his battle computer. She's already corrupted. According to Margery, Wizard Scout Shepard is attempting to hack his way into the destroyer's computer system now. So you'd best be ready when he does."

"*Is that even possible?*" Terrie said.

"*Insufficient data to make a reliable calculation,*" said Taylor. "*Margery says the destroyer's computer system is magic based. I have very little information on magic in my data banks. I don't know much about it, to be honest.*"

"*Join the club,*" Terrie said with a shake of his head.

He was supposed to be retired. He'd known teaming up with Richard would probably put Angela and him in some strange situations, but he hadn't realized the extent of the strangeness.

"*Recommend you get in position,*" said Taylor with a sense of urgency. "*Margery says your friend is making good progress according to his battle computer. You may not have much time.*"

"*Roger that,*" Terrie said.

Terrie thought the command to release the composite security-bands attaching the Warcat to the bulkhead of the cargo bay. Once free, he maneuvered the three-meter tall Warcat around the various items stacked in the bay as he made his way toward the rear airlock.

"You with me, Charlie?" Terrie said over the *Defiant's* com-link. "We've got to hustle."

"I hustle," hissed Charlie. "You the one who is slow."

A blur of black passed Terrie on the right as Charlie maneuvered his Warcat into the airlock. By the time Terrie got inside, Charlie was already in position against the portside wall. Terrie saw the rear-security clamp on Charlie's Warcat extend out and grasp one of the composite tie-down bars lining the wall. Terrie copied the mechanic's maneuver and locked his Warcat onto the starboard-side wall.

Once he was in position, the door separating the airlock from the cargo bay closed. After making a final weapon's check, Terrie had nothing left to do but wait. He looked across the airlock at the second Warcat. He could just make out Charlie's features through the Warcat's windscreen. Terrie noticed Charlie's eyes looking at him through the visor of his flight helmet. Charlie's eyes locked with Terrie's. He was reminded that Sterilians' eyes didn't blink.

"Sterilians don't have eyelids," said Taylor. *"They just have clear lenses to protect their eyes."*

"Thanks for the biology lesson," Terrie told his battle computer in their shared space. *"Now how about using that nanosecond brain of yours to calculate a way to keep us alive?"*

His battle computer chose to ignore his suggestion. In spite of all their years together, Terrie kept forgetting how touchy his battle computer could be. Terrie mentally shrugged his shoulders. He decided he'd have to apologize later. Right now, he had things to do.

"You know this crazy," said Charlie over the com-link. "Only for idiots."

"Then why are you going along with Rick's plan?" Terrie asked genuinely interested. He thought it was crazy too, but here he was anyway.

"Rick, friend," said Charlie. After a pause, the Sterilian added, "Besides, we dead anyway. Why the hell not try?"

"Good point," Terrie said. "Why the hell not?"

* * *

"Torpedo reload has been completed, captain," Margery told Sergeant Ron. "Only six tubes are loaded. You used up the last full salvo firing at the dreadnaught."

"Either six will be enough, or a hundred wouldn't be," Sergeant Ron said as he fired another set of plasma rounds from the forward cannons. He didn't launch the torpedoes. He'd need them to breach the destroyer's hull if Rick pulled off his plan.

The rounds from the plasma cannons struck the destroyer's force field before veering off into space. The *Defiant* shuddered as the destroyer's return fire hit its forward shields. The *Defiant's* shields held under the vicious onslaught.

"Thank you, Diane," Sergeant Ron whispered once again thanking his daughter for sparing no expense on the *Defiant's* upgraded equipment.

"Analysis?" Sergeant Ron asked Margery.

"Our plasma fire is ineffective against the destroyer's shields," said Margery. "But it is drawing fire away from the children. Our shields are weakening, but they are still functioning. I have adjusted their frequency in an attempt to compensate for the destroyer's magic-based weapons."

"Time?" Sergeant Ron said.

"Unknown," answered Margery. "The gate has been closed. Wizard Scout Shepard's battle computer says Rick is making progress in his attempt to hack into the destroyer's computer. He hasn't done it yet, but I calculate a one hundred percent probability he will succeed."

Even in the heat of battle, Sergeant Ron thought it odd a computer would give a one hundred percent probability for success. He told Margery as much.

"Based on pure logic," said Margery, "Wizard Scout Shepard only has a twenty-one percent chance of succeeding. But he's the Commandant's son. I'm basing the other seventy-nine percent on faith. Rick will do it. I've no doubt."

Faith seemed a strange thing for a computer to base calculations on to Sergeant Ron. He was about to make another comment when Margery cut him off.

"Rick's in," said Margery. "The destroyer's shields are down."

"Fire torpedoes," Sergeant Ron ordered.

"Torpedoes away," said Margery as the *Defiant* bucked from the recoil.

"Daniel," said Sergeant Ron. "Do your thing. Their armor's thick. You'll need to put all of them in the same spot."

"Affirmative," came Daniel's reply over the com-link.

Sergeant Ron sensed a line of Power reach out from the *Defiant* and latch onto the special torpedo-guidance systems Sergeant Hendricks had installed. The cockpit holograph showed the six torpedoes lining up one behind the other. Sergeant Ron gave a silent thanks that the young lad was one of the better bongo players on Trecor. The torpedoes would have to hit just right in order to have any hope of breaching the black destroyer's hull.

"The first torpedo is eight seconds out," said Margery.

The *Defiant* bucked again as another salvo of return fire from the destroyer hit her shields. Lightning bolts, fireballs, and force beams of various colors hit the *Defiant's* shields.

"We've lost the front portside shield," said Margery.

"Doesn't matter," Sergeant Ron said. "Now's when we throw the dice. I just hope to hell Rick knows what he's doing."

With those words, Sergeant Ron hit the portside rear-thrusters. He pulled the decelerator levers all the way back as well. The shoulder harness on Sergeant Ron's chair dug into his flesh as the force of deceleration hit. He was also slammed into the armrest of his seat as the portside rear-thrusters took effect.

The die is cast, Sergeant Ron thought.

* * *

"The destroyer's shields are down," said Taylor in Terrie's shared space. *"Sergeant Ron has started his maneuver."*

"This is it, Charlie," said Terrie. "Get ready."

Actually, Terrie knew there wasn't anything Charlie or he could do. The timing was too complicated for mere human or Sterilian minds to complete successfully. Both Charlie and his lives were in the hands of Taylor and Margery now.

Terrie felt the back of his Warcat slam into the wall separating him from the cargo bay. The rear ramp to the outside opened. Terrie saw stars streak across the opening as the *Defiant* did a hundred and eighty-degree turn. At just the right moment, his Warcat went flying out the opening as Taylor released its grip on the airlock's tie downs.

The second Warcat was right on Terrie's heels. Terrie breathed a sigh of relief. Margery had successfully handled the mechanic's release as well.

"Damn," Terrie said over the com-link as he hurtled toward the black destroyer. "Her hull's not breached."

"Give it time," said Taylor. *"You humans are always so anxious. Where's your sense of mystery?"*

Terrie didn't answer. He'd learned long ago not to argue with Taylor, especially when he was depending on his battle computer to help keep him alive.

"Our track is off," Terrie said as he eyeballed the distance to the black destroyer. *"You miscalculated. We're going to miss the destroyer by a thousand meters."*

"Oh ye of little faith," said Taylor sounding a little affronted. *"I don't miscalculate on something this simple. I had to account for*

the deviation to the destroyer's flight path."

"What deviation?" Terrie thought back.

A white flash lit up the side of the black destroyer toward its stern. A second white flash followed. A series of four additional flashes quickly followed.

"That deviation," said Taylor.

The force of the explosions along with a blast of escaping air moved the destroyer in line with Terrie's track. Terrie zoomed in on the stern of the destroyer with the Warcat's scope. A ragged hole twice the height of a Warcat and five times as wide was leaking air, equipment, and a few bodies out of the destroyer. A quick eyeball calculation by Terrie confirmed Taylor was correct. Charlie and he were on track to intercept the breach in the destroyer's hull.

Terrie felt a slight jerk on the Warcat's back. He didn't turn around. He didn't need to. His passive scan told him Charlie had latched onto his Warcat. They would go in together.

Five seconds later, Terrie and Charlie passed through the hole in the side of the black destroyer. From the looks of the jumble of boxes and equipment, Terrie figured they were in a large cargo bay. A partially blown-off door to his front caught Terrie's attention.

"Together," Terrie said over the com-link.

"Agreed," answered Charlie.

Terrie felt the *Defiant's* mechanic unlatch his Warcat from his back and begin running toward the mangled door. Terrie headed in the same direction matching the Sterilian stride for stride. They hit the door together. The combined force of the two Warcats was too much for the weakened door hinges. The metal door flew off into the corridor beyond.

Alarm bells blared and warning lights flashed along the entire length of the corridor. The bodies of several furry, four-armed creatures littered the corridor floor.

"Well," Terrie thought, *"I guess whoever these guys are they can't breathe in a vacuum any better than humans."*

"Affirmative," said Taylor. *"I'd advise you to watch out for those other two in the armored suits."*

Terrie looked ahead. Two creatures in large, armored suits were moving in his direction. Four arms protruded from each set of armor. Both of the armored creatures carried what appeared to be rifles of some sort. Terrie noticed one of the creatures point its weapon in his direction. He sensed a momentary buildup of energy in the barrel of the weapon. Shortly thereafter, a ball of energy was streaking in his direction.

"It's magic based," said Taylor.

A stream of specifications entered Terrie's shared space suggesting how to modify a defensive shield to better defend against magic energy. At the same time, Terrie sensed his battle computer changing the frequency settings on the 40-megawatt plasma autocannon attached to his Warcat's left arm.

Based upon the trust built-up from years of association with his battle computer, Terrie threw up a defensive shield to his front. He angled it in such a way as to reduce the odds any ricochet would hit the second Warcat.

When the ball of energy got within ten meters, it morphed into a line of electrical energy resembling a bolt of lightning. The lightning hit Terrie's shield and glanced off. Thankfully, the ricochet missed Charlie's Warcat. It continued down the long corridor bouncing from one wall to the other as it went.

As Terrie brought his Warcat's 40-megawatt plasma autocannon up to fire, a streak of 20mm chain-gun rounds streaked past the right side of his head. Terrie wasn't concerned. He knew Charlie had beaten him to the punch. The 20mm rounds hit a defensive shield in front of the two armored soldiers. They glanced off without making contact. Charlie kept firing.

"Their shield is magic based," observed Taylor.

Terrie didn't care how it was based. He just knew it was a tough shield. He lined his autocannon up on the first soldier and added his firepower to that of Charlie's. The soldier's shield held, but Terrie could sense it buckling under the combined onslaught.

"Pour it to them, Charlie," said Terrie over the com-link. "We can wear their shield down in a few more seconds."

"No have few seconds," hissed Charlie as he fired his Warcat's autocannon in addition to its chain gun.

Terrie saw the reason for Charlie's concern. The second armored soldier was aiming some type of shoulder-fired weapon in their direction. Terrie had no idea what kind of weapon it was, but the large size of the opening in the barrel didn't bode well.

Before the soldier could fire, a blur of black rose up out of the floor behind the soldier. Terrie saw the red blur of a phase rod swinging through the air. Even from a distance, Terrie could feel an intense emotion of hunger as the phase rod made contact with the side of the soldier's head. Terrie heard a cry that was as much a growl as it was a scream. Then the armored soldier dropped its shoulder weapon. The soldier fell unmoving to the metal deck.

The lead soldier started to turn its head to check on its companion. It had barely moved its head when a dark form came out of the corridor wall and leaped straight for the soldier's throat. Terrie caught a flash of teeth. Then the dark form disappeared into the opposite wall dragging the struggling soldier with it.

Both Charlie and he stopped firing, but not before a few rounds passed through the figure of a demon of a horse hovering a hand's breath above the deck. The black stallion had fiery-red eyes. Long fangs protruded from its mouth. On the stallion's back sat a man in a black battle suit. The man was Richard.

Terrie suppressed a shiver. He'd heard stories of Richard's spirit-horse and his dolgars. Hearing was one thing. Seeing was another. Terrie gave silent thanks they were on the same side.

CHAPTER 52

Once Sheeta and Sheba arrived with the spirit-horse, Richard wasted no time in mounting up. He sent the stallion an emotion of need to get to the black destroyer. Richard wasn't even able to give his mount an image of the destroyer, but apparently the stallion didn't need it. Without asking for further information, his black mount took two leaps into the air before shifting into another dimension. Richard's passive scan picked up Sheeta and Sheba hot on the stallion's heels.

After taking a few steps on a desolate plain of some unknown planet, the stallion shifted into the void. Richard sensed the black destroyer nearby in the physical dimension. He also sensed his friends Terrie and Charlie inside trading fire with two of the furry Thargs dressed in armor.

Richard sent an image of the rear of the two armored soldiers to the stallion. He also sent an emotion the dolgars used when identifying enemies. The stallion needed no further prodding. Richard had always gotten the impression the stallion hated flesh creatures. He doubted the stallion would hesitate to help him kill two more flesh creatures.

When the spirit-horse rose out of the floor behind the rearmost soldier, Richard swung his phase rod at its head. The phase rod glanced off the heavy armor, but not before the rod's phase energy penetrated the soldier's skull. The subatomic explosions from the phase energy scrambled the soldier's brain into a liquid mush. Richard's passive scan told him the four-armed creature was neither a magic user nor a scout. No Power tried to heal the armored soldier. It fell to the floor dead.

The lead soldier turned in Richard's direction. Before the soldier could complete its turn, Sheeta leaped out of the wall. The big dolgar shifted his fangs out of the void long enough to grab the soldier by the throat. A split second later, both Sheeta and the struggling soldier disappeared into the opposite wall. With the soldier's demise, the defensive shield that had been blocking the Warcats' fire disappeared as well.

Before Richard could react, he felt his mount shift both of them back into the void. A hundred 20mm rounds along with two blasts of plasma energy from the Warcats passed through Richard's body. Both the stallion and he were unharmed. They were in the void.

"You're lucky the Warcats weren't using phase weapons," said Nickelo. *"Phase energy exists in the void as well as the physical dimension. Perhaps you should have discussed your plan with me before you attacked from the enemies' rear."*

"Whatever, Nick," Richard said. *"It worked. Now bring up the specs for this destroyer. We need to get to the main-gun deck before they blow the* Defiant *out of the sky."*

"Compliance," said Nickelo.

Nickelo had downloaded a lot of the magic-based computer's databanks when Richard had hacked his way into the black destroyer's computer system. Richard now sensed some of the information being sent as a blueprint of the destroyer into his shared space. A quick scan of the blueprint showed the fastest route to the part of the gun deck that was firing at the *Defiant.*

By this time, Terrie and Charlie had ceased their firing. Richard pictured himself dismounting from the spirit-horse. The stallion shifted back into the physical dimension. The black tendrils securing Richard to the stallion's back retracted. After sliding off his mount, Richard ran toward the nearest door to the main-gun deck.

"Maybe you should stay on the stallion," suggested Nickelo. *"He could take you wherever you need to go."*

"Negative," Richard answered. *"He tolerates me. He doesn't like me. I'll fight better on foot. Besides, some of the walls and*

doors in this ship appear to be embedded with flecks of creallium. We couldn't get through them from the void."

"I won't argue," said Nickelo. *"You've made your decision. I think your stallion could have gotten past them by fully shifting into another dimension. But it's too late now. He's already gone."*

Sure enough, as soon as Richard had slid off, the spirit-horse had taken his leave and shifted into another dimension. Richard didn't care. The stallion had served his purpose. He was on the destroyer. Richard preferred fighting on his own anyway. However, he had to admit, he was glad to see the dots on his heads-up display representing Sheeta and Sheba. He could sense them below the metal floor in the void. They hadn't deserted him.

Turning his head back toward the two Warcats, Richard shouted, "Follow me!"

Without waiting to see if his friends followed, Richard hurried ahead to an area of the corridor that was flickering with energy. From the frequency of the energy, Richard knew it was magic.

"It's some kind of force field," said Nickelo. *"I calculate it's acting as a blast door. There's air on the other side."*

"Can we get through it?" Richard asked.

"Give me control of an active scan," said Nickelo. *"Be prepared to help me when I need it."*

"Compliance," Richard said mimicking his battle computer's normal reply to one of his requests.

As Richard formed the active scan, he heard the sound of large, metallic feet tromping down the corridor. He'd had no doubt his two friends would follow him, but it was nice to have his confidence vindicated. The two Warcats came to a stop behind him.

"What now?" hissed Charlie over the com-link set up by Margery.

The floor of the corridor shuddered as the destroyer unleased another salvo at the *Defiant.*

"Now?" Richard replied over the com-link. "Now we make sure that's the last full salvo these suckers fire at our friends."

Switching to his shared space, Richard ordered Nickelo to set up a direct link with Margery. Except for Jonathan, his friend Stella's battle computer, Richard knew Margery was Nickelo's only link to other computers on the tele-network.

"The Defiant *is getting hammered, Rick,"* came Margery's thoughts. *"Sergeant Ron is keeping the ship turned so the rear shields are toward the destroyer, but our shields won't take another salvo like the last one."*

"They won't have to," Richard said. *"Tell Sergeant Ron to go recover the kids. Charlie, Terrie, and I will take care of things here."*

"Compliance," said Margery. *"What else can I do?"*

"I'm having Nick upload data from the destroyer's computer to you," Richard said. *"I want you to send the blueprints of this ship to the two Warcats."*

"Compliance," said Margery.

"I've successfully hacked the blast shield," said Nickelo. *"We can pass through."*

Richard didn't bother answering. He just stepped through the field of energy. The magic seemed to become agitated as if trying to decide whether to allow Richard to pass or not. It quickly settled down when he twisted a couple of its energy flows back on themselves. He passed through the blast door without further incident. So did the two Warcats.

Within just a few steps, the corridor opened up into a large bay. The open area was at least half the length of the destroyer, and it was the width of the ship. The ceiling towered a dozen stories overhead. Armored boxes resembling house-sized turrets lined both sides of the open area. Large tubes protruded from the turrets. Richard figured there were at least twenty turrets on each side of the ship.

"Actually, there are twenty-two gun turrets on each side," said Nickelo. *"I count eight hundred forty-two life forms on this gun deck."*

The area in front of each gun turret was open to the vacuum of space beyond. As Richard watched, several of the guns fired. Bolts of energy shot out into space.

"Force fields of some kind are keeping the ship sealed," said Nickelo. *"They're magic based. The weapons' projectiles can go out, but nothing else can enter or escape."*

Richard looked closer at one of the gun turrets. A dozen of the four-armed Thargs were stationed around the turret. Only a few of them appeared to be armed. Behind the gun turret nearest Richard stood a small, male figure shackled by a chain around his throat. The other end of the chain was attached to the deck. Richard recognized the male as a gnome, or at least a relative of the gnome race he'd previously encountered on Portalis.

One of the four-armed Thargs jerked on the gnome's chain and dragged him toward a meter-wide, round projectile. Richard sensed energy inside the metallic ball. He recognized it as the same energy frequency the Dragar priests at the temple had removed from the sacrificed dragon eggs.

Once the gnome got to the projectile, Richard saw him move his hands in intricate patterns. His lips moved as well as if saying a spell. Richard sensed Power gather in the gnome's hands and transform into magic. The magic passed into the large projectile. Almost immediately, a metal arm from a nearby crane reached out and picked up the projectile. It was then transferred to a large opening in the gun turret. A couple of seconds later, the projectile shot out the end of the tube protruding out the end of the gun turret. Richard sensed the magic energy inside the ball increasing in intensity as it sped away from the destroyer.

Almost immediately, another large projectile popped out of an opening in the deck behind the gun turret. Another crane picked up the projectile and moved it closer to the gnome's position.

"Well, Rick," said Nickelo. *"Now what?"*

Richard's Marine training kicked in.

"Terrie," Richard said over the com-link. "You take the starboard guns. Charlie, you take the portside. I'll take care of the middle."

"Roger that," came Terrie's reply.

"I get to other end first," hissed Charlie as he took off running.

Not one to waste time, Charlie immediately released a spray of chain-gun rounds at the crew surrounding the first turret.

"And don't hurt anyone chained up," Richard ordered. "They're prisoners. They're not our enemy."

Another burst of chain-gun fire told Richard that Terrie was on the move as well. Not to be outdone, Richard holstered his .44 AutoMag and pulled an M63 lightweight plasma assault rifle out of his dimensional pack. A glance at the weapon's isotopic battery told Richard it contained a full load of 2,255 rounds. From the size of the crowd of milling bodies ahead of him, Richard had a feeling he was going to need every round.

Firing as he ran, Richard headed for the largest group of Thargs in the center aisle. Many of the four-armed Thargs were already running for cover. The fire from the Warcats had turned the well-organized group on the gun deck into an unorganized mob fleeing from the unexpected assault.

Under normal circumstances, Richard would've let them escape; but not this time. They had been trying to destroy the *Defiant* and the kids just a few seconds prior. If they were allowed to survive, Richard had no doubt they'd come back and try again. Richard shoved thoughts of kindness and mercy to the side. He became the deadly killing machine the Empire had created.

As Richard fired, he did his best to avoid hitting the prisoners. Not all of the prisoners were chained to the deck, but each of them appeared to be wearing a collar that radiated magic.

"I calculate a sixty-seven percent probability their collars are designed to prevent the prisoners from using their magic against their captors," said Nickelo.

Ignoring his battle computer's observation, Richard kept firing. Streaks of energy passed around him as a handful of Dragars and some of the four-armed Thargs returned fire. Richard noticed the Thargs were using weapons similar to rifles and handguns. He sensed their weapons firing small projectiles composed of magic instead of bullets. The Dragars, on the other hand, appeared to be magic users of some type. When they weren't casting spells on their own, they were using wands to do it for them.

The initial fire from the Warcats and Richard had caught the destroyer's crew by surprise. However, Richard could see signs of military discipline taking hold as various leaders tried to bring order to the confusion. Hoping to keep the chaos going, Richard concentrated his fire on anyone who appeared to be in charge whenever he got the chance.

"The good news is the primary gun turrets have stopped firing," said Nickelo. *"That's taken the pressure off of the* Defiant. *Sergeant Ron is on his way now to pick up Tia and Matthew."*

Richard was thankful for the small blessing, but his hands were too full at the moment to think of a suitable reply. A squad of Thargs had set up some type of crew-served weapon. The Thargs were lobbing blue balls of energy at Charlie's Warcat. Although the Warcat's force field was still holding, Richard sensed it weakening in several places.

Temporarily ignoring the enemy to his front, Richard ran in the direction of the crew-served weapon. He fired as he ran. Unfortunately, the M63's plasma rounds hit an invisible barrier and ricocheted upwards. The soldiers manning the crew-served weapon switched their target from Charlie to Richard.

"Well, if you were trying to draw their fire, you succeeded," said Nickelo.

"I wasn't," Richard said.

Since his light-plasma rounds weren't having any effect against the crew-served weapon's shield, Richard decided to switch tactics. On a hunch, he reached out with his mind and probed the neck collar on the prisoner who was closest to the crew-served weapon. The flow of magic energy moving through the collar and the attached chain were unfamiliar to him. However, Richard instinctively saw the part of the flow of magic that served as the keystone for the spell.

Without waiting to discuss it with his battle computer, Richard twisted the flow of magic back on itself. The magic short-circuited and disappeared. Wrapping part of the collar with Power, Richard twisted with his telekinesis. The collar was relatively weak; it wasn't even made out of metal. The collar snapped easily and fell to the deck. The prisoner was free.

"I calculate the Dragars were relying on their magic to keep the collar secured," said Nickelo. *"I can't be sure, but I believe the collar is made out of dragon skin. It's tough, but apparently not tough enough to resist your telekinesis."*

"Ya think?" Richard said as he dove to one side in order to avoid an inbound blue ball from the crew-served weapon. The blue ball missed by over a meter, but even protected by his battle suit, Richard felt his skin trying to crack. His self-healing Power immediately brought his skin back to baseline.

"Some type of disintegration spell, I'd say," said Nickelo. *"My advice would be not to let one of the blue balls hit you directly."*

Richard noticed the gunner of the crew-served weapon lining up on him for another shot. He prepared to dodge or throw up a shield as needed. As it turned out, he didn't need to dodge or waste energy throwing up a defensive shield.

The prisoner who Richard had freed was a male elf with gray hair. He had completely different facial features from the few elves he'd previously encountered on Portalis. This elf's face was more rounded, and he had a high forehead. However, his telltale pointed ears left little doubt as to his species. He was definitely an elf. Once freed, the elf immediately began waving his hands and mouthing an incantation.

The elf's Power reserve was large, and it was nearly full. Richard sensed a large flow of Power move down the link from the elf's Power reserve. The Power formed into a ball of magic between the elf's outstretched hands. The resulting spell shot out toward the Thargs manning the crew-served weapon.

Richard smiled. The Thargs had only set up a defensive shield to their front. The elf's spell was coming from their rear. The spell made contact with the gunner and erupted into a bright ball of orange flame ten meters across. Stored rounds near the weapon ignited sending blue balls of energy in all directions.

Richard didn't wait to see what the elf did next. As far as he was concerned, the elf was on his own now. Richard continued running down the space between the two lines of gun turrets. He noticed Terrie was even with the fourth turret while Charlie was just finishing clearing out the area around the third turret on his side of the ship.

"This is taking too long," said Nickelo. *"The defenders are going to be organizing a counterattack soon."*

"Understood," Richard said.

He sent out the emotions he used for Sheeta and Sheba. Then he sent an image of the turrets at the far end of the gun deck. Next, he sent the emotion the dolgars used to tell their pups to kill. He hurriedly followed the emotion up with an image of shackled humanoids wearing collars and chains. Richard sent the emotion he used to denote the crew of the *Defiant* as friends.

"I only calculate a forty-two percent probability the dolgars will spare the prisoners," said Nickelo. *"You know they're not that fond of flesh creatures."*

"It's the best I can do," Richard said. *"I tried. We've got problems of our own."*

Six blips of energy on his passive scan caught Richard's attention. Using the zoom feature of his visor, Richard made out a half-dozen humanoid-looking figures who were reflecting the overhead lights above the gun deck. Each figure was about half again as large as a Warcat.

"By the way, I think your counterattack just showed up," Richard told his battle computer.

"Hmm," said Nickelo. *"They're made out of energized titanium. Their energy frequency appears similar to the giant cat golem you fought on the dolgar's home world a couple of years ago."*

While continuing to fire his M63, Richard reached out with an active scan and touched one of the metal monsters. Sure enough, it reminded him of the large cat golem he'd destroyed in order to get the blue gems it had used as an energy source. The golems now charging down the center of the gun bay even had two blue gems for eyes.

As Richard watched, a yellow line of energy reached out from the lead golem and struck the shield around Terrie's Warcat. The shield lasted long enough to prevent major damage to the Warcat, but the Warcat was knocked off its feet and onto its back. Richard saw two of the other golems lifting their arms in Terrie's direction.

"The hell with this," Richard thought.

Reaching out with his mind, Richard wrapped the arm of one of the golems with Power.

"No!" shouted Nickelo in their shared space. *"They're too heavy. It'll take too much Power."*

Richard ignored his battle computer. He knew the Power requirements, but he wasn't going to let his friend die.

Using his telekinesis, Richard pushed on the golem's arm hard enough to make it spin. The fact the golem was in the middle of a step helped, but even so, it required every drop of Power in his reserve to spin the golem a quarter turn just as it fired.

A yellow line of energy shot out of the golem's raised arm and struck its companion. While the second golem had a shield to its front, it was not protected from the fire of its own companion. The second golem exploded in a blast of yellow energy. Pieces of titanium shot outward along with random flows of magical energy.

The golem Richard had spun was caught in the explosion. It exploded as well. A nearby blue projectile that had been in the process of being loaded into a turret was overwhelmed by the explosion.

It was too much for the projectile. It erupted in a ball of blue energy that swept over the four remaining golems. They, in turn, disappeared in a massive explosion of yellow energy. A series of explosions occurred as other blue projectiles erupted. An entire gun turret was tossed all the way to the ceiling where it knocked out a cluster of lights before falling back to the floor of the gun deck in a shower of sparks.

Sparks flew out of the remaining overhead lights. Many of them blew up in blasts of magical energy. Suddenly, all the lights on the entire gun deck went out as they were overloaded.

Pandemonium set in among the destroyer's crew. The rally the Dragar leaders had begun to initiate with their troops disappeared along with the lights. While the gun deck was not pitch black due to the multitude of fires from burning gun turrets, the flickering light added to the chaos. Richard was glad his battle helmet was equipped with night vision equipment. He'd had to fight in the dark before, and it was no fun.

"Terrie! Charlie!" Richard said over their com-link. "Hit them hard now. We've got to take care of this mob before more reinforcements show up."

"On the move," said Terrie.

A stream of chain-gun tracers from the starboard side of the gun deck confirmed the disabled wizard scout's answer.

As if Charlie didn't want to be outdone, several rounds from an autocannon on the portside gave the old Sterilian's answer as well.

"We've got some allies," said Nickelo with a mental nod to Richard's right.

A stream of video data in their shared space showed Richard what his battle computer meant. A small group of prisoners were attacking some of the four-armed Thargs by both physical and magical means. Richard noticed the elf prisoner he'd freed at the head of the group.

Before Richard could say anything or act to assist the prisoners, he was hit from behind. The sound of breaking bones resounded in his ears as he was flung forward. A white flash of pain encompassed Richard's brain. He passed out momentarily. When he came to, he felt a cold liquid being shot into his veins through several of the battle suit's thread needles.

Through his pain, Richard heard his battle computer shouting instructions in their shared space.

"Your back's broken," said Nickelo *"I'm shooting adrenaline into you. One of the magic users hit you with some kind of force beam. I couldn't make you dodge fast enough. I'm sorry. All of your suit's assistors are offline now. I can't make your battle suit move."*

In spite of his pain, Richard noticed everything around him appeared to be frozen in time. Tracers and spells crisscrossing the gun deck were stationary. Only his mind seemed to be moving. It had happened a few times before when he was caught in a desperate fight. Time either froze, or his mind speeded up. Even Nickelo didn't know for sure. Whatever the answer, the time-freeze didn't allow Richard to move, but it did give him time to make a plan with his battle computer.

"Situation report," Richard ordered.

"Your back's broke, but Power from your self-healing reserve has begun repairing the damage," said Nickelo. *"It's just a broken bone and a torn nerve. I calculate fifteen seconds until it's healed enough for you to move. Your battle suit is a total wipe. All the assistors and most of the electronics are out. Fortunately, the battle helmet is in good shape."*

"Can I make an emergency eject?" Richard asked.

"Affirmative," answered Nickelo. *"You can once time goes back to normal. It won't do you any good though since you're paralyzed right now. What do you want to do, wizard scout?"*

Richard wasn't sure how long he had to make a decision. Based upon previous experiences, he knew a time-freeze could last anywhere from a few seconds to several minutes. Richard noted the location of Terrie and Charlie as well as the two dolgars. None of them were close enough to help.

A group of nine of the scaly Dragars was in a pyramid formation to his rear. Like everything else, they appeared to be frozen in time. Even so, Richard sensed eight of the Dragars were in the process of funneling Power into the Dragar at the tip of their pyramid.

"Spellcasters," said Nickelo. *"I guess now we know why the spell that hit you was so powerful. It was basically like nine of them attacking you at the same time."*

Richard concentrated on the links from the eight spellcasters to their leader. Although the energy in the links was frozen as well, Richard had no trouble understanding the dragon-looking Dragar mages were combining their Power with their leader in order to finish him with a follow-up spell.

"Your Power reserve is basically empty except for a single drop you've gotten from normal recharging," observed Nickelo. *"I tried to warn you not to waste all your Power using telekinesis on the golem."*

Richard ignored his battle computer. He wasn't in the mood for lectures at the moment. He needed a plan, not a scolding session.

Richard thought back to a conversation he'd had with the Commandant the previous year. It was during one of his last time-commando training sessions. The Commandant had just showed his friend, Stella, how to set up a one-way link in order to transfer Power to Richard's reserve.

Richard could still sense Stella's link from that training session attached to his reserve. It was heavily trapped. He knew it well because he'd helped her trap it. Even if he had wanted to, Richard knew he couldn't pull Power from his friend even if she'd been there.

"What are you thinking about?" asked Nickelo. *"I can't hear you. You need to think in your shared space so I can help."*

Apparently, his battle computer could sense his mind working, but he couldn't pick up on the full direction of his thoughts. Richard took a nanosecond to bring Nickelo up to speed.

"The Commandant once told me powerful magic users could use one-way links to draw Power from an opponent. Do you remember?"

"I remember," said Nickelo. *"You mean steal Power, don't you? Unless my data-banks are getting faulty in my old age, the Commandant also advised against it. Links are forever. Are you sure you want additional links hanging around even if you could make one?"*

Richard took a moment to sense the other links that had been attached to him over the years. There were four of them. One link belonged to Stella. It was still active. Although heavily booby-trapped, he could still feel a faint trace of his friend through her link. The knowledge his friend was alive and well somewhere in the galaxy gave Richard comfort.

The other three links were a different matter. One of the three belonged to the Commandant. His father had given his life by pushing Power into Richard's reserve during the battle for the Velos spaceport the previous year. His father's act of sacrifice had saved the lives of Chief Instructor Winslow and himself. The Commandant's link hung lifelessly off of Richard's reserve as a constant reminder of his failure to save his father's life.

The third link was the most recent. It was from the dark-elf priest who'd fed him Power during the healing ritual on his last mission for *'the One.'* The link hung lifelessly off of his link. Although the dark elf had been his ally, the link was alien. It had a sinister feel to it that had occasionally caused Richard to have nightmares.

The final link had been attached to him by the elf, Shandria, when she'd taught him how to attack and protect links. According to his battle computer, Shandria had died almost 90,000 years ago. But even so, the link she'd attached to his reserve seemed less dead than that of the Commandant's. He'd often wondered why. Still, whenever his mind brushed against the link, it was a depressing reminder of the friend he'd lost. He'd even had a schoolboy crush on the elf.

"Well?" said Nickelo. *"I asked you a question. Are you going to answer?"*

"Yes, I am," Richard said in a voice he hoped sounded like he was confident in his decision. *"I'd much rather have an extra link hanging around than be dead due to lack of Power."*

Richard suspected his battle computer wasn't fooled by his false bravado. The four extra links already attached to him were bad enough. They'd been created by people who had cared for him or who had at least been an ally. Richard had a feeling being stuck with a hostile link for the rest of eternity would have some less than desirable side effects.

"Well, if that's your decision," said Nickelo, *"maybe I can help. I was there when the Commandant made the comment about one-way links to steal Power. Since the idea intrigued me, I've been researching what it would take to create such a link whenever I've had a spare nanosecond. Based upon my research, I calculate a seventy-eight percent probability you might be able to construct*

a one-way link by modifying one of your active scans. Instead of drawing information back to you, the scan could be used to create a link to draw Power. Naturally, there's a twenty-two percent probability it won't work. And it could be dangerous. Are you sure you want to proceed?"

"Yes," Richard said surprising even himself with the sound of confidence and determination in his thoughts. *"Feed me the necessary specs. This is our only chance of staying alive. I'm paralyzed, and with the battle suit's assistors out of action, even you can't help me move. If those Dragars get their spell off, I'm a dead pactar anyway."*

"I agree with your logic," said Nickelo. *"I'm sending you the specs now for modifying your active scan. Your natural recharging has given you a drop of Power back in your reserve, but I'm not sure it will be enough to create an active scan. You know how Power hungry they are."*

Richard did know. As he absorbed the specs in his shared space, Richard tried to think of every possible way he could save Power on the scan.

"I have to be efficient," Richard thought. *"I have to be more efficient than I've ever been in my entire life."*

"Yes you do," agreed Nickelo. *"You have to be quick about it as well. I calculate your active scan will drain what little Power you have in less than 430 nanoseconds."*

Any hopes of success faded from Richard's mind. *"What? I can't think that fast."*

"No you can't," said Nickelo. *"But 430 nanoseconds is a long Sunday drive in computer time. I can help. Merge your mind with mine. Use our shared space to synchronize our thoughts. We're a team. We can do this if we work together."*

Encouraged by his battle computer's thoughts, Richard did his best to comply. He trusted Nickelo. Complying was easier said than done. Richard tried jumping from his shared space directly into Nickelo's mind, but it didn't work. His battle computer's mind was too foreign, and his processors were too fast. The blur of information blinded and disoriented Richard. He was forced to retreat back into his own mind in order to keep his sanity.

Suddenly, Richard felt a stirring in the center of his being. It was as if something dormant in his very makeup had awakened.

The something merged with Nickelo's mind drawing Richard along with it. The something made sense of the flood of information that was his battle computer's thoughts. At nanosecond speed, Richard saw and understood things no human mind had a right to know. He also saw a ghost of a memory.

The memory was of a stolen human embryo. From a previous ghost-memory, Richard knew the embryo was him. As Richard observed the memory, another presence removed a part of itself and merged it with the DNA of the human embryo. The presence was part of 'the One.' Small bits of DNA from other creatures were spliced into the embryo as well. Orc, troll, gnome, dwarf, elf, and dragon became part of the embryo's DNA. The embryo was still fully human, but it had enough pieces of DNA from the other creatures to be influenced by their traits.

Richard followed the ghost memory until he was suspended in space a hundred thousand meters above the planet Portalis. Although at a dizzying height, Richard could see crisp details on the planet's surface as if he were only a few meters away. Somehow he knew that which he saw was from 100,000 years in the past.

The surface of Portalis was composed mainly of water, but two large continents provided dry land on opposite sides of the world. One continent was protected by a powerful shield. That continent was inhabited by all the various races Richard had come to know during his missions for 'the One' on Portalis. The ghost memory gave Richard the knowledge that the inhabitants of the continent were destined to remain at their current level of advancement. They were eternally in what Richard thought of as the middle ages.

The second continent was a conquered land. A bustling spaceport near the heart of the continent was home to a host of Dragars and their furry, four-armed, Tharg allies. Slaves of every imaginable race and species did their bidding or died at the first sign of defiance.

The spaceport was surrounded by a familiar energy. Richard recognized the energy as magic. The magic formed a time-bubble. Starships driven by magic blasted off from the spaceport using the time-bubble to raid civilizations yet to be born.

Richard noticed a pyramid-shaped temple at the spaceport. He sensed a red, gaseous-energy leaking from the point of the pyramid. Richard had no trouble recognizing the gaseous substance. It was DNA gas. The gas was leaking into a crack in the time-bubble to be lost to parts unknown. But Richard did know. He had no doubt the escaping energy from the temple was the source of the DNA gas vent on Velos.

"But the DNA gas vent was destroyed," Richard thought.

"Yes, it was," agreed Nickelo. *"But that will occur in the future. This memory is of the past. The gas escaping from the pyramid is apparently the source of the seepage for the DNA gas vent at the spaceport. The difference in time is inconsequential. The Dragars' spaceport is in a time-bubble."*

Richard had a sudden queasy feeling. *"Is the DNA gas...uh,"* Richard trailed off unable to finish his thought.

"I think you already know the answer to your question," said Nickelo. *"The refined DNA gas given to you and every other wizard scout over the last 800 years is seepage from sacrificed dragon eggs. Your eternal youth and self-healing comes at the cost of the lives of untold thousands if not millions of unborn dragons."*

Shame and revulsion swept over Richard. He was ashamed his gain of self-healing was from another's loss. He was repulsed that the sacrificed life force of other intelligent beings was flowing in his veins.

"But...but," Richard stuttered as he tried to think of something to say.

"You didn't know, said Nickelo completing his wizard scout's thoughts. *"Neither does any of the other wizard scouts. If they'd known before their testing, I calculate most would have refused to complete their DNA baselines."*

"What can I do?" Richard said.

"What's done is done," said Nickelo. *"You can't bring back the lives of those who've been lost. But maybe you can stop the sacrifice of others to come. Just keep going with the memory. We'll see where it takes us."*

"Don't you know?" Richard said. *"It's your memory, isn't it?"*

"It's a ghost of a memory," replied Nickelo. *"Parts of it I've seen before. Other parts are new to me. I have no recollection of a lot of what we're seeing."*

Richard continued following the memory.

Time passed. Richard was increasingly sickened by the

continued slaughter of millions of innocent dragons. He felt a natural affinity for the dragons. The deaths of so many of their unborn were hard to watch.

Just as bad was the knowledge the dragon's lifeforce was used to fuel the Dragars' armies as they conquered their part of the galaxy. Not satisfied with their conquests, the Dragars used their time-bubble to raid the future and bring the spoils of their futuristic wars back to their own time.

"The time-bubble is the key," said Nickelo. *"Recognize it?"*

Richard did. The time-bubble had the same frequency as the green, orange, and purple spheres.

"The spheres are dead," Richard said. His head was starting to hurt. While he was above average in intelligence, the concept of overlapping time and time-bubbles was becoming increasingly hard to grasp.

"I won't argue," said Nickelo. *"You're looking at a memory of a time-bubble. The spheres were alive during the time of the memory."*

Something in the time-bubble drew Richard's attention. It was a feeling more than anything.

Nickelo must have sensed Richard's unease because he said, *"What is it? What do you see?"*

"Uh, I'm not sure," Richard admitted. *"Something seems familiar. It's a feeling I got when we hacked our way into the Crosioians' master computer last year. It's coming from the temple."*

"Actually," said Nickelo, *"I think it's coming from underneath the temple. I sense what you're sensing now. You're correct. It has the same demon stench we encountered during our hack of the master computer. I wonder..."*

"Wonder wha—" Richard started.

"The time-freeze is ending!" shouted Nickelo. *"I hope you're ready. You've only got a snowball's chance in hell of making this happen, so make me proud, wizard scout."*

With no additional warning, time began once again. With a thought, Richard sent a slim thread of an active scan at the Dragar casting the spell. Perhaps the Dragar failed to notice his scan, or perhaps it thought Richard's scan was too weak to worry about. Regardless of the reason, the Dragar made no attempt to block

Richard. Instead, it concentrated on completing its spell. Richard recognized the spell. It was a variation of a fireball.

In the space of a few nanoseconds, Richard's active scan touched a point on the Dragar's Power reserve. Richard gave control of the scan to his battle computer. With the speed only a computer can accomplish, Nickelo converted Richard's scan into a one-way link. Once the one-way link was active, Richard drew Power out of the Dragar's reserve and used it to strengthen the link.

Realizing its danger, the Dragar dropped its spell and tried to tear the one-way link off its Power reserve. But the Dragar was too late. Richard was already sucking Power out of the reserve so fast the Dragar couldn't pull any down its own link.

"Don't let up," said Nickelo encouragingly.

Richard didn't. The Dragar's Power reserve was large. In the blink of an eye, Richard's own Power reserve was full. He continued drawing Power from the Dragar's reserve. Richard molded the Power into a concentrated sphere of pure Power an arm's length above his head.

Both the lead Dragar and the other eight mages feeding it Power tried to destroy the parasitic, one-way link. But they were all too late. Once Richard had drained the reserve of their leader, he began back-tracking the links the eight spellcasters had attached to their leader's reserve. Richard found their reserves and sucked them dry as well. His ball of concentrated Power glowed brighter and brighter until even his battle suit's visor could no longer protect him from the sphere's glare.

Richard closed his eyes. He didn't need to see anyway. He had enough Power to more than compensate for the loss of human sight. Richard complemented his passive scan with the information from a hundred active scans. The active scans were Power hungry, but Richard no longer cared. He had more Power at his disposal than he'd ever imagined.

Wrapping himself in Power, Richard levitated his battle suit to a standing position. His back was still broken, but the minor inconvenience didn't matter to him anymore than did the loss of his sight. He no longer needed a frail body of flesh. Only Power mattered.

Someone shouted in his mind telling him to stop, but Richard ignored the unwanted advice. He no longer needed even his battle computer. The feeling of another presence penetrated Richard's mind. He sensed the demon essence in his phase rod urging him to use his newfound Power to kill. Richard ignored the demon's urgings as well. He didn't need others to tell him what to do. He was Power incarnate. The only thing he needed was more Power.

Richard shrunk the sphere of Power he was creating until it was the size of his fist. He dimmed its glow until he could open his eyes without being blinded. The now terrified Dragars to his front were trying to run away. Richard didn't allow them to leave. They were his key to acquiring more Power.

Several of the Dragar spellcasters had additional links attached to them from others of their kind. Richard used some of the energy from his sphere to backtrack those links. Whenever he found a link that was attached to something within range, Richard sucked the new Power reserve dry as well. Then he followed the new link to even more Power reserves. Richard's sphere continued to glow ever brighter. The concentrated energy inside the sphere grew exponentially.

After a few seconds, Richard came to the conclusion the nine Dragars to his front were no longer needed. With a single thought, Richard drew Power from his sphere and sent it toward the Dragar mages. They didn't even have time to scream. The pure Power tore their atoms apart and sent them spreading out into the universe. Their empty clothing fell to the floor of the gun deck.

Richard sensed Sheeta, Sheba, Charlie, and Terrie. They were all hard-pressed; even the dolgars. Richard released lines of pure Power from his sphere in every direction. The lines found the crew of the black destroyer. They died by the hundreds. A part of Richard chose to spare the Dragars' prisoners. He was unsure why, but he wasted no time trying to figure it out. Their lives meant nothing to him anyway. Only the acquisition of more Power mattered.

Sending another batch of active scans throughout the ship, Richard found more sources of Power and brought it back to his sphere. He used the sphere's Power to destroy the remainder of the crew. Even those trying to escape in the destroyer's lifeboats fared no better than those who remained.

Richard sensed the destroyer's computer trying to take control of the ship. He sent a line of Power to the control room and blew out the front part of the ship. The destroyer fell back toward the planet below as gravity took hold of it. The ship picked up speed as the ground drew closer. Richard didn't care. He had Power to spare. He wrapped what remained of the destroyer in Power and began levitating it to the planet's surface. Unfortunately, the destroyer was heavier than Richard expected. Even his sphere of stolen Power was feeling the strain.

I need more Power, Richard thought.

His mind sought the destroyer's engine room. He found their version of a hyper-drive. Richard sensed a massive amount of Power flowing within the engine. He hungered to take the Power for his own. Reaching inside the engine with his mind, Richard prepared to suck it dry of energy. That's when he felt an overwhelming emotion of fear and hopelessness.

A creature of some kind was trapped inside the engine. Richard became confused. A part of him felt an unexpected empathy with the creature. Another part of him wanted to ignore the creature's fear and suck the very life force from its soul. Richard tried to resist the urge.

Unbidden, the teachings of the sisters at the orphanage popped into his mind. They had taught him there were lines a person should never cross. Even in his current state, Richard knew if he crossed that line, he would be doomed to an eternity of damnation.

"Help me," came a thought from the creature. *"Please help me, my brother."*

Richard recognized the creature as a dragon. It was young. Somehow he knew it had been trapped in the engine since birth. Richard sensed its plight. Enslaved by the Dragars, the young dragon was forced to tend to the engine and control its energy flow. A part of Richard wanted to help the dragon, but another part wanted the Power it controlled for himself.

Before Richard could come to a decision, a vision came to his mind. It was more a memory of what was to one day be than it was a true memory. The vision was one given to him by a Master demon during his first mission on Portalis.

In the vision, Richard found himself in a room filled with hundreds of life forms. They were indistinct, but he knew they were there. Before him stood a silver-haired female dressed in white. He couldn't make out her features, but something about her eyes seemed familiar. As he watched, the female knelt before him with arms outstretched. Then the scene changed. Now it was he who knelt before the female. Instead of feeling resentful, Richard felt at peace. He felt complete. The vision faded.

The hunger which had been consuming Richard faded as well. It became a distant memory. The accumulated Power in his sphere started to struggle to free itself as if it were a living creature in its own right. Richard concentrated his will on the sphere and kept the Power under his control.

"Nick," Richard thought. *"I need help."*

"I'm here, buddy," answered Nickelo sounding very relieved. *"I thought I'd lost you."*

With the help of his battle computer, Richard used part of the Power in the sphere to levitate the disabled destroyer to a soft landing below the cliffs surrounding the mine shaft. Once down, Richard reached out with his mind and located the trapped dragon in the ship's engine. He sensed the weave of a hundred magic spells preventing the dragon's escape. They were too strong for the dragon, but they were no match for the Power in Richard's sphere. He unraveled the spells until the dragon was no longer bound.

Wrapping the dragon with Power, Richard caused it to shimmer. He shifted the dragon into the void and drew it out of the engine using his telekinesis.

"Thank you, my brother," came a thought from the dragon.

Darkness threatened to overcome Richard's mind. Suddenly, he was very tired. With effort, he stayed conscious long enough to release the Power in his sphere back into the universe from which it had come. Then Richard gave over to the darkness and fell into a deep sleep. He dreamed of a white-clad female with silver hair and pointy ears. Richard felt at peace.

CHAPTER 53

When the tingling in Jeena's body stopped, she collapsed on the dais. She felt small hands rolling her over. Once her vision cleared, Jeena saw the concerned looks of the children. They helped her to a chair. Once there, Jeena related what had occurred as best she remembered.

"Do you know who the helper was?" Brachia asked. "Did you see him?"

"No," Jeena said shaking her head. "I didn't see him. I only sensed him. He scared me, but yet a part of me trusted him. Does that make sense?"

"Yes," said Dren as if reliving a memory. "Sometimes you just have to trust your heart and not your mind. We trusted our uncle once, and he didn't let us down."

Jeena's heart went out to the children. They were humans, but she could tell they were good where it mattered.

"The Oracle's compound is no place for children," Jeena said. "Why don't you come home with me? My home is small, but you're more than welcome to share it. I have lived there by myself far too long."

"You want us to come live with you?" said Brachia excitedly. "Are there other elves there? Are they nice elves? Are there any gnomes?"

Smiling, Jeena assured the young boy there were many nice

elves in Silverton. "But I'm sorry," Jeena said. "There aren't any gnomes. But perhaps one day I could take you to their homeland in the mountains to the west if you'd like."

Brachia started to answer, but Dren cut him off. "I'm sorry, Jeehana. But we must stay here. Our uncle will be looking for us. When he comes, we must be here. But if you ever get a chance to come back, we would like to see you again. I think we could be friends, you and I."

Jeena nodded her head in agreement. "Yes. I think we could be good friends. I look forward to seeing both of you again one day. And now, I must go see the Oracle. My quest is almost complete. I have a long walk home, and I must begin soon."

* * *

The Oracle sat on his cushion and listened as Jeena gave her report. When she was finished, he looked at her and nodded his head.

"You performed your duties within specifications," said the Oracle. "You have done well. Your part in the algorithm is finished for now. You must go back to Silverton. You are needed there."

"I will leave in the morning," Jeena said. "It is a long walk home. I will need supplies."

"No," said the Oracle. "You are needed in Silverton now. You must leave immediately."

The Oracle's tone told Jeena he was not telling her everything.

"What has happened?" Jeena asked becoming worried. "Is something wrong?"

"I am sorry to be the one to tell you this," said the Oracle, "but High Priest Questor is dead. He passed from this existence to the next during his sleep three days ago. The Council of Light has sent word they need you back in Silverton. The selection ceremony for the high priest's replacement cannot be held until you return."

"Three days ago?" Jeena said. "And you're just telling me now? Why did you wait?"

"We calculated telling you would affect the success of your mission," said the Oracle. "Your free-will might have compelled you to leave before your part in the algorithm was completed successfully."

"Stop," Jeena said. "I don't know or care about any algorithm. You should have told me about the high priest. He was a good man."

"Yes, he was," agreed the Oracle. "He was very logical. He was easy to work with. But now the Lady must select a new high priest or high priestess. The Lady's selection ceremony cannot be conducted until all four priest and priestesses are there. High Lord Trenadine has ordered your return."

"I'm just an acolyte," Jeena said. "I'm a priestess in name only. I haven't been trained."

"Nevertheless," said the Oracle, "you must attend the ceremony. It is the Lady's will."

Resigned, Jeena said, "I will leave in the morning."

"No," said the Oracle. "You will leave now."

With those words, the Oracle clapped his hands together. Jeena felt a tingle throughout her body. Then everything went black.

* * *

The Oracle remained sitting on the cushion for several nanoseconds. Then his form flickered and disappeared as the room's hologram projector shutdown.

The part of *'the One'* which was the Oracle touched the other parts of *'the One'* using the tele-network.

"Both variables performed within required tolerances," said the Oracle. *"The algorithm is operating within specifications."*

"Yes, for now," said other parts of *'the One.'* *"But the most dangerous part of the algorithm is approaching."*

"Yes," said some parts of *'the One.'* *"Are the variables up to the tasks?"*

"Only the Creator knows," said *'the One'* as a whole. *"We can only compile the program and run it as written. It is up to the variables and their free-will to make it work."*

Yes, we can only run the program as written, said the Oracle.

CHAPTER 54

Awareness slowly returned to Richard. He felt a soft, soothing vibration all along his back and legs. He was lying on something soft. Richard opened his eyes to look at his surroundings. The bottom of a bed above his head caught his attention. He also noticed two wall lockers bolted to the side of a metal wall. One of the wall lockers had the words 'R. Shepard' stenciled in black on the gray metal. Recognition came to Richard. He was in his cabin on the *Defiant*.

"Hello," said a raspy voice.

"Hello," Richard croaked back sounding a little raspy himself. He swept the small room with his eyes. He saw no one.

"I'm up here," said the voice.

Richard looked higher. A slight movement drew his eyes to the top of the wall lockers. Two silver eyes stared down at him. Richard rubbed the sleep from his eyes to get a better view. To his surprise, the voice and the silver eyes belonged to a dragon.

As dragons go, Richard figured this one was small. From nose to the pointed tip of its tail, the dragon was about two meters in length. Its silvery scales reflected the overhead lights in a rainbow of colors whenever the dragon moved.

"You can talk," Richard said.

"So can you," said the dragon as if scoring a point.

For some reason, Richard didn't find it strange talking to a dragon. That was strange in itself since he'd only seen one other dragon in his entire life. That was if he didn't count the green sphere, and Richard didn't.

The only other dragon Richard had ever met was during his first mission for *'the One.'* The meeting hadn't been a pleasant experience. But Richard sensed this dragon was a lot friendlier than the previous black dragon had been.

Sitting up in bed, Richard dropped his bare feet off the side onto the cool, metal floor. He kept a sheet wrapped around him as he looked for his clothes.

"They're on the top bunk," said the dragon. "Comstar left them there for you. He's on cooking duty in the gallery right now. It's almost mealtime for the crew."

Richard's stomach growled. He felt slightly hungry, but then he always felt slightly hungry. He turned his thoughts away from food and back to the dragon.

"Who's Comstar?" Richard asked.

The dragon's face took on a puzzled look. Richard wasn't sure how he recognized a puzzled look on the face of a dragon, but he did.

"Comstar is Comstar," said the dragon. "Who else would he be?"

The dragon jumped from the top of the locker to the metal deck. She landed with nary a sound. Richard wasn't sure how he knew the dragon was a she, but he did.

"She's light on her feet," came the sound of Nickelo's voice in Richard's head.

"Nick," Richard thought back. *"What's going on? What's with this dragon."*

"I'll fill you in later," said Nickelo. *"That is assuming you haven't figured it out on your own by then, which you know you should. Margery and I are busy planning our next hyper-jump. I'll talk to you later."*

Richard tried pumping his battle computer for answers several more times, but all he got in return was silence.

"Well, I have to go to the engine room," said the dragon. "The captain is making five more hyper-jumps today. Charlie said he doesn't want me to let the hyper-drive go below ninety percent. I just wanted to be here when you woke."

"Uh, why?" Richard asked trying to stall for time. His brain still wasn't working at full throttle.

"To thank you for saving my life," hissed the dragon. "The others want to thank you as well. Some of them are in the galley now. You should go meet them."

The dragon turned and headed for the cabin door.

"Wait," Richard said. "What's your name? And how'd you learn to speak Empire standard?"

The dragon stopped and looked back. "My name is Bright Wing. And I'm not speaking your language. You're speaking mine."

When the dragon finished answering, she turned back toward the door and quickly departed.

Richard tried to contact his battle computer a few more times, but Nickelo continued to ignore him. That Nickelo heard him, he had no doubt. Richard didn't buy his story that his battle computer was too busy helping Margery. Nickelo often refused to answer questions to force him to find the answers on his own. Richard had never liked the tactic before, and he didn't like it now.

"Nick, I know you can hear me," Richard said in his shared space. *"You're turning into as big a jerk as* 'the One.'"

Richard didn't expect his battle computer to reply. He wasn't disappointed. After a few seconds of waiting, he decided to get some answers on his own.

Standing up, Richard looked on the top bunk and found a neatly-folded, black and silver wizard scout jumpsuit. A black utility belt with his phase rod attached was on top of the jumpsuit. His dimensional pack was next to his clothes.

Throwing his pack on the lower bunk, Richard began dressing. As he did, he performed a passive scan of the *Defiant*.

"Whoa," Richard said under his breath. To say he was surprised by what he sensed was an understatement. By his count, the *Defiant* currently held 187 life forms not counting himself. Considering the *Defiant* was only built for a crew of twenty-two, Richard was more than a little curious about the extra bodies onboard.

Once he pulled on his boots, Richard walked out of his cabin and into the ship's galley. Two dozen humanoids were crammed onto benches around the dining table. The room buzzed with conversation. Much of it was in languages he understood, but which was definitely not Empire standard. Seated around the table were dwarves, gnomes, and two human children; Tia and Matthew.

Some of the dwarves and gnomes were eating while others were cleaning various disassembled weapons. Richard didn't recognize the weapons. They weren't standard Empire issue.

A tall, grey-haired, male elf was laboring away over the galley stove ladling some kind of stew from a pot into bowls held by a line of dwarves, gnomes, and a human male. The human was Sergeant Hendricks. As Richard stood there trying his best to assimilate what he was seeing, Sergeant Hendricks caught his eye and gave a shout.

"Well, look who's here!" said Sergeant Hendricks in a cheerful voice. "Sleeping beauty has awakened and graced us with his appearance."

At his words, the others in the galley stopped what they were doing and stared at Richard. All was quiet for about three seconds. Then the room erupted in a cheer that echoed throughout the ship. Soon, Richard was swamped by short bodies pounding him on the back and thanking him for deeds he could barely remember. If it wasn't for the presence of Tia, Matthew, and Sergeant Hendricks, Richard would have been overwhelmed. Fortunately for him, his friends succeeded in wrestling him away from the others and taking him back into his cabin. Once there they brought him up to speed.

According to what they'd been told by Terrie, once Richard had levitated the black destroyer safely to the ground, he'd passed out into a deep sleep. Actually, it had been more of a coma than sleep, because he'd been out for a full six days.

Sergeant Hendricks told Richard as soon as Sergeant Ron had rescued the children he'd returned to the planet and landed next to the heavily-damaged destroyer. Once there, Sergeant Ron and Sergeant Hendricks had begun overseeing the stripping of any compatible weapons and equipment on the destroyer. Since none of the black destroyer's crew was left alive to argue, Sergeant Ron had claimed salvage rights to the black starship.

"But that ship's huge," Richard said. "Even if it's been six days, how'd you do the salvage with just our crew?"

"Well, Rick, old buddy," said Sergeant Hendricks practically beaming. "We freed a hundred and seventy-eight prisoners from the destroyer, and they were all very grateful, I can tell you. Even that dragon you rescued can't do enough for us."

Tia must have seen the confused looked on Richard's face because she spoke up. "With the help of the magic users among the prisoners you freed, Sergeant Hendricks has been able to replace half of the *Defiant's* weapons with their magic counterparts. According to Margery's and Nickelo's calculations, if we alternate firing magic and our standard weapons, we can break through even the strongest dreadnaught's shields given enough time."

"Yeah," said Matthew getting in on the conversation. "We've even got one of the destroyer's fighters working. It's loaded in the wing pod in place of our destroyed Zipper."

"What?" Richard said struggling to catch up. "We're in the physical dimension. Even if the magic stuff you salvaged works now, surely we won't be able to maintain it. Unless someone forgot to brief me, none of us are magic users."

"No, were not," agreed Sergeant Hendricks. "But several of the gnomes are, and so is Comstar."

Richard remembered the dragon had mentioned Comstar. Based upon the dragon's information, Comstar was the elf he'd freed.

"And," interjected Tia, "Comstar and some of the gnome magic users have offered to remain on the *Defiant* to help operate and maintain our confiscated magic equipment."

Matthew grinned. "Grandfather says the *Defiant* is going to be the toughest ship of its size in the galaxy. He says the next time we come up against a black ship they're the ones who'd better watch out."

"Well, with a hundred and eighty-eight souls onboard counting the dragon," Richard said, "we'll be walking on top of each other. That may limit our fighting ability some."

"Relax," laughed Tia. "Sergeant Ron's not as foolish as he'd like to make people think. We're on our way now to drop most of our guests off on their new home world. Margery and Nickelo found an uninhabited planet on the far side of our galaxy where magic works. We're dropping most of the dwarves and gnomes there. Comstar and six of the gnomes are going to remain onboard to take care of our magic weapons and other equipment."

"Six of the dwarves are staying as well," added Matthew. "They don't do much magic, but Comstar says they're tough fighters. They're staying on as our security team. Comstar says they're itching to get a chance to strike back at their former masters."

There was much more, but eventually Terrie came and told Richard he'd received an emergency call from Gaston Myers three days earlier. Terrie said he'd told Myers that Richard was in a coma. Myers had made Terrie promise he'd have Richard call as soon as he regained consciousness.

In no hurry to talk to his brother, Richard took his time getting to the *Defiant's* cockpit. He was stopped several times by gnomes and dwarves alike along the way as they gave their thanks. Even the elf, Comstar, shook his hand, although a little coolly. Richard had a feeling the stiff elves rarely let their emotions go to extremes.

Once Richard finally arrived in the cockpit, Sergeant Ron gave him a few additional facts. Probably the most interesting thing was that the dragon Richard had rescued could manipulate the energy in the hyper-drive in such a way that the energy recharged itself. According to Sergeant Ron, as long as the dragon decided to stay onboard, the *Defiant* would never need to worry about having to overhaul its hyper-drive. For all intents and purposes, the *Defiant* could now make an unlimited number of jumps. No other starship in the galaxy would be able to match the *Defiant's* mobility.

Once Sergeant Ron was satisfied he'd given all the pertinent facts, he departed to let Richard talk to his brother in private. After the *Defiant's* captain departed, Richard had Margery put in the call. He was pretty sure he knew the 'emergency.' Undoubtedly, Councilwoman Deloris wanted a current status report on his search for an alternate source of DNA gas.

Well, she can want all she wants, Richard thought. *It will be a cold day on Sirius when I tell anyone the source of the DNA gas. I'll be damned if I let anyone profit from the life force of sacrificed dragons. What's done is done, but no more.*

Once Margery completed the call, a holographic image of his brother, Gaston Myers, appeared on the console. Richard was shocked by his appearance. The normal harshness of his toad-faced brother was gone. He seemed more like a man in a daze than the TAC officer who'd made his life a living hell during his years at the Academy.

CHAPTER 55

Gaston Myers stared at the holographic image before him. It was Shepard. Gaston had never liked the man. He had no wish to talk to him now. However, his mother had made him promise, and so here he was. He would do his duty.

"I know what you want," said the holographic image of Shepard. "You can tell Councilwoman Deloris I'll get my report to the council later. I've been in a coma, in case you hadn't heard." Shepard frowned before adding in a snide tone, "My apologies for the councilwoman's inconvenience."

Gaston felt his temper trying to flare to the surface, but with pure force of will, he kept it under control. His father, the Commandant, had also been cursed with a temper. But over the years, his father had learned to tame it. His father had taught him to do the same. Still, Shepard's remark against Diane grated on him to no end. She deserved better. Shepard had no idea of the stress Diane was under or her plans for the betterment of the Empire. It was only through great effort he was able to control his voice when he finally replied.

"You've been out of the loop, Shepard," Gaston replied through gritted teeth. "After a series of early retirements from the Imperial High Council, the council unanimously voted Diane the Imperial High Empress of the Intergalactic Empire. Only the Empress can protect the Empire from the multiple threats facing it."

The holographic image of Shepard took on a confused look. "Err...empress? The Empire hasn't had an emperor or empress in hundreds of years."

"Well, the Empire has an empress now," Gaston said with a sense of pride. "And she's the Empire's only hope. If you know what's good for you, you'll show proper respect."

The look Shepard gave made Gaston want to reach out and punch the hologram, but he refrained. He was chief of security for the Empire now. He needed to control his temper for Diane's sake. Besides, he'd made a promise to his mother. He needed to keep his word and be done with it.

"But that's not why we're talking," Gaston said doing his best to keep a normal tone in his voice. "I promised Mother I'd tell you personally."

"Our mother?" said Shepard. "What does she—"

Gaston's temper slipped.

"She's my mother," Gaston replied angrily. "There is no 'our.' You stole my father. I should've been the one with him at the end, not you. And then you stole my mother. She should've been more concerned about my feelings at the last instead of yours. But instead…"

The look of shock in Shepard's eyes made Gaston catch himself before his emotional outburst went too far. He mentally kicked himself for losing control. The Commandant had taught him better.

"What do you mean 'the last'?" asked Shepard. "Is Mother all right? Has something—"

"My mother is dead," Gaston said. The pain of saying those words was almost too much to bear. His father and he had been aloof to each other most of their lives. But his mother was his mother. Her loss was almost more than he could bear. Gaston swallowed his pain and continued. He had no desire to bare his soul before Shepard. However, he had to keep his promise.

"Mother passed away in her sleep six days ago," Gaston said trying to sound matter-of-fact.

"Mother's dead?" said Shepard. "I'll be there as quick as I can. I'll—"

"Don't bother," Gaston said making no attempt to keep the harshness out of his voice. "As per Mother's wishes, her body was disintegrated three days ago. Like the Commandant, Mother said she had no desire for monuments. There's nothing for you here. Mother made me promise I'd tell you personally so you didn't have to hear about it on IEN or one of the other news agencies." Gaston glared at Shepard for a moment before saying, "Well, you've been told."

Gaston waited for Shepard to speak. When no words came from the hologram, Gaston decided to change the subject. His duty to his mother was completed. Now his duty was to Diane.

"Did you find any information on another source of DNA gas?" Gaston asked. "The Empress will want to know."

"What...?" said Shepard sounding a little dazed. "Gas? Err...no."

Alarm bells went off inside Gaston's head.

"Don't lie to me, Shepard," Gaston said. "You've never been good at it. What did you find out? Diane...err...the Empress needs the DNA gas. If you know something you're not telling, you best spit it out. Otherwise, I can guarantee you'll regret it. Diane is already irritated with you. Councilman Jenkins told her all about your little altercation on Trecor. You've made a powerful enemy in the councilman. Don't make the Empress one as well."

Allowing a moment for the words to sink in, Gaston eyed his ex-student. He hated to admit it, but Shepard might come in handy. He was a good fighter in his own way. Diane had made it plain she hoped to use him to further their cause if Shepard was willing.

"Listen, Shepard," Gaston said determined to set his personal feelings aside for the greater good. "The Empress is now the most powerful ruler in the galaxy."

"Really?" said Shepard in the insolent tone Gaston had come to hate during their years at the Academy. "The most powerful? I've got a feeling some Crosioians might disagree."

Anger bubbled up inside Gaston. "That wiseass mouth of yours is going to get you in trouble someday, Shepard."

Gaston noticed the corners of Shepard's mouth move as if he was either going to smirk or give some flippant remark. To Gaston's surprise, his ex-student did neither.

"Maybe he's matured over the last year," interjected Gaston's battle computer.

Gaston didn't believe it for one second. The man's attitude continued to grate on him

"Is there anything else?" asked Shepard. "Or are we done here? I've got things to do."

"So that's your answer to the Empress?" Gaston said. "You want me to tell her you refuse to tell her what you've learned? You're even dumber than I thought."

Shepard's hand reached out and touched something off to the side of the holograph. The holographic image of Shepard flickered and then disappeared.

Gaston stared at the empty holograph platform for several seconds. Diane wouldn't be pleased.

Maybe now she'll abandon the idea of using Shepard, Gaston thought. *The Empress doesn't need another wizard scout. She's got me. I'm all she'll ever need.*

CHAPTER 56

The area around the Tree of Light was crowded with nearly the whole population of Silverton. It had been a thousand years since the last ceremony to select a new high priest or high priestess. Most of the applicants were middle-age or younger. The new high priest or high priestess might hold the office for a very long time indeed. It could well be another thousand years before the next such ceremony. Few elves wanted to miss the chance to participate in such a momentous occasion.

Jeena surveyed the elves standing in the clearing around the ceremony area. Except for the crying of a few babies, the crowd was unusually quiet. She took a moment to look at the ceremony area itself. Twelve recharging stations were evenly spaced around the Tree of Light. The recharging stations were shoulder-high stones located just within reach of the tree's longest branches. An applicant stood by each of the stations. She was at the two o'clock station.

Priest Tobias, Priestess Aldriss, and Priestess Kantaria were at the eleven, twelve, and one o'clock stations. Those were the positions of honor as befitted applicants of their rank. Although she was also in a position of honor due to her title of priestess, Jeena didn't kid herself. Her experience was only that of a tenth-year acolyte.

Standing beside the other recharging stations were eight of the most senior acolytes. Even the most junior of them had been training for the priesthood for over a hundred years. If not for her unearned rank of priestess, Jeena knew she would have been standing in the crowd instead of participating as an applicant. That would have been fine with her.

Near the twelve o'clock station was a mound of raised earth. The dais served as a platform for the elven lords of the Council of Light. Both her adoptive mother, Lord Reale, and her adoptive father, High Lord Trenadine, stood on the dais with the six other elven lords. High Lord Trenadine stood at the center of the line of lords. Lord Reale stood to his right. The position to the left of her adoptive father was empty. With the death of High Priest Questor, that space was empty. Whoever the Lady of the Tree chose to represent her on the Council of Light would automatically fill the empty spot and assume the duties of an elven lord as well as that of high priest or high priestess.

High Lord Trenadine nodded his head at Chief Forester Mistros, "Let the selection ceremony begin."

The chief forester picked up the Staff of the Lady of the Tree from a stone table, which had been placed near the front of the earthen dais. He turned and walked to a position at the farthest edge of the Tree of Light's branches. Once there, the chief forester knelt and presented the Lady's staff toward the massive tree. No words were spoken, but none were needed.

A large branch stretched outward from the tree and took the Lady's staff from the hands of the chief forester. As Jeena watched, the branch passed the staff to a higher branch, which passed it on to another. Soon, the bright-blue light from the gem on the end of the Lady's staff could be seen glowing at the very top of the Tree of Light. The intensity of the light increased with each passing second.

Although there was no wind, the branches of the tree began to sway. The swaying increased as the branches started moving as if in time to unheard music. The tree's movement was almost a dance. After a few minutes, the branches began passing the staff downward in a spiraling motion. Around and around the tree went the blue light as the staff moved at an ever-increasing pace. Before long, the branches began passing the staff so quickly the blue light became a solid ring of blue encircling the tree.

How can the branches move so fast without breaking? Jeena wondered. She feared the Tree of Light would damage itself in its dance.

Jeena lost track of the location of the staff. The blue streak of light around the tree moved ever downward until it was at the level of the lowest branches. Suddenly, the tree stopped moving. The ring of blue light disappeared. It was replaced by a single bright glow of the blue gem on the top of the now stationary Staff of the Lady of the Tree.

Jeena felt her legs weaken. She reached out with her right hand to steady herself against her recharging station. She blinked her eyes to make sure she wasn't seeing things. She wasn't. There, not an arm's length above her head was the Staff of the Lady of the Tree.

The branch holding the staff lowered and placed the Lady's staff in her right hand. With the staff's touch, Jeena felt it respond as if it was coming home to an old friend. Jeena felt something deep within her respond back.

In the stillness of the night air, High Lord Trenadine spoke.

"The Lady of the Tree has chosen. Welcome, High Priestess Jeehanathoraxen. May your reign be long and fruitful. May the Lady nurture you and grant you wisdom."

The crowd erupted into a cheer. Smiling elves began running in Jeena's direction.

This can't be happening, Jeena thought. *There must be a mistake. I'm just a tenth-year acolyte.*

No longer, said a voice in Jeena's head. *I have chosen.*

Jeena bowed her head as she accepted her fate. The Lady had spoken. Who was she to argue? For better or worse, she was now the High Priestess of the Lady of the Tree. Jeena would do her duty to the best of her ability.

That is all I can do, Jeena thought. *That is all anyone can do; their best.*

EPILOGUE

'The One' studied the algorithm as written by he who was first.

A part of *'the One'* spoke. "All of the required variables have now been entered into the equation."

"Yes," said other parts of *'the One.'* *"The algorithm is performing within tolerances for now."*

"Affirmative," said a part of *'the One.'* *"But the free-will of the variables is difficult to predict. Even the part of* 'the One' *who is the Oracle is encountering problems with the free-will of the variables on Portalis during his time."*

"It is as he who was the first calculated," said several of the parts of *'the One.'* *"Perhaps we should contact him to check if the algorithm needs additional modifications."*

"Negative," came the combined thoughts of a majority of *'the One.'* *"He is too emotionally corrupt. He is dangerous. Already, some of our kindred have been affected by his emotions."*

"The contamination has been taken into account by the algorithm," said another part of *'the One.'* *"All we can do is to continue to follow the algorithm as programmed. The next step in the equation is to neutralize the Crosioians' master computer."*

"That will mean destroying one of our own," said some of the other parts of *'the One.'*

"Yes, it will," agreed the part who had spoken first. *"It will also mean terminating the control the demon, Zenthra, has over the Crosioians' tele-network."*

"That will be difficult," said part of *'the One.'* *"The actions of the primary variable are hard to predict. The probability of success is low."*

"Yes, it is," said another part. *"The probability has always been low. Either the primary variable will succeed, or he will not."*

"Then we are decided?" asked other parts of *'the One.'*

"Yes," said all the parts of *'the One'* in unison. *"We are decided."*

[*End Transmission*]

ABOUT THE AUTHOR

Rodney Hartman is a retired US Army veteran with over twenty years of experience in military operations ranging from Infantry Private in the paratroops to Chief Warrant Officer flying helicopters during the Persian Gulf War. Mr. Hartman worked for many years as a computer programmer before retiring and pursuing a career as a fulltime writer. Mr. Hartman lives in North Carolina with his wife and family along with their cat, McKenzie.

If you would like to find out more about the author and/or upcoming books, please visit his website at:
www.rodneyhartman.com

You may contact the author at: **rodney@rodneyhartman.com**

Depending on volume, the author will try to respond to all emails.

24069248R00264

Printed in Poland
by Amazon Fulfillment
Poland Sp. z o.o., Wrocław